REAL FUN

anəgram/ fju:n(ə)r(ə)l/

anagram funeral

'I didn't think that would have happened'

by

Philip Marks

with illustrations by

Christopher Murphy

CONTENTS

LIST OF FULL PAGE ILLUSTRATIONS

INTRODUCTION

Auctions of any sort are exciting and fun and, with no previous experience of one, I went to an agricultural sale. The lots going through the three auction rings were huge, hundreds of sheep and what seemed to me to be herds of cattle, all split into manageable packaged numbers. It was wonderful to see the skill of the auctioneer, enthusiastically gesturing here, there and everywhere from high up at his lectern, looking like some fearsome preacher, or worse still the mortar-boarded school headmaster of my youth. How he knew who was bidding, and for what, the Lord only knows – the twitch of a newspaper, the touching of the side of the nose, the flick of a finger. He could pick up these signals effortlessly, whilst still burbling away at speed in what sounded like a complex and unfamiliar foreign language. His talk was punctuated by the odd firm landing down of his hand-held gavel and words such as 'Sold, Hayhurst'. The next lot would then be speedily and unwillingly ushered in and off we would go again, the pen gates clattering open and shut with the efficiency of the valves of an engine.

Having recently lived in a flat in Manchester without so much as a window box, we had bought a house at the end of an easily missed and pothole-strewn lane in deepest coastal Cumbria, with a good-sized garden and small orchard. It was only on the day we moved in, when I was greeted by our new neighbour, Sooty, that I learnt that this was not entirely accurate. Sooty was a retired painter and decorator who, I found out later, lived for (and largely in) his vegetable patch and adjoining garage, surrounded by copious amounts of home brew and associated brewing paraphernalia. After we'd exchanged pleasantries and handshakes, Sooty asked about my plans for our new place.

'Well,' I said, 'just a spruce-up for now, the usual decorating, get rid of the woodchip. Maybe look at a new kitchen when funds allow,' I joked.

I immediately thought I had possibly just put my foot firmly in it there for starters, as it suddenly occurred to me that Sooty was just the sort to be happily living in a wall-to-wall woodchip house.

'Oh yes,' Sooty had replied out of politeness, 'but what are you going to do with the jungle?'

'Jungle,' I replied, in what sounded even to me like an enquiring, questioning, if not slightly surprised tone. He gestured with his finger to a point past my garden and orchard and into the wilderness beyond, over the garden wall. I didn't want to admit it, but I wasn't aware that the so-called 'jungle' had anything to do with me. I waffled on a bit in the hope that he wouldn't twig that I didn't know anything about this land, the 'jungle'. I had simply assumed it was a very distant unknown neighbour's land. Anyway I thought my waffling good enough to have done the trick and that I had indeed covered my lack of knowledge and got away with it, until towards the end of the encounter when Sooty said:

'Yes, I used to go in there for my blackberries and elderberries for my wine years ago but you can barely get through the gate now, terribly overgrown, it's a good three acres.'

I think I replied, or more likely uttered, something along the lines of 'Er…' followed by a nervous 'Oooh'. What was an acre? I wondered.

Sooty knowingly looked at me and smiled.

'You didn't know you had all that as well, did you?' Thankfully before I could answer he went on cheerfully, 'Best get on,' while turning for home.

'Okay, thanks, bye,' I said. His arm came up in acknowledgement and he was gone. I often thought, after that, that Sooty quite deliberately hadn't given me the chance to answer his question, and indeed had let me off the hook, aware of my obvious embarrassment at not knowing I had acquired the jungle. I instantly liked him. He was a nice man and was to become a good friend.

He was also, of course, right. I had had no idea the jungle was ours. Better go and see Sam, I had some news…

I always had a tendency to buy things that I neither understood, had read the small print of, had the slightest idea what to do with, nor, on some occasions, even wanted. I bought a 12 bore shotgun before ever touching or firing one, simply because I had 'moved to the countryside now'. My long-suffering wife, Sam, bought a 20 bore shotgun simply to maintain some form of parity and both were housed under the bed, one on each side. This was long before the days of locked shotgun cabinets.

Well, this time it was the turn of the buying of sheep. I had bought a house with land that I was nonchalantly unaware of and had assessed - from extensive experience gained looking out of the window of the car as a boy on Sunday drives in school holidays - that on land there were sheep. Sunday drives were a common bewildering affliction parents frequently wielded on their offspring; the irritating unnecessary weekend 'treat' of driving simply because the car had been invented and they were lucky enough to have one. This habit of flask, travelling rug and thumbed route map in motion (the original 'must have' mobile accessories) developed long before the awareness of greenhouse gases and global warming. It was simply a frightfully easy way of polluting for fun and often simply wasting both fuel and time, not to mention one's life, whilst also providing the added thrill of a journey where the point of departure doubled up as the destination, therefore offering some limited economy. It was on such trips that I observed open fields and sheep. This was the extent of my agricultural knowledge at this point, and with this knowhow and memory at the forefront of my mind clearly the solution to the overgrown jungle was sheep. Job done, end of story, how hard can it be? It wasn't long before I had my answer to that one.

Standing at the ringside at the auction in our lookalike Barbour jackets, trying hard to look as knowledgeable as we could, or at the very least not as obviously green and out of our depth as we were, Sam and I looked like twins. The pen gates crashed open once more, and I saw two panic-stricken ewes with 'lambs afoot'. The smallest lot of the day, and hopefully the cheapest I thought. I didn't know that 'afoot' meant more in the countryside than just the imperial measurement it sounds, an imperial measurement which was going to feature frequently and with importance in my near future. If I had known then, what I know now …

With the blurred fast-speak of the auctioneer ringing out, which everyone else appeared to understand, I threw up my hand aloft and left it there until other bids petered out.

'Sold!' shouted the auctioneer. 'Name?' he bellowed across the assembled crowd.

'Jeffries,' I replied, while checking around me that it really was me he was addressing, and lo and behold I owned some sheep. True to form, and in keeping with my ill-prepared purchasing history, I had never so much as even touched one.

This whole environment was alien to Sam and I. I was the classic only child public boarding school product, and Sam was from a similar school regime. Even our accents must have given us away, if the jackets had not already done so.

To all intents and purposes that was the end of Master Philip Jeffries OR, although he was to reappear from time to time, when required or necessary.

Philip Jeffries, a typical English public schoolboy twit, had suddenly, in one fell swoop by changing his postcode, become me.

That is when it all began…

Chapter 1

THE AUCTION

The name 'Gefry, Gefry' rang out across the holding pens, now choked with adrenalin-fuelled animals being acquainted with their new owners, who themselves were climbing all over the sheep pens prodding and poking their newly purchased business partners who bleated loudly in protest. The cacophony rising upwards was quite deafening, only beaten by this stockman shouting 'Gefry'.

Why were all the shepherds and farmers wearing wader-type leggings? I had noticed this attire in the selling ring, as most of the farmers and their associates therein spent an inordinate amount of time looking at me, rather than the sheep. They were having a laugh at our jackets and corduroys, I had thought naively. My new wife, Sam, was with me and I realised that she was more likely the object of their obvious interest and whispers. I often said to her afterwards that I could probably have got a good price for her on that day because she had certainly got their attention, and she would no doubt have got a good 'prodding and poking' too!

From nowhere this great gnarled weather-worn hand clamped my shoulder, and the presumed farmer said, 'Your name Gefry, son?'

'No,' I replied. 'Jeffries.'

'He won't bother 'bout that, lad,' said the pipe-wielding giant. 'Think he's a-looking for thee, to pick up them Suffolks.'

What on earth was a 'Suffolk'? Other than a used-to-be-sleepy county in the South? I thought I had bought two sheep 'wit' lambs' and hopefully not more unseen distant land.

'Gefry?' the stockman said. I later learned he had worked at 't'auction' since 'afore the war'; which war I never found out, but it was obviously not recent due to the evident age of the man.

'Jeffries,' I replied.

Even after a full twelve years of a school where you were only known by your surname (I had indeed run the risk of forgetting my Christian name more than once before now) I missed the stockman's ask. Surname fine, but I missed the pronunciation by a mile, to my shame. My local dialect would have to improve that was for sure, and quickly as it turned out.

'Back tha' trailer up ter ramp over thee'are,' he said, as he tapped his stick on the back of one of my new pride-and-joy purchases, who were in a small pen with a piece of tatty blackboard hanging on the gate simply saying in chalk 'Gefry'. This immediately explained my new-found name.

Next the stockman said, 'Give us tha paperwork, lad.'

'Sorry,' I replied, 'paperwork?'

''As tha paid for tha sheep, lad?'

'Paid?' I replied.

'Aye, paid fo' t'sheep. They don't give 'em away, tha knows!'

'Oh no of course, got it, how do you do that, sir?' I enquired.

'Tha not bin afore 'ave thee, lad?'

I thought that by now my blatant inexperience, and inappropriate clothing, would have been a bit of a giveaway if not glaringly obvious, but clearly not. Either that or the stockman was simply too busy to have noticed my obvious shortcomings, or too polite.

'Go up to t' office, they'll sort yer.'

'Okay,' I said, 'where's the off—' But he was away into the melee poking his stick at some more unfortunate sheep and shouting another indecipherable name. I was obviously dealt with.

I set off to the office without the slightest idea of where it was. The draughty building seemed to consist solely of tube-like constructed walkways with pens apparently popped in wherever they could get them, bursting and bustling with people climbing everywhere, squeezing and prodding sheep, lifting their legs up and rooting in their mouths. Quite what this inspection was for I knew not; I'd just bought mine as seen. There were animals seemingly by the thousand, and consequently rivers, even deltas, of urine as a result. I had a look at a passing farmer's leggings and thought: hmmmm… the penny was beginning to drop concerning the suitability of my attire of new jacket, corduroy trousers and polished footwear. I feared for the future of my footwear, which, in particular, was unlikely to survive the testing ground conditions. If these conditions were a measure then these were certainly all healthy animals judging by what issued from them, their back ends working overtime through stress. They only had three ways of showing their concern and obvious displeasure at their surroundings; firstly exhaustive piercing bleating, secondly the production of steaming rivers of wee, and thirdly the landscape of droppings through which the rivers flowed.

I thought I'd look for an office sign, as everyone was tearing about hectically and it was difficult (and seemed rude) to interrupt with what to the assembled was likely to be such an obvious question. Finally I saw it in the distance. It was a poorly maintained, frail sign swinging at an angle on one of its chains, the other dangling aimlessly, but its message of 'Office' was still intact. I immediately felt sorry for this forlorn piece of metal, a distant shadow of itself in its heyday, when it would have swung proudly from where its much needed information - second only to 'Toilets' I imagine - was imparted. If the sign could speak, it occurred to me, it might have thanked me for probably being the first person to use its services in years. This sign was certainly my port in a storm and I was very grateful to it. The office was the most important place at the auction. It was where the farmer's life blood was shed by the auction secretary, who by now wanted to see the colour of the money. I'd made it to the office. As I passed under it, I whispered a thank you to that sign.

I entered the tatty but comparatively quiet corridor and joined the orderly queue of muttering farmers as they passed the rusty, albeit functional row of tea, coffee, cola and sandwich machines. I thought it would take a brave man to tackle any of the above, particularly the sandwich machine. I'm sure the refreshments were fine but their dispensers' condition made my new friend, the office sign, look in first-class order. However on the evidence of the neighbouring overflowing bin, they had all done good business. I noticed the farmers were getting quieter the nearer to the office they got. They were more subdued, edgy and less boisterous than out in the body of the building, but then it dawned on me that this was the painful bit. The money moment. In their world this was, after all, their equivalent of the holding pens and queue at the abattoir…

I got to the front surprisingly quickly.

'Yes?' the (on first impression) austere lady said.

I answered, 'Good afternoon, dear lady, I should like to pay for my sheep.'

'Lot number?' she said. Not for the first time that day I simply repeated the question with a quizzical look.

'Lot number?'

'Yes?' She repeated her question as I had. I realised quickly, as her tone had already changed in our so far limited and matter-of-fact exchange, that I was perhaps not dealing with a patient lady. Mind you, I have to say in her defence that these farmers, buyers and dealers were a rum lot and that's no lie. Reminiscent of that bar in *Star Wars*, there were all sorts to deal with and no doubt she needed skin of leather and selective hearing as some of her clients' language was a little choice, usually only heard by livestock.

She went on, surely thinking 'I've got a right one here'

'Don't you have the lot number for what you bought?'

There was no dressing it up, I thought of trying to, but it would have been futile in this case. There was no easy answer. 'No,' I reluctantly admitted.

Her not unexpected disappointment was plain to see. She turned on her swivel chair to her computer, or what appeared to be left of it.

'Name.'

'Jeffries,' I said. She typed furiously.

'You sure it's Jeffries?'

After my mistake with the stockman, I was about to offer the alternative spelling and pronunciation, but she was well ahead of me.

‘Got one under “Gefry”,’ she said.

I thought my name had simply been spelt wrongly when chalked on the board on the pen, but it now appeared the spelling error ran deeper and was in the computer’s innards as well.

‘What did you buy?’ she said over her shoulder.

I said quite confidently, ‘Two sheep, with four lambs at their feet.’

‘Got it, two Suffolks, lambs afoot,’ she replied remarkably quickly, then paused before saying, peering quizzically at me, ‘What did you say? “Lambs at their feet”? You are not from round ‘ere, are yer, luv, with an accent like that?’

I drew breath to offer an explanation, but before I could reply she had moved on. Time really and clearly was money here.

‘That’s one hundred and forty-four pounds, cheque, cash or card?’

Puzzled, I said, ‘No, no, sorry, seventy-two, surely…’ The straightforward maths of this still hadn’t dawned on me. (Sometimes I think I’d miss a moving train.)

She simply repeated, ‘One hundred and forty-four pounds. Bid was seventy-two each.’

EACH!! Each… 'Oh good' I thought, my clear misunderstanding of the very basics of how auctions operate now obvious even to me. In an effort to conceal my naivety, stark financial panic and inexperience as best I could I said;

'Of course a hundred and forty four, silly me'

There was no point in looking, I knew I only had one hundred pounds in the world and this was the cash in my pocket. I had thought the one hundred quite a fiscal achievement, as it was the wrong time of the week, the wrong time of the month, and the wrong time of year for my cash flow, and, as usual, another wrong year...

I nervously said, 'I'm afraid I don't have that much.' I wondered if there was a returns policy on one sheep after the sale, but I somehow doubted that there would be, and thought it safer not to ask.

'Card cash machine over there,' she said while notably and deliberately moving my paperwork to one side.

'Thank you,' I said.

She continued rather than replied with a loud, 'Next?' Again, I was obviously dealt with. This whole place ran at a faster pace than I was used to; a well-oiled machine it most certainly was.

Now I was in trouble, the expression 'none and slim' came to mind as it summed up my cards chances in not only that machine but any machine, and I had left 'slim' at home. Ice cubes, hell and all other such expressions came to mind, indeed the ice cube may indeed have had a chance that my card sadly did not.

The trusty chequebook was the farmer's preferred weapon of choice for payment, as it delayed the dreaded hour when cash would actually have to leave their account and pocket, but I had not brought mine. I knew exactly where it was though, usefully on the kitchen worktop in readiness for its trip here. There was no 'wind' behind my cheque either, but I would, as the farmers, have time to regroup before the funds were actually called upon. Sam, I thought? I wonder if she has any money. She was my only hope.

The return journey back across the auction hall to our pen, well our sheep's pen, was very similar to the outward bound trip. The rivers of urine were however noticeably deeper and faster-flowing now though and the mountains of droppings higher.

'Sam, Sam!' I shouted, unheard in the chorus. She was leaning on our pen to protect our purchases, not that they were under any imminent threat yet.

As I approached she said, 'Where have you been?' I didn't answer that for the moment, it would soon become clear.

'Sam? Have you got any money?'

'What?' she replied impatiently. She was busy with her new charges, who had soon rightly overtaken me in the pecking order.

‘Money,’ I said. ‘Have you got any?’ It really was becoming a day of repeating myself. I could feel the panic showing on my face.

‘Money,’ she said.

‘Yes, money, tokens, anything – I haven’t got enough,’ I pleaded.

‘How much do you need?’

‘Fifty quid should do it?’

‘Okay,’ she said, ‘hang on.’

I was relieved as the thought of being thrown out, banned or worse, even the leg stocks, had crossed my mind for bidding without enough money. I tried to reassure myself that such punishments must have been long banished, but it did feel very Dickensian in there.

She reached into her ever-deep pocket and handed me the funds; it has to be said with understandable resignation. I’m sure she believed she had married an idiot, and although I lived in him, I more often than not struggled to disagree.

‘You’re a saviour,’ I said, already setting off for my second leg to the office. ‘Love you,’ I shouted back over my shoulder, which interestingly wasn’t reciprocated. I made it back to the office marginally quicker. I was definitely showing improvement at hurdling barriers. (I learnt later that these barriers were actually called ‘hurdles’, and with good reason.)

The queue had thinned a little by now and I soon faced round two with the lady behind the glass. Her face didn't drop as far as I thought it might on my return.

'Hiya,' she said almost joyously. 'Where have you been, printing it?'

Quite floored by the change in her manner, I replied, 'If only, I wish.' We chuckled together.

'Now that will be one hundred and forty-four pounds, please, luv.'

You could have knocked me down with a feather. I had wrongly marked her down like Matron at school, a merciless, unsympathetic uniformed lady, military in look and nature, a robust nurse of her day, but I was wrong about the auction lady: she was lovely. Her job and environment undoubtedly required a hard initial exterior, her clientele were no walk in the park, and the pace was fierce.

'Sorry if I was a bit off with you earlier,' she said. 'We get really busy little spells in here and you caught one, and getting money out of most of the miserable sods in here is like pulling teeth in the main.'

'No need to apologise to me, my dear lady, it was I that was at fault.' I handed over my one hundred and fifty pounds and she quickly opened her wooden till drawer, in which there was more cash than I'd ever seen, and handed me my pound coin and fiver change. The printer on the desk behind whirred into action with the characteristic racket.

While it was doing its stuff, I said to my new-found friend, ‘I bet mine was the smallest purchase of the day, wasn’t it?’

‘Yes,’ she replied, ‘by some way.’

We laughed and I said, ‘Probably took the longest to process as well, did it?’

She looked very knowledgeably over her glasses and replied with a mischievous smile, ‘I’m saying nothing.’ She turned round to the printer and retrieved my ‘paperwork’ and handed it to me.

‘That stock fellow will be happy with me now?’ I said.

‘Jimmy.’

‘Jimmy?’

‘His name.’

‘Oh, thank you, and thank you for being patient with me. Sorry for the delay earlier.’

‘Don’t worry, my pleasure, see you again, bye-bye luv.’

‘Bye,’ I replied and I hoped she picked up the affection I had developed for her; she clearly was able to suffer fools gladly. She had turned out to be a port in this storm of animals and humanity for me, and things unbeknown to me were only to get worse. Jimmy would definitely be pleased with me though, I thought, grasping my paperwork. I was more than a little proud of myself. A little slip financially, granted, but all in all a good effort, I mused. I also knew I would likely be the only one that thought this an unchallenged success, but I could live with that. I had learnt something here about auctions and how they were run, farmers and folk, which was all good. Unexpectedly, I really liked the lady in the office; I think she recognised my raw naivety and felt sorry for me. I have often wondered since if she caught sight of the state of my shoes and corduroys. I hoped to perhaps meet her again someday. I felt she would have had some tales to tell and I would have loved (I think) to have heard what she really made of me that day. But 'see her again' I never did.

Jimmy spotted me on my return to Sam.

''As tha got t' paperwork, lad?' he asked.

'That I 'ave, sir,' I replied, and after all my travels and effort, he just stuffed it unceremoniously into his body-warmer pocket, not even looking at it. ('That I 'ave'? Did I really say that? I was pleased I was picking up the lingo. It could do no harm to my non-existent credibility)

'Back tha trailer up, lad.' Even Jimmy seemed more relaxed now the major push was over. 'Trailer, lad,' Jimmy said again, staring at me with increasing impatience, so off I went between the flared-nosed cattle and equally flared-nosed truck drivers to get my 'trailer'.

If there had been a trailer attached to my car it would have been a surprise, no, more a miracle, because I did not set off from home with one. I didn't own one, so quite why I went to get it as instructed is open to question and beyond even me too. It just seemed like the thing, well the only thing to do, and he had told me to. In general, after strict schooling, it was my second nature to do as I was told and it was not always the best course of action. The wagon drivers were all jostling for position to get to their lorries to remove their two or three hundred or so purchases first, or as soon as. 'Time's money' and all that.

As I navigated the throng, one thickset farming sort hollered at me, 'Bit o' luck money, lad?'

What? What was he was talking about, 'luck money'? I had not the slightest idea. I even turned round thinking he must be talking to someone behind me, but he repeated, 'Bit o' luck, lad?' He rubbed his fingers together in front of me. Oh money, he wanted money, I thought with a question mark. My five quid seemed to do it, (Sam's change). He briefly explained that he had sold my sheep to me, clearly enabled by 't'auction'. The 'bit o' luck money' was apparently a quaint, if expensive I thought, traditional good luck gesture given by the purchaser to the vendor. I rather thought I was the one in need of the luck with my new sheep. To this day I'm not sure what luck money is, and have no idea who the bloke I gave Sam's fiver to was. He may have been an enterprising fellow who was just going round asking everybody for all I knew but I suspected not, although I was obvious and easy pickings for initiation jokes I was quite sure. I would have thought so if in their shoes…

I knew my stockman would not be happy when I was stopped again by a large portly 'owd 'un', a term frequently used for the retired farmers and 'fathas' by their sons and daughters. They attended the auctions simply because it was all they knew and to keep their beady eyes firmly on how the 'young 'uns' were doing. He was wearing overalls, which had seen better days, and I somehow knew he was going to offer me his depth of knowledge, like it or not.

'You buy them two Suffolks wit' lambs, lad?'

'Yes,' I said with, it has to be said, a combination of both pride and trepidation in my voice.

With his huge rough fingers tucked into what was left of his lapels, he drew breath through his pipe smoke and began to pontificate. 'What you pay?'

So much for confidentiality, I thought. Besides he already knew. Even with my inexperience I knew he knew. These 'owd 'uns' didn't miss a thing. He just wanted me to say it, and know he knew, to give the knowledge and wealth of experience which he was undoubtedly about to impart all the more credence. Nothing was to stop him having his penn'orth. Besides, no doubt everyone else had heard it to exhaustion, and it was my turn to be induced.

'Seventy-two pounds,' I said 'each.'

'That's it, lad, what I thought,' he replied and went on, 'Seen you coming, they have, lad, seen it all afore wit' you 'obby farmers, seen you coming.'

I couldn't take issue with the man about being an ''obby farmer', and indeed positively basked in the promotion from blithering idiot. He indeed would have had a field day if he had known that I had never so much as intentionally touched a sheep. I might have rubbed up against one or two thousand on my trip to the office, but never deliberately laid a hand on one.

'Ney, they's not worth that, lad, seventy-two pund, you've been done there.' I thought I'd been 'done here' too, with my luck money investment, but hey-ho.

'Aye, seen you coming...' I was interested to now learn the magnitude of my financial error. I did not have long to wait for the punchline to come.

'Yep, lad, had yer - thee'are, not worth a penny o'er seventy-one.'

With considerable relief at this result I pressed on through the crowd. I didn't tell the 'owd 'un' that I could have paid thirty-two or one hundred and two pounds, and would have been none the wiser. As to the sheep's value I cared even less, my purchase was based on two simple needs. The first solely my lawnmower theory of getting, and keeping, the grass down in 'the jungle', the second it was the only lot of two sheep going through on that day. Besides his one pound variation in what I had paid paled into insignificance compared to the fiver 'luck money', and the small matter of my seventy-two pound misunderstanding.

I'm not sure when it dawned on me I had simply been swept along by this tide of humans and animals, but dawn on me it did. You couldn't help getting the impression that a lot of the older farmers just went to the auctions 'fer crack', and were intermingling 'wit' udder 'owd 'uns' and each had a view on what seemed to me every animal in the place. It was their theatre, their coliseum, their monument to their lifetimes. During my brief visit I had been treated to every animal smell and sound imaginable, made to feel that I looked sufficiently out of place to merit interest from all who saw me, and learnt how it was 'lucky' to give passing strangers money for no obvious reason. Now I was being told to go and get, and had indeed physically set off for, a trailer - that most obvious and basic prerequisite of any level livestock purchase - which I didn't have… and I loved it.

More genuine folk you couldn't meet. 'Get what you pay for' you certainly did. Have you ever walked your dog into a field full of cows? It is not recommended but suddenly you, for no reason other than your presence, merit the unwavering focus of attention of every cow, and can feel their eyes boring into you from every angle. They are not of course looking at you but the dog as their perceived enemy. Cows have clearly never heard of roast beef or chilli con carne, as they see the dog as the threat, not the human. It was a bit like the feeling you get in the tap room of some old country pub, when it falls silent as you walk through the door..

I was halfway to my vehicle when I realised that I was going to have to break the news to a likely by now impatient Jimmy that I didn't have a trailer. Sheepishly I weaved my car slowly through the various lorries and Land-Rovers with their trailers duly attached. There were even trailers with trailers attached to them being reversed with bewildering skill that boarded on just showing off, but none of this was actually going to lessen or divert the ridicule to come when I met the stockman, trailerless. 'Rabbit in the headlights', 'dog in the cow field', 'loneliness of the local country pub'… it felt like all three.

I reversed up to the ramp in my car, which was getting ever more attention. I did think: this is not good. Even I was beginning to see this wasn't going to be easy and couldn't end well. There were now three complications. Firstly no trailer, so the sheep would have to get in the car. Secondly I had never handled a sheep, and from their obvious staring panic in the sheep pen they would very likely, even to the untrained handler, be less than keen on the idea of getting into the aforementioned car in an orderly fashion. Thirdly, (and I'm not entirely sure why I had forgotten this) Purdey was also in the car. Sadly 'Purdey' was not the prestige shotgun of that name, more of a… how should I put it… well a young boisterous Gordon Setter.

Purdey was incapable of containing excitement, full stop. From dawn till dusk she was quite mad, hyper, and had she been human would have been diagnosed with some form of disorder without doubt or hesitation. In her world simply waking up was fantastic. She would accelerate and fly into the car to come out with us, often crashing into the opposite door (deceleration not being a technique she had given any thought to), even when she didn't know where we were going. But now we had taken her to, in her view, doggy Disneyland, she was simply beside herself. With all the sounds and views and smells the auction animals offered she was becoming uncontrollably delirious. Little did she know at this stage with whom she'd be sharing her lift home. Then, of course, there was Sam, my resigned, long-suffering and often disappointed wife and best friend. Where she was going to sit I did not know (I was wrong about that as it turned out).

I don't think that stockmen are given to speechlessness as a rule, but I rather think I had now caught both his and most of the other farmers' and farm hands' attention. They were getting on with their tasks, but were a tad quieter and more distracted: you could sense that they all had one eye on the unfolding pantomime - the centrepiece of which was sadly me. Some of the assembled had even stopped what they were doing and were leaning on their ever-present sticks. PJ strikes again, I thought, wishing I was somewhere, anywhere, else. I don't think I'd ever felt quite like it.

The stockman looked at me and said with a forlorn question mark in his voice, 'Trailer?'

I didn't know whether to blag it or not with remarks like 'Oh yes, knew I had forgotten something, always doing it' or 'No, no, always just come for a few animals in t'car, hardly worth bothering wit' trailer'. I decided against this strategy. It would surely make a bad situation worse and it wasn't going to work. Confidence and I had parted company for the moment. My predicament wasn't helped by the thought that someone in the now extensive assembled crowd was bound to notice that my car did not even have that most basic of farming assets and trailer essential - a tow bar.

Finally the solution was clear: send in the cavalry. Introducing stage right Philip Jeffries, my public schoolboy alter ego twit and saviour. I went for the PJ tried and tested posh clown impression.

‘I’m sorry to say, guys, I don’t have a trailer, or indeed a tow bar. I have made the classic mistake of the hobby farmer in that I didn’t really want to buy any sheep today as I’m not ready and haven’t a clue what I’m doing. Today was a recce if the truth be known so I would not be, and look, so obviously stupid when I came for real. I just had no idea that the lots would be so big, so when my two popped into the ring I thought it was fate. I’m an idiot!’

PJ further addressed the assembled crowd, this part of the impression being designed to gain their sympathy, so they might take pity on me.

‘Could anyone give me a hand loading these?’

I wasn’t hopeful, as these giant lifelong sheep farmers probably wouldn’t be seen dead doing something as unprofessional and ridiculous as loading sheep into a family car. They would possibly be running the risk of never living it down in their country locals, the stuff of folklore. I hoped they would like to be part of the unfolding story, which was looking more likely by the minute to be retold for years to come.

The silence was broken by laughter then the shout, ‘Come on, lads, let’s load this lad’s sheep for him.’

‘Thank you, thank you,’ I grovelled.

'You're all right, lad, you're not t' first and dare say won't be t' last.'

'Least you've had the balls to admit you're a plonker,' was one playful shout. (I was just glad I apparently, and surprisingly, wasn't the first.)

'Flip me' (I didn't say that, even a public schoolboy wouldn't say that, or more likely especially a public schoolboy wouldn't say that).

'You are a strong lot.' I also didn't say. I was trying not to sound like John Inman or David Walliams, and that the nervous embarrassment of the whole situation appeared to be manifesting itself in my language. As the first giants' gnarled hands grabbed my purchases by their wool, I decided that compliment and flattery was my best technique, and the reappearance of the public school twit had saved the day. I am sure all my new chums saw right through it though. They were just decent folk, and I had perhaps broken their long day up with a bit of light relief. Wasn't every day they got an idiot there with a darling in tow I imagined, so I have to say I felt I had got off lightly.

My two newly purchased lawnmowers with four big legs and eight little legs underneath reluctantly made their way to the very different looking trailer. Trailers they had come to tolerate, but a barking car was a quite new proposition. They didn't have much choice though with my new found burly friend's help; they were quickly manhandled towards the boot (small mercies it was an estate car). There was a drawback to the open plan nature of the roomy inside though as it gave Purdey absolute access to her new chums. My loader's great hands lifted the bums of the sheep off the ground, and into their new temporary accommodation and surroundings. I was soon to learn that sheep are heavier and stronger than I thought.

Sam shouted through the front car window, 'PJ, get the travelling rug.'

What? I thought. We had a travelling rug? I thought only elderly aunts and uncles in old Ford Escorts had such things. This 'travelling' rug was a remnant from Purdey's puppyhood, and was under the seat. Sam was always more organised than I.

'What for?' I protested. This was no time for a picnic, I thought.

'Just get it and hold it onto the head rests and keep Purdey in the front seat,' came my reprimand and her cry from somewhere now in the thick of it at the back of the car, the burly crowd quite enjoying her getting stuck in, clinging on to a lamb. The assembled seemed to like a practical good looker, which Sam certainly was. And they were right about her being practical. Had she organised the day it would have gone like clockwork, but I had. She suffered me in silence, but I am under no illusion that her true thoughts and words would have been quite specific and choice. But animals were involved now and her priorities were, quite rightly, her lambs and their mums.

Purdey was no longer a dog, she was an astronaut, going stellar with excitement, and showing the classic characteristics of weightlessness by bouncing off the sides, seats and indeed the ceiling of the car at one point whilst tethered to me. Gravity did not appear to be affecting her any longer in the slightest. I was quickly finding out how strong this 'puppy' was too.

Trying to hold her torso under one arm, whilst fitting and adjusting my tartan travelling rug sheep-and-dog-proof screen with the other, was no mean feat. At the same time the car was bouncing and rocking in unison with the loading procedure behind. I was also learning quickly how loudly a panicked mother sheep could bleat in an enclosed space, especially directly into your ear.

Finally the boot lid closed, signalling that they were in. I wound down my window as I felt duty bound to thank my new found friends, albeit over the back of a now almost unrecognisable, rabid-looking, eye-popping dog, in imminent danger of heart failure.

'Thanks, thanks, chaps, well done, couldn't have done it without you.' There was never a truer word or understatement spoken. With that and Sam putting the final touches to my quite futile attempt at a barrier, we were nearly done.

In a last attempt at humour I added, 'Can you come to my place to unload them?'

I got a chuckle then one chap shouted back, 'No, no, but I'll sell you a chuffin' trailer.' For this he got rapturous laughter from all around, including Sam and me, and rightly so.

Sam jumped in the driving seat. She really did want to go now. (Oh and without being unnecessarily specific, he didn't say 'chuffin'', just in case you were in any doubt).

We slowly pulled away.

‘Well,’ I said to Sam, ‘that wasn’t too bad?’

I just got glanced at with ‘that look’. I don’t think she had ever been more embarrassed; I likely was not going to live this down in a hurry. I think if she hadn’t been driving her response might have been otherwise.

‘What’s that all up your arm?’ I said.

‘One of the sheep relieved itself as I was pushing it through the door,’ she replied. Were her teeth clenched? I didn’t know but suspected they were.

‘Well you can’t blame it,’ I said. ‘It’s not every day that you and the family get shoved in a car by the arse end. You’d think they would be happy, it being a family car,’ I chirped in an attempt at humour.

‘It might even be lucky,’ I said, pensively soldiering on. ‘You know, as rumoured, when you are lucky enough to be under a relieving bird?’

The look returned, this time with venom. It’s time to shut up PJ, I told myself. Quit while you are ahead, lad; well if not ahead, not an irretrievable distance behind.

I was far from convinced that Sam agreed with my assessment of ‘wasn’t too bad’.

I now found myself clinging on to Purdey for a secondary reason. It wasn’t just to stop her from trying to visit our guests, who had very nervously retreated as far from us as possible to the back, like the gold bars on the coach in *The Italian Job*. I was, it could be said, cowering behind

Purdey to protect me from Sam in case she should lash out at me. Fortunately for me she wasn't taken to physical violence, but on this occasion I wouldn't have been surprised or blamed her. Sam was coping well, though: she'd been massively embarrassed, ogled intolerably, covered in shite and was forty-nine pounds lighter for her trouble, and it was all undoubtedly my fault.

We pulled gingerly out of the auction gates, and I said 'Bye' to the passing gatepost. All in all I felt we had been amongst friends.

It soon became clear that this was to be the longest ten miles in a car we had ever travelled. My concerns for the upholstery were going to be the least of my worries. Purdey had settled a little, downgrading from the excitement level of astronaut to that of just criminally insane, and was still desperate and fighting to look around the blanket to see her playmates. I, meanwhile, was trying to do my level best to encourage her front legs and feet off me, in the forlorn hope that they'd consider joining her back legs in the foot well of the car.

Sam was steering her way through Corcastle town centre, trying to avoid any sudden movement and changing traffic lights. Roundabouts were particularly testing as with the increased weight we were tending to lunge a bit, like a ship half full of water. I hadn't checked the tyre pressure recently; in fact I hadn't checked the tyre pressure ever, it was just one of those jobs you know you should do, but you never do. Big Suffolk sheep, well any sheep, were much heavier and larger animals close up than I'd thought, especially in my current position of looking up one's nose as the travelling rug was slowly falling down. Admittedly it could have been worse, it could have been facing the other way, and the rug hadn't collapsed completely… yet. Mummy sheep don't look terribly friendly, fluffy or cute when you have just kidnapped them and their offspring, in what must look like a space ship. I suppose you can't blame them for that.

'Not far from the motorway now, love,' I said to Sam by way of encouragement. 'How are you doing?' All the car windows were open a tad for air, so it was a little like talking in a wind tunnel.

'Okay,' she said. 'Just you keep your eyes on those sheep.'

'Righty-ho, love,' I replied. It was not what I wanted to say or meant. Sod the sheep, was what I wanted to say. I was underneath a furry straining lunatic, which was producing saliva on an industrial scale. This 'thing', that used to be such a cute puppy, was sapping my strength and taking all my concentration to prevent her planned, no doubt murderous, incursion into the back of the car. If I didn't sweat my balls off, they would probably be trampled to paste by this ballistic dog jumping up and down on my seat dangerously close to my personal assets. The travelling rug screen had now collapsed so the opposing sides - the front and back opponents - now had an uninterrupted view of each other. The car was now more like the pitch. I turned round astride the dog to stop an advance, at which the sheep pushed hard against the back door. I hoped that the lock was latched properly, or it would be carnage. Keeping my eye on the sheep, as Sam had suggested, was doing no good at all.

As we joined the motorway beads of sweat were running off my forehead. So far we'd managed to pull off this stunt not only without any preparation, but also on what was one of the hottest days of the year.

Sam said, 'Need a drink when we get home.'

'You're not kidding,' I replied flippantly 'could murder a cider.'

'Not you' came the robust reply, 'the sheep'.

Suitably chastised I tried to subdue Purdey a bit with bribery, a chew. Wouldn't you just know it, lamb flavour. I ask you, the one chew I didn't need in the packet that day was lamb-flavoured, anything else but not lamb. Mind you, with modern food flavourings, ours and animals' alike, I imagined this was the nearest this chew ever got to a lamb and vice versa.

On the motorway things slowly became a little quieter as all the assembled, Sam and I included, settled a bit, realising that we were all in the same boat as it were and there was nothing any one of us could do about it.

Shortly after we had got going on the motorway we were overtaken slowly by another family car, complete with family. Two small children's noses were glued to the car window, and there seemed to be a good deal of pointing and discussion going on. I thought: What are they looking at? The sheep appeared to be looking back at the children. I imagined that if they had had a sign it would doubtless have read along the lines of: 'Help, we are being kidnapped, babies on board!' We were just lucky sheep can't write, I thought mischievously.

You would have thought by their faces, that that passing family had never seen a car on the motorway with sheep in it before. Strange…

If you heard what we did next in a car that did not happen to have sheep in it, you would immediately pull over to take a look, then likely ring for roadside assistance suspecting a significant journey threatening water leak. But if, (like normal people), you were travelling in a deluxe family estate car with sheep in it, then you wouldn't take it to mean there was something wrong with the engine. Every few minutes, it seemed, the bump, bump sound of the sheep's back legs adopting a wider gait could be heard, shortly followed by a catastrophic water leak. Purdey's odour alarm would immediately go off, and my heart sank ever deeper at the thought of the clean-up job that was inevitably going to ensue. You know they say it takes weeks to get the smell of milk out of your car if you are unfortunate enough to spill it? Well believe me I can beat that… That dear car never recovered from that day.

We finally turned into Cliff Field, our home and now the sheep's home too. I got out with an exhausted panting dog to open the five-bar gate and she bounded through it, no doubt planning her next ambush when the sheep were released. She was having the time of her life.

Sam backed the car up to one of the outbuildings. I quickly organised a bit of straw for the floor while Sam got a bucket of water. We opened the car boot door and the first sheep flew out, jumping high from the car into the building with little concern for her new charges, like a mini point to pointer. She was soon back for her babies though. The second one was less convinced about this move, believing she'd had enough excitement and changes of accommodation for one day, and deciding the car would do for now as she seemed to have got quite used to it. With the boot open, this one and her two adorable offspring reversed hard up to the back of the front seats, and looked to be staying put. Mum's facial expression and nostrils seemed to be saying to me something along the lines of: 'And who do you think you are?' I had the uneasy feeling that cooperation was not on her agenda.

While this stand-off continued, Sam was dealing with the water trough. She must have noticed or sensed my nervous reluctance to do anything and said, 'Just get in and shove her out, you wimp.'

So, as instructed, I cautiously climbed in to one side of the car. Mum looked at me still with that 'just try it mate' look on her face. I climbed farther in saying, 'Shoo, shoo, Mrs Sheep.' What on earth was I saying?

'Come on, you tart, PJ, shove her out,' encouraged Sam, grinning far too enthusiastically. She looked completely at home, and must have done this in a previous life, I thought.

I made one more move forward, at which the now newly named 'Mrs Sheep' decided it was time to go. She brushed heavily passed me, bleating, and her two offspring scampered after her. Finally they were all out.

We shut the building's lower stable door, and just leaned and watched. It was great, a truly Christmas card view, albeit without the tinsel or even being December. The little ones were soon launching themselves at their mums' mini traffic-cone-shaped teats with such ferocity it would have made a lady wince; it was making me wince too for what it is worth. Sam said forlornly but with understanding to the lambs: 'oye, be more gentle you.'

Well you can imagine how much attention they paid to that. We watched our new investments until the mums had had a drink of water then left them in peace to settle in.

I said apologetically, 'Sorry about the money, Sam.'

'That's okay,' she replied. 'I had half a mind that you wouldn't have a clue how much they would be, or have enough money with you.'

'Thanks, 'I said. 'Here's your pound change.'

'Oh great, thanks,' said Sam, laughing.

'Call it luck money,' I said.

'More bad luck money with you,' she retorted.

'Unkind, but true,' I replied, both of us now having a good giggle. I was blessed with the most understanding girl on earth. I noticed then we were holding hands; we hadn't done that in ages.

Little did we know then that these were just our first new business partners, and over time we were to graduate to Jacob sheep, Gloucester Old Spot pigs, turkeys, chickens – well the whole amateur shooting match really.

Sam was the best thing that ever happened to PJ, albeit if their relationship started at a well-attended ten pence per pint Guinness night at uni, to which she went with her then long-standing boyfriend. Terrible stuff Guinness, it delightfully fills one with groundless confidence. It should never have worked or happened but, as for so many of us, the reasons we are together or form relationships are not often clear and often best forgotten.

Boyfriend duly faded as he chose Sandhurst over his university course, and PJ moved up the queue. They say opposites attract, well it could not have been more true in this case. Sam was mature and professional, PJ never; Sam very much a morning person, PJ a night owl. The list went on.

I did try to alter what traits I could to bring our paths closer together, but again failed spectacularly. I could do little to alter my immaturity and chaos, but I did think one morning I could become a morning person in an effort to impress.

Sadly impress I did not, but leave a lifelong impression on the poor lady I did. It was one of those 'best laid plans' stories really.

I secretly elected to rise before Sam, as quietly as a mouse, and make her breakfast. Well not a full breakfast in bed (she indeed wouldn't have eaten anything I cooked, nor would she have believed I did not have some dreadful confession to make, and wasn't just 'soft-soaping' her) but perhaps coffee I thought after she awoke. Simple enough, what could go wrong?

I boiled the kettle, got a mug off the 'mug tree', put in a teaspoon of coffee from the jar, then the milk, carefully remembering some unlikely old wives' tale about burning or scorching the coffee granules, then the boiling water. I wanted this to be just right.

The drink, although visibly hot, appeared, it had to be said, a little pale in colour and not being an expert at the time I simply assumed that I was light on coffee and strong on milk. This I do remember thinking was easily solved - more coffee clearly required. I duly dolloped in a further good measure of coffee and stirred furiously. To my concern and puzzlement, there was little or no improvement in darkening the brew.

However, it was what it was, as they say, and after placing the mug on a suitable small tray with a selection of very boring biscuits I was ready. I duly tiptoed up like an excited child with a pressie or a puppy with a toy for its owner.

Sam was just coming round with a bit of a stretch, and a 'Good morning' soon followed. It was then that I struck.

'Stay there, dear lady, oh and good morning,' I said.

'What are you doing up?' she sleepily but already sounding suspicious said.

'Don't you worry, you just enjoy your coffee and I'll make a start on the jobs…' And I was off.

Moments, only moments later I heard what could only to be said to be a medical emergency from the bedroom, so I turned and ran back in. Sam was choking or worse, she just had to be from the loud spluttering sound.

I was greeted by Sam sitting bolt upright, wide awake, arms flailing about, making some very peculiar movements with her mouth and almost shouting 'Eeerrrggh' or something similar, her tortured eyes rolling demonically and more worryingly in my direction.

'Aaggghhh, what is that!!??'

'What is what?' I stupidly replied, compounding the stupidity by cottoning on and saying, 'It's your coffee, love' (already employing a rarely used defensive title for Sam, something was quite obviously amiss), 'I thought it would be a treat, hot coffee in bed?'

'Treat!' she shouted and raced past me to the bathroom. After considerable sound effects which are best imagined, she reappeared and without speaking marched down to the kitchen. I followed sheepishly but blissfully unaware that I had done anything wrong. What was worse was I was beginning to suspect that Sam knew or had a strong suspicion of what the problem was. Worryingly she still didn't speak. Still nonchalantly unaware of my crime, I saw Sam reach up to the cupboard and retrieve the jar of coffee granules. She placed it in front of her on the worktop and immediately reached back up again. This time she brought down a further container, then in one motion turned to face me and, shall we say, firmly placed it down next to its partner in crime. (I am deliberately and carefully avoiding the 'slam' word, as that would not reflect the message she was conveying and was far from her nature.) Quite calmly, it has to be said, she said, 'Please don't ever, I mean ever, get up early unsupervised again, thank you.' With that she went back upstairs.

My crime was still not at all obvious to me, but that was soon to change. The jars were, to be fair, similar…ish, both glass and labelled. Admittedly one most definitely had a red lid, the other not quite so red, well quite bright green really, and one lid was round, the other quite definitely hexagonal. Still I was a little in the dark…

It was only on reading those very telling words 'Nescafé' and 'Bisto' that the full extent of my crime was clear.

In PJ's defence apart from the shape, lid colour, brand labels, not to mention contents, the two jars were all but nearly identical.

The way she had silently presented the two jars spoke volumes about her cool crisis-management skills, no words required, argument necessary or denial opportunity available, just simple fact.

That was the end of my being-a-morning-person attempt. The old expression 'If it ain't broke, don't fix it' was adopted.

Sam always remained superficially calm, at least on such occasions, and had had her fair share of my disasters, but for some reason was still with me, so by my standards today had gone okay… by and large.

As we started our morning rounds, by then all was well with the world. And what's more I had finally touched a sheep, albeit involuntarily.

I didn't dare look in the back of the car, that treat was for another day…

…and I had thought that coffee had stayed unusually pale…?

Chapter 2

TYLER

Stan was a builder, a great guy, a bit older than me, about five years or so at a guess. He lived in Westlet, the village a couple of miles from us here at Cliff Field. We had met in the local pub. I am a firm believer that if you want anything anywhere simply go and ask in the nearest local pub, the Google and Facebook of their day. Westlet was the nearest village with a pub and no exception. Quite why it was called Westlet is not now completely obvious. It has a front if you like, where the sea used to be, but over the years its muddy little estuary has silted up. Where there was sea there is now marsh; some people now jokingly call it Grass-side, which is undoubtedly more accurate, if a little unkind. The best guess is that the name came from the estuary, an 'inlet' on the west coast, but I never really knew.

When we moved into Cliff Field it soon became obvious we were in need of a builder. I'd said to Sam I'd have a go, but she flatly declined. Her decision was a bit harsh, I felt, but I knew the source and whence this opinion of my building skills arose. What had happened previously was not exactly a demonstration of my finest practical skills. Sam and I were both geologists by trade, in fact we had met in the geology department at university. I have often since wished I'd had a childhood fascination with history and biology, rather than geography and geology, as now I've become interested in history, and, as the years progress, increasingly dependent on biology, particularly mine. Hey-ho.

In our Manchester flat, which was some way removed from a blueprint of a glamorous first home, there was a tired 1960s fire surround - I'm sure state of the art then, but now it had sadly had its day.

Sam had been the driving force behind the move to Cumbria, deeply impractical geographically for work purposes, but we deemed the likely commutes worthwhile, the 'pros' of youthful energy and optimism just outweighing the far more sensible 'cons'. She had spent her childhood holidays in Cumbria, and indeed produced her geology dissertation in the pouring rain in some remote deserted valley and old miners cottage. She had, however, rediscovered an old slate mine and its associated spoil heaps, which became the perfect hunting ground for the stone for PJ's project.

The car hadn't liked that trip either, but the stone was duly sourced from rich pickings of finest Lake District green slate. It has to be said the rock was dusty and the car's suspension no doubt suffered - but at least it didn't urinate.

Rock sourced and retrieved, we laid it out in front of the fireplace to be dressed, like a debris field from some sunken vessel. It wasn't a working fire so our creation was just to be a 'feature'. Needless to say though I had turned our smart lounge into a bomb site. I had totally stripped the room to do this work and it was now just an area of old bare floorboards, rock and dust, more like a long-forgotten outbuilding.

Assembly began. I bought some cement from the local builder's merchants, Sam selected the stones and I stuck them where required and when allowed, as Sam was far better at planning, visualising and indeed executing this sort of thing than I, and besides wanted her lounge back. We were delighted with the outcome (it did look good, even if I say so myself); the 'feature' became the focal point of our living room, long before the word 'feature' in home design became popular.

We were out with friends one night months, if not a year later, and we all had 'new to us' properties with various works required. One had had a fitted kitchen, another a new loo and so on. Not to be outdone I chirped up that we had 'done' our fireplace feature. I explained the sourcing of the stone, but added I was a bit disappointed with the cement as it had set a bluey colour and was extremely hard. I jokingly said I thought it must be because I'd used outdoor cement. One of the assembled said he wasn't aware that there was indoor and outdoor cement. The most knowledgeable and oldest DIYer present, (that much he made sure we all knew), confirmed there was no difference in cement for use indoors and out. Fillers yes, but cement no.

'Cement is cement,' he said and that's it. Oh it must be something else then, I conceded.

'Well...' he said. I was not getting off that easily, I knew he was going to love sharing his superior knowledge with us all, probably at my embarrassed expense, and how right I was.

'What ratio did you use?' he asked. I didn't know what he meant.

Over my forkful of chilli con carne, I simply replied, 'Ratio?' with a not deliberately puzzled tone and without unnecessary interest or encouragement.

I still had absolutely no idea what he was talking about. I thought ratios were something to do with gears or another irrelevancy one had to be able to quote, not understand, in physics lessons at school and that was as far as that went.

'Yes, what ratio of sand to cement did you use?' Clever Clogs went on.

'Sand to cement?' Interesting idea, I thought if irrelevant.

Clearly the man was an idiot. To glue wood together, I use wood glue; if I want to make a model I use model adhesive; wall paper, wall paper paste and so on. It therefore follows that if I want to glue stones together I use stone glue, better known as cement. He clearly didn't understand.

'No, no,' I went on. 'I didn't use any sand, I just wanted to cement the stones together so I just used cement,' I explained as if talking to a child.

Well he positively guffawed with laughter. 'No sand, hear that, no sand,' he annoyingly repeated to the assembled... 'No wonder it went blue, it will have set like metal. I bet it's a sight stronger than your slate,' he said, loving every minute.

He did have a point though, that much I could immediately see, sort of an 'uh ohh' moment when you realise the error of over confidence. So I soldiered on: 'Well I wanted it to be strong.'

'It'll be that all right, you'll need dynamite to shift that. Just hope the next people in there like your "feature",' he mocked.

I had again served us up as the target for the butt of all the remaining humour that evening. Sam had just shaken her head and, I suspected, vowed to herself that building was another skill set to be struck off my dwindling list. On the way home I said to Sam in my defence that it didn't say add sand on the bag, but it did me no good. How was I meant to know that sand was a prerequisite? I would have put money on the fact that at least five of the eight around the table wouldn't have known that either, but they had kept suspiciously quiet. However I said no more, and we had all had a good laugh.

From that day forth Sam wanted a builder for what she couldn't do. I was never shortlisted for the job, and never entered the equation again.

I went to the local pub at Westlet one evening hoping to catch one or two locals having a quick pint before their tea. Inevitably these 'quick ones' ended up as nothing of the sort, when they rocked home some three or four hours later to find their 'dinner in the dog', who probably hadn't been walked yet, to add to the 'dirty stop-out's' misery.

There were four lads sitting at the bar that night, padded dirty trousers and tool pouches dangling from their belts like sporrans, a very promising start. These looked ideal candidates for my upcoming questioning.

I ordered my pint, had a swig, and said, 'Excuse me, lads, do any of you know a builder?'

There was a disappointing lack of response and 'stranger in a country pub syndrome' was evidenced by the stony silence. However after a short while the lad nearest to me, who had appeared the quietest when they were chatting before and lived under a hedge of mousey blonde curls, slowly and deliberately turned his head like in a Western and said, 'Who wants to know?' That was it, my Eureka moment. Stan and I had met! I had landed my builder with my first cast. Try doing that on Google…

Stan and I hit it off immediately and our relationship flourished. He came round to Cliff Field and we went through a list of priorities. He had a daytime building job and gave me a lesson in local dialect and expressions. A 'foreigner', like 'lambs afoot' at the auction, had a whole different meaning here. When he said he could ‘do a foreigner’ for us after he’d finished the ‘foreigner he was on’, well I have to admit to double taking, but after his explanation that ‘a foreigner’ was a job of work outside his employed status, all was well.

Over the next few weeks things moved swiftly and swimmingly. Our milkman, who was in fact the local farmer, on hearing I had bought some sheep (I was learning that news of any nature seemed to travel faster than light here), descended almost immediately on Cliff Field to help me and assess my purchases, and I am sure check on their well-being and my understanding of husbandry practices. I couldn’t help thinking he had come to have a laugh in a good-natured fashion as well though, as what I happened to have done by making this purchase qualified as news, or more like gossip round here. Peter brought his neighbour, Wool, his expertise well-advertised by his name. They were a visually amusing pair, both dressed in tatty overalls that fitted only where required and, thank heaven, provided modesty (but thankfully ‘stock was quiet’ was the expression) and almost matching shiny-with-wear flat caps. The major, and obvious, difference betwixt the two was that Peter was nearly as wide as he was tall, a champion rural wrestler no less. In contrast Wool was a gangling tall man with hands like dinner plates, who towered over him. They effortlessly manhandled and tossed our uncooperative new charges onto their backs, leaning them against their legs during their extensive no-holds-barred inspection. They checked the unimpressed beasts end to end and they got a clear bill of health. During the whole examination Wool enthusiastically sucked on his pipe. Reading between the lines they were more than a little surprised that I had happened to buy some on-the-surface sound stock, and that they had found nothing catastrophic, concerning or - probably to their likely disappointment - amusing at all, but that was without doubt beginner's luck.

Over the following years these two and their families welcomed us into the farmers' social inner circle and became firm friends and invaluable 'consultants', to say the least. To say they were a couple of local characters was, I very soon found out, an understatement. We had some rip-roaring dos. They certainly knew how to stage a knees-up. My unusual and unexpected introduction to sheep had, without me knowing, acted as my farming initiation ceremony, and my way to acceptance.

Peter and Wool had shown us the basic checks – mouth (broken teeth apparently gave some clue as to age, a bit like us in many cases), feet, foot rot and so on. These were the pre-flight (pre-purchase) checks we should have done at the auction, as all the waterproof-wearing professionals we saw were doing.

'We'd know foot rot when we saw it,' they said, soon corrected to 'when we smelled it' as it issued forth the most appalling smell, as the name foot rot alludes to. My new charges did not have it but we were informed we would likely encounter it in due course. The back squeezing and pushing down we had seen at the auction was a condition thing but more relevant to fat lambs to see if they were ready for the off (the plate), a deplorable thought with such delightful youngsters. But 'We din't make t' rules, lad, just play by 'em,' I had been reliably informed at the auction, but this unpleasant, uncomfortable harvesting was far enough away to be put out of our minds for the time being …

I don't remember ever seeing Wool without his pipe, or if forgotten, a roll up.

The sheep settled in well, sitting in the sunshine in the orchard gently chewing, each with their two youngsters curled up beside them. They looked picture-postcard idyllic, the epitome of contentment. I often thought where's a camera when you needed one? Oh for a modern mobile phone…

Sam, in her spare time, was looking for agricultural courses for us to go on to learn sheep husbandry and so on for ourselves.

The sheep lawnmowers had done a good job on the grass; in fact its availability was becoming limited. Stan was building the car park retaining wall when I took him a beer one lovely summer's evening. Whilst sharing a beer, we discussed how he was getting on with his day job, how his family were, and generally put the world to rights.

I said at one point, 'I think I'm going to have to put the sheep in the jungle.' Sooty's christened name had stuck.

'What, in there?' said Stan. 'You're joking, aren't you? Have you been in there?'

'Yes,' I said. 'It's a bit overgrown.'

‘Bit?’ exclaimed Stan, laughing, ‘Put the sheep in there and you’ll never see ‘em again.’

‘Why?’ I said with obvious puzzlement.

‘PJ, you ever got a sticky bomb stuck on yerself when you were a nipper?’

‘Yes.’

‘Well what does it stick to?’

‘Well, my pullover or something?’

‘Yes, yes, exactly, but what does it stick to?’

‘Er…’

‘Wool!’ he bawled at me. ‘The stuff the pully is made of. That ground in there, in yer jungle, is just briers and thistles and crap. Sheep will be stuck solid in minutes, like your pully and the sticky bomb, and if you don’t spot ‘em and help ‘em they’ll dee.’

It had never occurred to me that sheep could get stuck. What had evolution been up to? Surely they would just eat everything in sight. Mind you, briers can’t be easy on the palate and stuck they certainly can get, as they were to prove to me on a number of occasions in times to come.

Stan had settled back down now from his bewilderment at my stupidity, and I got us another bottle of beer – those Continental beers are lovely, but they don’t last. Stan was quite well-spoken but was well known to fit in the odd choice expletive into his sentences. It quite became him though and was somehow never offensive; it just wouldn't be Stan without them. He never let me live down the one time I offered him a coffee... admittedly almost unheard of, but I didn't know him well enough at the time to offer otherwise and it was morning, which said far more about PJ than Stan. The reason he never let this slip was that he never got it; I simply forgot and brought beer. That much PJ could be relied upon.

Stan playfully cautioned others over the coming years if the offer of coffee was made - 'still waiting for mine'. How Sam wished she was too.

'You need Tyler,' said Stan, who had now adopted the position I first saw him in at the bar - the pub bar, albeit temporarily, now having been replaced by the wall he was building. The pub bar would, no doubt, feature later in his day too, I was sure.

'Tyler,' I said, but who or what was Tyler?

'Tyler,' Stan said. 'I'll bring him with me tomorrow. I'm off now.'

'Okay,' I replied, 'see you then,' and he was gone. Well at least I now knew that 'Tyler' was male, presumably a life form, and could get or be put into a car. But more than that, I knew not.

The following teatime I saw Stan approaching so went to open the gate for him. Stan drove what remained of a Vauxhall Astra Estate. Maroon was its long-forgotten colour; it now had that greyish pale sheen of a weathered maroon. He had two children at school who, on the occasions that Stan took them to school in the car, had to sit on upturned yellow builders buckets, between the mattocks, shovels and picks, where the back seats used to be. The estate boot area was especially reserved for his cement mixer. Mine was for sheep so I couldn't talk – both our cars could be said to be utilitarian. His kids, even at their young age, had enough pride to insist on being dropped off round the corner from school lest any of their chums should see them getting out of this vehicle. Westlet had locals such as Stan, and a good retirement population, but also it was very desirable to Corcastle's young commuting professionals. As a result quite a few of the children were delivered to school in Range Rovers and the like. Stan's car, when performing his parental role, was therefore nothing short of an utter embarrassment to his offspring and best left undiscovered by their friends for street-cred reasons, whatever they were.

Close behind Stan another engine could be heard following. This was a silver Vauxhall Cavalier SRi, (emphasis on the 'was'), which on first inspection made Stan's car look quite acceptable. No, more than that, even almost 'showroom' in condition in comparison. Although probably similarly faded, the silver colour did not show it. One thing was beyond doubt even to the layman - this car was definitely not legal. As it approached, you could hear it sometime before it actually materialised. There was a crescendo of noise: quite clearly the front part of the exhaust was no longer friends with its rear counterpart. Neither were scraping on the ground, but judging by the angle of the rear tube it would not be long. As I closed the gate, any niggling doubts about the legality of the vehicle rapidly vanished. The back lights did not work on the driver's side. I knew this as they were not there, their absence advertised by the significant dent nearby and the 'bird's nest' of exposed wires blowing in the slipstream. This poor saloon vehicle, I later learned, had happened upon its present owners who could not or did not distinguish its capabilities from that of a farm tractor or stock car. Its 'sump' must have been made of granite, the pounding it got positively racing across rocky outcropped fields. They had tested that poor Vauxhall car every bit as much and as harshly as Clarkson and his *Top Gear* chums had their famous 'indestructible' Toyota. But remarkably it rolled in behind Stan. Not perhaps the flagship advert Vauxhall might like or envisage, but an advert for resilience it undoubtedly was.

The two vehicles came to a halt in the car park, brake discs rubbing on one of them, but which I knew not. But hey, who was I to say anything about cars; my urban taxi was no longer the rose it used to be, after my recent passengers. I felt my car was amongst suitably abused friends though and fitted in quite well, and contrary to Stan's kids' view, its use as a sheep trailer did my 'street cred' the power of good in this company.

'Hi, PJ, oreright' said Stan as he climbed out of the builder's merchant's, closely followed through the buckets by 'Buzz' his chunky Springer Spaniel. 'Springer' being the complete understatement for this rocket powered adorable blur. Buzz, single-handedly reinvented the word 'busy'. It getting light in the morning was enough to ignite the firework she lived in, and set her tail and nose in almost involuntary perpetual motion.

‘Yes,’ I said. ‘Fine thanks, Stan.’

‘Brought Tyler,’ Stan said.

‘So I see,’ I replied. At this Tyler joined us, disembarking without the door falling off, which would not have surprised me, cigarette glued to his lip. A visibly older black Labrador peered out from under what little remained of the interior, but his new surroundings were apparently neither justification nor motivational enough to move.

Stan said, ‘PJ, Tyler.’

‘Hi’, I said, offering my hand.

‘Alright,’ acknowledged Tyler, and as we shook hands I was immediately struck by his grip. With no more ado, that was obviously sufficient and local formalities concluded.

‘And who have we hear?’ PJ moved toward the dog in an attempt to break the ice.

‘Oh that’s owd Strom’ replied Tyler ‘doesn’t come out wit us as much naadays’. The black, white bearded, snout twitched briefly at the mention of his name, signalling mild interest and recognition, but that was enough effort for one day.

‘Beer, chaps?’ I asked.

‘Aye, thanks,’ came from Stan, but only a slight smile and almost puzzled nod from Tyler, which I took to mean yes. The question simply wasn’t worth asking Tyler. I soon learned it as good as ran in his veins, and he would have thought the question absurd.

At the house I said to Sam, 'Stan has brought his mate Tyler to look at the jungle. You coming?'

'Yes,' she said.

'Grab a couple of beers, I've got the other two.'

'Okay'

We approached the lads who were leaning over the gate separating the jungle from the garden and chuckling.

'Beer, chaps,' I said and they smiled approvingly, whether at the beer or being called 'chaps' wasn't clear. No doubt I'd find out.

'Tyler,' I said. 'This is Sam.'

'Hello, Tyler, how are you?' Sam greeted him.

'Fine, thanks,' he said. 'Very nice to meet you, Sam.' Oh yes, I thought, he can speak then…more than my grunted 'Alright'.

Sam then largely took over. 'So, guys, what do we do with this lot? I've got scissors but that's about it.' We all laughed. She went on, 'We want to get the sheep in there quickly, as the lambs are growing well.'

'What are the boundaries like?' asked Tyler.

'Well I couldn't get to the far...' I said, but it was soon clear I was superfluous to the discussion now and was cut off.

‘Not bad,’ said Sam. ‘Bit of a scramble but I got round them this morning. Lots of patching up to do but nothing I can’t have a go at.’

Now hold on, when had she been round them? I knew Sam had always been a morning person, and me a night owl, but I knew nothing of this inspection. I guessed she would likely have taken a look long before I was up. Tyler was visibly impressed.

‘So what do you reckon?’ said Sam.

‘Can’t come tomorrow, I’s got to finish one at Stockbridge.’ he said, although mysteriously his answer seemed to be directed at Stan largely, and for his benefit.

‘Can get here day after, Sam,’ Tyler said.

‘Great,’ she replied.

‘I’ll bring blade, reckon, Stan?’

‘You’ll need it, T,’ said Stan.

“Got to finish one at Stockbridge”. One what? I wondered. I must have missed something - perhaps he was cutting another field. I didn’t ask, as on past PJ performance it would likely only advertise further gaping holes in my understanding of all things agricultural. The encounter and formal business apparently concluded between Sam and Tyler, from which I had largely been excluded, was drawing to a close. I was still clearly superfluous at this point but my suggestion of more beer received overwhelming support. Well I might as well do something. I left the three to plan their assault on the jungle.

Walking back to the assembled I was trying to weigh up Tyler. He'd be a bit older than both Stan and I, I guessed, but trimmer. Quite a wiry sort and judging by that handshake I suspected you would rather have him on your side if the need arose. He had long, almost black hair, rugged good looks, a deep voice, the obligatory cigarette, tanned skin, grubby oily jeans and an armless red T-shirt which it had to be said had seen better days. He had a bit of a North American Indian look about him if you like – I should have disliked him already, but I didn't.

When I got back with the other beers, it was to the; 'Yes, yes,' from Sam, 'that will be great, T.' Single-letter-name terms clearly already established.

Stan said, 'Well, must get on, got a wall to build.'

'See you then, Stan,' we chorused. Although he was only going one hundred yards or so, we sounded like he was setting sail on an expedition.

'Well, Tyler,' I said, 'we'd better talk money.'

'Don't worry about that,' said Sam, firmly shutting me up. 'It's all sorted.' Oh, righty-ho then, I thought. Superfluous was becoming my middle (who was I kidding), my first name…

It was all arranged. Tyler was to start the day after tomorrow, when he'd finished that one at Stockbridge.

Whatever that 'one' was…

Chapter 3

THE PIVOTAL MOMENT

Everything was going well. Stan's wall was nearing completion and he was to alter the old pig pens next in readiness for the future.

Tyler was well into the jungle; often you could only see his progress by the wisps of smoke rising in the distance. I was never sure whether this smoke was from tobacco products or the pyres from the cut briers. His bladed strimmer whirred away destroying everything in its path; soon Sam's extra grazing would be on line. Tyler had all sorts of power tools - chain saws, mowers, trimmers - all piled in the car. Also an extensive collection of hand tools, picks, spades, and mattocks, as well as greengrocer grass. I had to look twice at that: greengrocer grass? What on earth did he have greengrocer grass in the car for? That was to remain a mystery to me, for now…

Most of this equipment was shoved into his Cavalier SRi interior - like Tutankhamen's tomb, looking as chaos but with some order if only to the occupier - the remainder being in the boot. Tyler's car was unbelievable, not in a condition I had ever seen a car in before or since. Spectacular is not too strong a word; even the floor was chock-a-block with petrol cans, sticks, and empty cigarette packets. One day there was even a shotgun balanced on the top of all this. There was one notable anomaly I had noticed in the maelstrom, simply the number of assorted tape measures? I mean how many tape measures do you need to successfully operate a mower? The answer wasn't obvious.

I asked Stan one day what Tyler did. He clearly didn't have a job in the normal sense of the word, due to the random times he came and the condition he was often in, demonstratively having cider and sherry on board as his favourite travelling companions (Guinness being reserved for special occasions - twice daily in the pub), but what did he do?

It was clear however that whatever Tyler didn't do, he appeared single handily (later it emerged not all the credit was his as it was indeed a joint effort with his father) to have developed the expression 'UV' to describe a vehicle. Nothing more was required of a vehicle and no further prefix; the word 'utility' was enough. This duo over the years turned any car, van, alleged four by four (for not long usually) into ‘utility vehicles’. Quite why car manufacturers spent millions and went to all the trouble of making different models for different human purposes was lost on Tyler and his dad. Had they ever needed a tank they would simply have attached a gun to what was parked outside the house at the time - matching a vehicle to its required ‘use’ simply never crossed their minds. It was the turn of the dearly loved (once) SRi now. Four wheels was not even mandatory in this (through necessity) frequent car acquisition process. PJ would have fully expected them in a Trotters three-wheeler if one had come their way on the day the previous incumbent UV died.

‘When he’s not in t’ pub,’ laughed Stan, ‘he’s a groundworker, good un at that mind.’

‘What’s a groundworker?’ I asked.

‘He works with ‘is old fella on the farms and that; drains, hedges, fences, anything. ‘Is dad runs local shoot at Westlet Ruins an’ all.’

“Westlet Ruins” was a farm with a good helping of medieval ruins, hence the name.

‘Where does he live?’

‘Oh in Westlet.’

‘Wife?’ I questioned.

‘Nooh,’ said Stan, ‘they long divorced ‘im, lives with his dad.’

(They? Ermmm, no further information was forthcoming, well not then anyway).

The shoot explained the shotgun at least. Judging by the car I didn't dare think what their house might be like. I did have the good fortune, or misfortune, depending on your point of view, of visiting the said house some weeks later. It did not disappoint.

Tyler emerged from the jungle. He was running with sweat, wearing only a hi-vis waistcoat-type jacket to fend off the protesting briers, and was ready for the beer I was primed with.

'How's it going?' I said.

'Hot,' he replied as he discarded his jacket. ''Nother couple of days, and we should have a way into that clear bit in the middle.'

'Great,' I replied. 'I'll come and have a look, I'll get changed.'

'Can't stay tonight, PJ, be back in a couple of days, busy tomorrow.'

'Okay. See you then.' Lighting a cig he was away.

I had a sales job, so I was a 'suit' when appointments arose. The rest of the time was largely my own. It was commission only and I did not enjoy it, so I used to pull the stops out when required or when the dreaded targets had to be met. I went into the house. Sam worked from home but had finished for the day. She had a management job at which she was very professional and was the undoubted breadwinner of the household. I had had a good job as a geologist with the National Coal Board but had been made redundant when Maggie Thatcher and Arthur Scargill fell out in the 1980s, and the coal industry was their victim, metamorphosing from being the provider of fossil fuel to becoming just the fossil.

'Hi Sam,' I called, 'the lads have gone, what do you fancy for tea?' We checked the sheep had some feed, and had a quiet night planning our next project around the house.

About nine o'clock Sam was about to feed Purdey before I'd take her out. Purdey had got quite used to her new chums in the field now, so we could have a wander and a look at Tyler's handiwork.

I returned from my walk to find Sam on the phone.

'PJ, it's for you,' she said, so I duly stepped up.

Ever heard of pivotal moments …?

Chapter 4

THE INITIATION

'It's Tyler,' whispered Sam, covering the mouthpiece.

'Tyler,' I mouthed. 'Is he leathered?'

'No, doesn't sound it,' mimed Sam in reply.

'Hi, Tyler, how's things?' I said gingerly.

'Alright,' he replied in his usual manner.

'What can I do you for?' I said.

‘Well you can stop calling me Tyler for a start PJ, T will do. Have you got any time tomorrow?’

‘Yes, can have, what’s up?’

‘Can you go and dig a grave for me at Levant?’ Levant was a small village about ten miles north of Westlet.

‘A what?’ I said.

‘A grave,’ he replied.

‘Where?’

‘In the ground in the churchyard,’ he said, laughing.

‘Very funny’ I reluctantly admitted.

‘Two have come in at the same time; one on answering machine tonight. Old fella can’t help. He’s got to go to Ruins, as the pheasants are arriving.’

‘Right.’

‘Can I come round to yours now - got some stuff for you - and tell you what to do?’

‘Please do,’ I said nervously, a grave for a real-life dead person? Oh dear I thought… what was I getting myself into now?

‘See you in a minute,’ he said.

‘Okay,’ I replied and put the phone down.

Sam said, 'What's to do?'

I replied, 'Well you are not going to believe this, but I'm going to dig a grave!'

'Huh,' she said laughingly and then, far too quickly to be completely comfortable with, 'Well you've dug your own often enough, you should be a natural.'

Nice, I thought. It suddenly came to me that that must be what the 'one' was he had needed to finish at Stockbridge when we'd first met, and why it was directed at Stan, as he would understand. Gravedigging would have been a tough thing to explain to an outsider. He was round in what seemed seconds. I met him in the car park.

‘I didn’t know you were a gravedigger,’ I said.

‘Yes,’ he said, ‘got collared into it when Dick died.’

Dick who? I wanted to ask but that could wait for another day.

‘Come in, let’s have a glass.’

We went into the kitchen. The cooking range was on, currently our only form of heating, and T started on my instructions. Sam made some brief notes; she was so organised it was embarrassing.

I chirped up saying that my mother was thirty-six when I was born in the 1950s, a positively veteran age in those days for motherhood. As a result I had had what seemed like an endless supply of elderly aunts, uncles and the like who were all popping their clogs whilst I was young. My mother insisted that after every funeral we went back to the grave and arranged the flowers in their correct hierarchical order, and noted whom the tributes were from. Not sure this information was ever used but she did it as a matter of course every time. It fell to me to do it for her not long after, when she passed away at fifty-four. I was trying to give Tyler some ‘curriculum vitae’ credibility when it came to familiarity with graveyards, but I had a feeling I was going to get a lot more familiar with them shortly.

‘Levant graves are on terraces down from the back end of the church,’ said T. ‘Your grave is on tier two towards the left as you look down with the church behind you.’

‘Not sure I like the expression “your grave”,’ I said. We giggled.

'You know what I mean,' said T. 'I went up there tonight and took the grass off for you so you won't get mixed up. It's a new one.'

'New one?' I interrupted.

'First one in, not a reopen, just a straight double,' T replied. 'Double is dug for two as name suggests. I've cut the grass to the hole size that you need so just go straight down, six foot two long by twenty-nine at the shoulders. Don't taper it, no coffin shape, just do a rectangular hole.'

I was brave enough to assume the 'twenty-nine' was inches, but I said nothing. It would have made me look ridiculous, I thought.

'I don't suppose you have a mini digger, do you?' I asked forlornly.

'Huh, I wish, you'll be lucky,' was his reply. 'Dare say where all your relations went was a big town cemetery, all dug with mini diggers?'

'It was,' I confirmed.

'Not here. The only reason the Council use us is 'cause there's no way in for mini diggers into these small old churchyards. I can dig one on my own but Council need three men, battened, buttrussed holes, planks, supported sides, even scaffolding below eighteen inches deep, for all the health and safety stuff. Council couldn't afford to do what we do,' said T.

'So "health and safety" applies to their staff, but not to you?' I asked.

'Yep, seems to. Our risk, no compensation or time off.'

There was little more to say on the subject, it was just ridiculous. It was reassuring to know that coffins would be left on top if it weren't for Tyler and his dad, as the Council simply couldn't afford to do the job under their own compliant Health and Safety 'job prevention' rules. Whoever said this is a mad world…

'How many churchyards do you work in?' I asked.

'Seventy-two,' was his immediate reply. Blimey, I thought.

'What's a reopen?' I asked.

'Don't you go worrying about that,' said T. 'You will find out soon enough.' I got the distinct but worrying feeling I would, as this already sounded like it may not be a one off.

'Right,' said T, finishing his wine. 'That's it, I think.'

'Hang on,' I protested, 'what time does it have to be ready?'

'Doesn't matter,' said T. 'It's fer next day, just so long as it's dug tomorrow, shouldn't take you long.'

I wished I shared his optimism.

'You got a spade, haven't you?'

'Well just a garden one,' I answered with a raised eyebrow as to its likely suitability.

'That'll do,' he said. 'Oh and yes I've set the box up for you.'

‘Hold it, what box?’ I asked. He kept introducing new, and not at all obvious, terms into the conversation.

‘The box is to put the soil in instead of just chucking it on the neighbour. You’ll get it when you see it,’ he added reassuringly. I was flattered and not a little worried by his confidence. ‘You’re lucky as well,’ T said. ‘The weather forecast is okay too.’ As an afterthought he asked, ‘You got a pick?’

‘No,’ I said.

‘I’ll give you one of mine,’ which he duly did.

By now I was distinctly worried and out of my depth; this training course had been less than comprehensive.

‘Where do I park?’

‘Just on road outside church,’ he replied.

‘I’ll make you some sandwiches,’ said Sam.

‘I think you’d better go and dig it, Sam,’ I replied. ‘You’re far more practical than me.’ Nobody disagreed – worryingly – but we all laughed.

‘I’ll pop in and see you during the day. I’m not far away at Kelsy,’ said Tyler.

‘See you do,’ I said as we got to his car.

‘Here’s a tape, just in case,’ he said.

‘Thanks,’ I said. ‘You will come and see me, won’t you?’ I said nervously.

‘Don’t worry, I will…and thanks. Got me out of a spot’

‘No problem,’ I lied.

He got in his car and with a beaming smiled shouted to Sam, ‘Don’t let him wear that bloody suit, Sam, will you.’ We all laughed.

‘Leave it with me,’ she said.

‘I’ll see you tomorrow, T.’

‘Bye,’ came the reply.

Sam was laughing as he drove away.

‘That will sort you out,’ she said with nothing short of mischievous glee.

‘You’re not wrong, not sure I’m in his league for fitness,’ I agreed. The heaviest thing I had lifted in years since Sam’s ‘PJ building ban’ was a pen.

‘I know,’ she said, laughing all the more. That yet again wasn’t very helpful…

Well at least that had sorted that out. I was not to wear a suit and at last I had an explanation for the tape measures and greengrocer grass in the car, also as to why Tyler was so fit and strong. I wished he was a man of a few more words though. This training had not been comprehensive or practical and into the deep end I felt I had most definitely and unceremoniously been chucked!

I actually felt quite privileged to be asked though. It is an important job, so either he thought I would do okay or he simply couldn't get anybody else. I hoped it was the former. I'd always thought that gravediggers had a mystique for the general public. They certainly did for me, a bit like surgeons and pilots, holding an unaccounted for fascination as we know they are there, and what they do, but not who they are, or how they do it. We never really see them; they are always behind the scenes but of pivotal importance. Well now I had met a gravedigger in Tyler, and by tomorrow night hopefully I would be one… (or a trainee emergency one at least!)

I arrived at Levant at about a quarter to ten, duly equipped with my spade, tape measure and sandwiches that Sam had made as promised, which I thought better to leave in the car for now. I parked outside the church as Tyler had said, armed myself with my spade and tape measure and set off. It suddenly occurred to me as to whether I was in the right place. I'd forgotten to ask Tyler if there was more than one church in Levant. I put my tools back in the boot and decided to do a recce, so as not to unnecessarily embarrass myself should I meet someone in a graveyard whilst clutching a spade and clearly not knowing exactly what I was doing. I could feel the long arm of the law on my collar already.

So I wandered down the church path until I saw the start of some form of terrace. Continuing, I could see one below it and one below that also. I walked along the second tier and lo and behold there it was, my grave with the grass removed and box installed, just as T had described. As I retreated to the car, I read some of the headstones. I loved that - it was fascinating stuff: they all told a tale and recorded a life if only briefly. So all in all, a good start, at least I was in the right place. I got my stuff out of the car. Here we go. Tyler had advised stout boots rather than wellies.

'Wellies in the wet, boots in dry,' he had said, more as a statement of fact gained from years of practice than advice. Good coming from him, I thought, as nine times out of ten he appeared wearing well-used trainers.

I placed my tape measure on my neighbours' headstone. They were a married couple, Howard and Elsie Templeton. It was a lovely day, which I remarked on to my new-found neighbours and now workmates.

Tyler had told me to create a step edge, whatever that was, and work back from it. The first five spadesful across the head end went just like digging your garden, but instead of turning the soil over, you threw it into the well-placed box on the right-hand side of the grave. Tyler was right-handed as was I, which was lucky as we had never discussed it. I didn't really like (well, more wasn't comfortable with) the terms 'head end', 'foot end', and 'toe end'. I thought this a little biological for me and a reminder that there was actually a person to be laid here, not just a box.

Whilst I was digging away I was trying to think of alternatives. 'Top and bottom' were possibilities, but might lead to all sorts of confusion, I thought. I smiled imagining coffin measurements given out by 'bottom' size. That would end in tears one way or another for sure, despite all the doubtless humorous innuendo. I'd never really understood, though, why in this modern world ‘across the shoulders’ was still a coffin measurement? Indeed it was, as in ‘used to be’ and probably should be, the widest part of the box as our skeletons suggest. But with all the media coverage of obesity and the like, and from just ‘people-watching’ observations (that pastime that none of us admit to enjoying, it not being PC), it is all too clear from the ‘live’ evidence on the high street, the shoulders nowadays often appear to be considerably less wide than the middles or bottoms on display, so perhaps in the future coffins would indeed be pear-shaped and expressed as length and bottom width? Just a mischievous thought to while away the time. Gravedigging provides lots of such time, I later learnt.

We in the UK appear to follow the US, trend wise. We eat their imports - Big Macs or Kentucky somethings - and we are slowly, or not so slowly in many cases, turning into them in a ‘you are what you eat’ fashion. Our American cousins had to get this coffin-shape problem sorted out years ago: the fat American is a caricature, like it or not. So all we need to do is look across the Atlantic for the future solution to disposal? The ‘casket’ is their answer. Americans clearly have lost their shoulders and are now straight rectangles, the same width from head to toe.

What about ‘bow and stern’, I thought, with ‘port and starboard’ instead of ‘shoulders’?’ Good idea for mariners perhaps or ‘up and down’ for the airmen? No, that sounded too much like exhumation. Well I had tried to help the industry’s future on my first day, but concluded that things were probably best left alone, a further example of ‘if it ain’t broke don’t fix it’.

I looked at my progress: not bad, I thought. I was about four spades deep and 'edge cutting' now was making more sense. Because of a spell in a previous life (admittedly not an entirely appropriate expression given my current situation) in the Opencast Coal Mines of wildest Scotland, I knew that a similar system was used on a vastly grander scale. So, I thought, provided I treat the whole exercise as digging a mini opencast coal mine everything will be fine… surely?

'All right' woke me from my daydream. I froze, and felt my eyes immediately widen.

'All right?' I slowly, deliberately and not so calmly asked myself that very question as the words sank in.

No! No! I wasn't 'all right', not all right at all, far from it. I hurriedly assessed my situation. I was:

1. On my own.

2. In a grave in a deserted rural graveyard (where you could hear a pin drop).

3. Someone had just spoken to me…

There was no getting away from it, I repeated to myself that someone had just spoken to me! My heart was suddenly playing tunes in my chest, and even Usain Bolt would have had to keep up and couldn't run as fast as I wanted to right then.

After what seemed like ages and gathering all my non-existent courage, I turned to look up and behind me. I was greeted by the vision of a World War II pilot in his faded RAF demob suit looking down at me. Oh my goodness (I didn't say to myself…at all!) a ghost on my first day! I must have looked terrified, my eyes were staring and fixed again like a proverbial rabbit in the headlights. I don't mind admitting it took a while before any form of rationality returned.

'All right,' the vision said again. 'Good day for it?' I wanted to poke him just to see that my finger wouldn't go in, or worse through, but he looked solid enough.

'Yes, thank you,' I said nervously as I climbed out. Quite why I said 'thank you' I didn't know. Thank you for half scaring me to death perhaps? I did think though that I must remember to cut a step as Tyler had said, in the side of my hole.

'Where's Tyler?' said the man. I relaxed as he appeared to be alive.

'Tyler? Oh, he can't make it today,' I replied.

'Where's Alf?'

'Oh he couldn't make it either,' I said. 'He's having his pheasants delivered.'

''Im and 'is bletherin' pheasants,' the figure, sorry, man said. 'Who are you then?'

'I'm PJ,' I replied.

‘P what?’

‘PJ, sir, just initials,’ I confirmed.

‘Huh, reet then, ’Igginson’s me, I’m doin’ funeral.’

His pipe now firmly between his teeth, he went on, ‘Just wanted to make sure it were getting done. Them two, Tyler and Alf, are good lads, tha knows, but they can forget. Known fer it.’

‘Forget?’ I enquired

‘Aye, wouldn’t be first time we’ve had to dig a bugger in t’ dark. Knew it weren’t Tyler ‘ere though.’

‘How?’

‘No fags on tombstone.’ He laughed, I had to smile too as although I hadn’t yet seen cigarettes on a tombstone I felt sure I soon would.

‘How many you dug afore?’ asked Mr Higginson.

‘None,’ I replied.

‘Typical Tyler’ he cackled. ‘Should be a laugh then if nowt else. I’ll pop in to see yous later young fella te see ‘ow yer doin’. You do yer best, lad, I’ll keep an eye on yer, dunner worry.’

‘Mr Higginson,’ I said.

‘Aye, lad,’ he replied while lighting his pipe. He peered down at my handiwork so far.

‘How deep does it have to be?’ I asked. ‘Tyler just said a double.’

‘Typical ha haa’ he laughed, ‘couldn’t organise a piss-up in a brewery, that Tyler.’

Even then from my limited experience of Tyler I did think that was an inappropriate expression of his abilities. He would be very good at arranging the said piss-up anywhere, with or without the involvement of a brewery.

‘Just deep enough typically so they can’t get out,’ he continued, beaming from ear to ear. ‘I’ll let you know when I’s come back, jus’ keep goin’ fer now.’

‘Come back’, I thought, you may be lucky, I might well be packed up and ready for off, mate, at the rate I’m going.

(Mr Higginson clearly liked the word ‘typical’, needed or not.)

After this sort of a ‘comfort break’ I got back in, and wow, I wished I hadn’t straightened up so quickly. My back had been fine, but once you stop, you get reminders.

Well, it all was going smoothly now. The ground conditions were a little friable, but generally it was digging well. It was about then that it happened. I stuck the spade in and it seemed to slip off something, I tried again but again encountered significant resistance. Thinking I must be weakening I jumped on the spade with both feet: nothing was going to stop that. How wrong can you be, my spade turned into a pogo stick. Instead of going down, it was I that was flung upwards in what seemed like a classic equal and opposite reaction. It was only good fortune that the spade handle didn't knock my teeth out.

This was head-scratching land now; it looked like soil but dug like a very tough, dirty and unusually buried, bouncy castle. Before my spade bounced out of the grave completely I, in hindsight, made an absurd decision. I went to the car to get the pick. I got back into position and threw my pick with full force onto the earth. It immediately bounced out of the ground, brought my arms up to over my head then left me, landing a good way down tier three, clobbering a headstone in its flight. It would have been a fair attempt had I been an Olympic hammer thrower. I looked around just to check that nobody had seen. I had thought that the pick might succeed where the spade had failed, but you live and learn.

I got out and retrieved the pick, stopping on the way to inspect the headstone it had struck. Luckily there was no damage. I was grateful for all three not so small mercies; firstly that that could easily have been an expensive mistake had the grave stone been damaged, secondly nobody had seen me, and thirdly I hadn't turned a passer-bye into a resident...

This was now a mystery or had I indeed found a buried bouncy castle, four feet down in a graveyard? I wasn't uninterested in this phenomenon due to being a geologist, but the only rock that I had seen reflect a hammer blow, to the extent that the reflected hammer had hit its operator sufficiently hard mid-forehead to render him unconscious, was solid un-weathered granite. It has to be said that this had been an unkindly funny event to watch, which could so easily have been me. The university student involved was fine but we had all had some fun with him after that, about it actually knocking some sense in him rather than him out.

I began scraping the soil back as the offending material could only be just under the surface, and soon I felt something smooth and saw it was black; more interestingly it appeared to be rubber. My dad had acquired some old conveyor belt years ago, when we were caravanning near a limestone quarry in North Wales; it lasted as car mats for a good deal longer than the car concerned, and indeed him. From memory it appeared almost indestructible. Now I could think of no earthly reason why there was conveyor belt in my current location. As I continued to scrape, what appeared to be a blue sleeve fell out of the side of the grave like an arm. I jumped and immediately hoped again that nobody was watching, but it was soon obvious that it wasn't actually a resident or part of one, as it was a bright blue tube and had a concertina-shaped side. I seemed to have found the culprits for the unusual responses I had received from my spade, but time didn't allow for too much academic or archaeological research at this point. These obstacles had to be removed as progress on the current task had been seriously delayed; in fact, all but halted.

I exposed as much as I could of the conveyor belt as it went right across the grave and was diving towards the foot end with a fold in it, and the blue pipe simply dangling from the side. I slashed at the pipe using the side of the spade as an axe. It was moving too much, so I put my foot in the end of it to anchor it whilst still chopping furiously. This shattered a piece off but not enough. I had some gloves with me and started fiercely bending the pipe up and down, and from side to side, waggling it furiously like a dog trying to obtain ownership of a new toy from its owner. The pipe wasn't giving an inch, a bit like a dog wouldn't, and my attempt at encouraging the 'metal fatigue' effect on industrial plastic was also getting me nowhere, except for the slightest pale discolouration at the end of the 'waggle'.

The sweat on my forehead and the sore arms were just a bonus. If you didn't know better you would think this plastic was nearly new. I sat down on the conveyor belt, wiped my brow, and went back to the drawing board. Whatever this stuff was it was fantastically tough and completely alien down a grave, and was not for submitting readily.

I always did wonder where exactly that drawing board was that everyone went back to when they were stuck...

Surprisingly I found it wasn't uncomfortable sitting in a grave, and almost wished I'd brought my sandwiches. I could have had forty winks, as everything was beginning to hurt and it was a lovely day, and there was not a breath of wind or breeze down here.

I quietly wondered how Howard and Elsie were doing; we were approaching close friends now as we could only be inches apart. What trials and tribulations had life served up to them, I pondered. I was dangerously near to going daydreaming again, when I refocused on the immediate problem. I knew now that I had not discovered a new geological phenomenon, indeed a rubber moraine would be difficult to sell to the *New*

Scientist. No, this was manmade I concluded. It had taken me three years at university studying geology and eighteen finals exams to come up with this hypothesis - I knew my degree would come in useful one day for something.

But how was I going to shift it? Pulling was a no-go, a spade didn't work, and the pick had literally left the job and was out of the question. I needed a Stanley knife but could see the headline now: 'Man found digging in grave with Stanley knife'. This was undoubtedly the solution, but, in itself, posed a number of problems. Firstly, where did you find such a knife in a graveyard; secondly, the nearest DIY shop was miles away; thirdly it was a Sunday so we had to be gone by Evensong; and fourthly I had not a cent to my name to pay for such an item. I have to admit that I was trying to keep a level head but panic was beginning to set in. As it built I thought, my first grave and it looks like I may have to finish it off 'in't dark', as Mr Higginson graphically described earlier. My long forgotten optimistic thoughts of 'I might well be packed up and ready for off, mate, at the rate I'm going', came back to haunt me, now to be replaced by 'I might not be ready for tomorrow at this rate.'

It had become clear that my early optimism had been misplaced. At this point the strangest thing happened as I heard a thud to my right. I looked and there lay a Stanley knife, not a new one but a Stanley knife nevertheless. Oh thank you, thank you God, I thought, I'll be good from now on. My prayers had been answered.

Then I heard the laughter. I quickly stood up and saw Tyler splitting his sides, with Higginson not far behind.

'You bar steward,' I shouted at Tyler. 'You knew!' Sorry for the language, I muttered to my neighbours Howy and Else. This just made T laugh all the more.

Higginson said to him, 'You been playin' that old trick again, you mean git,' but Tyler didn't care, he was all but doing the 'dying fly' routine.

'It's better than that,' said T. 'He's a geologist.'

I instantly saw the funny side and joined in the laughter. A gravedigging initiation ceremony jaunt and, I conceded, a very good one at that.

Mr Higginson, guffawing at T's revelation of my past, and making the most of my situation said, 'Told you I'd see you later, lad, rubber stuff always at about four foot.'

'Indeed you did, sir'.

Without doubt though my prayers in relation to a Stanley knife had been answered, not as directly as I first anticipated, but with Tyler as the middle man.

At this Mr Higginson (or 'Iggs as he would for ever after insist) made his farewells and set off back to his home-made 'pop-up' Chapel of Rest in the corner of his joinery workshop. We could hear him chortling and mumbling to himself as he made his way, no doubt reliving the Stanley knife moment, and congratulating himself on the accuracy of his prediction of my likely progress, as he was spot on. There was no doubt that that tale would be retold into submission, of a geologist to boot.

Tyler said, ‘C’mon, let’s ‘ave some dinner.’

‘Shouldn’t we crack on?’ I said.

‘No, be all right, you’ve got on well, we’ll soon ‘ave it finished this aft,’ said Tyler. From Tyler that was almost a compliment. I thought we’d have our sandwiches in the car, but sandwiches weren’t in Tyler’s vocabulary or on his menu when it came to lunch.

‘Jump in my car,’ he said.

The Horse and Hounds looked very welcoming, if you were going for Sunday lunch with your Granny, but how welcoming it would be to two grubby gravediggers, I knew not. When I started brushing my clothes down as best I could, Tyler looked at me and said ‘Don’t worry it’s got a tap room.’

Something told me this was not his first visit.

We came out three quarters of an hour later with the benefit of four pints on board - two Guinness for Tyler (to keep his stomach settled and heartburn at bay was always his reasoning, not to say excuse) and two bitters for me. On our return I jumped into the hole and started on the conveyor belt with the knife with a new-found vigour, courtesy of best bitter.

I said to Tyler, ‘Are you off back to Kelsy now?’

‘No,’ he said, ‘that was the filling in today all done. I’ll help you with this. Have you taken any away yet?’

‘What?’ I replied. ‘Taken away any what?’

‘Soil, you divert. It’s not all going to go back in the hole after the resident’s in, is it? Think of the volume?’ This of course had never crossed my mind, I had to admit, and Tyler’s use of the word ‘volume’ surprised me, although it shouldn’t have the more I got to know him.

Meanwhile I was battling with this wretched conveyor belt. It had a fabric centre and I realised I was not making much of a go of it. Tyler, fags now safely installed with one in his mouth and the packet on Howard and Elsie, jumped in behind me and said, ‘Come here.’ I duly retired to the foot end of the grave and Tyler got on all fours at the head end. He pressed firmly down on the knife with those vein-covered arms, and cut it as easily as carpet underlay.

‘Just got to get through it and pull,’ he said.

‘Well you’re certainly showing me up,’ I said. Tyler was soon throwing rafts of conveyor belt out, and it wasn’t long before the blue tube got the same treatment.

‘Right,’ he said, grabbing the spade, ‘another eighteen inches or so and that’ll be it. I’ll dig it out, and you wheel all this lot away.’ At this he started throwing spadefuls into the barrow, like a machine. Strong wasn’t the word. I duly wheeled the excess away to the tip in the corner of the graveyard. All graveyards generally have such a tip, although I'd never noticed one before.

After about half an hour Higginson approached. Tyler leaned on the side of the grave, and I leaned on Howard and Elsie's stone, carefully avoiding the obligatory fags. Mr Higginson was no longer in his demob suit, but in what passed for (just) a dark grey suit.

'You finished, T?' he said, treading carefully around any mud in his noticeably shiny shoes, to avoid "getting 'em shittup", no doubt.

'Nearly,' said Tyler. 'You're dressed up, Higgs, what's to do?'

'Relatives,' said Mr Higginson, as unenthusiastically as imaginable. 'They only want to see Arthur tonight, don't they. Come up from away for t' fun'ral do tomorrow… I's got three in chapel o' rest at mo. I's just bin in and by God one of 'em's ripe, can't 'elp sniffin' 'em. It's ney Arthur nor Margaret, but Harry… terrible. 'Ave sprayed 'im with every air freshener I've got, screwed 'im down tight and put big sheet o'er 'im, and lit one o' them big smelly candle things an' all.'

I took that to mean a scented candle.

'Just 'ope' fer best that Arthur's lot o' relations don't notice. Some of 'em, bodies like, don't last, tha knows, go off right quick,' he continued unnecessarily, and I am sure with no scientific basis. 'I reckon it's summat to do with what they dee of, tha knows. I've never taken to this viewing bodies lark, can't see point.'

These were the sort of details better left unsaid by most, but this was 'Iggs, and that quite simply wasn't in his nature. In an earthy and inappropriately refreshing way, it would never have crossed his mind.

Too much information, I thought. No, I thought again, way too much, and not a conversation either I or Tyler were going to contribute to, for fear he would go further into it with more graphic detail. It had become clear that he would not get a job in the diplomatic service. All I could think of to say was 'Well, good luck with that, Mr Higginson.' I hadn't a clue what else to say, but certainly didn't want further knowledge of the contents or condition of his Chapel of Rest.

'Just 'Iiggs, lad.' Did no one use their full names up here? Mine had been shortened to PJ, then 'Iggs and T, it all really rather made a mockery of all the fuss parents put into researching names for their offspring.

'Thanks, Higgs, see you tomorrow,' I replied. T smiled.

'See you tomorrow, Higgs,' he said.

Higgs turned for away and then shouted back, 'Twelve, for half past, T.'

'Got it,' replied Tyler, and disappeared back into the hole.

'PJ,' he said, 'bring that tape and jump in.' I did. 'Put tape at end.' He put the tape measure down on the bottom of the hole. 'What was it meant to be?'

'Six foot two inches by twenty-nine.'

'And what you got?'

‘Six foot two inches long.’

‘Aye that’ll do, just check chest.’

‘Twenty and a half inches.’

‘Be fine. Chuck the pick and spade in t’ hole, and get them planks from behind box.’ This I duly did and covered the hole with the planks.

‘I’m about ready for off, T, I’m quite knackered.’

‘You’ll be all right,’ he laughed. I would have laughed too but I didn’t have the energy.

We gathered our bits and bobs, cigarettes first of course. I thanked Howy and Else for their company for the day and bade them goodnight.

On the way back to the car I said to Tyler, ‘When you said terraced, I’d gone all Chinese agriculture, and ice ages. Should be interesting, I’d thought.’

‘No,’ he said. ‘Sorry to disappoint, a bit more recent a deposit than that. 1974 actually, year I left school, they extended bypass on mosses. Some bright spark offered church if they wanted slope at back of churchyard terraced while they were at it.’

‘Church snapped their hand off as graveyard was filling up, and this would replace need for new land, for a while at least. Contractor didn’t mention, or conveniently forgot to mention, what they were going to terrace it with, which was any old junk they needed to get rid of, hence all the conveyor belt and stuff. It was all left to settle for a couple of years, so the contractors were long gone before anyone found out. That hole today was not too bad, had a lot worse in ‘ere. Sorry about the Stanley knife joke.’

‘Get off, great fun! Do you want me tomorrow for the funeral?’

‘If yer want, but don’t come in yer suit, we’re not attending. We’ll just clear it out, put grass round and that.’

‘Great…’

‘Be here ‘bout half eleven, should be okay.’

‘Okay.’

‘Sleep tight. Oh – and well done today.’

‘Cheers, and thanks for the beers at lunchtime,’ I shouted after him. Fag in mouth he drove away with that wry smile on his face and I followed.

I got back to Cliff Field, dragged myself out of the car and into the house.

Sam greeted me with, ‘How have you got on?’

‘I’m knackered,’ I said. ‘I haven’t worked that hard since doing that shift as a roughneck on the oil rigs.’ A job I had had about ten years previously. I was a geologist offshore and they were short of a roughneck one shift, and I got the job. One day was enough.

I slumped in the chair.

‘Oh diddums,’ said Sam. ‘Where does it hurty-wurty?’

‘If I could get up I’d put you over my knee,’ I said.

‘Oh would ya,’ she replied. Sometimes she had a mischievous streak, and thank you, missus, it hurty-wurted everywhere.

‘How were your sandwiches?’ Sam asked.

‘Lovely,’ I said, ‘I’ve still got them,’ and as for sleep tight, I surely did.

I was early the following day arriving at Levant. As I drove past the joiner’s shop where, from Tyler’s description, the very unsophisticated ‘Chapel of Rest’ was, I wondered how Higgs’ viewing had gone. Tyler had said the ‘chapel’ was really no more than a portion of the workshop, divided off with a partition, glazed with that glass-effect orange plastic stuff, and with a separate door and a plain wooden cross decorating the limestone window sill. It was clearly big enough to take three clients although that was its limit. No doubt we’d hear first-hand about the viewing later, oh joy.

T arrived soon after I did. ‘Morning,’ I said.

‘Morning PJ,’ he said, drawing deeply on his cigarette. ‘Sleep well did yer?’

‘You’re not kidding,’ I replied. He smiled.

‘Give us a lift with this, will yer?’

‘No problem,’ I replied. ‘This’ was what seemed like armfuls of greengrocer grass, some purple sheets, and a small wooden box with a handle on it. We set off to the grave. How Tyler could carry stuff in both of his arms, walk, talk and smoke at the same time I didn’t know. When we arrived at the graveside, he dropped the grass on the ground as did I, following his example.

He said, 'Grab t'other end,' referring to the planks. We lifted them off and put them behind the soil box. Tyler peered down the grave, as did I by his side. Quite why or what we were looking for I did not know; perhaps it was just a gravedigging ritual.

'Always have a look in when you come back, wherever you are, to see it hasn't fell in. Sides often collapse, depending on soil, it's a right job when they do.' This one had no such collapse. 'Just jump in, give it a final scrape, while I do grass.'

'Okay,' I said.

'The other thing,' T said, 'is check for life.'

'Life? In a grave?'

'Yep. Found a woman lying in one once.'

'What!' I exclaimed, spluttering.

He continued. 'Yep, a woman, live one too. Her lad had killed his self on his motorbike, deliberate accident. Had been diagnosed with some dread disease and didn't want to stay. Think he wanted to go out doing what he loved, drove into a bridge at full tilt.'

'Oh dear, but that is so sad,' I said.

‘Yep tis a funny thing grief.’ said Tyler. Now there’s a contradiction in terms if ever there was one, I thought.

‘But what was his mother doing?’ I enquired.

‘That was the sad bit,’ said T. ‘As I helped her out and asked if she was all right, she said she’d wanted to see what his view was going to be like… One-off that though.’

‘I’m very pleased to hear that was a one-off. What did you say?’

‘Nowt’ he replied ‘she was all right and apologetic and it was none of my business. Was just sad with her.’

Fair enough, I thought, what could you say? I noted how he said ‘sad with her’ though, and not ‘for her’.

‘You have to have an eye out and look in for other stuff though.’

‘Like what?’ I asked.

‘Hedge-pigs,’ he answered.

‘Hedge-pigs,’ I repeated.

‘Yes, hedgehogs, they fall in all the time. They have usually cleaned up any worms though.’ He laughed ‘always ‘ave some gloves wit’ yer, though, in t’ car. Mrs Tiggywinkle is lovely in a Beatrix Potter book but in reality they are prickly, uncooperative, worried little fellas. They don’t get it that you’re doing them a favour and saving their life. Lovely irresistible little faces though, they sort of have that "It wasn't me, honest" look about them.'

'You old softy' I said (agreeing entirely about how cute they were, but felt there was no need to tell Tyler that, men being men and all that nonsense.)

I duly jumped into the nearly ready grave. A few pebbles and bits had fallen in; I spaded them up onto the soil heap above. There were a few leaves, which I was picking up by hand, when the side of a purple sheet fell to greet me.

This was followed by, 'What are you doing?'

'Oh just tidying up a bit.'

'You were picking up leaves,' said Tyler.

'No, no,' I said, 'just tidying up.'

'Come on,' he said, 'it's fine. Did you see Roxy?'

'Roxy…music?' I guessed at, however unlikely.

'Very funny, nope Roxy the black and white cat; 'ave ta watch out for graveyard cats. Roxy is the one 'ere, and that's 'er Sunday name. If you 'ear 'em call for 'er it's Sox. The daft beggars often jump in, but can't get out - they don't think that far ahead.'

'No, no Sox,' I said, stupidly looking back in to check. Even I hoped I would have noticed a cat in my 'tidy up' but logged the warning.

‘Doesn’t it get to you?’ I asked.

‘What?’

‘Well this soil we are looking at here will never get looked at again by anyone ever, and I’m the first and last person to ever stand on it.’

‘What?’ repeated Tyler, quizzically.

‘Never get looked at again by human eye, and we did that. Out of seven billion people and five point two billion years so far, or thereabouts, I am the only human ever to stand on this bit of planet earth. Now there can’t be many places you can, with certainty, say that about, can there?’

From the expression on his face I do believe he hadn’t the slightest idea what I was talking about, and thought me quite mad.

‘Come on,’ he said. ‘Get out, we’ve got to finish off up here.’

‘Right,’ I said, just checking there were no leaves that we were about to confine to permanent darkness.

‘Here, come on,’ Tyler said. I could tell he was getting impatient with me now.

‘Can you give me a hand?’ I said, passing up the spade.

‘Where’s the step you cut in the side?’

There was no dressing it up, I’d forgotten.

‘You’ve forgot, haven’t you?’

‘Mmm…’ was the only reply I could muster. It was like being found out that you hadn’t done your homework by the Headmaster.

‘I told you never to forget the step, ‘cause when you’re on your own, you could really be in bother.’

‘Have you ever done that?’ I enquired.

Tyler just looked at me. Of course he had, I thought, but admit it, never…

Once I’d surfaced, Tyler showed me how to put down the remaining purple sheets, then planks around the now ‘grave’, not simply hole, to hold the sheets down, then the greengrocer grass, again held down by tucking it under the planks. Important, Tyler had said, when the weather was inclement, which more often than not it unfortunately was. The planks, he explained, made the top of the grave look smart and linear, and supported the vicar and subsequent mourners throwing in their soil. The greengrocer grass was obviously meant to look like grass, and the purple sheets to look sombre, reverent and religious, to create the impression of a cosy resting place. The overall effect was one of respect for the imminent and solemn event the grave was to host. The wooden hand held box was charged with sand as the grave soil was too wet and claggy on this occasion. Two pristine white ropes in a less than pristine carrier bag had been conjured from nowhere, and were coiled at either end. We were done, and a smart job it was too even if I say so myself. With twenty-five minutes to the funeral, we hid the spades under the grass covering the soil box. We went back to our cars, and moved them round the corner. Some of the funeral guests were already arriving.

Tyler said in a loud whisper, 'PJ?' He was gesturing for me to go to his car. 'Jump in. Time for a quick sherbet in t' Horse.'

'Pardon?' I said.

'Beer,' he replied.

'Have we got time?' I enquired, but we were off.

On the way he said, 'When you were messing around in that hole rescuing leaves and wasting pub time, was the ground disturbed?'

'Disturbed?'

'Yes.'

'Well no, I don't think so…'

'You sure?'

'Yes' I would have noticed, surely, had it been otherwise. 'Why?' I enquired, now panicking as to whether it should have been, or should not have been. Had it to be ruffled up for some reason that I had missed and should have fixed? To stop the coffin slipping perhaps, but slipping to where? Even to me this seemed a long shot.

'Why?' I repeated with more urgency.

‘No, doesn’t matter,’ said Tyler. ‘Just allays think be a good way to dispose of a body if you had to? Just dodge yer merder victim in just before funeral. Who’s going to look under a coffin in a churchyard?’

I instantly thought he was right. Tyler, who was now my new best mate, not only had the physical strength to do me in, but also the perfect place to conceal his crime. That would make a really good Miss Marple or Midsomer story, I thought. He also worryingly had seventy-two churchyards with multiple graves in to choose from…

‘But you’ve never found anything like that,’ I said nervously with disbelieving tone, quickly followed by a questioning, ‘Have you?’

We got to the pub, and for the second time today he didn’t say a word.

In my mind I was already pacing up and down as Tyler ordered our second beer. Shouldn’t we be going, I was thinking. I was the guy that set off to catch a train the day before, unlike Sam who walked on to a platform expecting to step straight on to the train.

‘Stop fretting,’ he said, sensing my unease. ‘They’ll have gone in now, and be about half an hour with this fella.’

‘Which fella?’ I asked. Surely not the client, as I don’t imagine they have much say in the matter or are indeed in any manner of hurry. Perhaps Higgs?

‘This Vicar,’ said T, ‘he’s a two-pinter.’ Now, I could see little or no connection at all between two pints of beer, a vicar, and a funeral, and was curious to know.

‘Okay, let’s go,’ T said moments later. ‘See you, Bill,’ he said to the landlord.

I finished, well more gulped, my beer. Whatever Tyler was he was not a leisurely drinker, more of a ‘car at a petrol pump’ technique, an unglamorous pit stop. I said, ‘Thanks, Bill,’ and followed T out.

In the car I asked, ‘Okay, what’s a two-pinter?’

‘Vicar,’ T replied. ‘It’s how you measure the length of a funeral service. If it’s the regular vicar, and they’ve got a busy day, they can be one-pinters, they really skip through the service, two pints, slower and so on. Generally though, especially up here where they very often don’t get big congregations on a Sunday, some of older vicars, or them vicars what have been called out of retirement to do a one-off service, can give the congregation a right talking-to. I had one old fella once who was a four-pinter, even if you were drinking slowly.’ Which Tyler most certainly never did.

So it was explained and the mystery lifted: a pint was not only T’s favourite fluid measurement but also a unit of time. I worked out that one Tyler pint equalled approximately twelve minutes, which was an alarming pace of around five per hour. It struck me that if T worked alongside a regular four-pinter that, with cigarettes and travelling thrown in, he could end up making a loss simply by going to work.

On arrival back at the church we quietly walked past the door, the final hymn issuing forth, and went down to our hiding place. The hidey hole here was located below terrace two where our grave was, at the end of terrace three on the churchyard boundary where there was an old shed. It had been where the mower had been stored in the past, said Tyler. The shed was falling into disrepair as the mower operator had liked the churchyard so much he had made it his home. On his death contractors had taken over, as in so many places, and the shed was now redundant except for the odd plank and the like, along with a healthy population of spiders. T and his father Alf still mowed four churchyards nearer to Westlet but it was hard work and they were getting a bit much for his dad.

When in our position behind the shed I asked Tyler, speaking now in an unnecessarily reverent whisper, 'Why is there a hearse here?'

He leaned towards me, as if about to impart a secret. I reciprocated by leaning towards him; I was eager and all ears for the answer.

'It's what they bring the body in,' he said, as if sorry to break this terrible news to me, or as if it were a tightly guarded secret.

'Behave,' I shushed. 'I know it's what they bring the bloody body in yer daft egg. But why here?' I went on, not giving him the chance to say the obvious: we were at a funeral. 'The chapel of rest is only there?'

I pointed towards the end of the churchyard wall. 'And correct me if I'm wrong but that, some hundred yards away, is the church?'

'Yep,' said Tyler.

'Well, why don't they carry it or put it on a trolley?' I asked. A hearse on the face of it looked ridiculous.

'Vicar won't have it, insists on a hearse. Higgs is well brassed off about it. He doesn't have a hearse, none of the jobbing joiners-come-undertakers do, have to hire it from the big lads. Costs Higgs two hundred pounds for hire of a hearse per funeral. He had a right pop at him when he insisted.'

'I bet he did.'

'Aye, by all reports, vicar learnt a few choice words that day – they've never really got on since… Oh and you're on lookout duty today, when they're putting flowers on.'

'Lookout duty?' I queried. 'What's that?'

'Dick's invention,' Tyler replied.

What on earth was Dick's lookout duty? It had to be something to do with the purple sheets or greengrocer grass, surely?

'Good spot here, by the shed corner,' said T. 'After vicar's done his stuff, and the mourners are chatting and looking at flower labels and all that, on occasions ladies crouch down, reading wishes and what 'ave you. Sometimes 'as been known to get a glimpse of stocking top.' He grinned, brimming with male mischief and character.

‘For God’s sake, goodness’ sake,’ I corrected myself. ‘You’ve been doing this too long.’ I said. He grinned again.

Lighting a fag he said, ‘You’ll learn there’s few perks in this job. ‘ere’ he produced from the shed a bottle of sherry ‘get some of that down yer.’

‘And where’s that come from?’ I exclaimed.

‘Put it in here earlier when I brought ropes down.’ (That’s where they came from).

‘Aren’t you full of surprises,’ I said. ‘I came here today to inter dear Arthur and find myself supping sherry behind a derelict shed preparing for ‘Dick’s voyeur duty’, after having a jolly in the local? You couldn’t make it up.’

‘Good, i’nt it,’ said T, ‘and we get paid.’

‘They’re coming,’ said T. We involuntarily flinched as if we were hiding villains about to pounce.

I peered round the side of the shed; he made another ‘shh’ sign with his finger against his lips. So there we were, out of sight, leaning on the shed in the gentle sunshine, one of my feet propped against it, T happily smoking, and us both bottle-necking the sherry. Fair to say for those few moments we hadn’t a care in the world. We were proper Andy Dufresnes on a rooftop in *The Shawshank Redemption.* In my head I said a little prayer for Arthur to bless him on his way, and one for me as the language in my head had been deteriorating fast and perhaps you shouldn't really have this much fun in a graveyard...

The Vicar said his few words and the mourners threw in their soil from the hand box now being policed by one of Higgs's oppos, I think this one came with the car; the other helper brought the flowers down from the church and laid them to one side. At this Tyler peered out from our position and gestured to me, whispering, 'C'mon.'

I could now see how a lady could commit an inadvertent indiscretion viewed from our level, but thankfully none such today. I just thought it would be ten times more embarrassing for us to be noticed, two heads poking out from around the shed corner like two of the tatty urchins in *Oliver Twist*, than for any lady. I encouraged Tyler back with the sherry, which was not difficult. It crossed my mind to call him the Artful Dodger; on second thoughts that could be me, as Tyler would make a better Fagin. He was after all in charge, heaven help us.

We peered out from our bunker some minutes later, and the place had returned to its normal tranquillity. The grave's few minutes of fame and notoriety had passed, and its site was no longer the one of the orderly bus queue it had been moments before.

'Okay,' said Tyler, and we emerged as if going to advance. 'Just follow my lead, won't take long, and don't rescue any leaves or worms or we'll be here all day, right.'

We went to the hole. Arthur looked comfy, and had obviously been a well-loved man, judging by the number of floral tributes and handfuls of sand that had been thrown in. The ropes were still in the rings on the coffin; the undertakers had done the physical lowering, which Tyler told me later is always a blessing, and I'd find out why soon enough. We pulled the ropes out and the rings gently chinked back against the coffin, and put them in the sherry bag, beg your pardon, carrier bag in which they had come to keep them clean. T said he usually had to wash them after each funeral but sometimes you could get away with two. I'd never really thought - after any of the many funerals I had been to - about the ownership of the ropes, or realised that they had to be washed each time, but they were the gravedigger's responsibility, which made sense. I must remember, I pondered, if I am ever asked to do a funeral in the future, to put ropes very firmly on my 'must not forget' list. No ropes would make for a really unimaginable problem. This was the second entry in my list after 'dig a step' to get out while gravedigging in progress. A burial with no ropes, wow, what on earth would you do? What a thought…

Next the greengrocer grass, planks and purple sheets were removed and crudely folded. All very matter of fact; the grave was skilfully, quickly and unceremoniously 'undressed'.

'Okay,' said Tyler, 'let's have a fag break.' This we duly did, T leaning on Howard and Elsie and me just standing.

Lighting a fag he said, 'You ever smoked, PJ?'

‘Yes,’ I replied, ‘on and off. Started at school, mainly because it was frowned upon, well more than that, it was an expellable offence, and perhaps I was a bit rebellious at the time. My parents smoked too, but not much.’

‘Want one now?’ he offered. I thought: Get thee behind me, Satan, but wasn’t sure this was the right place or occasion for such a remark.

‘No thanks,’ I gracefully declined. I was over them for the time being.

‘Here, ‘ave a drink then.’ Which I did.

‘Should we be drinking this much? We’ve got to drive,’ I said.

‘Be all right,’ said T. ‘You’ll soon work it off.’ I wasn’t entirely sure he was right about that, but hey-ho.

‘Right,’ he said, ‘climb in.’ With that he climbed down and stood on the coffin and gestured for me to do the same.

‘Will it take our weight?’ I asked.

‘Yes, should do, ‘aven’t had a new ‘un break on me yet,’ came his answer.

That wasn’t very reassuring. I was at the foot end, and Tyler the head.

‘Now,’ he said. I felt a much needed lesson coming on. ‘We’ll stand here and shovel stuff in towards you and down. Make sure you pack and tuck it round the sides tight as you can, then there’s less to take away.’ That one technique and tip saved me tons of barrowing away over later years.

I had a final look at the polished wood in what had fast returned back to a hole in the ground from its briefly elevated status of 'grave'. With that we shovelled away, and yes, the soil and stones do thud onto the lid with a dull finality, but we always tried to keep this clatter to a minimum out of respect. It was a shame to see these flowers, caringly and lovingly thrown only minutes ago, just buried, but I suppose their job was done, their memory created.

'Cross,' I said.

'Cross what?' T replied. 'Me fingers?'

'No, no,' I said, 'Arthur Cross, that was his name, he was seventy-seven.' I had no sooner read and said that and the nameplate was gone.

It took about twenty minutes to fill in. Tyler told me to take what was left in the box to the tip in the corner. This I did along with that blessed conveyor belt and blue pipe. No way was I filling that back into the grave, as some poor soul was going to have to open this grave again in due course for Arthur's wife, who looked fine today - upset but fine - and it could be me, Tyler reminded me. Whoever it was though would no doubt curse me in absentia if we put it back, whether me cursing my own stupidity or another... We were soon putting the sod back on in the order it had been removed, tramping it down, and leaving enough of a bump up on top for the ground to settle. It is a misconception that this early settling is caused by coffin collapse; it is not, it is just the soil bedding itself down again. Admittedly not universally the case nowadays though with the perceived environmentally friendly cardboard and raffia coffins, as they collapse almost immediately, or very soon after the day.

My mother then ‘turned up’ in me as I arranged the flowers exactly as she would have done, and I hoped would approve. Arthur’s wife’s first, and so on. Tyler was a little confused by this attention to detail, but my mum would have done it this way, as she did for many and I had done for her grave. I did not know Arthur but that mattered not. I was once told there are no strangers in graves, just people we did not have the good fortune to meet. A noble thought, I remembered thinking, but nonsense really, as surely strangers and people we have not met amounted to the same thing.

‘Right,’ said T, ‘all done.’

Out of his view I made the sign of the cross towards Arthur, said bye to Howard and Elsie and thanked them for their company over the last couple of days.

‘Who are you talking to?’ said Tyler.

‘Oh,’ I said, ‘just thanking Howard and Elsie for their company.’

‘Who the…’ He was going to swear, I was sure, but he didn’t, ‘are Howard and Elsie?’

‘Oh, they’re Arthur’s new neighbours.’

Tyler just turned away and continued on his way with his barrow load of greengrocer grass and tools. I think my dead-leaf rescuing, flower arranging and now talking to the neighbours had got the better of him.

I followed on with my pile of greengrocer grass and purple sheets and at the top of the terraces I looked back down towards Arthur. 'Thank you and God bless you, fella,' I said, and was gone. It struck me whilst walking away that in this case of dear Arthur, he probably did have the last laugh. In essence, when I had muttered 'God Bless you fella', I made the simplest attempt at making with my hand the sign of the cross. "A Cross" was, after all, not only Arthur's name but also perhaps his last instructions "on the tin", if you like…

Back at the cars Tyler was laughing with Higgs. I unloaded my stuff and joined them.

'Well, young man, you're not a graveyard virgin any more,' said Higgs.

'No, sir,' I said, 'quite an experience.' 'Sir' was more my comfort zone.

'Aye,' he said, 'character-building stuff, and that's no lie. What do you say, T?'

Tyler acknowledged this remark, but said nothing.

As we parted company I said to Mr Higginson, 'Will you be needing us again this week, sir?' Immediately I thought it was not my place to ask, but nobody was bothered.

'Keen, eh, T?' said Higgs.

'Aye,' said T, 'he'll learn.' The two of them laughed.

'No, lad,' said Higgs, 't'other two are fer t' crem.' I was dying to ask him how his viewing had gone with the pungent Harry, but I thought it best not to. Doubtless it had gone without incident or we would definitely have heard.

Tyler said, ‘Jump in car, PJ, for a minute.’ This I did. He handed me fifty pounds in tenners. ‘There you go,’ he said, ‘thank you, you’ve done all right there.’

‘What’s this?’ I said. ‘No, no, you’re a mate, and God knows you’ve helped me enough.’

‘Its wages,’ said Tyler, with a ‘don’t ask again’ look on his face. Reluctantly I conceded but I hoped he knew I hadn’t done it for the money though, although it was very welcome.

‘Want some more sherry?’ he said.

‘No and neither do you,’ I said with new-found confidence. ‘C’mon, I’ll get you a pint closer to home, okay? How about the Swan, at Beckfoot?’ It was not far from Cliff Field or Westlet.

‘See you there,’ said T.

We had a pleasant couple of hours playing pool and darts, both of which T was quite good at; well I couldn’t touch him and I didn’t think I was too bad. I asked him how he had got all his churchyard work.

‘Off Dick, Dick’s round,’ was his reply. ‘Yes, old Dick.’ I remembered he had referred to Dick briefly before.

'He liked his beer as well, you know,' he went on. 'You'd know if Dick dug the one before you if you were on a reopen, as you'd find anything between four and eight beer tins in 'em… Chucked the tins in as 'is calling card.'

'Why did he give it up?' I asked.

'Joined 'em,' said Tyler. I must have looked puzzled. 'Died,' he said.

'Oh, how old was he then?'

'Late fifties'

'Oh dear - that's no age. What did he die of?'

'Cirrhosis,' said T. Oh great, I thought, it sounded and looked like heavy drinking and gravedigging went hand in hand. Over the years it became clear that gravedigging money was hard earned and a good percentage of it spent on booze of one sort or another. Cirrhosis was sort of an accepted occupational hazard. Cirrhosis indeed differs from many other diseases in that you actually have to go and physically buy it, the required volume being far from cheap. (Unlike most of the dread afflictions we sadly suffer from or become victims of, that are unavoidable and largely free…)

Towards the end Tyler asked me what I was doing Thursday; it was Monday now. Nothing, I replied and he said could I fill one in for him at Lowebraith, as he'd got two on that day. Yes, no problem, I said, with newly found, if groundless, confidence. In my insurance job the number of largely unnecessary 'if only' insurance policies I would have to sell (sorry, 'advise' upon) to generate commission of fifty pounds clear profit was not insubstantial, and the training to do it was tedious.

We went home after my losing at all the pub games. Well at least I went home, but I suspected Tyler would not get past his local in Westlet.

His last words to me out of the car window were, 'I'll ring you with the times. Tell Sam I'll probably get round tomorrow to do a bit more in the jungle.'

'Okay,' I replied and he drove off. He really must get that exhaust fixed, I thought.

When I got back home Sam had just been out with Purdey, who welcomed me with her characteristically enthusiastic over-the-top greeting, as if to say where had I been all her life. Sam asked me how I'd got on. 'Good,' I replied as we made our way to the kitchen, 'Yep, all right, job's a good 'un as they say in these parts.'

'Have you been drinking?' Sam asked.

'Drinking? Just 'blown the froth' off a couple on the way home, occupational hazard,' I said in an attempt at humour.

'Yeah and the rest,' was the knowing reply, 'you really ought to be careful, PJ, in the car.'

'Yes, I know, but it was T, you see, he brought a…'

My sentence withered away under her gaze of disapproval.

‘I don’t care if it was the man in the moon’s fault. You drank it, end of,’ she said.

‘Sorry,’ I said sheepishly like a scolded child. She was right of course.

In an effort to make friends again, I said buoyantly, ‘How much money did I cost you at the auction that day?’

‘Forty-nine pounds,’ she remembered instantly.

I pulled the ten pound notes out of my pocket and handed them to her. ‘Well there you go, fifty for you, so will you let me off now?’

‘I’ll think about it,’ was her reply. ‘I’ll let you off but consider yourself reprimanded and on a formal warning.’

‘Deal,’ I said, without hesitation (I was not going to get a better one). ‘Can I have my pound change though?’

‘No you bloody well can’t, now go and feed those sheep, its bell-ringing practice tonight. Grrrrrr,’ she said. I was forgiven, and she was back.

As an afterthought I said, ‘Tyler’s asked me to do another one, just filling in at Lowebraith, on Thursday.’

‘Great, go for it. Fancy you, PJ, earning money. Unheard of, I think I’ll have to have a lie down,’ said Sam. I had to admit there was undoubtedly more than an element of truth in what she said.

Well, I thought, on the way to tell the sheep my news, I had for the first time since school actually achieved something that was to me far more prestigious than O levels, A levels, degrees and so on (which all seem to be largely taken for parents so they can impress their counterparts at coffee mornings or bridge evenings and the like, and of very little actual use).

Now I had something I could be proud of. An unmentionable, conversation stopping career, apparently steeped in mystery. I wasn't a pilot, or a surgeon, but arguably the most mysterious of the three, I was a real life gravedigger.

Not long after my gravedigging initiation I attended a funeral. It struck me that we all have to attend these ceremonies from time to time; it was just that the 'from time to time' increased in frequency with age. It always amused PJ - to the extent of having to look away to hide it - when observing mourners congregating before a funeral just how many become both mime and lip readers. Many mourners acknowledge each other with a hushed and subdued half-hearted recognition which would have been an enthusiastic hug of a long lost friend if at a wedding. They immediately erase their natural and obvious involuntary pleasure at the sight of a loved or seldom seen one when remembering where they are, hoping nobody noticed this lapse in expected grieving. Confusion soon sets in at such times as to whether, after making this connection across a car park or aisle, the reason of it being a funeral itself becomes a little lost and more of an interruption in what often turns out to be a good day.

They then proceed, unnoticed in their eyes, to mime: 'Are you going to the pub after', with eyebrows raised in hopeful receipt of a positive response. This ritual serves largely only to advertise the skill of the ventriloquist. Often this exaggerated silent speak is accompanied by the raising and twisting of the wrist toward the mouth, signalling the drinking of an imaginary glass. If the required positive nod was received this would be greeted with a 'thumbs up' signal, close to the sender's face - intended as hopeless concealment so no one would notice - and an inappropriate ear to ear grin. The sender if accompanied would then turn to their partner and whisper in their ear 'have you noticed so and so is here', oblivious to the fact that their partner may indeed have noticed this 'secret' greeting, which was often second only in subtlety to a Maori Haka. You could only hope these senders didn't have jobs that required them to work undercover, or indeed played poker.

The only difference PJ ever saw in this ritual was if it were a licensed 'Funeral Tea' to follow. If it really was 'tea' the index finger and thumb may touch as in the holding of a tea cup, accurate enough then at least, if not secret.

This 'silent secret' greeting was common at every funeral. Although by definition funerals are undeniably sad affairs they are often preceded by weeks of family stress, trauma and torment, and the thought of a pint with friends often brought a welcome and necessary relief valve. Sad events though funerals undoubtedly were, it was human nature to make the best of a bad job and the ensuing buffets and shindigs could often be chatty affairs. 'You can't beat a good funeral'.

Quite simply, the funeral day offered us all a unique opportunity to renew relationships with friends and relations and to meet the other friends of the one we had lost, whom we would never have met in any other circumstance.

Nowadays it has become increasingly popular to 'dispose' of the client even before the service, as if they could really put a dampener on proceedings and take the edge off a good family 'do' (minus one). It wouldn't be the first time that a whole Church service was held for a table top flower display.

How apt it is, I thought, that one of the few anagrams of the word 'funeral' is of course 'real fun'. That always made me smile. Would even perhaps make a good title for a book?

Chapter 5

THE LONELY MAN

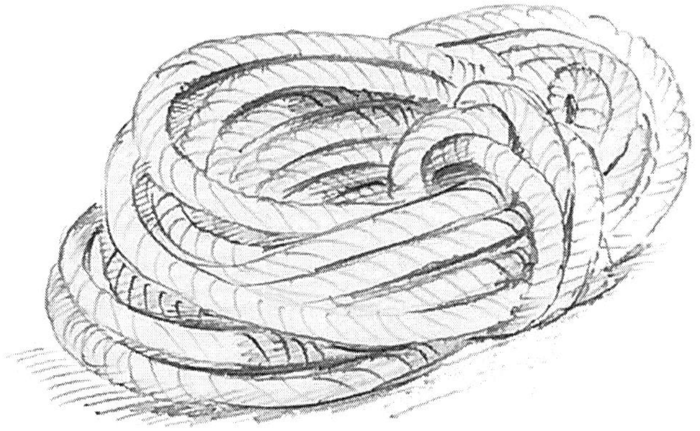

Sure enough Tyler rang as promised a couple of days later to tell me about the Lowebraith job. The funeral was at eleven and I was expected at the graveyard about forty-five minutes later. Tyler said it would all be set up.

This was a younger sister going in with her older sister, both of whom had been spinsters. They had lived together, and both had trounced the 'three score years and ten rule'. This was one of those where the younger sister was going on top of her older sister, who was now younger than her younger sister, who was now older than her. I thought the only two places that could happen were in a graveyard or a Ronnie Barker sketch.

Tyler had added, 'Hide behind the little chapel on the opposite side of the graveyard.'

'Okay,' I'd replied.

I arrived in plenty of time, at about eleven fifteen. The grave was a good two thirds of the way down the village graveyard on the left-hand side and against the wall. The church was in the village itself and this was the 'new' graveyard opened in 1901. I inspected Tyler's, always tidy, handiwork. There were a couple of leaves in the bottom but, had I tried to retrieve them, the planks, greengrocer grass and the lot would have fallen in as I was scrambling to get out. So these two leaves had to be left to their fate. They were in fact dead, too, so they fitted right in and were probably in the best place. The sides had held up though. Tyler had said it was a nightmare when the side or sides fell minutes before a funeral but thankfully no such drama today.

I was interested to note - as I was cautiously peering in to see the bottom of the grave - that it looked like soil. I had never looked down into an occupied grave before; the base simply had to be the top of the older sister's coffin. Tyler had camouflaged this beautifully and you really couldn't tell. There was no sign of the current resident's ground-floor accommodation. I must remember to ask him for tips on doing this as part of my training and development I thought, as I pondered why you didn't fall through into the coffin beneath. I learnt later that he couldn't show me that day because he had two funerals on at similar times and he was too busy. That lesson was for another day, but it was why Tyler had dug this one, as falling through (and unfortunately in) was a real possibility.

He showed me later his tapper, and the technique of tapping the ground to 'feel' for the already resident. Also, he said, you feel the ground begin to flex with the old lid beneath your feet. The tapper was an unglamorous top-weighted prong and when pressed into the soil you could feel, and indeed on more recent coffins hear, the 'clonk' of it on the wood, hence the name 'tapper'. This primitive technique was simple, like many things that work in life, but highly effective and told you when you were about two inches above. Other times, he said, you just fell through into them if the lid had rotted sufficiently, an unpleasant thought and not very reassuring.

Anyway I moved a rope slightly so its coil aligned perfectly with the one at the other end. This, I admit, was a completely unnecessary exercise. I just wanted to feel I had done something. I retreated to my assigned hiding place and settled down to watch; it was a little like being a bird watcher or a wildfowler in a hide. I noticed by the chapel wall a new-looking carrier bag behind one of Tyler's spades. Now don't get me wrong, I am not the sort of chap to go peering into discarded litter, but due to the newness of the carrier bag and the obvious logo of the local shop, I chanced a look. I still took the precaution of poking it open with a stick. Well, Tyler you bugger, I immediately thought. In the bag lay a new bottle of sherry. On the label was scrawled, with a pen which had obviously seen better days, 'Save us some'. What a good man, I mused.

I had always found the English language fascinating, not simply because of words that were identical, but with completely different meanings, 'lead', 'bark', 'pen' are all good examples and perhaps more suitably here, 'grave' and 'grave'. Also long or short vowels had always caused contention; just try to 'park' (another homonym) your car in the 'garidge' or 'garage'. I found it interesting that we had transposed this peculiarity into full sentences, which often stated the completely obvious: 'I took a picture with my camera', the obvious peculiarity here being sort of self-explanatory, as clearly without cameras pictures were called paintings or works of art…

'My dad was really good at playing the piano when he was alive'. Obvious problem here: he had, no doubt, been hopeless since he died?

'Mother said, in her lifetime'?!

Alternatively we often answered our own question. This was especially true around here, the standard local greeting appearing to be: 'Hi, how are you doing, all right?' I always felt a bit 'done' by this greeting as I considered the 'all right' was my reply? I thought this charming localism was at its funniest in the doctor's waiting room - always assuming someone dared to speak in the doctor's waiting room - when clearly geography would suggest that 'all right' was wholly inappropriate, and 'all wrong' maybe more accurate.

Nowhere did these instances of stating the blindingly obvious and answering your own question manifest themselves better than when you happened to be digging or filling in a grave. Lowebraith was to demonstrate this beautifully. The hearse and the following cortège, one family car in this case, arrived spot on time and the graveside service began. Wish I could say I didn't have a swallow of sherry, but I can't. There is a common denominator between elderly people's funerals, especially spinsters' or bachelors', and that is that there are typically very few mourners as the person concerned has outlived their generation. Any mourners there on these occasions were often care home staff.

The Vicar duly did her bit and the cars had gone almost as soon as they had arrived. When the coast was clear I emerged from my private cocktail bar to do my stuff. It was a lovely sunny day as I approached my client from the chapel side of the graveyard. It was a small coffin, and looked like it was resting in a dry dock, so there was ample room around the sides to lose plenty of soil. I repeated the routine I had been taught by Tyler, and stacked the ropes, grass, sheets and soil box neatly to one side. Although the gravedigging part of the funeral was not seen by the mourners, Tyler had said to me that it was no less important and should be carried out with due respect for the occasion. This I thoroughly concurred with. But the weather was good today, the graveyard quiet, and there was no tragedy attached to this lady's passing at her age of ninety-six. With these thoughts in mind I hopped in, and after reading the nameplate introduced myself to

Mabel and wished her well on her journey. I did my little routine of 'God bless you, Mabel' and made a cross sign in the air.

I started filling in around the sides and then on top. Tyler had impressed upon me the importance of being as quiet as possible when covering the wood – for no good reason really, just it was professional and avoided that hollow, final thumping sound.

Mabel was now reunited with her sister below her; this was their final joint resting place. Its depth had obviously been imposed on us by the first gravedigger, who had decided enough was enough when he or she dug the first hole for Mabel's sister. Mabel's grave was therefore not overly deep, so I could plainly see above ground and could myself be seen at my task.

At the point where Mabel's coffin was about to disappear for ever and I had covered it in soil but its shape was still visible, I noticed a gentleman at the top of the graveyard wandering slowly my way. I thought nothing of it at first; he was armed with two bunches of flowers so I presumed he was going to pay his respects elsewhere in the cemetery.

As he neared I could make out that he was an older fellow, with his best suit and flat cap on for this occasion of visiting the cemetery. At this point I got out of the grave, as it had become clear the destination of his flowers was very close to where I was as he was very definitely headed my way. I wished for him to have a moment of solace with his memories, without my clattering and interruption.

I stood with my back to the wall and my spade secreted behind me, my head lowered so as not to appear to be watching. Sure enough he paid his respects and arranged his flowers accordingly for Mabel's now next-door-but-two neighbour, but then he stood up and took a pace back from the headstone as if to salute it, which he did not do, but was in the position to if it had been required or necessary. There was definitely something slightly past-military about him.

Suddenly he addressed me: 'Me wife, this.'

Not expecting to have to engage in conversation, I must have sounded completely unprepared and simply stuttered, 'Oh, I'm very sorry.'

He moved across and down like a chess piece, careful not to stand on the graves. I remained motionless by the wall. The gent then positioned himself at grave number two, three away and two down from his wife; it was reminiscent of playing a game of battleships. He repeated his routine, arranging his flowers then standing back. Solemnly he said;

'Me mother, this.'

'Oh, I'm sorry about that as well, sir,' I replied. (What more could I say I thought? Nothing more came to mind, unoriginal now as it was).

Then to my surprise he addressed me further and asked, 'Someone else died, have they?'

He actually asked the question!

Given the sight of Mabel's still-open grave, my proximity to it and armed with my barely concealed spade despite my best attempts I thought it plainly obvious that it was very likely that indeed they had. But I had not the slightest idea of what to say. How do you politely answer such a nonsense question? My thoughts were on overtime, screaming possible answers at me:

'No, sir, I'm looking for rings.' (Possible? But very definitely illegal.)

'Yes of course they have, you silly old duffer, what do you think I'm doing this for, fun? The good of my health? Bizarre keep-fit?' (No, obviously not the done thing to make fun of the chap, this would be unkind; true, but unkind).

'What? Is that what is in these box things? Always wondered.' (Just plain silly, but arguably some merit as not as silly as the question).

'I do hope so, as I've just put two tons of soil on them.' (Better brain, keep it up!)

'No, but they didn't look too clever yesterday, so I thought I'd get ready.' (not credible, but not bad?)

However, in order to not appear unsympathetic to him or his day here, I simply broke my own rule and agreed with him and stated the completely obvious.

'Yes, sir, I'm afraid they have.'

I much preferred the first five answers to such a bewilderingly absurd question, and certainly hadn't helped matters by giving it credibility by answering it at all. But this answer had soon-to-be-felt consequences of starting the now rolling snowball of a particularly lovely example of the spiral dive of language when one piece of nonsense is simply compounded by the next. He went on:

'Aye, lad, 'appens to us all, all got to dee.'

What? I was simply lost for thoughts - I had quite given up on words… Had he now pointed this out to a gravedigger in his place of work? It was all too obvious that he had.

Was this revelation news or was he 'having a laugh'? In fairness though he didn't look the type for that. We were in a graveyard for heaven's sake; I was a gravedigger. I could see us being drawn into a further terrifying looming conversation about the completely obvious. I thought about replying, 'Yes, and it got light this morning and I reckon it may well get dark tonight,' but I didn't as it would have been puerile. I was beginning to understand the apparently mandatory sherry: the dead were fine but the living were positively crackers.

This sort of obvious questioning was often to provide both Tyler and I with a wry smile over the years.

Once in a small remote village churchyard we were just doing our stuff when a chap drifted in, visiting the graves aimlessly, he had no flowers or the like. He wandered our way while we were filling in and got to Tyler first. Without further ado or hesitation, he confidently said to him,

'Do you bury people here often?'

I immediately felt for him – just hard luck really. Wrong bloke to ask, I thought. I was now engrossed and looking forward to this, without being seen to be interested. Tyler stopped what he was doing, and standing on the coffin in the grave just looked at him with a curious expression. I watched excitedly, in expectation of what he might say if he answered at all. T, if anything, wasn't scared of a little humorous sarcasm. He drew himself up and said quite simply with a straight face, fag dangling as usual from the corner of his mouth,

'No, only once.'

Well it was all I could do not to laugh out loud, but I firmly bit my lip instead. I do not believe it was Tyler's intention to make the poor man feel foolish, well I don't think it was, as it was undeniably the only precise and indeed correct answer. The man had winced, but as if he had sucked on a lemon, and said apologetically and hesitantly, as the ridiculousness of the question dawned on him, 'Yes, yes, of course, only once. Silly me, what a question,' he reprimanded himself.

He was on a loser, a hide into nothing, because he did not mean 'Do you bury people here often?' at all. He meant were there often funerals in this remote little churchyard. And the answer to that was quite different.

Tyler to his credit threw him a lifeline by saying, 'Oh you mean are there often funerals up here?'

'Yes, yes, that's what I meant,' said the man with nervous enthusiasm, given away by his repetition of the word 'yes'. He was visibly relieved and grateful for Tyler's rope out of the hole he'd inadvertently dug for himself. The two of them had quite a conversation after that. It just goes to show that sometimes we say things that we do not mean at all.

On another occasion a stout gentleman approached me when I was digging towards the bottom of the grave. I was down too deep to see out, so the chap above can only have seen spadesful of soil being thrown up from below, a bit like watching a dog dig, but more leisurely. Looking down upon me, this apparent giant of a man said, 'Who's that for, lad?'

'Oh,' I stuttered, looking up as my digging ground to a halt. He had made me jump. Locals often used to pop into the churchyard when they saw us in attendance. It was just a gossip thing; any information from a gravedigger had to be right. It was always the same old village busy bodies, excuse the pun, who attended. You could hear them in the pub saying, 'It's reet, tell thee, got it off Tyler.' The name would add credibility to any forthcoming tale.

'Ramsbottom, yes, Ramsbottom, sir,' I finally replied, desperately trying to remember. This chap was lucky I knew this client's name and a bit about him. Often we did not.

‘What, what?’ said the man, with a degree of indignation. I thought: This repeating words thing must stop. ‘Not owd Rambo?’

‘Rambo?’ I replied thinking immediately of Sylvester Stallone.

‘Aye, Rambo, Tommy Ramsbottom, does all his drinking in t’ low house.’

The village concerned had two pubs - one at the top of the village and the ‘low house’ at the bottom.

‘I believe he did, sir, and I believe it is,’ I said.

‘What?’ exclaimed the man, distraught not at dear Tommy’s passing, but at the fact that he didn’t know about it, a serious credibility blow to a village know-it-all (you know the type).

‘Is he dead, is he dead?’ he went on, apparently genuinely shocked and upset, his thick frame shaking. ‘Is he… dead?’ I thought (it was me repeating things in my head now). Am I hearing things? What do you say? It is usually the police’s job to give such bad news, after no doubt years of lengthy training courses.

‘I’m afraid so, sir, I am sorry’ was the best I could do. It was no good joking about him not looking so good; all very difficult really.

‘Is he dead?’ to a gravedigger is as common as (I believe) the most frequently asked question, ‘How much is that?’ in a pound shop, and worse still we have all done it.

Another favourite we suffered from was, 'Do you ever see anything?' An uneasily asked question in a 'nudge, nudge, wink, wink' sort of a way. Quite what people, me included before doing the job, were expecting as an answer I know not. In fact the job held little morbid mystery or cloaked-figured misty romance of the films, and more just unforgiving hard graft.

I was praying my information and sources were correct and this grave was indeed for a Mr Ramsbottom and indeed the right Mr Ramsbottom at that. (Indeed 'Rambo 1' and not a sequel I thought mischievously). Frequently in villages there were people with the same or very similar names, and I did not have a Christian name for this particular client. It would not be the first such mistake, sad to say, in the debris field of Alf and Tyler's work, but to my knowledge they had not yet, at least, buried anyone who was actually not dead, referring back to Mr Ramsbottom's chum's original question.

That concept is of course a well-used nightmare to which no one would ever know the answer, and the foundation for the expression the graveyard shift. In Victorian times a bell string was attached to the recently buried corpse's finger, the string in turn attached temporarily to a bell on the surface for a specified time, after which survival of any description was not possible. The worker employed to listen out should any bell ever ring at night was said to be working the 'graveyard shift'. All being well nowadays our doctors are a little more reliably sure when one's candle has finally gone out - well we can but hope.

The consequences therefore of an information error at this point were unthinkable in the local gossip circle. Local folklore would never recover. The man, now over my initial information, continued,

'Oh, but I was only 'avin' a pint wi' 'im the other night,' he said, as if it were sufficient evidence and justification to prove to me that there had been some mistake and Tommy indeed was not dead. 'When did 'e die, lad?'

'End of last week I believe, sir.'

'Well I'll be buggered, just goes to show… What's 'e gone and deed of?'

This was where my information ran out, so I had to admit that I didn't know. I think he was disappointed that dear owd Tommy had forgotten to ask his permission before shuffling off this mortal coil.

Resignedly, he said, 'See yous later, lad.'

'Sorry to be the bringer of bad tidings, sir.'

'Aye, lad. It's not your fault.' Well that at least was a relief.

With that he left mumbling repeatedly, 'owd Tom Ramsbottom, nay, who'd 'ave thought. I'll miss 'im,' until he was out of earshot.

This human trait of perhaps being overcome by either the environment or emotion and talking nonsense as a result, even went as far as the printed word. One day whilst sitting in the car I asked after the day's client. Tyler didn't reply or utter a word; actions spoke louder than words was always his way. He simply passed me the local paper folded to the appropriate ‘obits’ page. He remarkably through years of practice could hold the paper, a cigarette and a bottle of sherry all at the same time. He signalled with one of the few remaining fingers not currently employed - not at the name but drawing attention to the age and announcement itself, as follows:

“Suddenly, tragically and completely unexpectedly at Christies after a long illness suffered well, aged 102”

Well it is all you can do not to raise an eyebrow. Emotion had certainly brushed sense aside and got the better of this author for sure, or some confusion with an air accident had crept in. Christies being a world renowned centre for the treatment of cancer and one hundred and two years was such a comparative joy that it really doesn’t matter what takes you. I had to smile - this announcement was just plain barmy on so many fronts, not to say all.

Tyler just grinned.

(You do wonder who lets them print the stuff…)

PJ was reminded of Mr Carrot’s observances of insurance claims,

‘I swerved three times before hitting the pedestrian’

‘I drove into the tree in my drive which I haven’t got’

…great stuff!

I asked Mabel for a break and went across to the carrier bag for some much needed refreshment by way of sherry. Wow, that was good. On my return

I continued to fill in, which did not take long, and put the grass back. Sad to say there was only one floral tribute from the care home so following my Mum's (Mimi's) job was easy. I had pulled the car down the cemetery after the chap who brought the flowers and paid his respects to his wife and mother had gone. I was loading up and minding my own business when this curiously quiet Cavalier SRi approached. Tyler emerged.

I said, with more than a little surprise, 'What? That exhaust's better?'

'Yes,' replied Tyler, 'one of the coppers who lives in Westlet mentioned it off the record in the pub – they are quite good like that.'

The local coppers drop hints, so as not to ruffle their own back yard as it were, as Westlet was almost a police dormitory for Corcastle.

'It's your charm, good looks and celebrity status that does it, you know,' I laughed.

'Bugger off,' he said, smiling. 'How've you got on?'

'No problems. Just one visitor after the funeral. I'll let you know about him over a pint?'

'Good idea,' said Tyler. 'That reminds me… any sherry left?'

'Loads,' I smiled, 'a real treat.'

'Let's go and have a swallow.'

I agreed and on the way across I thanked him for leaving the sherry. It was unexpected and welcome, I told him. He just smiled. I also asked him how he had got on with his funeral; an 'alright' was as much as I got. He had timed his arrival just right; I had just finished. I wondered if he had been watching from the top and leaving me to it. He never told me whether he had been; he just smiled mischievously, smoked and drank some sherry.

'Got a big do on week after next,' said T. 'It's at Preston Banks, going to be a good two-day job, horrible ground to dig and on a slope too. Will you be all right to give us a hand?'

'Yes, great,' I said.

'You haven't got to sell any of them policy things have you?' he said, referring to the expert professional financial advice that my sales manager told me I dispensed, which was the grown-up way of saying selling insurance. Just a straight deception attempt really, 'free financial advice' sounding as far away as possible from commission based insurance sales.

On more than one occasion PJ, the gravedigger, was to arrive in a suit and tie and leave in one. Changing clothes in the car in a graveyard, was never easy and indeed made one very uneasy - no trousers in a graveyard? Explanations would have to have been choice and creative, Officer.

PJ therefore often dispensed cover to the living in a suit, with pen and direct debit; and cover to the departed in overalls, with a spade and, I'm afraid, strictly cash.

'And miss working with you? You must be joking,' I said, half laughing.

‘Good. We’ll start on the Monday morning. It’s for Tuesday but if it’s like the last one, it will be a right sod, we’ll need plenty of time.’ I suspected plenty of sherry too. He sounded genuinely pleased that I could help. I was quietly delighted, but thought that was best kept to myself.

As we parted, Tyler said, ‘PJ, nearly forgot.’ He handed me fifty pounds. ‘Thanks.’

‘No, thank you,’ I replied.

‘Go and give it to Sam like a good lad, or do you want me to,’ he said, laughing. He’d got the measure of me, that was for sure, and of Sam.

This burial of Mabel reminded me of a similar situation some years later, when I was burying another very old lady. Sorry to say gentlemen, and although we all know it in our bones, I can verify from the gravedigger’s point of view that yes, the ladies really do live longer, often a lot longer. On this occasion the grave itself was about fifty yards from the church door and there were four mourners, the fittest three sporting Zimmer frames, and the fourth in a wheelchair, pushed by one of the care home nurses.

I had taken up position, my back against the wall next to a tree. I felt a bit like the hang man or executioner. Tyler wasn’t there that day, he was in hospital (which we will come to later - long-term, consistent, dedicated, nay even admirable, self-inflicted legal abuse caused him to require a service, in the same way as a car, from time to time). So I tried to be good and didn’t bring any sherry with me. The cortège followed their friend to her grave, the fifty-yard journey taking some twenty minutes or so. It is not often that the bier bearers have to slow down for the mourners to catch up but this was certainly the case here.

The grave seemed no bigger than a slot in the ground compared to some I'd dug, so it wouldn't take much filling in. It was one of Tyler's pet hates when the undertaker gave him oversized measurements 'to be on the safe side'. Sometimes we were told to dig a near dry dock for what looked like a canoe, and Tyler would get annoyed at the extent of extra material to dig out as this could amount to tons, unnecessarily dug out and moved for the same money. He could get quite vociferous about this, if only to me, but he was known to employ some very choice words and, shall we say, less than complimentary phrases. The undertaker's parentage and indeed conception were frequently the target of these verbal barrages to get his level of displeasure across.

As the mourners arrived at the graveside, and just before the vicar was to have his say, one of the older undertaker's crew came and joined me at my vantage point.

'I bet the singing was a bit thin,' I whispered to him.

This was a personal thing for me, always having been a supporter of a good tune and singalong of a hymn at a funeral, and not some long-resurrected verses from the past that nobody knew. Funeral congregations for the elderly were usually small affairs, simply because they had outlived their compatriots. Typically a funeral congregation would be made up of people who only darkened the doors of church for 'hatches, matches and dispatches', so they needed all the help they could get when it came to the selection and singing of hymns. The tried and tested classics with a strong tune were my preference, the ones we have all come across and often have a special place for any of us.

'Aye,' said the undertaker, 'we all gave it our best shot, but vicar's got a booming voice, saved the day, it was like a solo.'

PJ, by and large, liked vicars of all 'makes' across the board. They were a control on life for PJ, a 'constant' if you like, all round 'good eggs' in the main. The sort of person with unexplained enthusiasm for life that you want to know is just around if the need arises. If life were a pub quiz, you would want one on your team, offering an encouraging smile of friendly reassurance that they know something you do not or indeed the knowledge that is escaping you. You instinctively know the answer and team are indeed in safe hands, if not your own.

PJ found it disappointing though, even questionable, that out of all the sad statistics on suicide 'Reverends', as a profession, featured at the bottom of the list. The least takers? PJ never found this very reassuring, as they know it is better elsewhere and have the letters after, or titles before, their names to prove it. By-passing this life must have its temptations? (Therein, that word, lies the clue perhaps?)

In these days of 'e' everything, they are God's sales force of 'eLife Cover' for the soul if you like, just the 'e' in this case standing for 'eternal'.

In contrast Alf, Tyler and now me, simply peddled unglamorous 'cover' (still ‘eternal’ though).

Yes, concluded PJ before mentally moving on, there appeared to be no downside to tipping a nod to God from time to time, no harm done. True ‘life’ insurance (or perhaps it should be ‘death’ insurance) just in case?

As the burial ceremony continued, the undertaker leaned sideways towards me, and whilst respectfully looking straight ahead and without expression, he quietly and knowledgeably said almost in a whisper, ‘I don’t know why this lot are botherin’ to go home.’

Sadly he had a point (and I bit my teeth into my lip to avoid laughing)

It turned out that this undertaker was somewhat of a master of the stony faced one liner. On another famous occasion a portly mourner had taken ill at the graveside to the extent that the paramedics were called. What with all the hoo-ha, the soft ground and the sheer weight of the man, it was simply too much for the two lady paramedics to get him to the ambulance on their sitting stretcher. The fact that they were ladies was not an issue; this was an impossible two person job and more one for an entire rugby team. Besides they had quite enough to do supporting oxygen bottles and holding the heart monitors and so on.

Tyler and I were summoned from our hidey hole to help in the unfolding melee. With Tyler at the feet of this giant and me holding the handles behind his head plus the paramedics either side we shoved and pushed and crabbed our way out to the waiting ambulance.

Our undertaker friend held open the ambulance door (no mud risk to his suit almost certainly being his motive).

After we had done our bit and loaded our charge, we bade farewell to the paramedics, and silently wished the gent luck as he did not look well at all, and was clearly at risk or danger of coming back.

As we passed our friend returning to the job in hand, he said, again featureless of expression,

‘Don’t often see you lads carryin’ ‘um out’.

This time though I’m sure I detected the cracks of a wry smile as if he wanted to burst, which of course he never did.

Chapter 6

I DIDN'T THINK THAT WOULD HAVE HAPPENED

It was a Monday when Tyler and his dad Alf came down the drive at Cliff Field. I shouted, 'Morning, chaps,' as I opened the five-bar gate. They turned into the car park and got out. 'Fancy a brew?' I asked.

'Yes please,' times two was my reply, as they disembarked. This time it was Alf who was followed by a Spaniel who looked not dissimilar to Stan's Buzz.

'Cum 'ere' Max, t'owd lad' commanded Alf, to less than no effect at all as Max tore off and relieved himself against the house wall.

‘Sorry’ said Alf sheepishly.

‘He’s bonny, Alf’, PJ said as it was the first thing that came to mind, ‘thought it was Buzz’.

‘Max Buzz brother’, replied Alf unceremoniously as if one word.

‘I see,’ replied PJ, ‘great’. PJ didn’t know what else to say and instantly hoped the two didn’t go walking together as shouting for ‘MaxBuzz’ would sound more like ordering a new-fangled energy drink than calling two Spaniels.

When Buzz, Max and Purdey got partying together not much else got done. Stromble would have joined in the shinanigans, but was old and regal enough now to know better and just observe in supervisory capacity.

It should have struck PJ then that the polar opposites often displayed by Alf and Tyler were also reflected in their canine chums. Alf who was arguably the less fit (although not by much as the coming years demonstrated) had an uncontrollable whirlwind of a dog, and Tyler being of ‘match fit age’, the docile old fella. On the surface it looked as though it would make perfect sense to swop, they all lived in the same house-cum-kennel anyway?

I emerged from the house with two teas, sugar and a biscuit each - for humans and dogs.

‘Tea okay?’ I said.

By this time the two of them were attaching their trailer, which had slowly but surely been left at Cliff Field with such increasing regularity that it had all but moved in. It and the SRi were the other integral silent partners in this team, although mechanically not always that silent. Indeed if they had appeared in Reverend Awdry's Thomas the Tank Engine books world they would certainly have been allotted names and character.

The parking was a lot better than at T and Alf's house and we had no issue with space and the trailer becoming a resident. One had to avoid thoughts of 'Laurel and Hardy' watching them work together. It appeared that no sooner had Tyler put something in a secure position in the trailer than Alf would move it, for no logical or apparent reason that I could see. There were some choice exchanges between them during this procedure, but eventually all appeared to be well, with the greengrocer grass below the soil box and so on, and the load secured with ropes. The planks rested over the back of the trailer door with what was left of a hi-vis jacket tied to them as a token gesture to safety. There was a broken corner of plastic where the number plate and light board should be, but legality had never been one of this duo's stronger points.

‘Where to today chaps?’ I asked. Alf chuckled.

T said, ‘Just a quick reopen at Bellows Bottom.’

‘At where?’ I asked, a little bemused.

‘Bellows Bottom,’ he repeated. This was a new one on me. ‘Up behind Hilton,’ he said.

‘Okay,’ I said, ‘is that a joke, “behind” Hilton?’

‘No,’ said Tyler, ‘very funny’

Well, I thought, if you’ve got to be buried then Bellows Bottom, with the inevitable snigger value of the name, seemed as good a place as any - and funnier than most - and it being behind somewhere else just an added snigger 'bonus'. It also explained Alf's schoolboy-ish chuckle. Place names have always fascinated me. I wondered who or what Bellows was? Indeed to do a reopen of a hole in Bellows Bottom sounded far more like the task of a surgeon than a gravedigger and was almost too unpleasant a thought to bear. Particularly worrying, or cause for understandable considerable concern, if your name happened to be Bellow, I mischievously amused myself thinking.

'Easy digging, this one,' Tyler whispered. 'The owd fella's got more selective in his old age – you won't catch 'im on Preston Banks like you and me next week.'

'Oh right,' I said. I was already getting increasingly worried about this Preston Banks job, but this was temporarily offset as I was still amusing myself thinking that indeed what a blessing it was 'easy' to open the hole in Bellows Bottom.

Off they went, pre-flight checks done, which consisted solely of a quick twang on the trailer ropes hopefully securing the load.

As I watched them go off on their travels, I drifted off into a comparative daydream about people's preparations for work. For many millions the day starts with that infuriating invention of the Devil himself, the alarm clock, going off at some ungodly hour, which did little to welcome you gently back into the world from your cosy slumbers. After being jolted back to life, you jump out of bed already late, show yourself to the bathroom, put on the newly washed shirt, suit up, sort the kids, kiss anyone available on the cheek. Then shout 'see you later' to anyone that was yet human or just anyone, toast in hand, get in the car and into the dreaded traffic. Oh the traffic, the volume of which served as the only consolation: you were not alone in this madness. Well that and the radio 'travel' news, which would be far better named the 'stationary' news on most mornings, commenting on events betwixt the ends of the motorway car park.

Finally you arrived at work where some unappreciative boss was undoubtedly picking holes in what you did yesterday - or indeed in your whole career and raison d'être - to the point of destruction, just to justify their own elevated existence and position relative to some other faceless wonder further up the employment food chain. The human race and the rat race were so very true. This hopeless hierarchical system applied whichever rung of the ladder you were on.

Tyler and Alf's way was different: they had never heard of an alarm clock. They both had the body clocks of farm poultry (maybe a pheasant in Alf's case); they got up when it was light, rested when it wasn't. Wake up, have a fag (in Tyler's case), put on the same clothes as the day before or anything else that takes your fancy from the wide selection in the wardrobe, more commonly known as the floor in many households, visit the bathroom (or not in Alf's case). I always used to think from a certain manly aroma that surrounded Alf that he thought that 'BO' stood for 'Bathing Optional'…

Then it was breakfast, usually in the form of part of a pork pie, carefully marinated in the screwed-up plastic wrapper on the car dashboard overnight or longer in cigarette ash and heaven knows what else, perhaps on a good day washed down with some overlooked flat cider from an eighty per cent squeezed-empty bottle from the drinks cabinet. (The factory-fitted, onboard drinks cabinet on the Vauxhall SRi model – well more accurately this particular version of the model – was installed in the sea of rubbish behind the driver's seat.)

Another fag and you're ready to go. Alf and Tyler's clients were no less demanding than clients in any other job or profession. Admittedly they weren't particular on dress code, combed hair or otherwise, but they were sticklers for punctuality. That said, they never, ever complained.

I was pottering on in one of my outbuildings trying to mend something which was, no doubt, way beyond my capabilities, when about an hour after the two musketeers had left I heard what sounded suspiciously like their car on the drive. The SRi had a ruined sound as if pleading for clemency or simply oil and I duly went out to open the gate. It was indeed the 'gruesome twosome' but suspiciously minus one trailer, which immediately rang alarm bells. Now I knew where Hilton was, if not specifically where Bellows Bottom was, but enough to know that one hour was nowhere near long enough to get there and back and dig a hole.

'Hi,' I said to Tyler as he got out of the car. He positively glared at me and said nothing. Now I knew that I, perhaps for a change on this occasion, was not the target of his quite visible frustration.

‘What’s to do, and where is the trailer?’ I asked with concern. One always feared the worst with these two.

‘It’s ‘im,’ said Tyler, ‘the owd fella, he’s flippin’ useless.’ (I never heard him say the word ‘flipping’ and strangely enough he didn’t then).

‘Where’s the trailer?’

‘It’s all right, that’s at Bellows.’

‘What’s up with him?’

Tyler looked at me and said in a pathetic childlike voice, mockingly impersonating his dearest Father;

“I thought I’d put them in, but must ‘ave took ‘em out again at PJ’s, and forgot.”

‘Forgot what?’

‘The bloody spades.’

I quickly spun round away from him to conceal my spontaneous unavoidable grin. Two lifelong gravediggers – Alf had started on the Burma Railway during the war and Tyler had been digging since he could walk unaided – had apparently forgotten their spades.

‘And you can stop your smiling,’ Tyler quickly and forcefully said in my direction, having detected my manner.

‘C’mon T,’ I said. ‘You’ve got to see the funny side. Two, has to be said, experienced gravediggers forgetting their spades!? That’s funny, even priceless.' I was trying desperately not to start laughing profusely out loud. It would be like the Red Arrows pilots all running round the airfield wondering what they had forgotten.

'Aye,' he grunted begrudgingly, trying to sound more annoyed than he was. He was just too laid-back by nature to really get annoyed, and he knew I knew it. 'Well it's not funny yet,' he added.

But it was to me. We have all had to use the tools of our trade, whether it is a pen, computer, cement mixer or aeroplane, but gravediggers forgetting spades must rank in the top ten of the unforgivable list and finally I started laughing. Tyler reluctantly tried to hold a smile at bay.

Alf in the meantime retrieved the spades from where he had earlier left them, having lifted them out of the trailer for no obvious reason, and was loading them in stealthy fashion onto the car's back seat, or where the car's back seat should have been, the area currently occupied by a mower, of course. I think he was hoping that nobody would notice him.

'Do you guys want a brew while you're here?' I asked.

'Best not,' said Tyler, 'running a bit late now.' There was a small but surprisingly well-stocked ironmongers in Hilton, and it did cross my mind that it would have been far easier to have bought two more spades. Surely they would always come in useful if you happened to be a gravedigger. I thought it better to keep this idea to myself though, as they probably would not have had enough money with them. Forty fags and cider Tyler would certainly have had, but a spade to dig a grave he almost certainly wouldn't have been able to afford. I loved the lad to bits but his priorities, even by my hopeless standards, were sometimes open to question.

I couldn't let Alf off the hook completely, for Tyler's benefit at least. This whole episode reminded me of the time when Alf had shown me his 'best spade', one piece in each hand. That sort of said it all about Alf. I caught his eye and said in a questioning tone;

'Forgot the spades, eh, Alf. Gravediggers?'

He looked downwards like a schoolboy about to be reprimanded by a teacher (harking back to the good old days when children actually respected teachers or indeed any form of authority and didn't hold them in contempt).

'Forgot the spades?' I said again with a raised eyebrow.

He replied as if chastened, 'I didn't think that would have happened,' and boarded the car.

Well that was it, for the years to follow Alf would always revert to this phrase, as he probably always had, as it acted as a cure-all for him. It was never quite the right answer to anything but beautifully combined an implied apology with utter, almost childlike, bewilderment. It really should be on his tombstone, in due course. I'm not sure if he thought too much about when he used it, but he knew what he meant by it, and strangely enough, so did we. It usually meant some completely inexcusable and avoidable botch-up was about to be unveiled.

I thought this a clever phrase for dealing with daily living and got used to using it quite a lot myself, not necessarily out loud, but in those talking-to-yourself moments I hope we all have. Not long after Alf had introduced me to it, I left a pan of veg on the cooker. Usual stuff - veg knackered, room full of smoke, fire alarm wailing, pan base blackened and yes, water really does burn. The expression became a 'favourite things' line in my personalised version of the song from *The Sound of Music* when I played it in my head. I just muttered to myself, 'I didn't think that would have happened,' and bingo, all was well and righted with the world, misdemeanour over. The simple expression had definitely been awarded its place on my favourite things list.

There were reasonably frequent occasions when I would deploy this cure-all remark - when I tripped, stumbled, fell, bumped into something... Like us all, my first thought would be: Did anybody see me do that? My second: That was really stupid. Then the damage report: cuts and bruises, breakages and the like. 'I didn't think that would have happened' fits perfectly in these situations, and makes the whole event instantly even amusing.

Tyler and his dad set off again for round two at Bellows Bottom, Tyler sucking on a cigarette as if his life depended on it. He was letting his dad believe he was still mad with him, but he wasn't; he'd winked at me as they set off. He'd blow hot and cold sometimes but I knew he enjoyed making Alf squirm if just for a bit. He'd get some mileage out of this, but they would be friends again by teatime. Perhaps I was wrong about Laurel and Hardy, more like Harold and his dad, Albert of *Steptoe and Son* immortality.

This particular completely avoidable event reminded me of that old series of jokes involving a light bulb: how many and so on... Perhaps the gravediggers' version should read,

"How many gravediggers does it take to dig a grave?"

The answer is clearly three: two to dig the hole, and one to remember the spades...

(That was perhaps Tyler and Alf's problem - there just weren't enough of them).

A year or two later one afternoon Tyler was strimming something or other, and Stan and his wife popped in. We had all become firm friends by now and unbeknown to us this afternoon was about to become legendary. One of those unplanned events, which happen to us all from time to time, that just goes like clockwork, and far better than if it had be organised or arranged.

We had one of those picnic tables with seat benches attached, a 'one-piece' if you like. Stan and Helena sat one side and Sam and I on the other. Sam had brought down into the garden a demijohn of Sooty's best grapefruit wine. Clearly Sooty had gone tropical, from elderberries and peapods to grapefruit. He had got a job lot from one of his sources and donated one of his many demijohns to our cause, although not specifically for this spontaneous day. Unusually for Sooty the wine was quite good and even of sufficient quality to offer guests, albeit not very fussy ones.

This was great as I sensed Helena was never entirely happy when Stan announced that he was coming out to play with Tyler and I. This was our opportunity to put her mind at rest, and put the record straight. Sam and I would always be 'offcomers' in the local language here, but we had been accepted as far as you could be, and all was going swimmingly.

I had always called Helena as it is spelt, 'He-len-a', but she always corrected me, insisting it was 'He-leen-a'. This gave the others considerable amusement as neither of us would ever back down, yet another example of the delicious daftness offered by the English language. If her name had been just 'Lena', it would indeed have been 'Leena', but if it had been 'Helen', it would simply be that, and not 'He-leen'. This language impasse long existed between us, and we always playfully enjoyed reminding each other of it.

Anyway, on this sunny afternoon, we were all pleasantly chatting and having a generally good time. Tyler returned to the table for frequent fag breaks and to charge his glass, but had the bit firmly between his teeth with his strimming and we didn't want to stop him from this unusual show of determined enthusiasm.

For a laugh Stan took to emptying (by drinking from) Tyler's glass in order to confuse him. This worked for a couple of times, as it was clear from Tyler's face that he didn't remember whether he had finished his drink or not when returning to the table and simply poured some more. Clearly this ruse would not work well, or for long, as Stan was getting more and more inebriated and more and more sloppy in the execution of his joke, and drink was far too serious a thing for Tyler not to start carefully monitoring. Stan had underestimated the simple potency of anything that emerged from the dark secret depths of Sooty's garage. ABV was indeterminate; besides, Sooty wouldn't know or have the slightest interest in what it stood for. Sooty had indeed always had a faded newspaper cutting of a picture of the space shuttle stuck on his brewery garage wall. I never knew why as a painter and decorator, but on this afternoon it became obvious, as clearly it was to remind him he was making its fuel.

When we found ourselves sucking on the demijohn's sediment it became clear that it was time to draw proceedings to a close. Tyler playfully confronted Stan after reviewing his wine-level monitoring activities by questioning (as opposed to asking) of Stan if he had perhaps been drinking his ration of rocket fuel. Stan denied the charge and, trying to extend the level of amusement and add authority and gravitas to his defence, attempted to straighten up in his seated position. This was intended to show not only the seriousness with which he was taking Tyler's complaint but also to demonstrate and confirm his sobriety, drinking ability and prowess to the assembled - as if it were in doubt (a common fault amongst drunks). Clearly this display was overambitious and a stretch too far as, at first attempt, he simply and quite gracefully slipped backwards off the bench, and fell 'thump' onto the grass below, his curly mop of blonde hair, head and back now firmly on terra firma whilst his calves were on the seat where he had been sitting. He had adopted the position and posture of an astronaut on the launch pad, not dissimilar to the space shuttle, which made the fuel discussion all the more potent.

Well, laugh wasn't the word. None of us gave a fig whether he was hurt or not, and had we been concerned it would not have mattered as we were incapable of offering aid, disabled by laughter and tears. We indeed laughed till it hurt. The silly grin on Stan's face was a picture, and Heleena quite rightly mischievously never let him live it down (neither did Tyler). When I was able to compose myself enough to speak, I said, *à la* Alf, 'Well I didn't think that would have happened,' which was for once a complete understatement, and added to the hilarity.

I perhaps should have said, 'I never thought that would have happened,' not referring to Stan's acrobatics, but to the fact that Stan was drunk and Tyler wasn't!

That role reversal had never happened before or indeed since; again the stuff of folklore.

I was never entirely sure we completely convinced 'Heleena' that afternoon that her husband was in safe hands, but he was allowed out to play again (not that week though, sanctions had been understandably imposed).

Chapter 7

THE PICNIC

The day to go to the dreaded Preston Banks was upon us. Preston Banks Church was on a small hill. From the shape of it at best guess it was a glacial drumlin. It stood out for miles in the surroundings, so this largely rural parish could see their church like a beacon. It even had one of those large fluorescent crosses on the top part of the tower so it, and its message, could be seen from far and wide, night and day. I always thought such illuminated crosses were a bit naff, for want of a better word, and this example did nothing to change that view, rather it reinforced it. The approach was a tarmac road across a field with cattle grids at either end. The road climbed the hill following the gentlest of nature's routes, weaving up the contours on its ascent up to the churchyard entrance.

As we approached the top cattle grid it became evident that we were not alone. I peered out of the window over the top of the door from my unorthodox low viewpoint. My seat in Tyler's SRi had decided to fully recline itself so I had had a leisurely trip. In fact, on this one occasion, I was quite grateful that the church had the cross, as it had been all I could see on the approach, not unlike following the Star in the biblical story. When I had protested my new seating position to Tyler he had simply replied, 'Oh it does that, I'll fix it.' No timetable was set for this maintenance repair though, and compared to the other visible and audible niggles on this vehicle no doubt the seat would rank alongside emptying the ashtrays in importance and status and be seen as utterly cosmetic by 'Alf & Son', so I wasn't going to hold my breath. It wasn't uncomfortable though. I dare say my position was only marginally less laid-back going to the church for the funeral than that of the client in the hearse.

Backed up to the church doors there was a new long-wheelbase Land Rover with attached shiny double-wheeled stock trailer. We looked the poor relations with our barely recognisable SRi, and our, I hesitate to say, trailer, which compared to the Rolls Royce version of the one in front of us, was a positive ruin. The Land Rover and trailer pairing was so long that they restricted the access between the front of the vehicle and the wall to such an extent that we could not get through.

‘I’ll go,’ I said to Tyler, who nodded as he was lighting up. As I went round the front of the Land Rover, fully expecting to find a director and film crew for the advert, Tyler appeared around the other side of the trailer. He was to fashion what the Arctic is to the Antarctic, simply poles apart, with his torn armless red top with assorted dry mud patches, and his torn and weather-damaged jeans with his left knee visible. Nowadays, in this crazy consumer world, he might have paid a fortune for this look at the local designer menswear shop. (But he hadn’t, his clothes, like him, were the real deal). I never will understand the market for tatty clothes, it is quite beyond me. Tyler the mad fool had bought his jeans, albeit some time ago, brand new and undamaged; quite unheard of now it would appear. He still had a great figure for forty-something and even his top looked like he could be modelling it. I should have hated him, but again I didn’t. Mind you he was a walking advert for looking fit, plenty of appetite-suppressing medication, more commonly known as cigarettes, naturally tanned skin, and lots of exercise. I often thought from his example that the best way of keeping fit and out of a grave was very definitely to stay in one…

I went to the back of the trailer and a very grand but practically dressed lady, with country-set type waistcoat, pleated skirt, paisley headscarf and stout shoes, was just emerging from the church interior armed with a bunch of what looked like flower stems and a pair of secateurs. She clearly modelled herself on HRH the Queen whilst doing the horses. No film crew was there and I admit to being a little disappointed: her ladyship could surely have been the star. I noted that I should see if Land Rover had any vacancies for 'location finders', as the vehicle looked great here. Worth every penny.

'Ex—' but I didn't get the opportunity to go on with my '—cuse me' and following question as she interrupted,

'Hello… splendid, are you the gravediggers?' she said, peering over her half-moon glasses attached to her by a chain, and looking me up and down.

'Er, yes,' I said, feeling like bowing and saying 'Ma'am' all of a sudden. This lady had presence, whatever that might be. It was my intention to introduce Tyler as the gravedigger, but the opportunity didn't present itself, and she mistakenly took me as the lead.

'Was told to expect you. Now you will be in need of knowing where to go and dig I imagine. I've selected Teddy's plot myself.'

'Oh,' I mumbled inadequately.

'Teddy's my husband, you know. Yes, been a bit of a delay getting him back, you know, yes, a wonderful man, ticker trouble, you know… Never had a problem till he got to his eighties, you know. Bless him, he would have been ninety next week, you know, and it's our sixtieth wedding anniversary soon too, you know. We are having a joint do.' Hang on, did she say 'we are having a joint do'? (Surely not, did she just say 'a joint do' - she couldn't have. It must be me?)

‘It is such a shame he won’t be coming. Still, never mind, it can’t be helped.’ (‘Never mind, it can’t be helped’!? I again repeated her words in my head. It wasn’t me…?)

‘He was a Justice of the Peace, you know. I was his second wife, met him while I was the Mayor.’ Now why didn’t that surprise me? ‘He died on our annual jaunt to our lodge in Canada, you know. He loved it there, you know,’ she said through the misty eyes of fond memory. ‘He wouldn’t have wanted it any other way, you know.’

We of course didn’t know, and she had certainly exhausted the expression to the point of submission. Her reliance upon it was so completely misplaced as to how on earth could I or we know, or be expected to know, any of the above? I had only just met the lady. Well not really met, more simply ‘approached’ and she was yet to draw breath long enough for me to comment, let alone introduce myself ‘you know’!

It was clear that the time delay between Teddy’s passing and now had helped her to get over her grief, if indeed there had ever been any. She was very matter-of-fact and didn’t seem very sad or upset to me at all. You could be forgiven for thinking she was actually thoroughly enjoying herself, whistling as she went, most probably dreaming about fillings for the vol-au-vents at the up and coming ‘joint do’.

Tyler smiled at me out of her sight, and touched his forelock. I mouthed a suitable expletive to him, and he turned towards the car and laughed quietly.

‘We can’t get the—,’ again she was ahead of me,

‘Oh sorry,’ she said. ‘You can’t get past, can you?’ Then at what seemed like the top of her voice she hollered, ‘Bertie, Bertie! Oh where is the wretched man when you need him?’

After a while a little, almost bedraggled, obviously browbeaten man appeared from around the back of the trailer.

‘Ah good, there you are, where have you been?’ She didn’t require or want an answer, and likely would only have got ‘hiding from you’ if Bertie had been normal, I mean honest.

‘Have you unloaded all the flowers now?’

‘Yes, Ma’am,’ he replied diligently. Great, somebody said ‘Ma’am’, I thought.

‘Kindly move the vehicle so these gentlemen can get through. They are the gravediggers, you know.’

We were announced like celebrities to Bertie, who nodded at us in acknowledgement and recognition. We didn’t deserve the acknowledgement, but I imagine he wouldn’t have heard the last of it from Mrs Mayor if he had not.

‘Yes, Ma’am,’ he replied. I guessed Bertie would likely say a lot of ‘yes Ma’ams’ in a day, followed by a ‘three bags full’ in his head. He did seem very slight of frame and stature to be driving such a colossal vehicle and trailer. I half felt like offering him a leg-up or ladder.

‘Thank you, Ma’am,’ I said. She didn’t bat an eyelid. She must be very used to it, I thought. I kicked myself as I knew Tyler had heard, and it would have registered a bull’s-eye on his take-the-mickey-ometer. It would surely be logged as material for my future discomfort, I feared.

We squeezed through the available gap provided by Bertie’s surprising manoeuvring skills and Land Rover’s exemplary power steering, and headed off along the graveyard path, probably intended to be wide enough for nothing more grand than a horse-and-cart hearse when built, but a smidge too narrow for a car. The road was poorly tarmacked of old and had quite a camber on it as well, which, by the sound of things, was introducing itself to the SRi’s long suffering sump. At a point known only to him along the path Tyler unceremoniously and unannounced turned ninety degrees sharp left and floored the accelerator, in order to start the ascent to our destination. We were running on grass now in a clapped-out saloon car, with no doubt dodgy tyres, uphill and with an overloaded trailer.

Fortunately, or otherwise, Tyler was an old hand at this, and fag in mouth he said, over the now screaming engine, ‘Not too bad today, quite dry, should get up a bit.’ Sure enough about fifty yards short of our target the wheels began to spin. Tyler switched the engine off immediately and pulled on the handbrake for all he was worth.

I was beginning to learn that gravedigging, as a career, had very little to offer. There were absolutely no promotion prospects, pay rises or fringe benefits. We just asked the undertaker for our fee and he paid what he thought it should be, which rarely matched, and any 'misunderstanding' was always in his favour. They say that you will never meet a poor bookmaker; well the same could be said for undertakers. Unlike bookies though their concern was not whether they would win but when, as of course they only dealt with dead certs so to speak. Bookies did, albeit occasionally, have to pay out, but not so with undertakers. This job, however, did offer variety though, as you never knew where you would be or whom you would meet from one week to the next, or indeed which emotion would be tested and how hard. We simply followed the Grim Reaper's last trip out. I thought of drawing a map once, to see whether his approach was simply random or he used Google Earth. I never did though.

Generally self-employed gravediggers were groundsmen, or maintenance men, who filled in their time with mowing and 'foreigners' and the like, so were always ready to produce a grave at short notice. Usually we got several days' notice of an interment, but only a few days due to the sell-by date of the product, if you will. The product's shelf life was limited, not to put too fine a point on it.

But intriguingly we had known about the Preston Banks job for a fortnight or more. This was deeply suspicious. Was some poor soul expected to be 'Midsomer' murdered by their nearest and dearest? Or was there another explanation? I mentioned this to Tyler, who dismissed my concern with ease.

'No, you daft beggar, they've not planned to murder 'em, just be relations going on holiday or some such, usually is.'

‘What do you mean?’ I said in a tone of disbelief. ‘You mean they postpone a funeral just to go on holiday?’

‘All the time,’ said Tyler.

‘But that’s awful. Aren’t they meant to be, you know, sad? Surely means they don’t give a fig.’

‘Yep, you seen the price of them holidays though?’

‘Never mind the price of the holiday!’ I exclaimed. I was quite outraged that people could be so mercenary.

‘Shocked you that has it, PJ?’

‘I’m almost speechless,’ I replied. Having been to my share of relations funerals, I had never heard of such a practice.

‘Yep, pop ‘em on ice in the freezer, last for months, years ‘appen.’

I still couldn’t get over it. While the relatives were sunning themselves in foreign climes, their deceased granny was freezing her whatnots off at the undertakers. Just didn’t seem right. In this modern world you apparently simply freeze your granny if required, take the kids out of school (term times being no longer a consideration), and jet off to suit the ‘special offers’. Quite crazy. It did strike me that if one was fortunate enough to have had the privilege of a regular sex life and consequential family, it was only right one should pay more for a getaway during school holidays, and spare a thought for those with either a less fortunate or productive relationship, their only consolation being marginally cheaper holidays in school term time. (Which in the scheme of things is no consolation at all).

This day had become almost too much for me to bear. Firstly I had learnt that package holiday deals were more important that funerals, and then that 'it was a shame' that the corpse wouldn't be there for his party, but 'the show must go on' and why cancel a good shindig just because the main man had inconveniently decided to die? I hoped dear Teddy had sent Mrs Bucket, sorry, Mrs Mayor, his apologies.

Her ladyship came up to our position to instruct and pilot us in to Teddy's selected (by her) last resting place. Whether it was to be hers too you could not help but feel rather depended on whether she met a replacement companion for her Canada jaunts. We followed her up the steep graveyard path. The graves were arranged in lined terraces down the side of the hill; it was certainly another spectacular spot to be enjoyed only by corpses. Carrying all our stuff up here was going to be daunting before we started. Preston Banks' reputation was beginning to manifest itself.

Mrs Mayor marched ahead. I noticed even the seams of her stockings (that was an assumption) were straight, 'military fashion' and all that. I was carrying a 'few extra pounds' (that lovely almost slightly shy but meant to be charming mischievous expression for 'fat' used on modern dating sites) and was blowing a bit as a consequence on the ascent. Tyler, however, wasn't and had the added advantage of using his lit cigarette inhaler on route (how did he do that?). If he was swimming I'd swear he would have to keep one arm up out of the water to keep his fag dry.

We stopped at the junction of two paths near the top where there was a park-type bench with a brass plaque. I was looking forward to reading it although now was not the time, but I felt sure that the bench and I were to become firm friends over the next couple of days. Our guide gestured to a plot nearby saying, 'What do you think?' I was almost flattered that a lady of such obvious standing would ask our opinion. She made it worse by adding, 'You are the experts.' Well, he is really, I thought, but Tyler seemed quite happy that I was dealing with the negotiations. I kept my 'expert' view to myself, as it involved my preference for the grave being positioned right by where our car was, which was far more accessible. Or even indeed sending good old Teddy to the coffin miniaturisation centre in Corcastle, more commonly known as the crematorium, thereby reducing the required size of the hole a great deal.

She looked at me expectantly.

'Well?' she questioned.

'Ermmmm' I said, 'It looks lovely, and a fabulous view.' ('Lovely'? 'View'? Had I really used those absurd words about a grave? I believe I had). It occurred to me that if seen from above we would have looked a very unlikely group.

'Good, good,' she said, 'yes a super view. Teddy will like it here.' I gave up thinking we were all quite mad. I don't suppose our approval of the plot bore any weight whatever, but it was nice to be asked, and as for Teddy, he didn’t have a say in the matter at all, and was in all likelihood enjoying a well-deserved rest. But whether he would ‘like’ it here, I doubted.

‘Well, don’t let me keep you, must crack on, flowers beckon,’ announced our leader. With that she began her descent.

Keep us she wasn’t, as apart from our expert view, we hadn’t done anything yet.

I joined Tyler on the memorial bench.

When she was out of earshot, Tyler said, ‘You tart, you’re right at home with ‘er sort, aren’t yer?’

‘No, no,’ I said, ‘I can just mix with anyone.’

‘Oh yeah,’ said Tyler mockingly.

‘Yeah,’ I said, ‘mix with you, don’t I?’ He smiled but that was all.

‘What a view Teddy will have,’ I said mimicking her ladyship.

‘Aye,’ said Tyler, ‘Beats me as to why he or this lot need one up here though.’

‘It is a good job we never actually see our clients,’ I said.

‘Why?’

‘Well this guy is a Justice of the Peace.’

‘What’s that?’

‘Well,’ I said, sticking my neck out a little knowledge wise, ‘he’s a magistrate, he might well recognise you.’

‘You can get lost,’ he said, laughing (again not exactly what he said).

Tyler was, unusually, currently enjoying a hard and well-earned break from being banned from driving so I didn’t pursue it, this ‘break’ having already lasted longer than expected by most. He didn’t strictly speaking ‘drink and drive’, the risk of spill wastage being unacceptably high. On the occasions he had correctly been stopped it was not for driving offences, but for unrelated misdemeanours (easily avoided ‘slip ups’ by his ‘admin’ department that he didn’t have). No tax was one, and dodgy – well, more accurately, absent - tail light another. But the give-away was the opening of the car window, officer - that poor unfortunate car, to add to its ailments, smelt like a night club at closing. Tyler surprisingly had never been far over the limit but just, by miscalculation, enough.

‘I take it we have to carry the stuff up here?’ I asked stupidly.

‘Well we can get the car up to about there’ he pointed ‘then it’s Shanks’s pony. That’s if ground’s all right to get up, if it’s rained you’re knackered. Don’t want to ruck the grass up either wi’ t’car, Vicar will ‘ave a paddy and we’ve got to get out of ‘ere tonight. C’mon, milord, let’s be ‘avin’ you, t’ain’t going to dig itself.’

‘Milord?’ I wish. Right then I really did wish. A real ‘My Lord’ wouldn’t have to do this.

When we got back to base camp, we had a look back up to the summit.

‘Fills you with dread, doesn’t it?’ said Tyler.

‘It does…’ There was no getting away from it: this looked daunting. ‘I can see now why you call the place difficult.’

‘No, no, PJ, that’s not the difficult bit, the place or the lugging, it’s the diggin’ that’s the bad bit.’

I had quite forgotten about the diggin’. I now knew why the Council didn’t want this sort of work. You would never get a mini digger up here. We knew the only reason that we had a job at all was that local councils couldn’t, and indeed wouldn’t, dig graves by hand because of health and safety and all that. You can only imagine the bad-back-claims bill and pensioning-off pay outs. Not to mention the totally unnecessary shuttering in most cases, oh and of course the hard hats under open sky for the four fellas watching almost goes without saying. The job would simply have been unaffordable.

‘We better get on,’ said Tyler. ‘The royal family have put us back an hour or more.’ Tyler reached into the car as I was going to the trailer ‘to get on’ as instructed.

‘Oy, oy,’ he said. ‘Where’s the fire?’

‘But you just said we better get on,’ I protested.

‘Yes, yes, but get some of this down yer first.’ The sherry made its appearance. ‘We’ll take this to that bench,’ Tyler said, a wry smile on his face.

Suitably refreshed we returned to the trailer.

'First things first,' Tyler said as he loaded the side of the soil box on his back. I grabbed the next piece and followed. This was the easiest way to carry the sides, back and base of the box; you did look like Atlas with the weight of the world on his shoulders, but no one was looking. Tyler told me later you had to watch it up here on windy days, to make sure your wooden wing didn't try to fly. It was true Preston Banks would indeed have made a great hang-gliding launch site.

After about half an hour we had set up, pushed the trailer up against the wall at a respectful distance from the future mourners' position, and were ready to go.

'I'll get the grass off then we'll have a slurp,' said Tyler.

I sat on the bench and introduced myself to Ernest and Grace Applewood, in memory of whom this bench had been placed. It, and they, were to become welcome friends over the next day or so; at this point I didn't know just how welcome. I was sure they and their bench had been a port in a storm to many a weary visitor after the arduous ascent up here, and would continue to be so well into the future.

Grass dealt with, Tyler sat with me.

'You can see the sea from here,' I said.

'Yeah, it's good, i'nt it,' Tyler said as he offered me the sherry.

‘Yes, it’s grand,’ I said. (‘Grand’? Blimey, my Grandfather was with us – he often described quite unsuitable things as ‘grand’.)

‘We’ll do this one in shifts, it’s going to be hot. I’ll start,’ Tyler said. With that he went the few paces and I heard the spade slam into the ground. ‘PJ, can you get the mattock and pick from the trailer, we’re going to need ‘em.’

‘Okay,’ I said and duly did so.

This was a double grave, for dear Teddy and for her ladyship Mrs Mayor I imagined, barring a future suitably qualified husband, and no doubt when she instructed God that she was ready to attend him.

It soon became clear that Tyler’s prophecy was to be borne out: this ground was tough, hard compacted clay with boulders, the sort of stuff you might study as a geologist, but not deliberately get up close and personal to with a spade.

I watched the expert, and expert he was. Whatever Tyler was or wasn’t in the scheme of things, boy, that man could dig. He was podium material, had it been a sport. He had almost immediately changed to the pick as his weapon of choice, and was wielding it from full swing, thudding onto the clay below. There was going to be no clear face to dig against here, I thought.

This wasn’t a spectator sport. Indeed it was uncomfortable watching, as Tyler was wearing his preferred trainers, tatty ones at that. The thought of him missing… you daren’t go there, it made you shiver.

‘Tyler,’ I said, ‘that looks hard.’

‘Worser than rock,’ he replied, ‘just absorbs. You can hit it as hard as you like, makes no difference. Just got to get a bit of a start – ‘ere you are, ‘ave a go.’

I stepped down the few inches’ progress he had made so I could give it a try. If he was finding it tough I was worried I had little hope. Bang!! I slammed the pick down. It didn’t vibrate up your arm like in the cartoons, it just did as T had said, ‘absorbed’. I continued and slowly you could get a sufficiently big dint in the stuff to get the mattock in, you could then smash that down and wiggle it a bit, loosening perhaps a bit the size of a house brick. After a few of these the spade could be employed to remove the almost exfoliated spoil.

Tyler had retired to the bench for a rest break. You guessed it, fag and sherry. I shouted across, ‘Hope you’re leaving some of that.’

Laughing, he replied, ‘Don’t panic, got another one in the car.’

Now, perhaps with hindsight, I should have known that. I soldiered on. It was a lovely day, warm with a bit of breeze, thank heaven, but undeniably hot doing this type of work. After twenty minutes or so I looked up but Tyler had gone from the bench and was nowhere to be seen. Probably gone off reading gravestones, I thought, another gravedigging perk. Some on occasions were quite interesting and even funny.

He returned from his walkabout, and I asked, ‘Have you been stone-reading? Find any good ones?’

‘No,’ he said, ‘been to the Gents.’

‘Oh good,’ I said naively, as I could have done with a pee myself. ‘Where are they?’

‘Oh,’ said T, ‘just over the top there – it’s the big building with “Toilets” written on it.’

‘Great,’ I said, and we swapped the mattock and I duly set off for the loos. I got to the top of the hill and looked for the building, but could only see the most wonderful view and no sign of a building at all.

Ouch, suddenly it dawned on me, the lovely man, the so-and-so (neither exactly what I thought). Now I had fallen for that, I think the expression is hook, line and sinker. I could have kicked myself, would I never learn? I found a convenient bit of wall, where the only onlookers were the sheep in the field adjacent, but they were soon back to their chewing, the grass being clearly much more interesting than I. When I returned Tyler was standing up, leaning his leg on the bit of graveside we had exposed, laughing like a drain while smoking the obligatory fag.

‘You—’ I protested. My language was clearly suffering and deteriorating in this job, it had to be said.

‘Fell for that one, big-style, you daft b…, didn’t you?’ he laughed. ‘Really think there would be a toilet block up here? S’pose you were hoping it had showers too?’

I laughed, but I didn't mean it and difficult when biting your lip in irritation with yourself. I really had made a bozo out of myself there, and that's no lie. I could already hear him telling the tale in the pub.

'Not too bad here though,' said T.

'Sorry?'

'Just saying, toilet job. Not too bad here, good wall out of sight. Many the time not even got a wall, some places nowhere, no handy car parks or trees, nothing.'

'Yes, but most churches have loos nowadays.' I contributed.

'True. And most of 'em are locked an' all, thieving and all that nowadays. Besides, not all the graveyards are near church.'

'I see…'

'Yeah, aye, not bad here, otherwise you just have to pee in the hole.'

'What,' I nearly screamed. 'In the grave?'

'Where else?' Was the obvious answer.

'Oh God!' I exclaimed. I had never even considered this difficulty or solution, and it flowed from him (excuse the pun), so easily and without emphasis as to point to its accuracy.

'Isn't that sacrilege? Must be sacri-something?'

'I dunno … but when you've got to go, you've got to go. You dig out the wet bit then chuck it in box - needs must.'

‘Enough, fine, fine,’ I stopped him. I had got the picture, and further description or information was not required. For PJ ‘needs and must’ would not enter a sentence in this context unless in the car and driving home for the purpose.

‘You are winding me up, aren’t you, like the loos on the hill?’

Tyler just looked at me and raised his eyebrows. I had a really bad feeling that, unusually, this time he wasn’t.

This was beyond the pale. What with freezer-friendly package holidays, parties for, and including, the deceased and now this lavatorial revelation, I was not sure I was cut out to be a gravedigger.

The sun was ‘past the yard arm’ I was reliably informed by T.

I once more had no idea what he was talking about, but it must have had some significance. We both retired for a sit-down with the Applewoods and a slurp.

‘Do you have a thermos flask, T?’ I asked.

‘Yeah, still ‘ave.’

‘Don’t you use it?’

‘When I’m with th’owd fella,’ he said as if it that should be obvious.

‘Oh does he like a hot drink?’ I naturally asked.

‘Dunno—'

‘You don’t know?’

‘No, just use it to decant me sherry so he doesn’t give me grief.’

I give up, I thought. That wasn’t what I was getting at at all, perhaps I was being overoptimistic and should by now have known better.

I had been meaning to ask Tyler something for some time and now seemed as good as any. After all we were in such a lovely location, among the ranks of the dead, and on such a lovely day and when - other than the blessed ‘digability’ of the terrain - all was right with the world.

‘You scared of dying, Tyler?’ I asked.

‘Why d’you ask?’ T replied. He didn’t seem either surprised or concerned that this question had appeared apparently out of the blue as it were.

‘Well, crosses everyone’s mind from time to time and I just thought with your job and that?’

‘No then,’ he answered and went on. ‘Well not much, prob’ly no more than next man, no good dwellin’ on, it happens to everythin’ livin’. No good fretting over what you don’t understand and can’t change, nowt you can do about it.’

‘True enough,’ I said. I couldn’t think of anything to add to that, but it was clear he had considered the matter before, because that sounded an almost prepared, scripted answer.

‘Mind you,’ he said unexpectedly in a stroking the chin moment, ’don’t think I’m scared of deein’, just scared of not livin’, aye, scared of not livin’, that's it, things I'll miss, aye I'll miss stuff, that makes me sound like a right nosy beggar, don't it?' He chortled, the throaty chortle of the long term smoker.

'Change what you can, accept what you can't, and have t' wisdom to know difference, oh and do yer best by folk if poss. That's for me'

Well I hadn't expected the 'Serenity' prayer that was for sure. Tyler could always surprise, you could bank on that, and that was fun.

PJ asked his dad, Alf, the same question once. He, unlike Tyler reached to the shelf of stock answers.

'When lost me dignity PJ lad, be ready then, scared of dying without dignity.'

This, although a stock answer, left PJ with somewhat of a puzzle. The words 'Alf and dignity' no less than twice in a single sentence was noteworthy in itself, but to hear this voiced as his paramount concern about his dying was nothing less than a revelation, as he appeared to have carefully avoided, even escaped, the concept and any form of contact with it in life. I remember asking him on one occasion (I now know mistakenly) where the nearest 'loos' were? His reply was an outstretched finger to a clump of trees and a gesture to a shovel (presumably heaven forbid) if required. PJ found this all too much, quite horrifying and completely outside his comfort zone; the dead he could cope with but the living were quite simply revolting.

Tyler and I stood up together laughing at Alf's answer, me gently shaking my head, to get back to the job in hand. As for where the distinction between being dead and 'not livin'' in Tyler's case was I knew not, or more accurately maybe didn't understand, as he had so poignantly said in his original answer. But perhaps there was a distinction, and I suspected that he had been thinking about it over the years of digging more than he was letting on?

Progress was slow. This stuff wasn't for digging by the faint-hearted and it was tedious. From the ranks of graves already here, my goodness, some work and effort had gone on over the years.

'How many graves have you dug here, Tyler?'

'Dunno - dozen maybe.'

'A dozen!' I exclaimed. 'You've had to move some stuff here then?'

'Tell me about it …'

'Is it as hard everywhere up here?'

'Yep,' came my reply, followed immediately by a 'No!' cry after the next swing of the pick. 'I thought this was going too well.'

'What's up?' I said, looking down into what was beginning to look like a grave, fearing an emergency or foot injury in those trainers, and gravedigging offering yet another nonsense contradictory statement questioning 'what's up' whilst always looking firmly down.

‘Boulder, big ‘un at that, golly, that’s a nuisance, it’s no good it’ll have to come out.’ didn’t say Tyler in his initial immediate damage assessment.

I soon saw the smooth top side of the culprit appearing from the bottom of the hole like a whale’s back, and boy it did, even to my eye, look more than a little problem. In geology I could comment when seeing such things, but actually moving them was a skill set I didn’t have.

It struck me that it was a good job on such occasions that language offers escape routes for inner expression such as ‘go forth and multiply’ and individual words such as ‘kinnell’. At this moment on this day unusually the sky in colour matched the language very well.

‘My turn T,’ I said. ‘What’s the plan?’

‘Just keep chivvying away round it until we get it loose,’ T advised. I didn’t like his despondent tone.

‘Okay,’ I said. I did my half an hour then Tyler similar, by the end of which the rock was moving gently in its socket, like a hip joint.

‘Get in ‘ere,’ said T, ‘we’ll have to get this out together. Oh and bring a couple of planks with you please.’

While I was getting the planks Tyler lit up. I put the planks in the hole and hopped in. Tyler was sitting on the grass, his legs dangling into the hole.

‘This is where I miss jelly,’ he said, eating his cigarette. Now, this was no time to reminisce about childhood desserts, I thought.

‘Jelly?’ I queried, lost as usual, but already suspiciously concerned as to what he might mean. (Even I hadn’t bought my weak childhood dessert explanation).

‘Yeah, jelly.’ I still didn’t get it - he could see that by my blank expression. ‘Gelignite,’ he said. Well that was that mouthful of sherry down my shirt. It was suddenly clear it was my spelling of ‘gellie’ that was at fault.

‘You mean explosives?’ I snorted.

‘Yes, of course explosives,’ said T. ‘Th’owd fella used to have a licence after the war and he kept it on for doin’ drains on farms, across fields and that. Happen probably still got a stick or two at home, and did the odd grave or two with it, handy for big boulders, solid rock and the like.’

‘Has he still got it, the licence?’ I said.

‘No,’ said T ‘expired a bit back, new laws and that. Shame though, was right handy.’

On behalf of the general public, I was delighted with this news as the thought of Laurel and Hardy traversing the countryside loaded with dynamite was the stuff of cartoons. Sort of ‘Dad’s Army’ meets ‘Last of the Summer Wine’.

‘You didn’t really use it in graveyards, did you?’ I questioned.

‘Yeah, couple of times,’ said T. ‘Last time some rock chippings hit the vicar’s car over the hedge in t’ vicarage drive, he wasn’t best pleased, and it was a bit noisy.’

‘A bit noisy’! From my experience of the stuff in the opencast mines it was downright deafening; granted they would be using a lot more, but ‘a bit noisy’?!

This was up there with the most serious of understatements, I felt, a bit like telling the Captain of the Titanic that it was only a small leak. Was there no end to Tyler’s tales, exploits, skills and wind-ups? It didn’t seem like it.

We jiggled and fought with our rock for a further half-hour, until finally it was ready for removal, one plank under, then the other and so on, until we effectively walked it up the hole, securing it with a rope for the last foot. T jumped out and I took the weight until he hauled it up the last few inches and rolled it out onto the surface.

‘Blimey,’ I said, puffing and blowing, ‘the name boulder clay’s not wrong, that’s for sure.’

‘No,’ said Tyler. Even he was sitting on the grass without a fag; now that says it all about how heavy the rock was. ‘We’ll call it a day. I’ll buy you a pint in The Waterside.’

Now a pub at this moment I could use, I thought. The void left behind by this obstacle was substantial, so by tidying up the clay broken away from it we appeared to have made considerable progress for little effort in a short time. Good to finish on a bit of a high.

‘Well,’ Tyler said, ‘reckon we are about halfway, we’ll get it finished in time.’

‘What time is the funeral?’

‘Three o’clock.’

‘Bit late, isn’t it?’

‘Yeah, Willow said her Mayorship has delayed start, as some of the mourners had a long way to come.’ Well I suppose Teddy won’t mind bless him, he’s been hanging (well lying) around for weeks as it is.

With that we threw the tools in the grave, put the planks over to stop anyone passing falling in (as if) up here. The planks did serve a purpose though, because if there was a gap you could be almost sure to catch Mr or Mrs Hedgehog. We boarded the ‘gravemobile’ with all its hidden accessories and headed for the pub.

Tyler dropped me off at Cliff Field after we had had a couple of the most welcome pints by the canal. I was greeted by Sam, who asked how I was. My only reply was ‘knackered’. I did my few jobs at a snail’s pace. Sam had already done the sheep and chickens. As we were sitting down for supper - Sam made a fine gumbo - the phone rang. I was tempted to leave it, but Sam answered the call. I could hear the usual pleasantries and laughter. I could tell it was Tyler.

‘Here you are,’ Sam said to both of us at the same time and passed me the hand set. I was mid-chew on a piece of buttered French stick, very nice. I nearly spat it out.

‘You what?’ I said in almost impolite disbelief. ‘Tell me this is a wind-up, no, it’s not your fault, no need to apologise, all right, boss, I’ll be ready, see you then… Yeah, got it, we’ll need all the time we can get, bye.’ I returned the phone to its cradle.

‘I take it all is not well?’ questioned Sam.

‘That woman!’ I exclaimed.

‘Who? What woman?’

‘Mrs Bucket, that’s who,’ I said. I gave Sam the day’s low-down on Mrs Mayor and poor old Teddy.

‘So,’ I went on, ‘the undertaker, Willow, has just rung T to confirm that the grave will be finished, dressed and ready by twelve, midday.’

‘Well, surely that is okay?’ said Sam.

‘No, it’s not okay, the funeral is not until three o’clock! Sorry, not having a go at you, Sam. Just the digging is terrible, solid rock would be easier. At least that breaks, this stuff just bends. We would have stayed longer tonight if we had known.’

‘Known what?’

‘Known that her blinking ladyship wants to have a picnic around the grave from twelve till three? I mean I ask you ‘a picnic!’ As the guests dribble in from afar, they are to be welcomed to Teddy’s funeral with a glass and a cucumber sandwich, no doubt, at the graveside. She’s mad. Have you ever heard of anything so ridiculous? Tyler’s picking me up at five. Five! Is there a five in the morning?’

Sam was well aware that I wasn’t a morning person.

‘Well it won’t hurt you for once,’ she said.

I wasn’t so sure about that. It would be a close-run thing at that, as we had another three feet to go.

‘Oh,’ said Sam, ‘don’t know whether this is a good time, but your boss at the insurance office rang you today.’

‘Oh, what did she want?

‘Wants a meet.’

‘Well she can sing this week. I’ve got to get through tomorrow first.’

The shrill alarm went off at four thirty am. I hadn’t slept well. I never do when answerable to the devil’s clock but I knew I had to get up this day and sharpish, the reasons didn’t come much bigger. The royal funeral was on. I tiptoed across the bedroom floor, without making a sound.

As I got to the door Sam said ‘Good luck,’ and turned over. So much for my silence and attempt at ‘silent running’.

I got dressed on the landing. It was coal mine dark. I don't do getting up in the dark as a rule, but hey-ho this was a necessary exception, almost an emergency call out no less, if only to rescue a picnic. I got downstairs and into the kitchen, I switched on the light and put on the kettle. Purdey glanced up from dog bed heaven, opened one eye and gave me a disapproving look; it was clear she wasn't a morning person either. She was soon dreaming again, gentle little barks issuing forth from her, or what you could be forgiven for mistaking for a not very well looked after rug. This, along with some small but unmissable rapid leg movements, I think indicated as far as anyone could ever know that we were rabbiting, or in hot pheasant pursuit. Purdey thought it deeply unjust and not fair in the least when these, her feathered potential playmates, went loft side and airborne. Not cricket at all, as she would have had a chance but for this dastardly tactic.

Tyler appeared about quarter to five. 'Morning T,' I greeted him. 'Want a quick brew?' I didn't know that Neanderthal man spoke, but bang went that theory. He can…

'Mornnnunt, yep uggh.' I took that to be, 'Morning, yes please.'

Purdey gave us both a further cursory glance as if to say, look mad humans, can you lot just push off, or at least pipe down.

Tyler was worried, he'd left his fags in the car, and although he had one lit in his mouth, he had to go out and get the packet: sure signs we were in trouble that was for sure. T had upgraded the usual smoking level of serious to critical, and he was drinking (almost unheard of) tea.

'Cheers,' he said, coming back to life, and putting his teacup down. I handed him a chocolate biscuit bar, which he put in his pocket. Breakfast was over and indeed saved. 'Come on, this is going to be a bastard.' Motivation speech over, we were off.

I'm sure Purdey was delighted, if not her pheasant.

I assumed the space shuttle take-off seat position, as demonstrated by Stan that gorgeous afternoon that seemed a lifetime ago right now. I wasn't going to miss any view this time as it was still dark, but was in serious danger of nodding off, being nicely reclined with the heater on. Perhaps indeed this was all a dream. Oh I did hope so. We didn't speak; this job was going to be hard in the time we had, and we knew it.

On arrival at Preston Banks we got up as close to the grave site as possible in the car, which was a good deal easier than before as yesterday's Land Rover advert obstacle was not in the way. Tyler had gone noticeably quieter. He was often a man of few words, but this time it was different. At the graveside we moved the planks in a well-rehearsed fashion and without saying anything were both alarmed at how far there was to go.

'I'm in,' said Tyler. No question this time, he was going to be at the top of his game and I supporting him the best I could. 'You get the barrow ready to start taking this stuff away. The dump is up near the toilets.' That was the only funny thing said, although neither of us laughed. Tyler jumped in the grave and started downwards.

I took the barrow full of smaller stones away in search of the spoil dump, and that done I returned to Tyler. It was like watching a master, operating pick and shovel one after the other in a routine close to a dance. He was breaking the clay, loosening it and moving forward, then there would be a flurry of material expelled from the hole; he was barely coming up for air. Boy, could this lad dig, this was really showing me how to do this job properly; it was becoming clear that Tyler had introduced me to gravedigging through the soft underbelly of the job. After twenty minutes or so flat out, Tyler hopped out, wiped his brow and, after retrieving his fags from the neighbouring gravestone, sat on the grass. I handed him the sherry.

'Your turn,' he said. 'Dig out the loose stuff, and load it in barrow.'

'Wilco,' I said and got in. I was really going to have to put my back into this so I didn't look like the weakest link. Just before I got going, I said, 'Hope we don't meet any more rocks.'

'Not funny,' replied Tyler in deadpan fashion.

We alternated like this for the next two and a half hours, making good, and necessary, progress. Gravedigging, geology and *The Shawshank Redemption* were all illustrations of the consequences of pressure and time; at this point we were under a great deal of pressure with precious little time.

The Church clock tolled nine. Tyler was on shift, and I was on barrow duty. 'We'll have to take a load of this away,' he said. 'This stuff doesn't compact right well, and can take years to settle. The Vicar here doesn't like great mounds left on top, the grass mowing lads give 'im grief, so you keep barrowin'.'

Some spoil had to be barrowed away to accommodate the volume of dear Teddy, the soon-to-be resident. 'Okay,' I replied. At that very moment I noticed a well-dressed gentleman approaching up the path. 'Hey, Tyler,' I whispered. He looked up and over in the direction I was gesturing.

'Good morning, Tyler,' the fellow boomed out.

Tyler, climbing out, replied, 'Morning, Willow, less of the good.'

'How you lads getting on? Early start, I'll wager?'

I didn't know whether 'Willow' was the undertaker's real name, or a joiner's nickname. I guessed it was a wood nickname that had stuck.

'And morning...' Willow hesitated but was clearly addressing me.

T jumped into the pause in conversation. 'PJ,' he said, prompting Willow.

'Morning PJ,' boomed Willow. 'You haven't let this old bugger talk you into this daft lark, have you?'

Quite clearly I had, I thought, but simply replied, 'Well, for the time being, sir.'

‘Bloody hell T,’ said Willow. ‘Sir, indeed. Might just be poaching him off you, T. PJ, do you have a black suit, lad?’

‘And you can “sod off”, ‘scuse the pun,’ said T to Willow. ‘He’s alright where ‘e is’ They both laughed heartily, and I was flattered - I think…

‘I haven’t been called Sir for a while.’ Willow carried on. ‘You’ve never been called Sir,’ said Tyler in light-hearted protest.

‘I bet you fit right in with this posh lot today PJ,’ he said to me. I just laughed along. I’d spent years in the past trying to get a job and now two: they were getting like buses.

‘How’s digging, T? Always been a sod of a place.’

‘Well not too bad,’ said T.

‘Any rocks?’ asked Willow.

‘Just one, big bugger though.’

‘Well,’ said Willow. I think that was enough talking about rocks. He only asked out of politeness, I was sure, not interest. ‘Now you know what’s going on with madam, T, don’t you?’ he went on in a whisper as if he thought she might pop up at any time. I for one wouldn’t have been surprised. ‘She’s been a right handful, she has, ‘er ladyship, seen more of ‘er lately than me Mrs. Most expensive coffin I’ve ever sold though, can’t see the point meeself but who am I to complain? Ruddy lovely bit of wood, not that veneered chipboard us mere mortals get sent to meet our Maker in, oh no, this stuff should have been made into furniture fit for a manor. Was grown to look at, not bury. Lovely grain; bloody shame.'

We just nodded in agreement; there was nothing more to add. People spend small fortunes on coffins, which is a tricky one to justify when you think about it.

'Well, won't keep you further, lads, see you later and be finished by twelve, okay? There'll be a few extra quid in it for yous.'

'Thanks, Willow, bye,' I said.

Tyler said, 'See yous,' or something similar, and as he turned away he shouted, 'Save us a chicken leg, will yer.' We laughed, while chorusing out of his earshot 'bastard' under our breath. These undertakers were beginning to seem proper local characters to me, and Willow reinforced that thought and hadn't disappointed.

Our routine had been broken but that was all. T was straight back at it, no fag or sherry, and I barrowed away: this was going to the wire, or a photo finish at least. Things went well through to eleven am - we had both gone at it hard during our twenty-minute slots - when Tyler said, 'Jump in 'ere, PJ, at foot end, another foot down will do it.'

And so it was Tyler digging the head end, I the foot, and despite the few touches of our backsides against each other, it went okay. We finished about twenty five past eleven, thirty five minutes before the 'service' of the picnic not Church, and still with all the dressing of the grave to do. Tyler jumped out, using his pre-dug foothold, and I started picking up bits and levelling out little holes where pebbles had been. As one purple sheet came down so did the comment, 'What are you doing?'

'Oh, just picking up bits and levelling.'

'Just grab this sheet and see it is straight,' Tyler said impatiently. 'The first car's on its way up to church.'

'Okay,' I said, tucking the few bits I had rescued from their future of everlasting darkness firmly in my pocket. I straightened the purple sheets, Tyler gave me a pull-up, we together put all the greengrocer grass in place, hid the tools, positioned the ropes, all in double quick time, and Bob's your uncle, we were done. We both peered down into Teddy's final resting place and, even though I say it myself, 'job was a good 'un', as they say in the trade. We left then and saw Bertie and Mrs Mayor wandering up the slope. The routine was to go and see Teddy's coffin in the church, where it had spent the night, and then pop up to the grave for a canapé. Bertie was weighed down with a particularly large basket.

'Did we leave Mr and Mrs Applewood okay, with no mud on them?' I asked.

'I dunno,' said T.

'Should we have checked?'

'Don't you worry, too late now, I'm sure Bertie will sort it.' T was right. I was happy as I was sure I saw Bertie carrying a travelling rug, and Mrs Mayor would have thought of everything. As we made our escape past the

Church car park there was a fine, older Rolls Royce in the car park, and no sign of the new Land Rover. There was no guessing whose that was. We had to give way and pull off the single-track road up to the church for passing mourners, but then we were out.

Tyler said, 'Right, PJ. I'll buy you a pint in The Waterside.'

'Great,' I said. 'Aren't we a bit early?'

'No,' said T. I did have to admit to having a roaring thirst. Sherry is all very well but a thirst-quencher it is not.

'How long do you reckon we have?'

'Likely be half past four,' said T, 'so long as they don't stand around too much at the end.'

'Let's hope they get enough of that at the start!' I said. T laughed in agreement.

We got to The Waterside and it had turned into a very pleasant day.

'What yer 'avin'?' said Tyler.

'Do you know,' I said, 'I believe I'll have a cider with ice, please.'

'Oh very la-di-da,' said T, with a 'you posh tart' look on his face. There were one or two here with black ties, but we kept their secret. Odds on they were avoiding 'the picnic' - they probably thought it as bizarre as we did, although I would love to have gone, just for the small talk. One could mischievously imagine all the 'lovely view and place to be buried' and 'what on earth can we talk about now', 'don't get mud on your shoes dear' uncomfortable chitchat.

'Well, T,' I said, just polishing off my second cider: 'We can't sit here all afternoon or old Teddy won't get filled in until tomorrow.'

'What time is it?' asked T.

'No idea,' I replied, and got up to find out, as neither of us wore watches.

'Just coming up half past one.'

'Oh, it's another hour and a half till they start up the hill. Any ideas?'

'Well I noticed a sign pointing the other way at that last junction getting here. It was advertising an auction viewing today in Banks village hall. Shall we go there for an hour or three?'

'Are we too scruffy?'

'Well, well, that's never bothered you before, Mr Vanity.' A dirty look was my reply as we set off.

We killed a good hour or so there. I've always liked auctions, and at least at this one the lots weren't wandering about relieving themselves everywhere! I got chatting with one of the auction-house employees, who asked me what we were up to. I think from our appearance it was obvious we weren't looking for twisted-stem sherry glasses. If only he knew…

It was a pleasant chat about how they have to have eyes in the back of their heads looking out for people pilfering stuff, hence the locked cabinet in the corner of the hall with the expensive items in - silver, gold and the like. As we chatted it became obvious that our two jobs had a common purpose: the erasing or redistribution of a life. We disposed of the carcass and the auctioneer the possessions. Quite sobering and sad in a realistic sort of way, but just necessary services which we will all require in due course. However it appeared that auctioneering had its smile moments as well; the chap said that they had a behind-closed-doors category called 'lifers'. Lifers were items they had sold at auction, and retrieved again at a subsequent house clearance. The record, he informed me, was a little bedside chest of drawers, which they had sold no less than five times. The poor chest of drawers would, I'm sure, have got a complex about it had it been able.

It always struck PJ when attending people's 'Bargain Hunt' type auctions, as opposed to agricultural auctions, as to who bought some of the items or 'antiques' available for viewing? It is very difficult (even here) to avoid the use of the unsavoury word 'crap', but apologetically it fits the bill to a tee. In fact, perhaps even more interesting than the purchasers, PJ used to think of who actually got up in a morning and thought some of these 'good idea' items worthy of their time, and indeed life and manufacture. After all there are currently (although rising - some would say alarmingly - by the day) only seven point seven thousand million of us currently on earth (looks less scary in words without the zeros), but for the bizarre thinking portrayed and required behind the existence of some of these items, you could be forgiven for thinking that this number, huge as it is, is simply not big enough and there would have to be more. Some things the auctioneer had seen for sale over the years were 'unusual' (to be kind to them) bordering on just unashamedly quite barmy; others hid behind the cure-all term 'art', which, more-often-than- not was similarly crazy in topic or material, but with the addition of a marketing department (with notable exceptions of course, largely after the creator's demise). The coloured giraffe and orangutan Toby jug style ash tray described 'as rare' was always particularly memorable. The 'rare' was right enough, no kidding - a bit of a chin scratching surprise description for certain PJ thought. Although PJ had concern for the welfare of whoever bought that little treasure, it paled into insignificance as compared to the concern for the poor un-named soul that made it!

We returned to The Waterside at three-ish and Tyler said, 'We should be fine for a couple of pints.'

I returned to lager and we sat down. 'I know I'm not your keeper, T, and it is not my place, but driving...?'

'Yeah I know, you're right, it's not your business, but thanks though. Should be all right – we've a bit of working it off to do.'

I said no more, he knew the score. He didn't need telling twice, as unlike most of us he had buried more than one drink-drive victim.

We made a move at about quarter to four. As we approached the church the cars were leaving, so we waited at the bottom of the church drive until they thinned out. The Rolls appeared and Mrs Mayor went past. She saw us, though, and nodded approvingly in our direction, which was good of her. She did not have to. We acknowledged her and in that moment of a fleeting glance she looked for the first time genuinely upset. Perhaps it had finally sunk in and she would undoubtedly miss her Teddy. I am sure he'd been not only her soulmate and lifetime companion but also her purpose.

In that brief moment I learnt volumes about Mrs Mayor. Her real name we found out was Mrs Cynthia Amelia Harris-Elks, quite a mouthful, but a charming name in many ways. Behind all the airs, graces and trappings of wealth that she undeniably had, she was very much human and had to endure and be victim to the same rules of life and death as the rest of us. I reprimanded myself for perhaps having been a little uncharitable and turning her into an austere, matronly, no-nonsense lady. I liked her though, she restored one's faith - not sure in what, but definitely restored it - reinforcing the reality that there were no differences in either coffins or shrouds to set us apart from each other on our 'that' day.

(I did however mischievously wonder about the 'Elks' bit. Sounded awfully, to me, like it had been acquired as an add-on one way or another in her beloved Canada…?)

We went up to deal with Teddy. Willow had been right. It was, as far as these things can be, a beautiful coffin. The raised centre of the dark polished wood lid, almost cabinet featured sides, and the polished brass accessories any furniture would have worn with pride, all glinting in the afternoon light for the last time.

Tyler jumped in first and I followed. We stood on Teddy and gently covered the coffin. Tyler said through the obligatory fag in the corner of his mouth, 'Try not to scratch it.'

'Roger,' I quietly replied. I completely concurred with this instruction, as it was like standing on a posh sideboard and tipping soil and stones onto it, and just didn't seem right. As the brass plate was covered T said, 'We can go a bit quicker now.'

It was soon filled in and everything reloaded in the trailer. It was difficult to believe that the same filling material could be so willing to be returned home when you thought of the battle it had offered when being dug out. There was just one beautiful flower arrangement, with words on almost too personal to read without feeling intrusive. I said my usual 'God Bless you' to Teddy and we were finished. We were having a sit on Mr and Mrs Applewood, for the last time for now, when Willow turned up.

'Hi, fellas, well done, tough ask that. Here you go.' At this he handed Tyler an envelope.

'Thanks, Willow,' said Tyler. 'No surprise picnics next time, eh?'

'I'll see what I can do,' said Willow. ''Ere'– he handed Tyler a further envelope – 'bit extra.'

'Thanks,' said Tyler, as did I. I felt a bit like the headsman getting paid in *The Three Musketeers*, getting a bit extra for rowing the boat.

At this we exchanged pleasantries and Willow was gone.

We never got our chicken legs though…

It was at here at Banks, about a year or so later, when one of the realities of gravedigging hit Tyler and I hard. This job too involved delay, but not for trivial frivolous reasons. We had a shout to go to dig an infant's grave. She was just turned two. This was always sad, but clearly had to be done, as any other. The child's death had been quite unexpected; one of those incredibly and thankfully few in a million cases, as she had by all reports become very ill, very quickly. We dug the hole, not terribly deep, the day before as usual.

On the morning of the funeral, the undertaker rang to say it had been cancelled. Clearly, we thought, it had been switched to the crematorium, but we found out later this was not the case. We went and filled in the hole for safety reasons. The undertaker told us that the girl was a twin and, after her sudden death, tests had been carried out on her brother. He too had this rare complaint, of which his parents had been completely unaware, and he only had something less than six months to live at best. The baby girl's funeral therefore had just been postponed. The family had wished to delay until her little brother would so sadly inevitably join her.

Four and a half months later, he did.

We got the shout again and laid them to rest in one slightly wider little white coffin, side by side and together.

That was the day I learnt that gravedigging wasn't always a picnic.

Chapter 8

THE TITANIC

It was a grey, heavily overcast day when we set off for Crayston where we were going to finish a grave Tyler had started the day before, and set it up for the funeral that afternoon. It soon started to rain on the way; the weather didn't look hopeful at all.

There were two hospital-type oxygen bottles on the greengrocer grass in the back seat along with a closed 12 bore shotgun. It struck me that if this was to do with a leisure activity it must have a degree of risk with it, or perhaps there was more to digging a hole in Crayston than met the eye. I had to ask, as Tyler was yet again providing unfathomable puzzles.

‘Tyler what’s with the gun and oxygen?’

‘Don’t ask,’ came the almost sternest of replies.

Unable to let it drop, as I had already asked and having grown in confidence around Tyler, I said, ‘No, c’mon, spill the beans. Not taken up welding, have we?’

‘No, we flipping haven’t,’ he hissed back. (He didn’t say ‘flipping’.) The answer, as so often in life, was right under my nose but I didn’t see it at the time. ‘It’s th’owd fella,’ almost sighed Tyler with an air of resignation and defeat. I had already suspected Alf was involved. Usually, if two or more unrelated objects were together in an unexpected place, he’d be in the mix somewhere.

‘What’s he been up to?’ I said. ‘Not been shooting rabbits on the Ruins again and then trying to nurse them back to life with the oxygen?’ I chuckled at the distinct possibility.

‘Could have bin, knowing ‘im,’ said Tyler, smiling.

I for one couldn’t think of a logical or rational explanation for this juxtaposition - oxygen and shotgun? The words ‘rational’ and ‘Alf’ in truth rarely appeared together and made for uncomfortable bedfellows in a sentence, and although as ridiculous as my rabbit resuscitation explanation was, it was a starting point.

‘It was crows he was after, down near pond, bin taking his ducks again,’ Tyler explained.

The 'pond' was the local tarn on the farmland where Alf managed the shoot. Alf used to release reared ducklings onto the tarn when they were fully feathered but hadn't got the hang of flying yet. In the couple of weeks after release, they became fair game for crows, so Alf used to shoot the crows, or at least attempt to because despite the war a crack shot he was not. Alf ran the syndicate, tending the pheasants and ducks at dawn and dusk, and to his credit many times in between. When the shooting season arrived he switched to shoot manager, and many successful days would be had. He'd never shoot his own birds though, never. By the time the shooting season started the birds and Alf had simply been through too much together…

Crayston nestled in a river valley east of Corcastle, and from Cliff Field it was about fifteen miles. These miles included a couple of 'B' roads but mostly 'A' roads, or you could hop down one junction on the motorway if you wished. Imagine my surprise therefore as I was jolted out of our Alf conversation by a not insignificant pothole as we turned off the generally accepted main road.

'Where are we, T?' I asked, as looking around I could only see fields.

''Bout halfway,' he replied.

'Yes, but where?' I asked as we vibrated across a cattle grid. I noticed the grass was growing in an ordered way up the centre of the road, replacing the white-painted lines and cat's eyes on the imposter of a main route we had turned off.

‘Has there been a diversion? Why aren’t we on the main road?’ I went on.

‘This is the quickest way,’ said Tyler. Now not wanting to state the obvious but this, unless generations of road planners had got it seriously wrong, could not conceivably be the quickest way.

‘Which year?’ I asked mockingly. ‘Before the main roads were built?’

‘Just is’ was my less than comprehensive explanation.

‘But this is a farm track, horse-and-cart land,’ I protested.

‘Quickest way,’ repeated T as we hit another sizeable pothole. This could only be the quickest way in a light aircraft, but I left it as I could see we were going to have to agree to disagree on this one.

I returned to the safer territory of why Alf had a left a shotgun and oxygen bottles in the car. ‘Did Alf get any crows then?’

‘Well it’s not quite as simple as that.’

Well, there was a surprise - I don’t think. It simply never was with Alf.

‘Mother’s out of hospital for a bit.’

‘Sorry T, I forgot to ask after her, and whether she’s in or out at the moment.’

‘Don’t worry, PJ, I don’t know where the bloody woman is half the time meeself. Sometimes she’s in and sometimes she’s not.’

Tyler's Mum had the quite unusual name of Amona. I'd always thought T looked a bit North American Indian, with his strong features and almost black hair, and his Mum's name only added credence to this thought. None of this was ever mentioned though, and whether Alf had met Amona in Burma I knew not. Anyway Mona, the shortened version, was at home at the moment and according to local gossip she had lived up to her name all her life (A moaner), but I didn't know the lady and had only met her once or twice, so cannot confirm that or otherwise.

There was one occasion though when I called for Tyler so we could go and do a job, and she had answered the door. I remember a portly lady with a significant chest size and yellow cardigan, which was highlighted largely because on that day she had chosen to wear most of her obviously recent refreshment on it. First glance impression was of soup that had missed its intended target, her mouth. Whether she knew or cared about this spillage was open to question. From the overall look of the garment, it wasn't the first. I asked if Tyler was in, and felt like a little boy asking his chum's Mum if he could come out and play. Severe would be the word for her, I think. Or maybe just scary will do.

She had always suffered with her lungs from working in the Lancashire cotton mills years ago, and her condition was sadly getting steadily worse, necessitating the frequent hospital visits. I did think living with Tyler wouldn't help her on the passive-smoking front – she was likely on twenty a day just watching TV – and Tyler was generous to a fault with his endless supply of smoke. But clearly that was none of my business.

‘Th’owd fella had thought last night would be a good idea to get her out for a bit,’ said Tyler. ‘He reckoned on a ride out in the car to Ruins farm on concrete road.’

This ‘concrete road’ was infamous - concrete it was, road it wasn’t - and it connected the various parts of Ruins Farm. It was due to its history and original purpose (not to its cracked uneven surface of today) that it qualified for the term ‘road’, but it had certainly seen better days. And when I say cracked, picture the last television pictures you saw of a road which had recently had the misfortune of suffering from a severe earthquake. That will give an idea of this road’s quality and serviceability. It was, in parts, more of a series of broken wobbling concrete rafts than road.

Not the perfect surface therefore to take a terminally ill (as it turned out) lady, or indeed anybody, for a run-out. The sheep feeders were alongside it in places so these bits of ‘road’ were particularly messy, ankle deep in fluid slurry if the truth be known. To anyone else certainly this was not an obvious place for either Mona or the saloon SRi, but this was Alf.

‘’Cause ‘er lungs are knackered,’ T continued, ‘she has to have oxygen on hand all the time, so he put oxygen in back and muther in t’ front…’

I interrupted by saying, ‘Oh that’s why he’s fixed the front seat’s reclining feature then.’

‘Well if you call putting a brick somewhere underneath it as fixing it, then yes, it’s fixed. Now on the way down concrete road fatha saw two crows in field on me muther’s side of car.’

‘Did he get them?’ I asked

‘Hold on. Just ask yourself what you would have done,’ said T

‘Well, not sure. Go back later to see if they were still about?’

‘Fair enough, not bad, PJ. Or would you open the car door very slowly and quietly, and try to get a shot off over car, or over bonnet?’

‘Er, yes, might do,’ I said, although I was by no means an expert at such a covert military sniper manoeuvre.

‘Me too. So what does th’owd fella do?’

Could have been any number of things, knowing even the little I knew of Alf.

‘Well, doesn’t do that, not fatha. He tells me muther to wind her winder down; so she’s holding the oxygen mask to her mouth with one hand and winding down winda with t’other.’ Besides holding on to dear life itself by a shoestring by the sound of things, I thought.

‘Then the daft bugger reaches across her wi’t’gun and lets fly at them birds giving ‘em both barrels through winder from in t’ car.’

‘What!!’ I spurted out. ‘I’m surprised she didn’t have a heart attack on the spot! The bangs would be enough.’ This was again the stuff of Disney. ‘Did he get them?’

A knowledgeable ‘what do you think’ look was the answer. I had to admit I hadn’t been overly optimistic. ‘No, they flew off happy as Larry without a care in the world,’ said T. ‘Did get something though. Been in front of you all the time.’

‘What?’ I enquired, as there evidently were no dead animals at my feet or anywhere else.

‘Well the daft old beggar lined up his shot, looking along gun barrel to bead at end, while resting gun on car door.’

Tyler was right and the answer and explanation had been in front of me all the time. This temple to neglect that they called a car was now minus one more thing: a not insubstantial door mirror had been blown to smithereens and converted into a jagged edge of plastic, right under my nose. We laughed and spontaneously chorused together, ‘Now I didn’t think that would have happened.’

We arrived at Crayston a few minutes later buoyed up by this tale of Alf’s latest exploits and I remember thinking he should write a book. It was a good job – our spirits were going to need all the lifting they could get; it wasn’t raining any longer, it was throwing it down in stair rods.

We sat in the churchyard car park, just listening to the rain. Tyler cracked open his thermos. Thermos? I thought. Well either he’s not well or was expecting his dad. He had a slurp then offered the thermos to me, lovely room-temperature cheap sherry.

I said, ‘Expecting to be with dad, were you?’

‘How did you guess? It’s ‘cause mother’s home. I said you wouldn’t mind coming instead.’

‘No, no, of course, not at all. He’s picked the right day to miss.’

‘Jammy beggar.’

‘Yes.’

‘Now,’ said T, ‘we’ll sit here for a bit to see if this lot goes off. I’d nearly got it finished yesterday so shouldn’t be much to do, but this water might have set us back a bit.’

‘Okay.’ We had about three hours till the funeral.

The rain didn’t ease. If anything it did the reverse. Tyler turned and kneeled on his seat; I could hardly see him through the smog. I said, ‘What are you doing?’

‘Do you have any idea how muddy and wet we are going to get?’

To tell the truth I did not. He shoved the oxygen bottles back as far as they would go – at least the mower had gone – and started rooting.

He handed me the shotgun. ‘Here, just open this. It might be loaded, watch yerself.’

I opened the gun and yes, sure enough it was loaded. 'Here, T,' I said, showing him.

'Stupid pillock. I've told him about that a million times...' Probably statistically unlikely, I thought. The modern word has made us forget the size of that number. But it's nevertheless an expression we all use as it gets the message across. (I couldn't count the number of people I had told a million times not to exaggerate!).

'The safety catch was on though,' I said.

'That at least is a change.'

'Well perhaps your message is getting through, albeit slowly.'

We could only hope it was, before Alf mistakenly shot either himself or worse still someone else, and also they couldn't really afford to lose too much more car. But after the war, I imagine Alf felt an empty gun to be of limited use.

Tyler had now gone mad. Still kneeling on the seat (the head rests were long gone), he was throwing stuff back over each shoulder and side to side; he looked like Yoda sorting out Luke Skywalker's rucksack in *Star Wars*. The call 'Hold this' became more frequent the deeper he got.

'PJ,' he said. 'Turn round so you can do your bit.' This I did, just hopeful that in this day and age no one would start peering through the window at us with a torch: it wouldn't have looked good.

'What am I looking for?' I said.

‘You’ll know it when you feel it.’ It sounded like we were in a film. I wasn’t convinced.

‘Any more tips?’ I asked.

‘Anything made of rubber.’ Could this get any worse? I wondered.

Then up went the shout: ‘Knew they were in ‘ere’ somewhere!’ Tyler came up grinning with a wader.

‘One wader, what use is that?’ I said.

‘Means the other one and the chest waders are here somewhere,’ he replied. When we turned back round from our trawl to face forwards, our haul was one pair of chest waders, two single waders, three parts of what was left of waterproof jackets, and three rubber gloves. We were one torso up and one glove down, so all in all not that bad.

We sat back in our seats, and Tyler looked more relaxed now, drawing slowly on his new cigarette and drinking from his thermos. Although we hadn’t done anything yet, we had about knackered ourselves sorting out the surplus store on the back seat. But it was no good: we had sat here long enough; so we started the not inconsiderable task of getting all this clobber on in the foot well of a saloon car. After all this, I thought, when we got out it had better still be hissing it down. I was not to be disappointed as we set off for the grave. You could be forgiven for thinking you were watching an episode of *Trawlermen*, as such a sight can only very infrequently be seen on land.

‘Bollocks,’ said Tyler as we reached his handiwork from yesterday. We moved the planks, and looked down but not far. ‘Don’t get in there,’ he continued quite firmly. ‘That was five foot deep yesterday, ’bout a foot to go.’

‘You mean that’s wat—'

‘Yeah, you bet it is, water, mixed full with soil that’s fell in.’

‘Well how are we going to get that out? We’ve only got a couple of hours,’ I said, stating the obvious, which I found so amusing in others but strangely not right now.

‘Don’t remind me… Can you go back to the car, get that bucket we found?’

‘Okay,’ I said, and off I went.

He whistled me. He was good at that and could do it with two fingers in his mouth; that sort that you could hear for miles. ‘PJ!’ he shouted. ‘Bring the thermos!’ I could see him lighting up as I walked away. How he was going to keep that lit in this rain was anybody’s guess, but I dare say he could keep one lit if he was drowning.

On my return Tyler had obviously formulated a plan. This I wanted to hear as this five foot deep grave was full to within about eighteen inches of the top.

‘Right,’ said Tyler, ‘I’m goin’ to start bailing out. You go and get as many planks, bricks, anything, as you can.’

‘What for?’

‘Just get them. I’ll explain later. Afore you go, grab hold of the braces on these chest waders in case I go under.’

‘Go under?’

‘Yeah, bottom will have turned to mud.’

‘Okay.’

At this T, sitting with his legs down the hole at the foot end, lowered himself into the water. If he’d worked for Dyno-Rod it couldn’t have looked any worse.

‘Just hope it doesn’t come up over the top of these,’ he said, ‘or you’ll have to get the coastguard.’

This was no time for hilarity, or perhaps it was, as if you didn’t laugh you’d cry. With me holding him back like a puppeteer with a positively huge yellow puppet, he lowered away almost suspended by the chest waders like a baby walker. Together we got him to about groin depth before he started bailing.

‘Thanks, off you go and find that stuff,’ my lookalike deep-sea diver said.

‘Okay,’ I replied. I went through the car, removed Alf’s seat-reclining-prevention feature (brick), and got a few bits of ‘three be two’. I went round the back of the church, and found four good planks; this was becoming quite a good harvest or, more aptly, trawl. As I wheeled my prizes back towards the grave, there was a lull in the downpour. I’d like to say ‘and the sun came out and all was well', but this was not the case, though a definite lull there was. Tyler was heaving bucket load after bucket load out of the hole, over the foot end and down the slope. This particular graveyard had a significant slope to it, and the water flowed away freely and beautifully, forming a small but obvious delta system on the grass, the water depositing its complement of silt.

'That's a lovely delta you're creating there, T, looks like you are in the Med.'

'Well we're not, 'ere give us a pull,' he said, not amused. I got hold of Tyler's arm and helped him out.

'Well that's gone down quite a lot,' I said.

'Yeah, it's the best we goin' to be able to do. I'll have another go in a bit, it'll be coming back.'

I passed him the thermos, which he guzzled and sucked on like a newborn.

'Hey, steady on,' I said. 'That's all we've got.'

'No it ain't,' he replied mischievously. Would I ever learn?

He then pulled as if by magic from his sodden self a dust-dry packet of fags; now how he had done that? I didn't know. It crossed my mind he might be a marsupial with a fag pouch, a North American Indian marsupial, naturally.

'How long 'ave we got?' he asked.

‘About an hour,’ I replied. ‘Is it deep enough?’

‘Aye, have to be. Wish I’d done a bit more o’ it yesterday.’

‘Well you weren’t to know we were to have the wettest day since Noah was here, were you?’

He laughed. ‘I s’pose not. Anyhow there’s no way of making it any deeper now – just have to bed it down when it gets ‘ere. I’ll do a bit more bucketin’. You keep bringing anything you can find to stand on. Have you had a look behind church?’

‘Got them,’ I said. I think he was quite disappointed that I had found them. I could tell he’d been saving them as his trump card.

‘Ah, good, well find some more if you can. Try the old shed up there too.’

‘Wilco, boss,’ I playfully replied.

When I returned T was out and starting to position the planks and bricks around the grave.

‘PJ,’ he said, ‘go and find us some grass cuttings.’

‘Grass cuttings?’

‘Yes, grass cuttings, just get ‘em,’ T said, almost irritated. What on earth did we need grass cuttings for? Had he gone crackers? However, ‘Mine is not to reason why, mine is just to do or die,’ I quoted to myself. I filled the wheelbarrow with the freshest, today-soaked grass cuttings that I could find and returned.

'PJ, help us position these planks.' Tyler had built four corner supports for the planks from the bits and bricks. 'Trying to build it up,' he said. 'It's got to be strong enough to take vicar's weight. Don't want him falling in.'

Apparently, from the national gravedigging grapevine telegraph, an unfortunate Reverend down South had indeed lost his footing and done just that. He had ended up spread-eagled on his client in the hole. That must have been quite funny in that very British sort of way of finding humour in someone else's misfortune when there is little on the surface. It had taken the undertaker's crew and some burly mourners to haul him out. It occurred to me that, as the vicar stands at the head end of the coffin, a straight dive in would not only have been the most embarrassing moment of his life but would also have resulted in him, in relation to his client, being in an erotic position more commonly referred to by a number just shy of seventy; surely just the icing on the cake.

Anyway, back to our predicament. We got our stage up to about eight inches higher than grass level, and perfectly sound.

I said to Tyler, 'With a bit of training we could make it as roadies next.' I laughed.

'Just c'mon,' was my reply.

After it was all set - grass, purple sheets, ropes in place - we looked down. Since the pumping bucket had stopped we had lost a little ground, but it looked deep enough, didn't it? No, it didn't, I was just trying to be positive. It did look like a hole though and all being well, with such foul weather no-one would be there long enough to notice otherwise. It was time.

'Quick,' said Tyler, 'grass cuttings.' I wheeled them as close as I could. 'Chuck them in … No, no, not great clumps, just a scattering to disguise the fact that it is water.' Clever stuff, I thought, another trick of the trade.

At this point we heard the spluttering of some clapped-out diesel car. It was a blue Daihatsu 4 x 4 and it pulled up and parked next to where we were parked.

'Oh no,' said Tyler, 'just when you think things can't get any worse, and 'e turns up.'

By way of explanation there was only one person who would be seen dead in this particular leftover of a Daihatsu. It belonged, if anyone would be brave enough to admit it, to Ruins shoot, and was Alf's off-road runabout for feeding his pheasants. It made the SRi look positively cherished.

This vehicle was like the Toyota that Clarkson had tried to kill, although Alf hadn't found a tower block to be demolished yet. Clarkson and his team, nay, the nation would have been impressed at what this little fella had experienced and survived - there would likely have been two plinths on the *Top Gear* set. Why the producers hadn't simply saved licence payers money and given the Toyota to Alf was a bit of a mystery. Alf got out and wandered up our way. It was like *Trawlermen* versus *Scrapheap Challenge.*

I knew it was a pointless question as I said to T, with resigned inevitability, 'Is what's left of that blue thing road-legal?' meaning the vehicle, but perhaps I should have meant the whole package inclusive of driver too. Tyler just looked at me with his puppy-dog eyes and said nothing. He was right, that was a really stupid question, PJ.

'Thought I'd come and help,' chirped Alf, clearly unsure as to what sort of reception he was going to receive.

'What you doin' 'ere?' said Tyler.

'Thought you pair might need a hand wit' weather. Hi, PJ.'

'Hi—' I started.

'Who's looking after mother?' T asked him.

'Oh she's all right, keeps moaning about her hearing.' I wonder why, I thought? She can only have been inches away from that gun when it went off in the car, inches! No great surprise there though. I was on Amona's side on this one; poor woman's hearing was probably shot, excuse the pun, and she'd likely be dreaming of guns going off in cars for weeks.

'Well you might come in handy. This 'un's two thirds full of water – going to need all three of us to get it down.'

''Ey-up,' said Alf. People were beginning to arrive in the car park. 'We better scarper.'

Tyler did the last-walk-around checks and we went and hid in the cars, which were parked in the far corner of the car park as out of the way as they could be. We all three managed to get into the one car and before long we had steamed the windows up as it was still raining. Hopefully the relations wouldn't stand around, and we wouldn't be here long.

'You left the shotgun loaded again.'

Alf immediately spun round, as Otis to Lex Luthor in Superman, as if to rectify the position, but soon adopted his sheepish defensive mode as he realised it would have been dealt with. 'Oh bugger, did I?' he said. Here we go, I thought. 'Well I didn't think that would have happened.'

Yes, yes, I thought, he had to say it! Tyler ate two cigarettes, and had a swig from his thermos. He even said to Alf, 'Want some barely warm coffee?' Alf declined, but I accepted though. I thought: Blimey Moses, you're on thin ice Tyler, that offer was surely fraught with danger. I was going to ask him later. After about twenty minutes Tyler looked over the hedge. They had gone, he'd been right, they hadn't hung about. The warm pub and refreshments doubtless waited in the village.

'Right, let's go,' said T. I for one was looking forward to getting cracking; the soaking we had got before was now cold and damp, and utterly unpleasant. We all piled out of the car and set off.

The greengrocer grass where the mourners had briefly stood was thoroughly wet and quite muddy. The three of us started taking away the grass, sheets, and so on. I was surprised the sheets were still purple, as T had dyed them in a bucket, but it had obviously worked and stayed fast. To our surprise the coffin was just level with the ground-grass level. It can only just have looked conceivably like a hole, due to the decking we had built around it. The grave had clearly taken more water in the forty-five minutes or so that we'd been away from it.

'Bugger it,' muttered Alf gratuitously. I think it was his favourite word.

I said to both, 'This must have been more like a launch than a burial.' This warranted and received no response. I thought it funny though. 'So what's the plan?' I was again ignored.

The client sadly could not be ignored, though the coffin was bobbing about in its dock quite happily. I was surprised it hadn't sunk of its own accord, but it quite definitely hadn't, and of course there was no opportunity to bail out any more of the silt-laden water. It was clear even to my inexperienced eye that this client was going to need considerable encouragement to sink. Drastic action was going to be needed: there was no easy way of saying it but the coffin was floating proud of the ground, now all the paraphernalia had gone, which would never do.

T said to Alf, 'You, you get on the head end.' At this Alf did so. 'PJ, get on the middle.' Upon issuing his instructions T in turn stepped onto the foot end. It was slow at first but within a few minutes I do believe we were sinking, like going down in a painfully slow lift.

It must have been quite an inexplicable sight, three soaking-wet grown men, dressed in assorted clothing, standing in a row in a graveyard gradually, but definitely, descending below the horizon and into the depths below, in front of your very eyes.

As the client sank, a few grass cuttings began to come up around the sides, washing gently over the deck of the coffin. I was glad this wasn't a tight fit or it would have been more like a piston, with no gap up the sides for the water to flow, but slowly and surely we were going down and doing fine.

'When do you want us to start shovellin' dirt back?' said Alf.

'Not yet,' said Tyler, 'another foot or so.' It seemed to take us ages but probably wasn't long at all.

'Okay, let's go,' said Tyler like a rallying charge. I soon learned that that was not what he meant, rather 'let's shovel'. We started in sequence more by luck than judgement, to avoid the clashing of spades. There was no dull thud onto the coffin this time, just a gentle splash. This stuff was quickly building up round our feet and calves to the extent that you had to loosen a wader up and reposition on the now subterranean heap of soil you were standing on.

'Don't get stuck,' said T. 'It'll go like quicksand and suck you in.'

I knew this to be true, having been on an opencast coal site some years before. I went onto the site as the geologist with my clipboard, wellies and hard hat, and absolutely no experience. I had at one point to stand out of the way of the trucks, which were the size of a small block of flats, at the side of the site road, only for my welly to be sucked in and off by this viscous and vicious clay that the roadside had turned into. I felt a complete idiot on my return to the site office, with one welly on and one very bedraggled-looking sock. No explanation was required: all present, from manager to drivers, just laughed. I had been going to say I'd forgotten one, or only had one welly, but there was no point. They knew. I just laughed too. I wasn't the first, and dare say this clay had caught more than one of them out in the past.

Things in the grave were going smoothly, provided you were not the client I suppose. We were nearly down as far as he thought it would go, T said. It was prevented from sinking further by the certain build-up of mud below the box. It was still raining but not like the stuff of monsoons we had experienced earlier.

It struck me that coffins had to be reasonably watertight in the short-term because as this one was sinking, not a single bubble emitted from it; it felt like a cork just bobbing there, reluctant to leave the world above. I'm quite sure the client was the driest of the four of us, as for the time being we were like drowned rats.

This mud with the texture of wallpaper paste we were standing in was slowly thickening up (and it wasn't overwarm it has to be said) when Alf unexpectedly made a move. He was a strong wiry old fella, not carrying a lot of weight, and at first I thought he must have felt he was getting stuck. Unannounced to the rest of us, he quite suddenly got out. The consequence of Alf's unauthorised exit was that, as most of the trapped air was at the roomiest head end where he had been stationed, the coffin's head end reappeared out of the mucky depths like the aft end of the *Titanic.* T and I completely involuntarily slipped down towards the feet.

'What on earth…' shouted T as the Titanic deck lost any semblance of stability. 'What have you got out for my dearest sleepy (although now apparently illegitimate) father,' Tyler very definitely didn't say… Briefly the loaded grey sky turned blue.

I thought: don't dare say it, Alf, don't say it, the 'I didn't think that' line, not now, you'll likely be joining the client if you do.

Tyler was visibly furious, dad or not. The head end came up well clear of the water level with the soil and water mix guzzling now beneath with a sucking sound, whereas the foot end stayed down with us two standing on it. It stopped coming up when its length jammed it. 'You dozy b—' said T to his father, who had already adopted the naughty-boy-in-the-corner look. I was desperately trying to think of an excuse for Alf's behaviour but none was forthcoming or available.

'Why did you get out?' Tyler all but screamed at him

'I thought it would be enough,' Alf whispered at a barely audible volume.

'You thought it would be enough. Well it wasn't e-f-nuff, was it?' Tyler ranted as he got out of the grave. 'Dear oh dear…' Tyler very definitely didn't say. Throwing his spade on the ground, he fidgeted with rage and lit a cigarette.

‘Give us the thermos, PJ,’ he said with the rain dripping off his nose. We all three lined up along the side of the grave looking down: Compo, Clegg and Foggy. The head end was up at an angle. Now it looked a bit like the *Titanic* just before it snapped in half, perish the thought. Surely that wouldn’t happen? God, I hoped not. Now, though, the coffins deck plummeted away under the waves and into the invisible depths of the foot end. Tyler knelt down by the head end and reached down with his tape. ‘Two foot six inches, from grass.’ He stood up.

‘Dear oh dear,’ he didn’t say again. His language was certainly far more colourful than his surroundings. Staring forlornly at his dad as if looking at a new life form he simply did not understand he said, ‘It’s meant to be a double,’ he looked as if he could cry. ‘If it were a single we could get away without saying owt, but not a double. We come to bury his missus on top of ‘im now and ‘er ‘ead will be on surface.’

‘They’d notice that,’ chirped Alf. I nearly legged it; Tyler was in danger of committing patricide. I know he had thought about it… more than once. Alf clearly had no fear.

With this Tyler announced that he’d have to go and see the undertaker. ‘We’ll ‘ave to come clean … imagine someone doing reopen who didn’t know.’ He was of course right. That was indeed an unpleasant thought.

‘And you,’ he said to Alf, ‘better pray ‘e doesn’t want it up and out again. Now, you pair, look busy, pack the stuff up and don’t let anybody near that hole, no sightseers, right?’

‘Right,’ I answered, although I suspected the weather may have done us a favour in dissuading sightseers, as T had called them. People attending other graves likely wouldn’t be coming in this.

Once T had left Alf said, visibly relaxing, ‘Tyler shouldn’t be long. Undertaker’s just village joiner round corner.’

‘Oh, right,’ I said.

‘Don’t think he’s very pleased with me,’ said Alf a bit sheepishly.

‘Not sure he is, fella, no,’ I replied. I could offer him no solace, only sympathy. I felt sorry for him right then. He really was too old for this, and was a bedraggled skeletal figure soaked to the bone, who was only trying to help but had just been roasted for his troubles. He was a war-toughened man but the years were taking their toll, he should long be retired and relaxing, the heaviest and wettest things in his life being dominoes and a pint. We packed the soaking grass and sheets away. Even the ropes would need washing after this one; they were a rusty-brown colour. This was my first, admittedly brief, experience I was to have working alone with Alf. It was not to be the last, oh dear no it wasn’t…

Tyler returned and laboured his way back across to us. He had lost his waders now, and had his boots on again.

‘Right,’ he announced. The walk must have done him good: he seemed less traumatised, unless he had drunk the reserve sherry for medicinal purposes. ‘Just fill it in quick as we can with one of you’ – looking at me as I was the heaviest – ‘standing on head end just to see if it will go down a bit.' This we did. The client responded by returning perhaps six inches further into the watery depths but that was it; it had either jammed or was now solidly supported from beneath. With the three of us shovelling in silence I thought it is times like this I wish I smoked. It was obvious T wasn't speaking to his dad, but we soon had it infilled.

Tyler said, 'Undertaker was mad with himself about this, said it was his fault, we were lucky.'

'Lucky? Why? No? How?' I said, mystified by how it could conceivably be the undertaker's fault and how we on this day, in this condition, in this weather, with this job, could by any stretch of the imagination be called lucky was beyond me.

'No holes in it, undertaker said, should have put holes in it,' said T.

At the risk of seeming thick, I said, 'No holes in what?'

'In t'coffin, you duck egg,' didn't say Tyler calmly, as if it were the most normal exchange.

'What? In the coffin? Holes?' I shrieked.

'Yeah, weights 'em too if need be,' he said. 'Normally drills 'em, big 'oles at that, with a brace and bit if weather turns and there's likely water about as often is 'ere. Puts a few bricks in as ballast an' all, but he didn't today…'

Oh for all that is holy, I thought. Freezing bodies for convenience was bad enough, but drilling holes in them? The thought made me shiver.

Tyler smiled; he was clearly ahead of me: 'Before he puts the body in, you daft beggar. Holes in the coffin! But I shouldn't have told you that so soon, should have made yer sweat a bit more!'

Oh, thank the Maker, thank goodness. My imagination had gone into overdrive warp speed for a moment.

'Where?' I said, reluctant to let the matter drop. I still suffered from morbid fascination.

'In t' bottom where you can't see, leaves 'em a screw-turn loose on t' lid screws, to let th'air out.' A 'screw loose' I understood. You nearly had to have one to do this job. It was beginning to seem almost mandatory.

I have to say I was considerably relieved at that particular funereal explanation on this occasion. Mystery over, I had pictured coffins looking like Emmental cheeses coming down the church's aisle.

Tyler went on, 'He's going to tell the family and has already reserved the next-door plot for his missus. He thought we had done all right to get it as low as we did. He's had 'em left floatin' proud of the grass before he said, but thankfully not on our watch.'

'I didn't think he'd put holes in this 'un,' Alf muttered to himself in self-congratulation, and to demonstrate his wealth of experience and superior knowledge gained therefrom, as if it were obvious. (Yeah right, we thought).

We finished off, sloshed back to the cars and were done. I climbed out of my now half-full waders, tried to dry myself a bit with some dry greengrocer grass, and got in the car. I couldn't wait to get home and into the bath. Alf got in his vehicle, and before he started it T hollered at him, 'You playing dominoes in pub tonight fatha?'

'Yep,' came the reply.

'I'll see you there.'

'Okay.'

'Hang on.' Tyler got out of the car and went to Alf's window. ''Ere y'are,' he said, handing over some cash.

'No, no, I don't deserve it, lad,' said Alf.

'Well you're right about sommat at least,' said Tyler unkindly. 'Tek it, before I change mee mind! See you at doms.'

They were friends again and T had seen him right with the money, genuinely nearly bringing a tear to my eye. That was a relief as we had always suspected Alf had only turned up because he was skint but too proud to say as much. Even he would not have come in that Daihatsu lightly or if avoidable.

'Why don't you and Sam come to doms?' Tyler said, getting back in the car.

'Do you know, we might just do that.'

We got back to Cliff Field along the quickest 'M' rated farm track of a road in the land. It seemed ages since this morning. T paid me and I went in for that bath.

It struck me that that was the one grave I'd worked on without knowing the person's name, or offering my little 'God bless' routine. In all the panic and fall-out, and indeed mud on the sinking deck, I never read the brass nameplate…

It was a couple of years later that I was just passing on my way elsewhere, not digging, and I went back. The grass had regrown, the memorial was up and the sun was out. I went and read the name, apologised for the delay and hoped the slope was not too uncomfortable. I did my little cross routine and farewell. Here's hoping Anthony hadn't minded the wait…

Chapter 9

IN THE BLEAK MIDWINTER

There are a lot of places whose names sound similar, particularly on - let us say - older, less expensive landline answerphones such as Tyler and Alf's. There existed then, as now, state-of-the-art machines and this one of Alf's well I'm not saying it ran on valves and was a museum piece; it just wouldn't be long before it was. We must remember that these were the fledgling days of the communication revolution that we are now experiencing, days when mobiles were the size of breezeblocks, and computers had their own buildings. A different world but not so long ago.

Tyler rang me at Cliff Field, and said, 'PJ, got a problem.'

'What's up?' I asked.

'Got two on, day after tomorrow.' By now I knew he meant funerals.

'How can I help?'

'Owd fella's not up to doing one on his own any more… wondered if you could do one. You'll be on your own though.' This was quite a promotion as I had never done the whole job 'sod off to sodding off via sod back on' as it were.

'I'll have a bash, thanks for asking,' I said. I was really quite flattered.

'Can you use your sheep trailer?' asked Tyler. I had treated myself to one, and a tow bar, after the debacle at the livestock auction. (Sam had insisted in no uncertain terms, but you arguably couldn't blame her for that though.)

'Can't they get a hearse?' I said jokingly.

'Very funny,' Tyler replied, tolerating my nonsense, rather than laughing at it.

'Might be a bit big?' I said. 'But yes, of course, if you think it will be okay.' (Getting serious and 'growing up' was required, I felt, from Tyler's tone.)

'I'll bring box round to yours from cemetery at Seascale in the morning. You'll have all day to dig it – funeral's day after at one o'clock.'

‘Where is it?’

‘Tewthwaite, out on tops as you go out o’er Halgills Way. Don’t do many up there.’ Halgills was a small range of hills.

‘I’ll look it up on the map.’

‘You’ll find it easy enough…’ Well, I thought, I might provided I didn’t go the ‘quickest way’ route as of late.

‘Where are you going?’ I asked.

‘Oh I’m off the other side of Corcastle. That’s why I won’t get to you. They are both at one o’clock, and about as far apart as I do. See you in the morning.’

‘Okay, see you tomorrow.’

Morning came, Tyler arrived, and we had a brew while loading my trailer with my stuff - box, greengrocer grass, ropes, spade, etc. He gave me directions, to which I paid attention out of politeness and thereafter completely ignored after my recent ‘gate opening’ experience on the ‘quickest way’ to Crayston.

‘Oh,’ T said, ‘you’ll be needing this up there, bit o’ company.’ At that he handed me a bottle of Spar’s best dry sherry. ‘Don’t drink it all at once,’ he said, laughing, ‘just in case I turn up.’

Before long I was ready for off. ‘You might have a few problems,’ T said.

Oh, here we go, I thought, just drop the bombshell right at the end. 'What?' I said suspiciously.

'No no, don't worry, ground's okay for digging, it ain't that. Just I went up and marked the plot for you yesterday. It's only a single, but you'll 'appen be a bit deeper at head end than feet, bit of a slope…'

'Okay, should be okay,' I said. I was bordering on being an old hand at this lark now. How hard could it be? 'Who is it for?' I asked.

'Can't remember his name,' said T, getting into his car. 'Young lad, though, know that much.' His wheels were beginning to turn slowly when he added, 'Topped 'imself, by all reports, drank weed killer in his mum and dad's garden shed, paraquat,' and drove away.

That remark troubled me. This was my first suicide (well, not mine) and it was thought-provoking to say the least. I never liked the expression 'topped himself'. When did life get so bad or future so barren and hopeless that weed killer seemed a reasonable option or any form of good idea? What must that have done to his parents? If there was one thing I had learned from Tyler it was that gravedigging is a tough job on both muscles and mind. Sometimes for self-preservation purposes, you had to switch to autopilot and simply accept and do - not think, ask or analyse too much.

It was a cold winter's day. Tyler had said the sod might be frozen up at Tewthwaite. Time would tell. It was relatively easy to find, only a mile or so from the main road, and I weaved up the hill until I found a pull-in just over the wall from the churchyard, long enough for both car and not insubstantial sheep trailer. It was a double-wheelbase trailer, so parking wasn't going to be easy, but I'd been lucky: this pull-in was ideal. I climbed over the wall, which was also low enough to chuck my stuff over. I took in the view, which was quite spectacular - all countryside down to the distant blueish strip of sea.

What was it Tyler said? 'Bit of a slope'. Well, I could kill him now. I had never had the Eddie the Eagle view of a ski-jump slope, but what I faced now was as close to my imagined view of same as I wanted to get. Tyler's description was spot on. This was indeed a steep slope down from the road to a small chapel in the corner. I thought it quite ironic really that people paid huge amounts of money for their houses, and often prices were at a premium where a view was on offer. Yet we used large areas of land with spectacular views, not to live on but to bury our dead, who perhaps really couldn't care either way, although it would be nice to think they did and I was wrong.

I had a look around the graveyard until I found Tyler's grave-marker stick, right at the top of the descent towards the lonely little chapel in the corner, but thankfully not far from where I had been able to park. It did cross my mind to abseil down to the grave's position, but I stuck to the tried and tested setting-up procedure which was only hampered by the positioning of the box. The ground was indeed steep, hard, and bordering on frozen. I expected the first few inches to be the worst, provided Tyler wasn't winding me up about the ground conditions as well.

He wasn't: the grass and top inches were frozen but after that the digging went well. To get the bottom of the hole flat T was right, the head end was going to be a lot deeper than the foot, so I dug a grave-width terrace in the ground which meant I could dig the remainder flat. It took me about four hours, with breaks, to finish.

My breaks included a sherry with the audience of sheep over the boundary wall. I caught myself talking to them, asking them how their day was going - as you do - but they were disappointingly unresponsive. I was glad they hadn't heard of their relations kidnap ordeal that I had been involved in from the auction or they might have charged. I know that one shouldn't drink in the cold - lowers one's blood somethings and resistance - but my goodness it certainly warmed the cockles of your heart, whatever and wherever they are. It improved my day, keeping my spirits up, gave me something to look forward to.

One of the obvious things to do in a graveyard in these comfort breaks was to read the epitaphs on the stones. I often thought that, particularly in these remote locations, the only people to ever read them were probably the original relations, the stonemasons who fitted the headstones, and the likes of me and Tyler, anonymous ground workers. On this occasion I found a delightfully thought-provoking inscription in more ways than one, on an old table-top type stone slab near to the chapel. The stone was covered in ivy, with just the bottom part of the inscription visible. I carefully folded back the ivy, so as not to damage it. This inscription can't have been read for years as the ivy was thick in its diameter, and unless you were dressed in your scruffs (as I was) and had a spade to lean the ivy on, moving it would not have been an easy option.

After brushing the stone clean with my sleeve, I read:

HERE LIES ROBERT MASHITER

BORN THE 17TH DAY OF FEBRUARY 1800

DIED THE 17TH DAY OF FEBRUARY 1850

'BY SUDDEN DEATH I'M SNATCHED AWAY

DEATH SCARCELY LEFT ME TIME TO SAY

THE LORD HAVE MERCY ON MY SOUL

SO ABSOLUTE IS HIS CONTROL

REFLECT WHEN THOU MY GRAVE DOST SEE

THE NEXT THAT'S DUG MAY BE FOR THEE'

I had to smile at this. Not only had Mr Mashiter written or found a verse of Shakespearean quality, but also shared something else with the Bard. Mr Mashiter, as Mr Shakespeare before him allegedly, but not for sure, had died on his birthday. I carefully replaced the ivy, and I'd be surprised if it has ever been read since.

This inscription from the past spoke volumes. How true it was, as true now as then. Perhaps things had not changed as much as we liked to believe, each generation rather just tinkering at the edges. I imagined the young then, but old now, Mr Mashiter to have a wry smile on his face.

I covered up my grave for the night before leaving, and thought that the lad who was to become its occupant would be in good company with Mr Mashiter: he obviously had a great sense of humour.

That evening Tyler popped round to Cliff Field to see how I had got on. He and Sam enjoyed the story of the inscription.

Tyler said, 'So I'm paying you to have a jolly, supping sherry and reading headstones, am I?'

'Don't forget the talking-to-sheep bit,' said Sam. At that we all laughed. 'We'll have to keep an eye on PJ,' Sam said to Tyler. 'I've always had my doubts,' she continued, twisting her finger to her temple.

I gave Tyler my report: good digging, good smooth hole and how cold it was. It all seemed a million miles away standing around that warm cosy Rayburn.

Sam said, 'Would it help you two if I lent you my mobile phone tomorrow? I know I've only got one, but if it's any good you're welcome to it. Don't break it, though, it's not really mine, belongs to work.' (Sam was employed by a telecom-giant.)

‘Well it would actually,’ said T. ‘Give it PJ, means he can ring t’owd fella for advice if needed, God forbid! But better still I’m in Chevet, the other side Corcastle, and there’s a phone box at the church gate so I can ring him to see all is okay.’

‘Great, that’s sorted then,’ said Sam. ‘I’ll show you how to answer this one this time PJ,’ she said mischievously…

This was a reference to the last time she had lent me a work phone. She was coming back from London, and lent it to me so she could ring when approaching Corcastle. She duly did at which point I became an immediate laughing stock. These were the early days of mobiles, unlike today where people look like their phone would have to be surgically removed from either their hand or ear. I always wonder who all these people walking down the street are actually talking to. The phone that Sam had lent to me was one down from the old house brick, and I proudly placed it on the bar in the pub. It drew considerable interest as it was state of the art of its day, and I, a humble gravedigger, had one. I was quite sure some people thought: How has he got one of those? It would be a museum piece now, but back then it was a Bugatti Veyron.

Whilst on the bar it rang and I picked it up so as to answer it. As I put it to my ear it was still ringing. It had a keypad as on an old calculator, which by chance had also made no sense to me as a schoolboy. Phones stopped ringing when you picked them up, didn’t they? Well obviously not. Mobiles and my credibility duly left the pub with me as I retreated from the bar, tail firmly between my legs, with my still ringing phone. I had no idea how to answer the wretched thing, so I went home and rang its number. This was after Sam had given up. I pressed everything on it until I discovered the answer button. I then hopped it sharpish to the station to pick her up.

'Tyler,' Sam said.

'Yes?'

'Now, I feel we've known each other long enough, do you agree?'

'Yes.'

'Well, please don't be offended, but do you mind if I remind you not to forget to take some change for the call box, then?' Tyler laughed.

He said to me later, 'Good job Sam reminded me about change.'

'Well, I didn't like to say anything,' I said, 'but after the spade incident Sam isn't taking any chances.'

'That's fair enough.' T looked at me in a sort of assessing, weighing-up manner that was uncharacteristic. 'You are lucky to have her, you know, PJ…'

'You know, T, I am,' I replied. 'Was never sure what she saw in me—'

Quick as a flash T returned 'Funny that, that's exactly what I was thinking.' He then laughed characteristically, if a little more enthusiastically than was polite or necessary I felt. 'So are you set for tomorrow?'

‘Yes,’ I said, thinking: Who needs enemies? ‘I have got the ropes, sheets, and the hand-soil box for mourners. If we keep checking on each other, all should be well,’ I finished optimistically.

‘Hope so. I’ll give you a ring at some point tomorrow just to see you’re okay.’

‘Thanks. Hope yours goes okay too.’

‘Thanks,’ replied T, and went.

I got to Tewthwaite about nine o’clock in the morning. I was in a strange sort of a way looking forward to my day despite the tragedy and task in hand. Sam had packed me some lunch and I had a piece of pork pie on arrival, leaning on the wall. It was certainly cold and bleak up here today, with the long-distance view lost in the murk.

I jumped in the grave and sorted a bit of the side which had fallen in overnight. I levelled it up again then did my ‘spring clean’, leaves, pebbles and the like, until the base was perfect. I had remembered the step to get out this time as well.

I thought while setting the grave up that this family weren’t going to have much of a Christmas this year, after all they had no doubt been through. I took my time as there was no rush: Tyler had said one o’clock. I didn’t know whether it was a twelve thirty funeral for one o’clock, or a one o’clock funeral for half past, but no matter, I wasn’t going anywhere. At that point my phone rang. I answered it with my new-found how-to-answer-a-phone knowledge. It would be Tyler, of course.

'Testing, testing, testing,' the lady's voice said.

'Sam!' I said, with the enthusiasm of a little boy.

'Just wondered if you were all working in the new tech department. Reception and everything all right?'

'Yes indeed,' I replied. I was so high up here it should work, I thought, not knowing what proximity to an aerial was.

'Obviously remembered how to answer it then?'

'So far so good,' I chuckled in reply.

'Good luck today, PJ,' Sam said. 'Keep your chin up.'

'Wilco.'

'Ring me if you want to.'

'Thank you. Bye-bye, mate.'

I knew why she was concerned. She and only she knew what I was like: this lad's funeral would upset me, even though I didn't know him from Adam. It was just such a shame. I had never thought suicide as cowardly, as so many say, more immense misplaced bravery; however selfish it certainly and undeniably is, as we understand more now we realise it is often driven by intolerable anxiety and mental illness.

All was now ready. The grave looked smart (even though I say so myself) - well, as smart as these things can look. There was no one about and it was approaching eleven thirty am, so out of curiosity and for something to do I had a walk down to the chapel. Youngsters' funerals were always well attended. I suppose youth is the time of our lives when we know the most people; elderly relations are still with us, and school or university friends are still current.

It struck me immediately that this little chapel was going to be packed, and judging by the dimensions of the outside it was no Westminster Abbey. However I shrugged the thought off and went to the gates to the churchyard. Strangely they were locked, padlocked from the outside, but I shrugged this off too. I dare say I would have paid more attention had the gates been my only access, as that would have posed a significant problem earlier. It was odd, though, that the gate was locked so close to the time of the funeral. If people had to wait, they would have to wait outside. It wasn't warm; mind you it probably wasn't much warmer in the chapel itself. There would be no gas up here, and there was no sign of a Churchwarden or similar preparing what heating there might have been. Having done my rounds as it were and for what it was worth, I decided to go and pass the last few minutes until it all got going in the company and relative warmth offered by the car heater.

Twelve o'clock came and went with only me and the sheep to notice. Must be a twelve thirty or even a one o'clock funeral, I thought. They'd be getting here soon either way. My phone rang again. This time it was Tyler from the call box.

'All right,' he almost shouted. 'You there?'

'Yep, I'm here,' I replied.

'It works then,' said Tyler, another fine example of humans stating the absolute obvious, I thought. 'How's it going?'

'Well it's not.'

'What do you mean?'

'Well it's not,' I repeated. 'There's no one here and the gates to the churchyard and chapel are still locked.'

'Oh,' came the underwhelmed response followed by silence. Then, 'Well, I'm sure they'll be there soon,' Tyler said with questionable optimism.

'Yes,' I agreed, sure in my own mind that they would. After all, what other outcome could there possibly be? 'How are you getting on?' I asked.

'Fine, fine, my lot are in the church. If I get it done quick and they don't parp about at the graveside, I'll try to get up to you.'

'Okay,' I said, trying to hide my increasing concern. 'Look forward to it.'

'Bye then. Oh I'll ring you in half an hour to see how you're doing.'

‘Okay. Bye.’ Even then I could see this technology was going to go far. I wish I’d bought shares in it. A lot of them…

Twelve thirty pm duly came and went. With only the whistling breeze as company, I wanted to get on. This was getting to be more than a joke, it was cold up here. One o’clock came. By then I was running the car battery down listening to Radio 4. *World at One* could not have been a more suitably named programme. There was certainly only ‘one’ in my ‘world’ at the moment, I thought. No sign of Tyler’s call either.

I resorted to the sherry bottle for company. Again I wished I smoked, for something to do. Finally at twenty-five past one the phone rang.

‘Hello,’ said Tyler.

‘There’s nobody here,’ I splurted out, ignoring the pleasantries.

‘Nobody there?’ questioned Tyler.

‘Yeah, nobody here, got it in one, nil, niente, nada’ I said, the panic in my voice obvious. ‘It must be the wrong day, Tyler.’ After all that was the only variable.

‘Yeah,’ he said thoughtfully, then after what seemed like for ever he added, ‘either that or the wrong place.’

‘What!’ I believe I yelled down the phone like someone possessed. The sheep even looked up, nothing more though.

‘Well I got the message off the answering machine,’ he said. At this point I didn’t care if he’d received it by carrier pigeon.

‘So what?’ The phone signal hesitated so, in keeping with my height theory of phones, I climbed up onto the car bonnet.

‘Well it’s not the best answering machine recorder in the world. I wonder if it was Tewthcrake, not Tewthwaite, that it played,’ Tyler pondered. I hoped he was joking, but he was giving it too much serious thought to be joking.

‘Where’s Tewthcrake?’

‘Oh, about five miles further up valley from you.’

Well that was all, I could see it now, a huge gathering in such tragic circumstances coming out of the church not five miles away, everyone wandering aimlessly about looking for a hole, relations being consoled, floods of tears, ballistic undertaker, it was too terrifying a vision. The sensible part of me was saying this can’t be happening, the undertaker must have been to check, surely. Mind you, it had to be said he hadn’t been here.

Tyler said, ‘Don’t worry, there must be some explanation. Look, I’ve nearly finished here, I’ll get to you within the hour. I’ll be with you soon as. Bye.’

‘Bye,’ I said. It crossed my mind to volunteer to pop up to Tewth… wherever it was, to check, and was almost surprised Tyler had not asked me to. But the saying ‘rod for my own back’ flashed into my mind. Who would bear the weight of responsibility I was only guessing, but out of the gravediggers (which technically I was not), I would be the only one there so I thought better of voluntarily becoming the sacrificial lamb. To say I was stressed out would be an understatement, but it wasn't my problem, and I was sure I'd see the funny side in years to come. The poor mourners, and oh the undertaker in charge of such a monumental mess, well it didn't bear thinking about. I had another hopeful look down towards the chapel: nothing, diddly-squat, I could see the headlines now…

I paced up and down. Tewthwaite, Tewthcrake, Tewthwaite, Tewthcrake… You could easily see how they could get mixed up in plain speech, let alone on some antiquated answering machine. I was not hopeful any longer, resigned to the fact that this was not at all good. Everything was pointing to an unmitigated disaster.

Around quarter to three Tyler turned up. 'Oh dear,' he didn't say getting out of the SRi. He could see that his arrival had doubled the immediate potential congregation.

'Sorry I was a bit off with you on the phone T.' I had calmed down now. I just felt like the condemned man.

'That's okay.'

'I thought you were quite calm, considering.'

'I'm not now.'

'Well you hide it well,' I said, trying to reassure us both.

'Not really. I'm used to disasters, working with th'owd fella, but this has got me in a panic. I wish he'd listened to the message then I could have blamed him. The proverbial is really going to hit the fan on this one. Even if they do turn up it'll be nearly pitch dark before they're out.'

It had to be said that even on the Richter scale of Alf and Tyler fiascos this one was right up there, ground breaking. However at that very moment what looked like a cortège of black cars approached in the mid-distance.

'Ey-up,' said T,' what's this?'

Sure enough the hearse pulled up at the gates and a chap in his vicar's robes got out. It was bang on three o'clock. The stress that left us as that car stopped was tangible.

'You didn't hear the time wrong, did you?' It was the one variable we hadn't covered.

'No,' said T 'been going over it in my mind and that is the one bit I am sure of, one o'clock.'

There were only two cars with the hearse. Twelve mourners disembarked, shook themselves off and followed the coffin. All our troubles evaporated immediately. I for one had never been so pleased to see a coffin. We slouched down behind the wall. T lit a fag. 'Want one?' he offered.

'Yes, please,' I replied, 'but not just now.'

'You've done really well at this giving up lark, you know.'

'Thanks.' It had been about six months now. 'I haven't given up sherry though.'

‘No, ‘ere y’are,’ said Tyler. ‘I’m surprised there’s any left after the afternoon you’ve had.’ He smiled.

After our refreshments we stood up to watch. Where were all the imagined mourners? It would only add to the almost overbearing sadness of the situation if so few had bothered to turn up to celebrate the life of, and indeed remember and respect, the youngster and mark his tragic untimely end.

The cortège bypassed the chapel: that was a clue at the time, but I didn’t pick it up, it still hadn’t dawned on me. They made their way up to the grave led by the, even seen from here, very smart undertaker, and the parents obviously first in line behind the bearers. Dad had a firm hold on Mum and my heart went out to them; to the world they were leaving a wooden box on a hillside, to them they were leaving their hearts. The assembled did their stuff and were soon on their way back to the car. It was getting really cold now and the drab day had not improved on this bleak lonely hillside; you certainly couldn’t blame the mourners for their early retreat.

As the drivers were welcoming their passengers back to their cars – they had been ‘jacks of all trades’ today, driving, bearing the bier and lowering – the very smart individual who had led the cortège approached us. Our undertaker today was, Tyler informed me later, his first ever lady performing the role. She greeted us at our wall. My trailer was a good marker projecting over the wall as to our whereabouts.

'Mr Tyler,' the lady said in a quiet calm voice (did Tyler just run his fingers through his hair in an effort to smarten up? He did, I was sure of it, wait till I get him... I smiled inside), 'thank you.' She handed over an envelope. 'I trust this is satisfactory.' Tyler fumbled with the envelope. He was a wreck; the lady had really put him on his back foot. I would have laughed out loud had it been possible or appropriate.

'Yes, sir... er Mrs, um Ma'am, er Madam, that's fine.' (I wanted to laugh all the more at this faux pas!! He was writhing in his search for how to address the lady).

'I'm sorry,' she continued, as if oblivious to Tyler's ramblings (she was probably used to it. Although there was a glimmer of amusement in her manner, she was far too professional to admit to it) 'for the inordinate delay in arrival. There were some significant roadworks on the motorway, of which I was unaware. We set off at one o'clock as intended and it has taken us two hours to get here.'

'That's okay, sir'adam,' Tyler said. I thought: O blinking kay? I could have hit him. 'All's well that ends well,' T went on. Oh don't hold back T, that was really telling her, I thought. 'We were beginning to wonder what might have happened.' That's better I thought, let her know I've nearly had a breakdown and him nearly another suicide on his hands.

The undertaker bowed slightly in acknowledgement, tipped her hat and said, 'Well I'll take my leave of you gentlemen, we've a long return trip ahead and you have work to do. I do hope we meet again should the need arise.'

'Thank you, Madam,' said T (third time lucky). 'Yes, safe journey,' we chorused, and we nodded at each other. She returned to her car.

When she was out of earshot I said, 'You unmentionable tart, Tyler T.' (I would have used his surname if I knew it, or he had one.) 'Well that told her, you really gave her what for, didn't you, gone away with a right flea in her ear, she has—'

Tyler put his finger to my lips to silence me and showed me the envelope. 'That was the real deal,' he said quietly. It had to be said even to my uneducated eye this lady was not the jobbing village joiner who had dusted down their black suit and branched out into undertaking, as was so often the freely admitted case up here. The lady and her staff were exceptional, professional to a fault, and a credit to the industry. The industry shape of things to come perhaps (as Tyler had wishfully and quite cleverly remarked, I thought), and not far off as things have rightly turned out. But only the stuff of dreams for him then.

'Did you see the black ribbon on the back of her hat, looked like the Child Catcher out of *Chitty Chitty Bang Bang*,' I contributed.

'Aye,' said Tyler.

'She's been generous, has she?'

'Aye, more than.'

When I found out how generous, I was fine. I mean they were only a few minutes late and after all we have all been a little late, and things overrun from time to time. It had to be understood, they were only human, and it could happen to any of us. Besides, motorway travel was notoriously variable in its transit, carriageways routinely shut for no obvious reason. It often did seem like the usual week-long twelve mile 'exclusion zone' around a discarded broken wing mirror was a bit excessive though.

It was now our turn to close the day's proceedings. We were like robots that just did it. On looking down onto this coffin it was immediately clear that amongst the thrown-in handfuls of soil from the hand dispenser always offered to mourners, and the two already sorry and soiled-looking red roses, was a piece of paper. When I got in, standing on the coffin in order to shovel the overburden back without drama or clatter, I did not move or disturb the paper. It had landed there from the hand of a far more important person than I. But I did read it, through the dirt and around the rose stalk. It was simply folded and note-like in appearance. On the outside it said 'Mum's Chocolate Cake Recipe'.

Over the years we often saw grave goods thrown onto coffins, by relatives or friends, frequently poignant things - not supplies for the afterlife, as the Egyptians gave Tut et al, but more often mementoes of this one. Commonly an everyday favourite item: a cap, a hat, book, even a walking stick in one case or often just a touching note or meaningful saying.

PJ remembered a funeral once of a lorry driver, a big man, fifteen inches wide coffin at the foot end, thirty two inches at the chest. You could have comfortably had a bar snack opposite a friend on it. We had wheeled him to his resting place in the soft earth on the Victorian bier, the modern equivalent's wheels lost in the mud. He had had a heart attack at the wheel and gently rolled into the back of the wagon in front. On his grave PJ had put in pride of place a wreath shaped like a bone, a tatty well enjoyed ball and a paw shaped card simply saying:

'To my Dad, "Woof you" from your travelling chum, Poppi xxx"

He and his Poppi had been inseparable at home and on the road we later learned, and she had been with him in the cab, her heart clearly now broken too.

On one famous lighter-hearted occasion we peered into the depths of a grave to see a fully wrapped, brand-new, boxed bottle of eighteen years matured Macallan Whisky, clearly placed carefully on the lid and not dropped down. When I told this tale, everyone asked if I had removed it, nudge, nudge, wink, wink. No one believed I had not. Tyler and my reputations were not exactly shining when it came to the amber fluid and went before us. However, I swore then, and swear again now on my own Mother's grave no less, that I buried the whisky where it was placed.

I was sad reading this plain coffin on a bleak day on a random hillside. This lad's name was Ian Wood. He was twenty-six years old. I did my little routine and wished him well on his journey and expressed my sorrow that things for him had got so bad that he had not wanted to stay on our planet or with us any longer. I smiled and wished him well with his baking too, and thought his tombstone, when erected, would have about as much chance of being read as old Robert Mashiter's lower down. But I hoped that some bored gravedigger might read it in some hundred and fifty years or so, if burials were still allowed then, which I doubted. It might have to be left to a yet unborn sightseer who had come to see the view. Ian's young age would seem less tragic then as Robert's now, as he would have been long dead anyway. But it was my privilege to know his favourite cake was chocolate. I mischievously hoped he might bake me one when we met. Perhaps that should have been his inscription. 'liked my Mum's chocolate cake'.

PJ thought that if things ever get so bad (which they reliably do for all of us, it is part of the human condition) 'best advice' would be to walk to the railway line (provided it doesn't run past your window) - not in any way to stress up the train driver or staff or indeed emergency services, just to give yourself chance to change your mind, any and every chance… Remember not to be rash or rush into things: that rarely works in life, so make no exception. Change your clothes, insist on a blue shirt, anything, just create any form of delay and tell someone of your plan for the day. Strangely 'attempted suicide' is in many ways good news for relations and friends… they can work with that.

If you did however get to the tracks without changing your mind, keep walking to the next, as the first track is going the wrong way. If again this is achieved and impossibly there is a train in the same county, your phone is flat, and you did indeed find a blue shirt then check your lottery ticket as it is likely a winner. If not, you are on dodgy ground and it might just not be your day.

Ian's funeral had indeed been at twelve thirty pm as expected and was rightly packed to bursting, by all reports. It was just the seventy miles between the church and the graveyard that nobody mentioned, or was lost in dispatches. I wished his tombstone could have said 'Interred in the winter, after a funeral in Manchester', just to be clear, as well as the mention of his fondness of chocolate cake.

I always wondered whether it was the attractiveness of the undertaker or the amount in the envelope that placated Tyler so completely that day. I suspected the former: he was never any good with money…

We only ever did one funeral with a horse drawn hearse, popular through necessity in Victorian times and indeed at all times really before the good old internal combustion engine seduced us. However, they are becoming increasingly popular again and experiencing something of a renaissance. It occurred to PJ that our fine elegant lady undertaker today would look quite the part on such a vehicle and no doubt had.

Our experience of this delivery from an 'earse with an 'orse (quoting the undertaker who like 'iggs had never encountered the letter 'H' and sounded straight off the set of *'Allo 'Allo*) was, as these specialist funerals often are, very sad. A young mother with no understandable human rhyme nor reason to find herself where she was. She had just been in the wrong place on the wrong day and at the wrong time in a car. The horses were magnificent, their pink and black plumes matching the pink decorations and garlands of the wicker coffin and the mood of the day.

These new wood alternative coffins were becoming more common place too. One such time we had buried a cardboard one with lovely views round Westlet painted on it, but woven wicker and football club colours had all been part of this more modern trend of celebration and indeed conservation and 'carbon footprint' and so on and these products were necessarily getting more common. Woodland burials too had also just arrived. These modern ways however weren't popular with Alf; didn't suit the old school at all:

'Bletherin' things collapse overnight no bloody strength in um, forever gaan back to fill beggars in, level um up, it's findin' enough soil tha'noes and then there's travellin' they don't pay no more, and who's lookin at arty pictures on'th side when thear down thur?'

(Tyler always knowledgeably advised 'not to get him goin'').

Fair to say Alf simply 'didn't get um'.

A more politically correct or polite rendition of Alf's version of events may read; 'They have been known to settle at a somewhat quicker rate than their wooden counterparts'.

Alf's 'newfangled' coffins, (well 'caskets' is a better description regardless of material) did offer the gravedigger some small mercy in the way of their measurement, those standards that PJ had tried to reinvent on his first day. They were rectangular not tapered - a small difference on the face of it, but it meant that a whole two traditional measurements were redundant. No longer did graves have potentially five dimensions but three, probably the first recorded case of '3D' being the advancement on '5D'. A casket's grave had only a depth, a length and one width measurement as opposed to the always two, 'chest and feet' and commonly three if with the addition of 'head'.

Far easier and less biological or reminiscent of a person's actual shape, an important visual step removed thought PJ. Nowadays with the arrival of 'Amazon', when a roll of cling film arrives in a box the size of a coffin, requiring bearing on the shoulder into the house no less, our aversion to boxes has understandably lessened somewhat and they are no longer the visual threat they once were of old perhaps. It is almost a surprise when almost any delivery box doesn't contain a body or part as they are almost without exception always big enough. I wonder if Amazon do indeed sell 'small' parcel boxes on their site as a product? Perhaps they should order some…

I apologise for over-egging this difference in dimension and measurement of graves, but with Alf armed with a tape, the loss of two whole dimensions held importance beyond its station. Two complete: 'I didn't think that would have happened' opportunities gone in one fell swoop was far from being sniffed at as PJ was to find out in due course…

PJ was always pleased that funerals never did (and still largely don't) entice humans into photography, as everything else seems to deserve nowadays to be immediately unnecessarily shared with the planet. Even in these days where your average biro has a camera in it, at funerals it is thankfully still something of a taboo, rightly frowned upon, and broadly not the ‘done’ thing for a funeral to be recorded or remembered. Well not on Facebook or in that way anyway, such individual grieving memories being personal and private. Unless you of course are related to the Queen or of historic importance, then sadly there is the usual media circus.

It has to be said though that in the case of these horses it was almost a shame.

We are all too well aware that weddings are now exclusively the territory of the photographer, even the bride’s mother now playing second fiddle. Quite how photographers have achieved this position is, in PJ’s experience, something of a mystery, but achieve it they have, turning every wedding into as near to a Hollywood mega-buster as they will ever come.

It was funny though once when a lady Tower Captain bell ringer physically threw one such photographer out of the tower for purely safety reasons. The buffoon marched in unannounced and tried to lie down to take a picture upwards and between the moving ropes (it was only a shame that it was a ground floor ringing chamber was the consensus).

Hearses and gravediggers have a common denominator in a funeral. Everything else, people, Vicars, cars, buildings and so on, were multipurpose when it came to celebrations, and could and would be used on happier occasions, indeed even almost immediately in many cases going straight to the 'Funeral Tea' or even 'Party', whatever on earth they are, but they are rarely alcohol free and clearly served all day.

For the humble gravedigger and the hearse however, this was their one moment, their 'raison d'être', their day. No parties, warm reunions or canapes for them (just the odd swig of sherry, Embassy and a stale Scotch egg maybe).

After introductions on the horse drawn day and whilst PJ was inspecting these huge elegant animals during the service, (Tyler had snuck off for a sherry and a cig), one of the horsemen spoke eloquently and from on high, with the austerity and authority of a Judge, and in philosophical tone:

'Nature has taken its course, PJ'

After almost dismissively thinking 'obviously' due to circumstance, PJ did reflect and think that to be a surprising, very profound and potentially meaningful statement by the horseman, and was suddenly nervous of its deserved and expected response.

As PJ looked up at the top hatted gentleman for perhaps guidance as to where the conversation was to lead, trivial or otherwise, he beat him to it, angling his head in gesture and barely noticeable gentle nod, saying:

'Nature's course… behind the horse. You couldn't clear that up for me fella before they come out, could you'

Ah yes, silly me, immediately on seeing the steaming problem.

‘Ha Ha, yes of course Sir’ I replied, thinking it a shame I didn’t grow roses.

It was a close thing though as to what answer I was to give such philosophy and on such an occasion, and I had quite a feeling of relief.

(Shared by the horse no doubt; I’ll swear it winked at me.)

Chapter 10

ROUND PEGS IN SQUARE HOLES

Crocketford was a lovely little village secluded in the hills surrounding Corcastle. It was unusually easy digging too around here. When Tyler told me it dug like cheese, I frivolously asked him what sort, but now we were there he was right, it was great. We finished back-filling a grave there one afternoon on one of those good-to-be-alive summer days, despite being with someone who no longer was. The clay had dug in blocks; you could even do the grave sides with one of those half-moon-shaped tools for the edge of lawns, it planed off completely flat. You nearly had to reassemble the bricks of clay on top of the coffin, as they remained angular throughout and would take donkey's years to settle. It was like filling in a regular hole with huge sugar-lump-shaped spade-sized blocks; we would have been well advised to number them and fit them back together. If there were a graveyard in Legoland it would be thus.

When we had finished Tyler said did I want a pint before we went, as the village pub was just around the corner? It would have been rude not to, even life threatening for me. It wasn't really a question, it was an instruction thinly disguised as one and cleverly transferred any future blame onto me.

We sat on the benches outside the pub. Tyler had 't'owd Stromble' with him today. Such trips were increasingly rare, but from time to time PJ was assured 't'owd lad fancied a run out'. By the looks of him Stromble couldn't have cared less and have taken or left it, but it was good to see him for old time's sake. 'Thought t'owd lad would enjoy is bag of craklin's at pub' Tyler merrily said, betraying that this pint we were enjoying might not be quite the spontaneous opportunity as he had led PJ to believe.

PJ later learned that 'Stromble', whose name had apparently started life as 'Storm' (but evolved, obviously), was Tyler's soul mate. He had been a boisterous, big lolloping thing of a dog by all reports and helped in the digging of many a grave, whether as an observer or 'paws on' physically was never clear.

His digging days were over now but he did still attend on occasions, risking venturing out when his required criteria were met; the weather nice, the ground level, he could be bothered and conditions were generally favourable. Such coincidental occasions in the Lake District were understandably few and far between.

PJ learnt later that graves used to take a lot longer to dig in Stromble's heyday, Tyler spending half his time digging and the other half retrieving his beloved dog. He used to famously call Stromble with a piercing whistle, (that one where you put two fingers in your mouth). With this technique Tyler could call his dog in the next county, but this relied on the dog knowing that he was the intended recipient of the call and that its meaning was that his attendance was now requested, even required. Hearsay reported that Stromble never got the hang of the last bit.

We helped Stromble in and out of the SRi and he enjoyed his bag of pork scratchings and lick of Guinness from a wiped-out ashtray - you could tell by his Guinness lapping technique that this was far from his first time.

I had a foaming pint of beer and Tyler stuck to his Guinness. He'd said once that bitter didn't agree with him, he never went into details thankfully, well not then anyway.

'Do you fancy doing a quick cremated-remains hole on the way home?'

'Where?'

'Sholston,' Tyler replied. 'It's on the coast road, got to be done for one o'clock tomorrow.'

'Yeah,' I said, 'I'm in, great.'

‘It’ll give us a couple of hours extra on that other double tomorrow if we do this now. Won’t take long,’ said T.

We went back to the car, did our pre-flight checks on the trailer, loaded old Stromble, happy with his run out, but equally happy to be overtaken by sleep in the car. We quickly checked the grave again and all was well, the flowers and the tributes looking good in the evening sunshine.

We pulled into the small cemetery on the outskirts of Sholston. Again the dead had been afforded the most wonderful view. The cemetery sloped a bit right-to-left and a track went all the way round, about ten yards in from the boundary wall. We followed the road round until coming up the other side and stopped about halfway up, facing the gates again.

‘This is it,’ T said. ‘All the cremated remains go on this side between the road and the wall. Jump out and start looking for a marker stick.’ Tyler soon found it, just a small distance in from the side of the road. I hadn’t done one of these before so I found myself in uncharted waters.

‘So what’s the story with these then, T?’

Producing a packet of Embassy from his pocket, Tyler replied, ‘Oh, straightforward really, these can’t go wrong.’

I was confident enough now to say, ‘I’ve heard that before.’ He ignored me. Tempting and fate sprang to mind.

‘We’ll just dig a hole about eighteen inches long, a foot wide by about eighteen inches deep. Ashes come in either a case, sometimes wooden or that papier-mâché stuff, or in a plastic jar like them sweet jars when you were a kid. The plastic jars look terrible, not that it matters – often the undertaker or mourners just tip ‘em in. All of um will go in a hole this size,’ said T.

We cracked on. We just tipped the soil onto a board in order to keep the grass clean. Twenty minutes and we were done.

‘We’ve hardly earned a pint,’ I said to T.

‘Yeah I know, shocking i’nt it,’ he replied. We both grinned.

We covered the ankle-snapping hole with a piece of plywood that had been lying about in the trailer.

‘I’ve got some small bits of sheets and greengrocer grass at home. Don’t let me forget them tomorrow,’ said Tyler.

‘Will do,’ I replied.

We went along the coast road for about a mile or so, and where the road turned inland there was an oasis called ‘The Tides’. Stromble elected to stay sleeping in the car, but we again took up position in the pub garden, and had a lovely pint watching a lovely sunset. For quite a gloomy job we saw some terrific places and views, I said.

‘Do you know, Tyler, we ought to write a pub guide.’

‘Yeah,’ said Tyler, basking in the evening sunshine and paying no notice at all. Then after of a moment of reflection, he said:

‘We could, but there’s a lot you’ve not been to yet.’

‘Yes,’ I said, but I was miles away now, almost writing my new book. ‘We could call it “The Dead Good Pub Guide”. D’you get it, “Dead Good”, T?’

‘Yes, I get it.’ He was clearly completely underwhelmed by my comic genius. I smiled to myself over the invention of a first-class title, all in all quietly very pleased with myself. Tyler was noticeably unimpressed in the presence of such brilliance. He didn’t actually put his head in his hands but he might as well have done. Finishing his pint he said, ‘C’mon, Rowling, that’s enough literary genius for one night, let’s go.’

We left with me muttering to myself “The Dead Good Pub Guide” and smiling.

We got back to Cliff Field, where Sam exchanged pleasantries with us whilst on her sheep watering trip round the jungle.

‘I’ll pick you up early doors,’ T said, leaning out of the car window, ‘you’re alright it’s not silly o’clock.’

He had come to learn that I was not a morning person.

‘We’ll do two or three hours on the double then will pop out to Sholston and do the cremated remains. Got to be there for one o’clock, okay?’

With a shouted ‘Bye, Sam’ Tyler went off. Tomorrow’s double was nearby at Seascale, and there was no rush as it was for a funeral the day after.

Tyler picked me up just before nine. We went to Seascale and had a good three hours' digging before we had to go to Sholston.

'That'll do,' Tyler said. 'Loads of time – tomorrow funeral's not till afternoon. Let's go and have a quick pint in Tides, and we'll be right for one o'clock.'

We were soon on our way down the coast road. It wasn't as nice a day today, but not bad.

'Can be a right windy spot, this Sholston, you know. Ended up chasing the sheets across the cemetery last year, it was blowing such a hooley. It was only good luck they got caught up on another gravestone or they'd have been on their way to Ireland,' said a serious Tyler

'That's quite funny,' I said.

'What is?'

'The thought of you tearing about a cemetery chasing flying sheets, very non-PC 1970's slapstick. "Carry On Gravedigging". They never made that film, you could have been a star.'

'Didn't feel very funny. I missed 'em and fell over twice, felt like a right dork.'

I laughed at the imagined picture and indeed film. It would have been funny, likely a classic. We pulled into The Tides and had our quick pint. Tyler appeared to be able to swallow them whole, so he had another half while I caught up.

We got to the cemetery and hid the car the best we could. We moved the plywood hole-cover and set up the little grave, sheets, grass, soil box and all, and waited. It looked quite nice in a doll's house sort of way, a mini copy of a full-size cousin. From our vantage point we had a good view of the coast road and the cemetery gates.

Tyler lit a fag and I asked, 'Have we got any sherry?' Surely Tyler would have a slurp with his cigarette.

'No.' Was I hearing things, had Mr 'Tio Pepe' left the building?

'No?' I said in concern and amazement. 'Was the shop shut this morning?'

I had to get to the bottom of this: panic was beginning to set in, and unusually it was my panic.

Tyler seemed uncharacteristically calm. 'No,' he said. 'If you must know, I'm skint, I couldn't afford any.'

'Well you should have said,' I replied in alarm, already planning my rescue to the nearest Spar. It appeared I truly had become a Tyler recruit.

'Paid my fag slate at the newsagent's, and that was it.'

'Oh,' I said quite downheartedly. I had got used to this gravedigger's misbehaviour, as a perk of the job.

'You'll have to manage on cider,' T said.

Oh thank God, I thought to my disgrace. 'But I thought you had no money?'

'Not enough money to buy sherry,' said T. 'You asked if we had any sherry, you didn't ask if we had any cider. Couldn't afford sherry, but could afford cider. It's in bag behind yer seat.'

I reached round and got the three-litre bottle. 'What? Ten per cent ABV?' This wasn't cider it was rocket fuel, remembering Sooty's grapefruit creation, not quite as strong as sherry but far more of it. I had a slurp and Tyler followed. Our drink-affordability conversation over, we just sat there without a care in the world. Within moments we saw a hearse and cortège on the coast road in the mid-distance.

'Another one for the crem, Tyler,' I said confidently. I unscrewed the cider and readied myself for my next slurp. Whilst having a drink I suddenly became aware of a downward force on the bottle. It was Tyler pushing it down on the end with the palm of his hand. This necessitated my releasing the bottle from my mouth.

Tyler didn't say anything. His eyes were fixated on the windscreen or rather the sight beyond it. I lowered the cider, screwed up the top again, and put the bottle behind the seat on autopilot. The hearse and mourners hadn't driven past. I immediately understood Tyler's silence. There was no easy way to say it but they had driven into and around the cemetery to a point not far from us.

There were two black cars and no fewer than three private cars following in the cortege. The undertaker got out of the hearse, in which there was room for him and a small fold-down seat adjacent to the head of the coffin for the Vicar. Tyler and I still didn't speak, more like couldn't, I think. Could it be they had the wrong cemetery? I thought. But that was the last gasp of hope or lifeline for a condemned man - or men in this case.

We simply looked at each other blankly. I was trying to decide whether Tyler was in my bad dream or he in mine. It was as if time had stood still. We were frozen like a freeze frame of a film, quietly wishing we were somewhere, anywhere else, dead even had appeal. We all know of the expression wishing a hole would open up below us and swallow us up; well I have never known a situation where that was more apt before or since.

Better still for the said hole to miraculously appear and swallow that full-size coffin that had just joined us.

'You have got to be joking,' I finally murmured.

Tyler's usual alcohol-fuelled ruddy complexion had drained away. We had buried people that looked better than he did at that moment. This undertaker had arrived bang on one o'clock with the vicar, coffin, widow, grieving children, relations, next-door neighbours, the whole shebang, and all we had to offer was a very well-presented hole big enough for the deceased to put his toy 'Action Man' in. We had, in short, a hole that would barely take his size nines at a push. We just looked at each other.

The coffin was bedecked with floral tributes, and when I say bedecked I mean it wasn't visible at all, its presence assumed. There were even 'hangers on' on the roof rack. It appeared completely festooned, truly 'inter flora-ed'. There were wreaths on wreaths and endless bunches sprouting and springing forth from what appeared every angle, and 'DAD and HUSBAND' cleverly singing out in white capitals from either side.

For some unfathomable reason these loving flowers inexplicably made things look ten times worse. Unfathomable as they made absolutely no conceivable difference to the size of the approaching catastrophe, their presence being irrelevant for our purposes.

PJ perhaps unkindly hoped the client didn't suffer from hay fever (or the mourners for that matter). A sneezing vicar could never be good and he, in his 'alongside' seat, was right in the thick of the floral firing action, the pollen front line.

If flowers be a measure of love or regard gained in this transient life then this man must have been the Pope, PJ thought trying to drag amusement from despair. It was, however, indisputable that this man was deserving of deeply held affection, earned betwixt the two inevitables of birth and death, and was going to be missed.

They say 'death and taxes' are the only two sure things in life, but birth is the necessary third. PJ thought it only not as common in the saying because Whitehall have not found a direct way to tax it (yet).

To PJ the expression that ‘a picture is worth a thousand words’ suited very well here, as funeral flowers do just that, a visual display of grieving when words have ran out or are simply not enough. Flowers at funerals reflected different approaches and styles to dealing with sadness, PJ observed over the years. Some examples modest, even petite, others as today as flamboyant as a Channel Isles ‘Battle of Flowers’ float, sometimes comically looking like they might, by concealed pilot, drive off under their own steam if left unattended, to join a parade or compete in the nearest Red Bull Soapbox race.

Whether these tributes reflected the family or occupant was never clear and sadly went with them to the grave, as they say.

‘That’ll never fit,’ I said quietly, not intending to be funny, I wasn’t that brave. (I have blamed shock since.) I got a blistering ‘shut up’ and a look from Tyler usually only reserved for Alf: withering. This would have been hilarious if not so serious, or had happened to somebody else. It had been my turn this time to unthinkingly state the blindingly obvious and it was neither useful, nor received well.

This was going to be interesting. We both got out of the car and gingerly approached the undertaker, who had manoeuvred himself well clear of the hearse and following cars for us to have a chat. Surely we were going to get a right royal rollicking. I imagined the undertaker to be quivering with rage.

Tyler knew him, thank God. I wondered what he was going to say. I for one felt like a very small schoolboy who was in serious trouble waiting outside the Headmaster's office.

Tyler started proceedings. 'Derrick,' was his plain greeting. 'I don't know what to say.' This is where Derrick blows his top, goes nuclear, I thought.

'Hi, T,' said Derrick, quite chirpily, I thought, bearing in mind the visual seriousness of the situation. 'You didn't get the message then?'

T said, 'No, I'm sorry.' It was beyond obvious he had not and no conceivable need to ask, 'What message?'

'Look, thought there was a risk this might happen, think mess-up at our end,' Derrick reassuringly said. 'The grave is over there, it's marked, but you weren't to know. Could you have it ready by one o'clock tomorrow?'

'Yes,' said Tyler. We would have said yes to anything at that moment, jumping through fire hoops naked onto nails included I suspected.

'Can you start that one now?'

'Yes' said Tyler with subdued enthusiasm, 'of course'.

'Let me go and explain and get rid of this lot, and I'll come back and see you later.' With this Derrick went back to the cars, speaking to those inside one car at a time before moving off.

'Rather him than me,' said Tyler.

‘You’re not kidding,’ I replied.

We filled in the scratch we had dug for the cremated remains and set up in the body of the cemetery. The grave was marked where the undertaker had pointed.

‘What do you reckon’s gone wrong here then T?’ I asked.

‘Search me,’ he replied, sounding a bit down in the dumps, even for T.

‘Cheer up, it might never happen.’

‘Cheer up, cheer up? Now, Jeffries, just exactly what have I got to be cheerful about?’

‘Well…’ I was struggling, but I knew how much Tyler hated botch-ups. That was why Alf made T’s life so intolerable: he was a gravedigger and a good one, scruffy granted but rightly proud of his professionalism.

‘It could be worse,’ I said. ‘Derrick could have gone mental or it could have been our fault; and you have your health,’ I added, resorting to cliché for reasons I didn’t understand, again shock, I think.

‘What!’ he retorted with obvious irritated impatience. ‘My health! Well you better hope you’ve got yours as well fella.’

‘Why?’ I said naively.

‘Well, Einstein, the previous panic having evaporated, we’ve got to do this one and have you forgotten the other one we’re on with at Seascale, and both for one o’clock tomorrow? We’ll ‘appen be diggin’ all night.’ I had to admit in all the excitement I had forgotten about the Seascale job. With that Tyler positively plunged his spade into the ground.

'I hope this isn't th'owd fella's fault, takin' message and not givin' it me,' growled Tyler at the ground.

Oh please, I thought, hoping for poor Alf's sake that it was not. They blew hot and cold with each other at the best of times, but Tyler would momentarily go more than ballistic with Alf if it were his fault, that was for sure. Derrick had after all only said 'think mess-up at our end'…

About an hour later Derrick returned, not ranting and raving as one might have expected, but with an apology. He said that the family had decided on a cremation but had changed their minds after ordering the funeral. He had instructed us with a cremated-remains hole. He had then asked one of his crew to ring us and tell us of the change, but this had never happened. Great, I thought, Alf's off the hook. Derrick didn't say any more about that non phone call. If he knew whose fault it was he wasn't letting on. It could have been him; we all forget things. We said we were sorry, despite this, and asked how the family had taken it.

'Oh, not too bad, they were sorry about changing their minds. I think one or two of them saw the funny side, and one of the lads said his uncle, the deceased, would have loved it.' Well that was nice, I thought. 'Anyway, these things happen…' said Derrick, this laid back reaction only serving to give credence to my suspicion that it was him who forgot to telephone. He had been surprisingly very relaxed about the whole affair.

‘I’ll see you lads tomorrow.’

‘Righto,’ said T, and Derrick went.

‘Well,’ I said, ‘everyone seems to have said sorry to each other for this one. Nobody’s fault, eh?’

‘Aye.’

‘Yes. Only one apology left now.’

‘What’s that?’

I admit I was looking forward to this more than is normal. ‘“Oh, straightforward really, these can’t go wrong”?’

T looked at me quite sheepishly and said, ‘Who said that?’

‘You know very well who said that,’ I retorted, laughing. ‘I know, I know, I get it. Where’s scapegoat Alf when we need him?’

We laughed and chorused, ‘Well I didn’t think that would have happened!’

Alf was a genius. ‘I didn’t think that would have happened’ was beginning to make a lot more sense. Experience perhaps really is everything!

It was all very well that this ‘misunderstanding’, although serious, had ended satisfactorily if not happily. However, a reality check soon unveiled the harsh truth that we now had about twenty-two hours of almost continuous serious digging to do. Tyler would likely only ‘cheer up’ after considerable progress had been made, so it was to be all hands on deck that night.

The episode did remind me of one official at the local crematorium who always greeted the congregation wholly inappropriately, I felt, as follows:

'I should like to offer you all a very warm welcome to our crematorium today.'

The last time I had been was for my aunty Violet's funeral. We affectionately called her 'Aunty Violent', as she had built tanks - by hand I think - during the war and had been a big strong spinster. (Nobody had ever dared to ask her out - more chance of survival on the front likely).

I thought at the time that the official could have modified his greeting on that occasion, well more personalised it really as that would have offered a nice touch or final smile: 'I should like to offer you all a very warm welcome here today, especially you Violet.'

That always amused PJ, nearly as much as the irony when the same crematorium suffered a fault and burnt down not long after…!

'They didn't think that would have happened'

(There were thankfully no reported casualties although one badly burned body was recovered from the scene…)

Chapter 11

BIT OF A GIRL

Mardale was a small market town up in the hills on a terrace above the River Kent, a name, I always thought, that could easily cause geographical confusion in conjunction with a dodgy answering machine and operator. The graveyard offered a spectacular view of the river, the distant hills and the valley below. The view was named after an artist, who had reportedly been inspired by its beauty and painted it, thereby making it famous.

The phone rang at Cliff Field. It was Tyler.

‘Hi, PJ. You okay for Mardale tomorrow? Bit of fun for you there – I’ll let you know on the way. ‘Bout ten o’clock?’

‘Yes, no worries,’ I replied.

‘Great stuff, see you, bye.’

‘Bit of fun’ by their standards was more of a worry than harmless intrigue. I thought, well only tomorrow will tell.

Tyler was on time and we set off.

‘So what sort of fun is in store today?’

‘Well…’ Tyler paused to light up. ‘First we’ve got to do a reopen at Castlebrow, just this side of Mardale, then we’re off to Mardale itself for a new experience for you.’

‘What’s that?’

‘We’re going to dig one up.’

‘Dig one up!’ I exclaimed.

‘Yes,’ he calmly replied. Well that was the starting pistol. I was suddenly an extra in *Midsomer Murders*.

‘Why?’

‘You’ll find out,’ said T, grinning from ear to ear. Wasn’t he just a treasure and tease, I didn’t think.

The reopen went without incident except for the one visitor we got whilst digging, who was in fairness able to clear up one thing I'd noticed about the headstone when we arrived.

'Look at this,' I'd said to Tyler. 'How old is this lady we are about to bury?'

'I dunno,' was his uninterested reply.

'Well are you sure this is the right one?'

'Why?'

'Well, this bloke was born in 1886, right, and died when he was fifty in 1934. Well how can this be his wife? He's been dead for sixty-two years, she must be in her hundreds.'

Tyler took the point. 'Let me go to car. I've got a bit of paper wi' t' name on.'

He returned with a fag packet of a note. 'Richardson's t' name. Third row in from the path. Yes, this is it.'

The visitor that appeared was an elderly man with two walking sticks.

''Ey-up, lads, this yan for old Ma Molly then?'

'Well a Mrs Richardson, sir,' I replied. 'They don't tell us the Christian names as a rule.'

‘Ah,’ he said, ‘be old Molly then. I heard afore that she’d deed.’ My ears pricked up as maybe this gentleman had the solution to my perceived mathematical impossibility.

‘Do you know how old she was, sir?’ I asked. ‘Because we half wondered if we were in the right place as her husband died such a long time ago.’

‘Harry? He did that, lad. Mus’ be sixty year ‘appen. Molly, now well, let us think, she’d be a bit owder than me, and I’s eighty-nine, be ninety-two or so if she were a day.’ This still did not sound old enough to me, but it was all testing my mental arithmetic to its limit. I’d work it out later.

The man went on, ‘Aye, smashing couple, she’d be a bit younger than ‘im, tha knows, Harry would ‘a’ bin twenty or so years older than me. I used to work on his farm as a lad. Aye, very accommodating and understanding man, Harry,’ he mused. ‘’Twas allays said when copper come te farm about sommat once, all kids pushed thur noses te kitchen winder, one o’ them with small panes o’ glass, tha knows, nearly a little face in every little bit.’

‘When copper enquired about family’s well-bein’, Harry just said they were all fine, and when copper asked how many, Harry said seven and counting. Were not all his, tha knows. He told copper, pointing at ‘em in turn, that yan was thrown by butcher, that yan by posty, another by schoolmaster likely. ‘Twas allays thought in village that Molly was right friendly like, tho’ ne’er said… Harry were proud of lot of ‘em though, to him they were ‘is.’

Indeed Mr Richardson must have been an understanding and patient man; it rather sounded like Molly had been the more 'accommodating' of the two.

'How did he die?' I asked.

The old fella's tone changed. 'Terrible thing, shouldn't have happened, nice fella, didn't deserve it, just a cock-up with one o' lads who worked for him on farm, lad was never same after either. Lad left a bolt off on gate or sommat and Harry got gored by t' bull. Couldn't get out o' way, horns went right through him, they said, couldn't get 'is body off 'em.'

Enough, enough, I thought, mentally clutching my abdomen. I didn't want to hear any more of the gory, in its true meaning, details. His description was horrific enough.

'When's funeral, lads?' asked the man.

'Two o'clock tomorrow,' said Tyler.

'Thanks, lad, 'appen might pop by just to wish her off. Bye.'

'Bye, sir,' we chorused.

'Love them old codgers,' said Tyler. 'Such characters.'

'Yes, that's what I thought when I met you.'

'Yeah right, need you' he laughed.

(And we think we've invented promiscuity…)

There was no pub in Castlebrow, just a fancy hotel, so we headed to Mardale where there were a few. We settled into this country pub, brasses, open fire, the lot. It was about one o'clock.

Tyler said, 'Go steady on the beer, PJ, we've got to kill best part of an hour yet.'

'It's all right,' I replied, 'I've got some money.' Tyler had never been known to go steady unless funds didn't allow and certainly never the one to suggest such restraint. He must be ill…

'No,' said Tyler, 'we've got an appointment at two with the coppers.'

'Police?' I gulped, louder than intended. With Tyler's car we would probably get locked up there and then. I at the very least would likely be an accessory to some vehicular misdemeanour by association no doubt, and stinking of drink would feature quite highly on the list. But I was only guessing. My mind was racing.

'Yes.'

'What for?'

'They've got to be there by law while the undertaker shows us which one to dig up, and be there tomorrow when we rebury. Vicar will come to do his bit.'

I had to get to the bottom of things. 'So why are we digging it up?'

'Her,' he interjected.

‘Is it a murder? Wrong diagnosis? How long has she been buried for?’ I was conscious of issuing quick-fire machine-gun like questions. I had obviously been watching too much telly.

‘Calm yourself,’ laughed Tyler. ‘Nothing so sinister or glamorous, but as to when she was buried that I do know, September 14th last year.’

‘That’s very precise. How can you be so sure?’

‘Well I buried her, got the date from t’owd fella’s book.’

‘You mean you pair keep records?’ I said in astonishment.

‘He does… of a fashion. That was the second time.’

‘Second time?’

‘Yes. Her name is Elizabeth Tomkinson.’

‘So that makes this—’

‘Yes,’ interrupted Tyler, ‘the third time.’

‘Well how… don’t tell me, Alf’s records?’

‘No, ha haa, not this time. Everyone round here’s name is something-son, bit like Iceland, interbreeding of the past? Would have been like being on an island here years ago, middle of nowhere, no new blood.’

‘How do you know about Icelandic names?’ I asked through interest as I had been to Iceland on a geology trip, fascinating place.

‘Used to watch *Mastermind,* Magnus Magnusson and all that.’ Well Tyler really was full of surprises, but it had to be said he was no daft egg when it came to the pub quiz.

‘Well how did this happen?’

‘By all reports Mr and Mrs Tomkinson retired to Mardale a few years ago and after a good few years hubby snuffed it and she moved away, memories and all that. That was about twenty years ago. She had no next of kin and stated in her will she wanted to be buried back here with her husband. The first time we buried her was with a Mr Tomkinson by the wall about eighteen months ago. I remember the vicar dithering about whether he was the right Mr Tomkinson then. That vicar in due course left for pastures new and the new lady vicar was installed. Not long after she got here, she received a letter from the children of the Mr Tomkinson by the wall, asking who had been buried with their dad as that was their Mum’s plot, and she was still very much alive. So up she came! The second mistake was identified by one of the old girls in the town, who knew Elizabeth and her husband.’

Tyler took a final slurp of his Guinness. ‘C’mon, best be going, we don’t want to keep this lot waiting.’

On the walk across to the churchyard, I said, ‘Well how come a third time?’

Tyler said the old girl that knew them was right when she supplied the initial ‘G’, so they got him by his name G. Tomkinson (Gerald). ‘So in she went with 'im.' But then last week a newly retired bod who had joined the PCC was delving a bit into the graveyard records (this was a common occurrence amongst newly retired busybodies who wondered how things had conceivably functioned before their timely arrival, and was not always universally welcomed or necessary). But in this case lo and behold the newbie had annoyingly, but correctly, established that there were in fact not two currently single (as in buried on their own) Mr Tomkinsons in here, but three, two of the three inconveniently sharing the same names, both Christian and surname, so dear Elizabeth had been reburied with the second Mr Tomkinson and first Gerald Tomkinson. We were therefore now moving her into the grave of the other and second Gerald Tomkinson, who she was, by now, only alleged to have been married to. This would finally put her to rest, all being well, with her husband, or ex-husband, depending on your point of view. 'Till death us do part', well more 'Till death us do get together again' in Liz and Gerry's case, hopefully…

When we arrived our welcoming party was already there.

'Sorry we're late,' said Tyler.

'Good afternoon, Tyler, you're not, we've only just got here ourselves,' said the police officer. 'And you are…?'

'Philip Jeffries, sir,' I replied.

'Okay, welcome, Philip. Well here we go again then, chaps, bring her up. Will you be ready to move her by tomorrow? Give you a chance to get them both dug. Don't move her until we are all here though, just like last time. Shall we say three o'clock in the afternoon? Should be quiet round and about then. I'll bring the Home Office papers, Vicar, for you to scribble on them as before. Any questions?'

I later learned that you had to have Home Office approval before you are allowed to move a body once it has been put in the ground.

Tyler chirped up, 'Just one thing, Officer, could we move the reburial back until four, as we've got one at one o'clock at Castlebrow?'

'Oh Molly,' said the officer, 'you doing her as well?'

'We are,' said T.

'Well if that's okay with all present?' He waited for nods of approval from the vicar and undertaker. 'Well that's done then. Four o'clock it is, Tyler.'

'Thanks,' T replied, acknowledging all and we dispersed.

We returned to the car to collect our stuff and made a start. We had to dig down to Mrs Tomkinson, then cover it up, dig down to Mr Tomkinson and likewise cover it up. We took one each. So tomorrow we had to bury Mrs Molly Richardson, before digging up Mrs Tomkinson, moving her and burying her again. It was developing into a bit of a crazy day really.

We were to bury Molly, bless her, who had by all reports been a bit of a girl before she had died, then rebury Elizabeth in with her third chap, as she had managed through no fault of her own to become a bit of a girl after she had died…

Everything went as planned the next day. Elizabeth's coffin thankfully held together, for which we were grateful. It wasn't one of those increasingly popular cardboard or raffia affairs, or it would have been a different matter. Finally, she and her beloved Gerald, her real husband, were together again, after her adventures, as were Molly and Harry after an enormous sixty-two years apart. I hoped they were all pleased to see each other and had forgiven any absences.

I got it in the end; Molly was seventeen years younger than Harry, giving her a year of birth of 1903, making her ninety-three when she died. She was thirty years old when Harry died, and she brought up the seven children on her own and ran the farm, which was undoubtedly no mean feat. The old man had said she had no more children or relationships that he knew of after that appallingly dreadful accident that befell Harry those sixty-two years before. In death she had been completely faithful to Harry, just not in life. Dare say he wouldn't have minded. It's a funny old world, isn't it, thought PJ.

Chapter 12

TWO FOR THE PRICE OF ONE TWICE

Lower Huntsby was a place we visited reasonably frequently, but only when necessary of course. It was another village which had the church at its heart with an extended graveyard just outside the village, similar to those more common in Scotland. There was a graveyard immediately around the church, but it was long full and closed like so many. As the villages grew in Victorian times with the introduction of the railway, new graveyard sites had to be established. Lower Huntsby was a typical example of this, the new graveyard being established in 1901. It didn't do to dwell on why the place was called Lower Huntsby as an Upper Huntsby there was not. I never did work that one out.

These newer graveyards often had a better provision of tracks and footpaths and nearly all had a shed or chapel. Huntsby was no exception. It had a limestone road going around the boundary, with arterial paths branching off at regular intervals. Today we were just filling in a single, three in from the main track. The digging the day before had gone well. It was good soil that had held up overnight, which was always a bonus.

As was usual, Tyler and I were out of sight as the burial took place; this time behind the mower shed, which offered camouflage and a good view of the proceedings. It was pleasant sitting here in the good weather with the obligatory bottle of sherry, Tyler with his cigarettes and a noteworthy piece of overgrown graveyard in front of us: all was well with the world.

'What do you reckon happened here?' I said to T. 'Do you think the fella who mows it ran out of petrol?' I smiled, congratulating myself on my clever remark.

'No, sure it wasn't that.'

'How can you be so sure?'

'Because it's one of mine and t'owd fella's, we mow this 'un.'

'Oh,' I said sheepishly, although they had run out on many occasions of more than just petrol. Spades sprang to mind, so I didn't feel my comment completely unfounded.

As I was thinking this, Tyler said, 'Anyway what do mean ran out of petrol? 'Cause we didn't, as it 'appens, well not that day.'

'Well why didn't you mow this bit, if not petrol? It looks a mess, left like this.'

'We're not allowed to,' Tyler advised.

'What?' I exclaimed.

‘Local Parochial Church Council (PCC) decided that they wanted a ‘designated’ la-di-da wild area.’

‘What for?’

‘To encourage wild-flowers and butterflies and the like.’

‘What, by growing three-foot-high dead grass? You’re winding me up.’ I questioned.

‘No, I think they’re jumping on the bandwagon, if you ask me. Now don’t get me wrong, I’m up for this environment bit meeself, we are buggering planet up and that’s no lie, but there’s places and places, if you know what I mean.’

‘What? Do they really think graveyards could ever be environmentally friendly?’ I said. ‘I ask you. How environmentally friendly are they under the ground, water tables and all that,’ the geologist in me dropping into the conversation.

‘Don’t go there, best not, doesn’t bear thinking about,’ said T, pulling a face, ‘you don’t ‘ave to be a geologist to think that.’

‘It would be environmentally friendly if we grew buttercups on the M25 but it’s not going to happen, not to mention Heathrow,’ I replied.

‘Be double Brownie points for the chinless wonder whose idea it was, though, I bet’ said Tyler

‘Not only is church looking like doing their bit fer savin’ t’world, but they cut the amount they pay us too, so looking good in the Church books too. A round of applause all round, I reckon. Fact that looks a mess doesn't crop up.' (We smiled at the word).

'So you mean I could splash out a grand on my granny's headstone…'

'And the rest'

'To have it displayed behind three foot of dead grass and weeds?'

'Indeed,' laughed T.

'Well I think that's outrageous, and what about all the old stones. Look, they've vanished, and on top of that it makes the whole place look scruffy, uncared for. I mean, look at that military one over there, shining like a light. War graves folk won't let theirs be covered up. They do a fantastic job the world over. That should be the benchmark, in my book. That's how you do it.'

'You can get off your orange box with me, PJ. You're preaching to the converted. 'Ey-up?' He stopped.

We both watched as the coffin was unloaded, and then when all assembled were ready, it was lowered. We had a good view as we were looking from the vicar's end; the other three sides of the grave were flanked by mourners. After the usual proceedings - first the vicar, then the chief mourners and so on parading past throwing in their little handful of soil and then standing chatting for a few minutes - T said,

'They're off, best go and do our stuff. Fancy a quickie with the birds and bees before we go?'

‘Go on then,’ I replied. At that we shared a sherry.

When the coast was clear we went to the grave and everything was in order. I couldn’t personalise my little ceremony bit using a name though, because the nameplate was covered quite thickly with soil the mourners had thrown in, so the best I could do was a ‘God bless you, dear person’.

As we removed the ropes, the greengrocer grass, the purple side sheets, and finally the planks as normal, we were rudely interrupted by the unmistakable sound of a car horn. It beeped just once, but it was enough to attract our attention and was a long way from normal in a graveyard. It had been about twenty minutes since the funeral and the departure of the vehicles and mourners.

A grey transit-type van approached down the track that the cortège had left from. When I say approached, I mean approached as if ‘The Stig’ were driving it. Its alarming speed was far from the usual sedate pace at which vehicles normally travelled in such places. There was an arm waving furiously from the driver’s side. It was almost cartoon-like to watch. The van slammed on its brakes and shuddered to a halt just adjacent to where we were.

‘Stop, stop!’ came the shout from a clearly deliriously stressed undertaker, who almost threw himself out of the barely stationary van, with the vicar closely following as if in pursuit.

‘Stop, thank God,’ said the out-of-breath undertaker as he got to us, and bent with his hands on his knees, panting. ‘Sorry, Vicar,’ he said, his apology clearly aimed at the vicar for the 'thank God' remark and not the subsequent required running.

'On the contrary,' said the Vicar, 'thank heaven is quite appropriate. I was thinking the very same myself.'

'What's to do, Graham?' said Tyler. He was on first-name terms with most undertakers.

'It's the wrong one,' said Graham.

'The wrong place?' Tyler asked, as surely that was the only available variant that could be called wrong. 'Well this is where it was marked,' he went on, as the first volley of leaping to our defence.

'No, no,' said Graham, 'not the grave, Tyler, the body, the wrong body, sorry Vicar, I mean person!'

That as you can imagine is not verbatim, or chapter and verse, of what Graham actually said and he started apologising to the Vicar profusely for the language almost immediately. In Graham's defence it would have been very difficult to stay calm or say otherwise, this being one such collection of circumstances where swearing was difficult or impossible to avoid, shall we say.

Well this is going to be good, I thought.

Gesturing toward the Vicar, Graham said, 'The Reverend noticed as we were taking flowers off, and swinging the coffin over the hole, that the name on the plaque on the coffin was different from the name we had just held the funeral service for.'

'I threw some soil on immediately I saw it,' said the Vicar. He was almost congratulating himself.

'It's a good job the Reverend has lightning reactions,' said Graham. 'We've got the right one in the van. Vicar said we can swap it, that's right, isn't it, Vicar?' He looked up as if pleading to him for much needed confirmation and reassurance; even divine permission.

'Indeed, I did Graham. Not ideal, but I can see no other option' said a clearly uncomfortable and concerned man. PJ mentally added 'Not ideal' to the list of top ten of understatements.

'It's a good job your workshop's nearby,' Tyler said.

'You're not kidding,' said Graham. ''Bout knackered me getting back here in time though.'

After the recent goings-on at Mardale, we were well au fait with the relevant permissions required to move a coffin, regardless of the length of time it had been underground. But there was no time to tell the Home Office about this catastrophic admin failure and therefore no relevant permissions.

We looked at the Vicar as his colour drained away:

'Oh God-ood- ness, this is awful, but on my head be it, and… well… it's not been covered up yet,' he said to himself in justification.

On reflection I thought 'not covered up' did sort of qualify as 'not buried'. Although I think the Home Office Rule 'Letter of the Law' probably means 'not moved' once the coffin has touched down as it were. Not an altogether satisfactory expression given the current circumstances admittedly, as we covered up that it was not covered up…

The Vicar stood by as Graham went to get the bier. We were going to have to get this one out and put it in the van, then do the swap. We popped back to the shed, saying to the Vicar we were looking for a ladder. We weren't really: Tyler wanted a fag, and we both needed a sherry.

Out of earshot Tyler said, 'Well this is a new one on me …right mess up'

'No doubt we'll find out' I said.

T went on, 'I thought t'Vicar was a bit lively onto that soil box.'

'I sort of clocked that too, let's hope mourners didn't' I said.

We returned and arrived back at the same time as Graham.

'No ladder?' said the Vicar.

'Er, no,' said T, 'should manage though.' (A classic example of the need of a memory when employing fibs, but he got away with it).

'Right, what's the plan then,' said Graham.

'Well we will get this one out as quick as possible. Is your van as near as you can get it, Gray?'

'Well, I could come on the grass a bit,' said Graham.

‘Yes please,’ said T. ‘Nearer the better. I’ll get the ropes back on.’

The Vicar stood there uneasily, no doubt wishing this was all over. He was quite a young fella and this really must have been the stuff of nightmares for him. It would be for anyone.

Tyler hopped down onto the coffin (the Vicar visibly winced) and said to me: ‘Pass us a rope, PJ.’ This I duly did. Tyler had to kneel on the coffin to put the rope back on.

‘Bother,’ he didn’t say, which I duly repeated. This wasn’t something even T did every day and getting the rope back through the ring was a more muddy and fiddly job than you might imagine.

‘Sorry, Vicar,’ I said. He simply acknowledged me; he had that look of someone who suffers from sea sickness boarding a ferry. I am sure he hoped the language would not deteriorate further. It didn’t, but it proved a close call.

‘What’s up?’ I said.

‘The flipping’ (T remembered who was listening, thank heaven, if only just) ‘rings have bitten into soil at this end. Give us spade, will yer PJ.’

He took the spade and started to dig at the foot end into the grave wall so he could clear the rings. He looked like a lugworm-digger on the sands plunging down to catch his bait.

‘That should do it,’ he said, and finally came up victorious with the ends of his rethreaded rope. He repeated the process at the head end, which was far simpler, as the rope being tight at the feet meant the rings at the head were looser.

‘When is this one’s real funeral?’ said T to Graham.

‘Oh, not until the beginning of next week, I was going to ring you about that. It’s just a reopen over there’ he pointed up the graveyard ‘but I might as well show you now before you go.’

‘It’s a good job this one wasn’t a crem job Gray, or we’d really be in it.’

‘Yes, don’t,’ replied a thoughtful Graham. Small mercies, rare that they were, were very welcome at that moment.

‘Why?’ I asked the two of them, a little mystified.

It was Tyler who answered. ‘No rings on the ends of crem jobs P, no lowerin’,’ he explained. I had been abbreviated - whether that was a promotion or demotion wasn’t clear.

‘Oh, I never knew that,’ I said.

‘Why would yer,’ said T. ‘You’d not see they weren’t there unless you were at crem.’

I was in good company as the Vicar said, ’I’ve never noticed that either, to my shame, and I do both all the time.’

‘And we’ve been singing your praises about powers of observation and reaction times,’ I said boldly.

‘Obviously misplaced,’ said the Vicar. We all had a good laugh at that. I was getting to like this Vicar, he was a sport.

It was all pretty straightforward after that. Mind you, it took all four of us, including the Vicar, to lift the client out. We did try to keep his vestments clean, but to his credit he was on the tools and got stuck in. The graveyard was quiet, thankfully. We knew that if anyone had got this picture it might have embarrassingly ended up in the local rag.

We did the swap and the Vicar gave number two a blessing. There was no issue with the flowers now they were married to their rightful owner. Wrong coffin, right flowers so fifty percent not all that bad?

Graham said, ‘Thanks, Reverend, and you, lads. That was a close thing.’

‘May I ask how this has come to pass, Graham?’ said the Vicar.

‘Oh, my ex-apprentice joiner just got the wrong one out of our Chapel of Rest. There were two, and the young scallywag didn’t ask which one to put in the hearse. Nice lad, just a bit limited between the ears. My fault, though, I didn’t check. Back to the old adage if you want something doing, do it yourself.’ Graham laughed.

The language was very definitely for the Vicar’s benefit, as ‘young scallywag’ would, I’m sure, not have been what he had really called him.

The Vicar said, ‘Graham, I noticed you used the prefix ‘ex’, about your trainee?’

‘Yes’

'Do I take it you have fired him then?'

'Yes, sir, about twenty minutes ago, just before I left to come back here.'

'Well, Graham, has he been a good addition to the business until now?' said the Vicar with concern.

'Aye, has that, been all right. I'd had high hopes for the lad sir. He was well upset when I told him; well shouted it at him.'

'Well, these two gentlemen have worked tirelessly to help you out, and not forgetting they have still got to fill it in?'

'And if it wasn't for the Reverend's eagle eye,' Tyler interrupted, 'you could have been right in the proverbial.' I knew where the Vicar and Tyler were going now.

'You all want me to give him his job back, don't you?' said Graham.

'Well, Graham,' said the Vicar, 'a little bit of Christian kindness and forgiveness never goes amiss, and all is well now. And in your own words, Graham, you have stated that he is good and it was indeed your fault.'

Nicely put, Vicar, I thought.

'Give the lad his job back, Gray, you tart. You're only cutting off your nose to spite your face,' said Tyler, never one to mince his words.

'I couldn't have put it better myself,' said the Vicar. I was sure he could, but he was very polite. The archetypal diplomat.

‘Well better the devil you know, I suppose,’ sighed Graham in defeat. ‘Oh, sorry, Vicar,’ he added.

‘No apology necessary, Graham, very true.’

‘Well I’d better be off. I’ll go and get my lad back. He’s going to be busy tonight cleaning that coffin, got to be like a mirror again by tomorrow. Don’t suppose he will make that mistake again so it will be a learning curve. And I haven’t got another box. Lift, Vicar?’

‘Yes, I’m sure it will be beautiful once more when we meet next week – and yes please. I’ll see you two gentlemen next week and Graham, point of order, they are not boxes.’

‘Sorry, Vicar,’ Graham grovelled.

‘Look forward to it,’ I said.

The Vicar and Graham thanked us, and we reciprocated. I heard Graham ask Tyler if he could settle-up next week for both and he’d get a bit more for today’s debacle and fun and games. That was another one for the right mess record books. The four of us were bordering on firm friends by the time they left, thrown together by adversity. At least I could do my little ceremony now with the knowledge that the new resident was called Richard. I felt it all-the-more important on this occasion as he could do with all the ceremony he could get after missing out on the church one. The Vicar had done a good graveside sort of ‘field’ service, to his credit though - just no hymns, and I hoped he had attended his service anyway, in spirit if not in body.

‘C’mon you, first things first,’ Tyler said as he headed for the shed. ‘We’ll fill him in a bit.’

‘Did Graham say where the other grave was?’ I asked.

‘Yes, up there about five rows, given me the name.’

‘Now hold on, Tyler, you know what a mess everyone got into at Mardale remembering names?’

‘Nah, be all right, trust me.’ He had that ‘Terminator’ look in his eye, made worse by the fact that I knew ‘he’d be back’, next week at least.

‘Well how can you be sure, when they all end in ‘son’ round here,’ I said with obvious near panic in my voice. I was, on past performance, worried about this admin.

‘I’ll remember,’ he said.

‘Well I’m not sur—’ I started to say.

‘Rekininski.’

‘What?’

‘Rekininski. The bloke’s name. That’s half the reason the Vicar noticed it on the coffin ‘cause the service he’d just performed was for a Richard Brown.’

‘Oh,’ I said sheepishly. ‘Rekininski?’

‘Yes, and that’s also why I don’t need to write it down.’ Even I had to concede it was not a name easily forgotten or often heard in our neck of the woods. 'I'll check but if there do happen to be two Rekininskis when we come back, we will just have to sort it, right after I've eaten my hat.'

I nearly went into a sulk because he didn't tell me sooner.

'Got you going then, did I?' mused T.

'Moi? Never,' I lied and we smiled at each other, on our way back to infill poor Mr Brown.

Lower Huntsby was to throw a couple more challenges at us in those next weeks. One evening Tyler and Alf appeared at Cliff Field with an assorted shopping list of materials. A load of two-inch by one-inch rough-cut slats, a new box of small galvanised nails, and a large roll of chicken wire. It wasn't like the gruesome twosome to use anything new, so immediately suspicious and a mystery. I perhaps should have heard the alarm bells ringing then.

Stan was at Cliff Field that night. He was on with another foreigner for us on the pig pens and had got his lad with him.

'What are you on with, T, with all t' gear?' said Stan, with equal and knowledgeable suspicion. He was very particular in his work. I was as keen as anyone to know what Tyler's answer would be.

'We've got to make a pen for those daft buggers at Huntsby – they're a pain in the arse' said Alf, direct as usual and with uncharacteristic emphasis. It was clear that whatever this creation was to be, it did not meet with Alf's approval.

‘What for?’ Stan chirped up.

‘A flower-protection cage.’

‘A what?’ Stan and I chorused.

‘I know, I know,’ said Tyler.

Before he could go on, I said, ‘What, the place where they’ve got the wild bit?’

‘Yes, yes,’ he replied. ‘I’ve come here with me groundsman’s hat on for ‘em tonight. Thought I could lay it out ‘ere easier than at yom, if that’s okay, PJ?’

‘Of course,’ I said, assuming that ‘yom’ meant ‘home’.

Stan was by far the most practical of us and started asking sensible questions about dimensions and the like.

Sam appeared. ‘What are you lot up to, other than no good,’ she said, which got a laugh. She vanished and was soon back with some of those Continental lagers.

Stan’s youngster Adam looked on longingly, as we all do at fourteen, wondering if he could have a beer. ‘Dad?’ he said.

‘Not now, Adam,’ was the rebuttal. He looked downhearted, but Stan and Tyler were firmly in pencil and fag packet mode, designing their creation. I wondered if I might have more luck.

‘Stan,’ I said, ‘can your Adam have a beer?’

Stan glanced at Adam. 'Just one then, make it last and don't tell your mother.' That went for me too, I think, as I was inextricably linked in this supply chain. I opened a bottle and handed it to Adam.

'Thanks, PJ, wicked.' I felt like he wanted to scurry off and hide with this new prized possession, but he had a civilised sip, and sat on the wall. What the 'wicked' word was all about I knew not.

After ten minutes or so it was all hands on deck. The design team announced they wanted six panels making and a cage about five feet wide by eight feet long consisting of two end panels and two panels each side to use the wood efficiently and give it strength.

'When is the deadline, Tyler,' Sam said, always one to ask the pertinent question. Must be her management skills coming to the fore, I thought.

'Tomorrow,' stated Alf, pleased to put his five penn'orth in.

'Tomorrow,' I said.

'Yes,' came my reply.

'How long have you known?'

'Sin' yesterday,' said Alf. 'Couldn't get the stuff till today.'

That had cleverly, or unknowingly (I wasn't sure which), batted away my next question as to why so last-minute. It almost sounded like they might just have a credible reason for delay here, which for these two was unusual if not unheard of, as most delays were completely avoidable and, nine times out of ten, their own fault.

For the next three hours, before the light started to go, it was frenzied activity akin to *Scrapheap Challenge*, and we, as they, were against the clock. I was for the most part the gofer, as my shed was awash with tools in state-of-the-art disorder. The whereabouts of tools was solely influenced by where I last used them and therefore known only to me. I had fifteen hammers at my height, dead relative's tools and the like; by the next year I was down to half a dozen. They were not lost, I just couldn't remember where I had put them down. I imagine a few were along a new fence I had built, but I'd need a metal detector to find them.

Sam was in charge of unrolling and cutting the chicken wire, Stan and Tyler the frames, Adam was the runner, whatever that is, and Alf counting the cable ties (where he was considered safe enough and could do least damage). I was considered only marginally more reliable or useful than Alf, so it was fair to say that I surprised all present when I produced my contribution of an industrial stapler that I had built our dovecote with; it was 'mustard' for attaching chicken wire to anything, including the fast-developing required panels.

10... 9… 8… 7… There wasn't a countdown, but it felt like there should be. By dusk it was done, and loaded onto the trailer, ready for the following day. After lots of mutual appreciation and a couple more beers all was well and ready.

During the post-mortem I said to Tyler, 'What's a flower-protection cage for anyway?' its purpose having been almost overlooked in the excitement of making it.

‘The wild area,’ T said, ‘has attracted wildlife into the graveyard.’ Very good, I thought, the fact that it wass working was surely its purpose.

‘Clever lot at Huntsby, aren’t they? A wild area attracting wildlife,’ I said.

‘Shut up,’ said Tyler, unusually firmly. ‘It is attracting wildlife, but the wrong sort of wildlife.’

‘The wrong sort of wildlife? Did this ‘Church Council’ retire from British Rail perhaps, with the leaves problem?’ I surmised.

‘You’d think so…’

‘What exactly is the wrong sort of wildlife?’

‘Well, they wanted to encourage butterflies, dragonflies and the like…’

‘And?’ I interrupted.

‘’Old on, give us chance,’ said Tyler. ‘They’ve got rabbits and deer but not butterflies, and they want a cage for us, the gravediggers. Well not for the gravediggers…’ Although a case could be made for that, I felt sure, at least we would know where Alf was. ‘But for the gravediggers to use to put over the floral tributes on new graves, straight after funeral.’

This was an effort to stop the deer eating the said flowers as there had apparently been a complaint. After the last recent grave we did, the relatives visited the following day, as is often the case - indeed sobers them up in many cases - only to be greeted by a load of stems stuck into the tossed-about remains of the oasis blocks. The offenders were obviously quite partial to the odd chrysanthemum and assorted fresh flowers; they probably made a nice change from that dry long grass in the 'conservation' area.

'We have been summoned to go and tidy up the wildlife's work and deliver our cage for the future,' finished Tyler.

'A funeral sounds great fun if you're a deer or a rabbit,' I said. 'They must have thought a takeaway had opened. You could always send the owd fella there to go and shoot at 'em from the car.'

This got a ripple of laughter, much to Alf's embarrassment. I leaned towards Alf and apologised. He just coloured up and laughed with us; he had a surprisingly deep laugh for a little fella.

We delivered our cage and tidied up the mess left by the deer, but I thought at least the flowers were appreciated. Under our cage they would soon lose their appeal and look weary. If the deer had left it a day or two after a funeral, they'd have been away scot-free, but there was no talking to them, just they were so quick off the mark. Fresh veg.

Subsequently there were further reports of flowers going missing from Huntsby and the integrity of our cage was called into question. We checked it thoroughly, and apart from the odd crack, which we repaired, it was sound… and we were not the guilty party.

Months later we heard that, after an ambulance had been called for some minor domestic incident involving a lady in a nearby cul-de-sac, she had been discovered to have a living room decked out like a florist's - vases and all. The case of the phantom flower-thief was solved. If she had not broken a vase and cut herself thereby requiring the ambulance, no one would ever have known… All very sad really.

Huntsby provided us with another unexpected conundrum. We completed a routine, run-of-the-mill reopen and burial of a wife with her husband. All done and dusted. Well I say routine, but it did have a peculiarity. You can always tell when you are digging to reopen a hole, any hole, doesn't have to be a grave. There is always evidence that it has been dug before, and this evidence lasts for ever. Like a boulder that had had to be broken and that sort of thing. Typically, the sides of the new hole would fall in, exposing the original cut in the ground. When we were digging this reopen, no such evidence manifested itself. I couldn't stay that day, so T had continued alone.

Tyler had dug enough graves to know that this didn't feel right, to such an extent that he stopped digging. He rang Graham and expressed his concerns. Graham did what checks he could and gave T the reassurance he required, and so he carried on. When he got to the bottom there was no sign of the husband's coffin, even with the tapper or jumping up and down to see if the ground flexed, which would be the case if the first occupant had been buried deeper than was now required. My own mother's grave was a good example. It was hugely deep and dug for five. It was like looking down a mine shaft, as that was cemetery policy then. It meant there was plenty of room for future neighbours above, thereby getting the most ‘value’ from a single plot. With a deep original hole you might not get down to the incumbent, so despite his reservations, Tyler had continued with the guarantees he’d been offered.

Tyler telephoned not long afterwards. I was just expecting another job.

‘You know that one we filled in at Huntsby the other day?’

‘Yes,’ I acknowledged. ‘What about it?’

‘Well, Graham’s been on.’

‘Oh yes?’ I said, my senses immediately heightened after the ‘swap’ affair. ‘Him, what’s happened now?’

‘Well, not sure, but something’s up, or he wouldn’t have called us, but I’d have a fair guess.’

‘Do tell.’

‘Not yet, in case I’m wrong.’

‘Fair enough.’

‘Can you come tomorrow?’

‘Yes, no probs.’

‘See you in the morning then.’

‘Wilco…’

We met Graham at the graveyard. On first inspection the grave looked okay. The cage was in one piece, and had not been interfered with by either deer, rabbits or the lady at No 16.

'What's up, Gray?' said Tyler. 'Not the wrong one again?'

'Oh, don't remind me. Well no, not exactly,' said a nervous Graham. That sounded ominous, I thought.

'The son came to the shop yesterday to settle the invoice for the funeral; big lad, jolly fellow, farming sort, if you get my meaning, broad accent, well broad everything. I thanked him for his business yet again, and said I trusted everything had been satisfactory, to which he had said:

'Aye, grand, thanks, Graham, good do afterwards an' all.'

'Excellent, another happy customer,' I said, and we laughed together.

'Then, though,' said Graham, 'almost as he was readying himself to leave the office - I'd even stood up to show him out - the son said,

'Just one thing, Graham. I thought we were going to bury me mother wi' fatha?"

'Yes, we have, sir,' Graham had assured him, 'they are both reunited again now.'

'No they's not, Gray, beg to differ,' he said. 'Fatha were three in from path, and you planted muther by path. Not to worry, you weren't to know, there's no stone on th'owd fella.'

Tyler was beginning to grin, just slightly.

'It wasn't a reopen then?' he said. If you could put faintly smug vindication in a tone, he just did.

'No,' said a red-faced Graham. 'I'm sorry, Tyler. I could have died myself as he told me in the office, and he was so understanding; quite threw me'.

Feeling I knew Graham well enough after recent events, shall we say, I asked, 'How did this one happen then, Graham?'

'It is not completely my fault,' he said almost apologetically. 'It's down to Mrs Downey.'

I looked at T, he returned the favour, also more than a little mystified. Well that was okay then as long as we knew it was Mrs Downey's fault.

Tyler beat me to it. 'Graham, Mrs Downey? Who exactly is Mrs Downey?'

'Ah, sorry,' Graham replied. 'Edith, Edith Downey. She is the lady, well old girl, who has been on the Parochial Church Council since before Christ, who reckons to know it all. She's a well-meaning interfering old busybody, and the sooner she's on my client list the better.'

Tyler and I stood shocked. This was strong stuff: we'd assumed it was only the gravediggers that had such thoughts as a rule.

Tyler took over again. 'Blimey, Graham, she's riled you, lad.'

‘Yes, sorry, sorry,’ he said nervously, ‘but she’s a bloody nuisance. I specifically asked her to check the location on the map and to recheck after you called. She uses the original 1901 map. It is, well it was, a lovely document, copperplate writing, the lot, but she’s used Tippex and God knows what on it. Then she sends her husband, Lawrence, poor long-suffering Lawrence - lovely man, lost the will to live years ago but still does what he’s told - up here to put the peg in the ground, more where she wants them to be than where they should be. She’s just past it.’ He drew breath and swore again. Now this was not typical of our usually understanding Graham, not like him at all.

‘Isn’t the graveyard plan computerised?’ I asked.

‘No, no,’ said Graham, ‘we’ve pestered the PCC to do it, but she who must be obeyed says there is no need. Anyway no need, Edith can mess this up all on her own, without a computer.’

‘Maybe Lawrence put it in the wrong place, Graham,’ I said, trying to calm him down.

‘Philip,’ he said. ‘It is Philip, isn’t it?’

‘Yes,’ I reassured him.

‘Philip, if Lawrence should put a lump of sugar in his tea without using the tongs it would be on the agenda at the next PCC meeting, so no, it wouldn’t be Lawrence.’

Fair enough, I thought. That gave us a good assessment of dear old Edith.

‘Perhaps she does it to feel needed and important, Graham.’

‘I am sure you’re right, Philip, but you’d be less inclined to defend her if you knew what was coming…’

‘You’ve told ‘em we’ll move ‘er, ‘aven’t you?’ Tyler interrupted.

Graham responded with the nervousness of a schoolboy. ‘Well,’ he said shakily, ‘what else could I do?’

‘Uh-oh,’ said Tyler, ‘here we go again. This is getting ridiculous, what with seemingly randy wife in Mardale and you and your nameplates we’re spending more time digging ‘em up than burying ‘em.’ He laughed.

‘I’m sorry,’ said Graham.

‘You were right,’ I said to Graham. ‘I’m not as inclined to excuse old Edith anymore.’

‘When?’ said Tyler.

‘As soon as,’ said Graham. ‘I’ve asked the Reverend and he just said he hadn’t heard me, just do it, but don’t get seen.’

‘Oh great, don’t get seen!’ Exclaimed Tyler uncharacteristically ‘and just how are we going to do that without David Blaine or a magician?’

‘I don’t know, I’d hoped you might,’ said Graham.

I got the distinct impression that Graham and the authorities involved here underestimated just what a huge undertaking, well overtaking, this task was.

‘Where are we moving her to, Gray?’ T asked. Graham duly showed us an unmarked grave three in from the track as the son had said.

‘We can do the reopen now,’ said Tyler. ‘If we set up as normal, people will just think there is another unfortunate going in. Getting her up quick is the problem – if we set two boxes up so close together it will look like the plague is back. Can you get us a couple of your lads, Gray, and you, for tomorrow teatime?’

‘Yes. What’s the plan?’

We huddled together a bit, looking inwards and down. Goodness knows why, as there wasn’t anyone for miles; reminded me of night-time exercises in the school corps planning a stealth mission.

‘Late afternoon tomorrow you and your lads come up here. We’ll aim to slide her across the grass at dusk.’ Blimey, it sounded like a stealth mission now as well, I thought.

‘Do you want us all to wear black, put boot polish on our faces?’ I said to Tyler for a laugh. He just looked at me, brimming with contempt. The ‘need you’ look on his face was made all the funnier as it was clear that Graham was giving this serious consideration.

‘Wouldn’t bother you Gray, would it? I’ve never seen you in anything but black,’ I went on, turning the screw and wringing every ounce of humour out that I could. Well I thought it was funny, but it was soon clear I was on my own.

‘Shut up, PJ,’ Tyler said. That was me told. ‘We will dig her up putting the soil on some plastic on the grass so as not to mud it up. Your lads can wheel some soil from the new hole to this one, as there won’t be enough.’

We might need a conductor to pull this off, I thought, but we should get it done.

‘You’re sure the Vicar doesn’t want to say anything?’ Tyler asked Graham. Importantly, this was Tyler’s only verbal insurance against a likely prison sentence, or at the very least deep unforgiving suspicion and the end of a long downward career in a flourishing dying trade.

‘Yes,’ he replied confidently.

‘Well we’ll see you tomorrow late afternoon then.’

I asked Graham if the graveyard got locked at night, but he didn’t think so. It was all systems go for tomorrow then. Like a proper mission. ‘Operation Overland’ was born.

Sure enough it worked. We turned up shortly before Graham and the lads, who had been sworn to secrecy, and it all pretty much went like clockwork. It was going well into dusk when we slid Vera across the damp grass, like kids with a sledge, and finally laid her to rest. It was a good job there were five of us. Vera was no spring chicken and I’m no doctor, but she hadn’t died of starvation that was for sure.

Graham said, ‘May she rest in peace,’ finally, or again in her case I thought unkindly. I never liked the expression ‘rest in peace’. Personally,

I'm rather hoping there is something to do up, or indeed down, there when my time comes. Even should it be fire and brimstone, as reassuringly that means that one can still feel temperature and pain. 'Rest in Activity' or indeed 'Busy but in Peace' are better perhaps? 'Busy in Peace' sounded more like my shed, and perhaps that was more like more 'Hiding in Peace' in reality? Admittedly it doesn't have the same ring to it, but we would get used to it; after all, that is all we have done with the original.

We filled the holes in together; Tyler with one of the lads and Graham and I with the other. We were soon done and it was all hands on deck to clean up the grass where we had used the plastic, and replace the dreaded cage. We hoped no one would notice its location, and that of the flowers, had changed overnight, ever so slightly.

When the lads had got back into the van ready for home, Graham came across to us, but largely to Tyler.

'Thank you, guys, as ever. You've really got me out of trouble these last few weeks. Now what's the damage?'

'Well,' said Tyler, 'there's the swap job to settle up for—'

'Yes, yes—'

'So that's the single rate times two, for digging two. Then there's this one, or two, depending how you look at it, so we'll call that the same. 'ow's 'at, Gray?'

‘Yes, yes, that’s fine, Tyler, and thank you again, and buy yourselves a beer on me.’ At this he pressed an extra twenty pound note into each of our hands.

‘Thanks, Graham,’ we said, as his bill had been big enough. We shook hands and bade each other goodnight.

‘That was good of him,’ I said to Tyler. ‘He didn’t need to do that, but it was nice he was genuinely grateful, you know, there was real meaning in that T.’

‘You’ll have me in tears yet, you soft bugger, PJ. A poor undertaker there is not.’

It occurred to me that in the future only our little band of men, and I expected the lads wouldn’t remember, would know the location of a perfectly serviceable grave at Huntsby, which when if ever reopened, would fall away from the already dug sides. What a conundrum for the future gravediggers as they would dig down only to find it empty; a previously dug grave, mysteriously empty? It would certainly be a bit spooky and raise an eyebrow in wonder, but it would without doubt answer the age-old question ‘Is there anybody there?’, as in this case the answer would be a resounding no…

‘Well, two for the price of one twice. One got two Church services, the other got two graves,’ smiled T.

‘What did you say?’

'One got…'

'No, no, before that,' I queried

'Two for the price of one twice,' Tyler repeated

'Thought so … Very good that, James.'

'James who?'

'Well if that isn't the name of a Bond film, nothing is.' I said and we laughed.

Tyler, holding his newly rolled twenty-pound note pointing up to his mouth, blew, as if to blow smoke off the smoking barrel.

'You may well only live twice, fella, but dying you only do once, that's for sure. C'mon, Miss Moneypenny, the pub…'

Fancy Tyler coming up with a novel idea like that: I was shaken and we stirred…

Chapter 13

SIZE MATTERS

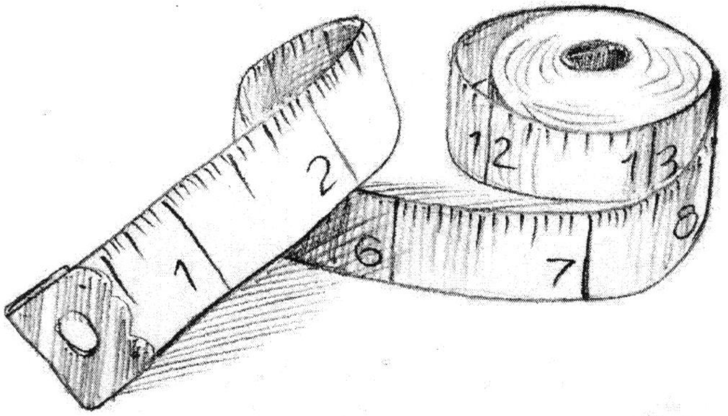

It was a lovely sunny Sunday afternoon. Tyler, Sam and I had been to the pub for a couple of beers. Sam and I had bitter, Tyler his usual Guinness. Back at Cliff Field Sam and I shared a bottle of wine, and Sam had got some Guinness in for Tyler. There was a metal and wooden bench against one of the building's walls which Tyler and I sat on. Sam settled on a lounger-chair thing opposite. It was a proper little suntrap between the building and an old static caravan that we kept quail in. We were just chatting and putting the world to rights, when quite unexpectedly Tyler dropped his beer and threw up quite violently, seemingly in one movement.

I jumped up for a bucket, for no reason or use as we were sitting on gravel, just one of those gut reactions - excuse the unfortunate pun. Sam, ever more practical than I, had gone like a flash and was back with some towels and fresh water. She wiped round his mouth, his head limp and lolling on his shoulders.

'He doesn't look very well at all,' I said, employing all my available medical knowledge and bedside manner, in what was another exemplary demonstration of the human talent for stating the blindingly obvious. You needed to be neither a detective nor a doctor to realise that Tyler was in trouble.

'Ring for an ambulance,' instructed Sam. She was a first-aider at work and knew the basics, so I did as she said.

Whilst waiting I thought the ambulance will never find either this place or us here. I knew houses with names rather than numbers always caused a problem for the emergency services anyway, but we were up a lane, off a lane and down a track. Even Tyler, who'd lived within a few miles of here all his life, hadn't known Cliff Field existed until he met us. After a speedy discussion with Sam it was decided that I should go and wait on the main road for the ambulance to direct it in.

Tyler wasn't presenting well at all. He was throwing up black stuff and it wasn't Guinness - that I would have recognised as it was not infrequent. This looked like congealed blood to me. I was no doctor, or indeed more usefully a vet, but we had had a sow pig produce something similar-looking once… before it sadly died.

I waved the ambulance down on the main road and ran in front of it to Cliff Field. It wasn't far, but nigh on impossible to find if you didn't know it was there, hidden in plain sight as it were.

The ambulance crew did their work, whilst asking simple direct questions. I suddenly realised how little I knew of my friend - sobering stuff…

'Age?' they had enquired. I didn't know.

'Existing conditions?' I didn't know.

'Medication?' Likewise, I didn't know. (I thought it was perhaps not the time to mention the almost intravenous alcohol and nicotine). And so it went on.

'Next of kin' was okay as that was Alf, but Tyler had two children of whom I knew nothing. Once he was loaded into the ambulance, masked up and dripped, they were off. Sam went with them and said she would ring when she knew what-was-what, and most importantly what we could tell Alf, because Tyler didn't look well at all. Indeed, it looked conceivable to me that he could soon be in need his own services…

I pottered on and did the rounds with Purdey. There was no getting away from it: I was worried about Tyler. He appeared physically fit in day-to-day gravedigging - far fitter than I - but his habits, well, were frankly terrible (and I was no saint). I was with him once when, about mid-evening, we dropped into the shop to get some fags, always the same brand. That was his fifth packet of twenty that day.

Sam rang about teatime. Tyler was fine and settled, but he was going nowhere for a while. She asked me to go and tell Alf but not to bring him down that evening, just to reassure him and arrange a time to go and pick him up the following day. Then she said could I come and collect her. 'Wilco,' I replied.

Tyler was asleep when I got there so we left him be. He'd been sedated so that he could sleep.

'Do they know what's up with him?' I asked.

'No, not conclusively, but the consultant has seen him. Looks like a burst stomach ulcer.'

'Well, we knew he was bleeding from somewhere,' I said, 'just like that pig,' I added very knowledgeably. I was quite pleased with myself over that, my shared-symptom diagnosis. I only hoped I would be wrong about the outcome, and that that was not to be shared as well. After all Tyler hadn't finished my training yet. He would have to do that before shovelling off - I simply wasn't good enough, or ready, to dig a grave for a gravedigger. Besides I'd miss him, the old rascal.

We went back the following day, taking Alf and also Tyler's son and daughter, who I had never met. They were eighteen and twenty respectively and both still lived with their mother. They seemed good sorts.

The son looked like a younger - almost spitting image - of his dad. We all sat around the bed in one of those semi-awkward situations of having nothing to say to one another, a bit like being in a doctor's waiting room.

Tyler was spark out of it. They had operated on him that morning and he sported a large bandage to show for it. When it became obvious that he wasn't going to come round in visiting time, or probably indeed that night, we all left. We each gave him the obligatory light squeeze of the hand and the ladies gave him a kiss on his cheek. We also left the again obligatory - almost mandatory - donation of a bag of grapes. I thought I might kiss him too, just for a laugh, but then thought better of it - if he came round the shock might kill him. It occurred to me that the last time Tyler had had that many grapes they had been processed into their liquid form, probably a contributory reason for his being in here. Not sure he had ever eaten one.

On the way out Alf collared me.

'PJ,' he said.

'Yes, Alf.'

'Had a grave come in and wondered if you could help me.' He sounded almost apologetic and quite sheepish.

'No problems, fella, when and where?' I replied with a confidence that surprised me.

‘I’m sorry to ask, but they are a bit much for me on my own now, if I’m honest, and I don’t know anyone else to ask. You know the ropes, yer see.’ Very un-deliberately droll Alf, I thought.

‘Don’t worry, I’d have been offended if you had asked anybody else,’ I lied. It did cross my mind that that I might live to regret those words, but hey, everything would be fine. I had to admit, though, to feeling a certain burden of responsibility descending on me. This was undoubtedly a promotion, but a not altogether welcome one. Some people really are indispensable, unlike the saying suggests, if only for a short time. It felt a bit like that feeling of joining a committee, then overnight finding yourself elected as Chairman or Treasurer – a common trick often employed by seasoned committee members on green, willing newbies. (PJ’s advice to any still enthusiastic lonely person was to join a committee and learn how good ‘lonely’ really is). Truth was I just wasn’t experienced enough to be the boss. Tyler had better not die. I wanted to kill him…

‘Know the ropes?’ I said to Alf. ‘Good joke?’

‘Oh,’ he said. He hadn’t the blindest idea what I was talking about. I wasn’t sure his mind was on our conversation - he was obviously worried about his lad.

‘Where is it?’ I continued.

‘Oh yes… It’s a new double at Quayside, just near the coast past Corcastle.’

‘Righty-ho. Can you pick me up?’

‘Yes, ‘ave to be early mind, funeral is in afternoon. With Tyler takin’ ill goin’ to be a one-day job. He was goin’ to do a bit day afore, but funeral’s not ‘til three so should be all right. Just give me time to do me pheasants in morning, and I’ll be wit’ yer.’

‘Okay, it’s a date.’

At this we said our goodnights, all agreeing to revisit Tyler the next day, hopefully with more success.

Alf was there bright and early at Cliff Field in the comedy car plus trailer. I crawled into the passenger seat, a bit like you see them crawling into hoarders’ houses in the documentaries. Before we set off, wary from previous experiences, I said to Alf:

‘Stop, hold on,’ (more ‘oddon’ in reality when deployed as one of Alf’s own expressions, obviously dispensing with the quite unnecessary ‘H’, which I turned on him. I thought if I spoke his language, I might get more accurate and usable results). ‘Have we got everything?’

‘Yes,’ Alf answered confidently. ‘Checked everything afore setting off.’

‘Spades?’ I enquired with well-earned scepticism.

‘Yep, everything,’ Alf assured me confidently.

‘As long as you’re sure,’ I said, deliberately labouring the point.

‘Yep,’ said Alf.

‘Okay.’ I replied trying to sound reassured. With that we set off for an unsuspecting Quayside.

(I think he said we had everything…?)

On arrival we parked at the church gates. It was about 8.30am. Lovely place once again with lovely views for the clients to enjoy, over the sea this time. It was a warm day with just a bit of breeze. We found our marker on the lower terrace; there were only two terraces.

Alf said, ‘Good digging here, better than Crocketford you did a bit ago. Bit softer than Crocketford, but still holds together, it’s like Play-Doh.’

We did the usual setting up of the box alongside the soon-to-be grave, carrying the required items from the trailer, and taking a different route each time so as not to leave an obvious track in the grass.

Alf was just going back to the trailer for the spades when I asked him, ‘Oh Alf, while you’re there, can you bring the tape measure?’ This wasn’t me being idle, I was busy sort of looking for the waste tip for the excess soil, but mainly enjoying the view, which was quite special.

He was back a few minutes later, spades in hand.

‘Have you got the tape, Alf?’ I asked.

‘No,’ came the unadorned, unashamed answer.

‘It’s okay, I’ll pop up and get it,’ I said, as the silly old duffer had clearly forgotten it or not heard my request.

He stopped me. 'No,' he said, 'we've haven't got one.'

'Sorry? "We haven't got one",' I repeated, not quite believing what I was hearing.

'I must 'ave took it out of the car to measure pheasant pen for more wire yesterday; must 'ave left it at Ruins.'

I left the 'must 'ave took it out of the car' remark alone, but if he could remember successfully measuring the pheasant pen, of course he must have taken it out of the blinking car. I stayed calm. This was my fault in part, as I did not do a visual check on a tape measure. There were usually a number of them, or at least one, and this detail had been, until that moment, the least of my worries. I had clearly been distracted thinking of 'spades' and the big stuff and had simply taken a tape as read.

I did not dare to think what Tyler would have said - that really didn't bear thinking about.

'Oh dear me,' I didn't say, not quite knowing what to do next. We were nowhere near a shop that would stock such an item and there wasn't time to make the nearly fifty-mile round trip to the Ruins. We could have gone into town, but the car was such a worry to me, and Alf's driving, as experienced this morning, was shall we say interesting at least. I wasn't at all sure town traffic was ready for Alf's road sense.in a built-up area. How we hadn't hit half the cars we encountered on the way I don't know. The reason we didn't hit the other half was that he would have had to have seen those first.

‘It’s all right, I’ve got a stick,’ Alf announced triumphantly. O praise the Lord, no problems now then, Alf has got a stick! What use ‘a stick’ was going to be was beyond me. I was slumping into despair already, and we hadn’t even managed to get the grass off before Alf had struck. It was so unfair, I thought, feeling suddenly terribly sorry for myself. I had done all the pre-dig checks imaginable. And this was my first ‘sherry free’ hole, but I felt that I might need some, purely for medicinal reasons, and we hadn’t started yet. I really was going to kill Tyler, just as soon as he got better.

‘The coffin,’ started Alf, ‘is six foot two long, be twenty-eight inch wide at shoulders, fifteen at foot, should be ‘bout right?’ The ‘should’ and ‘’bout’ were worrying. ‘Well me stick is six and a half foot, so if we dig it to length of stick, that should be reet. Me pick head is thirty inch across, so as long as pick goes down ‘ole wit’ a bit o’ room at wide bit job should be a good ‘un.’

This far from filled me with confidence, but sadly it was all we had. I took the grass sod off to the measurements of ‘a stick by a pick’. It rhymed, I thought, let’s hope that’s not all it did.

Alf lifted the sods away as I cut them and stacked them by the side of the box in order (I hoped). He was right about one thing: it was a dream to dig - it cut like cheese as at Crocketford, but was a lot lighter. I guessed it was an alluvial deposit.

Progress was fast. At about two feet down Alf asked if he could have a go.

‘Of course,’ I said, and off he went. You could immediately see where Tyler got it from. Alf was no slouch. His unimaginable (to us) training on the Burma Railway was clear to see and paying off, with his wiry frame chucking the alluvium out for fun. He was very fit for his age and wow could he dig. Meanwhile I went gravestone reading. I had more of a purpose than usual, as it was rumoured that there was a small one here in the oldest part of the churchyard which reportedly said:

HE WAS A PIG IN LIFE

HE WILL BE A PIG IN DEATH

I wish I could have found that gravestone, but I didn’t. I remember thinking those two characters must have had a great relationship. I’d wager we have all met someone like him in our own lives though - a bloke that deserves that description. But no matter, it was probably lost in the long grass. It was good enough somehow just to know it existed. I did get some smile-time just thinking that it was probably a blessing that the modern law no longer allows such personalised displays of view or affection, as in this case.

I did find one equally old gravestone, however, that had no inscription, just the outline of shoes going this way and that. It had been the cobbler’s stone in his shop, used to measure your foot size in order to craft your new shoes. There were shapes of all sorts from the outline of children’s shoes to giants, and the stone satisfied my gravestone interest for the day.

Between us we had it done in less than four hours, which for a new double wasn't bad. I wished we had had a mini digger. It would have taken no more than half an hour, but then there would have been the problem of no access, and of course the added bonus of no tape measure.

We trimmed the sides and base until smooth. We had a foothold to get out, two to be on the safe side, but it was such lovely stuff you could have carved an ornate staircase in it if you had wanted. The undertaker popped by to see if we were ready and complimented us on the hole. He said should be quite a funeral, 'a big fella', a remark that filled me with dread, until he added 'in the community'. I was so pleased he did.

Our client had been the Pilot of the Bay, the uniformed grown-up that boards and steers the ships and all that. Sadly he had not been retired long by all reports.

'We'll be well out of the way by three o'clock,' Alf said.

'Okay,' the undertaker replied and went on, 'Oh, Alf, can you shift your motor and trailer - there'll be our lot plus a load of cars, I reckon.'

'No problem, sir,' I said. 'We're going for a late lunch.'

'Grand,' came the reply. All went to plan after that. The grave was set up and looked fit for a king.

When we got in the car, Alf said, 'We'll go for a sandwich in t' pub, PJ, eh?' You could have knocked me down with a not very big feather. Alf had spent his life reprimanding Tyler for drinking in the day, and indeed I had never known him have a pint other than at dominoes. T would be spinning in his hospital bed if he knew.

We had a good wholesome sandwich with salad and not one, but two pints of foaming ale for me and Guinness for Alf. The love affair with Guinness seemed to run in the family, or more likely both their stomachs were knackered and it was just that Tyler had achieved his life threatening complaint level quicker as the war hadn't interrupted his consumption.

When our lunch was over I popped into the local shop, picked up a bottle of sherry, using the 'in case of emergency' as my enabler of an excuse, and noticed in one corner that there was a section of bits and bobs (pins, paperclips and the like) on a stand. On display was a folding fabric dress- or curtain-maker's tape measure, so I bought that as well, although not ideal and it was certainly sadly too late to use for our pilot. It struck me that indeed a 'curtain tape' could be seen as being quite appropriate for measuring graves, not ideal but well named.

We made tracks back to the church. The undertaker wasn't wrong – there were cars everywhere and it was a dead end. I thought that too was quite suitably funny, a graveyard in a 'dead end' and a 'curtains tape'? We managed to get along right to the end of the road and parked just into the sand, where others wouldn't risk it. The service was in full swing. It was only a small church and the mourners spilled outside, issuing out of the church doors like a lava flow. There were hundreds there. I prayed to God, knowing he was busy elsewhere up in the church, but I still prayed that

Alf's less than state-of-the-art measuring of 'a pick and a stick' had worked. The consequences of them not doing so were unthinkable…

We sat in the car waiting and Alf broke the silence by saying: 'Did one at the Cathedral once. That was embarrassing.' He'd put his deep voice on again, and a serious face. 'Wasn't my fault, didn't think that would have happened.'

His expression again. Of course it wasn't his fault, it never had been yet, so why break the habit of a lifetime. I was already waiting for another digging nightmare story... Please, I asked God, not now. I was stressed enough over Alf's stick as it was.

'Yes, they came for me. I was hiding behind the cemetery shed. Thought they'd go away, and I'd sort it later, but they didn't. That 'un wouldn't go in hole either.'

What did he just say? 'Either'? I died there and then. He seemed completely oblivious to what he had just said and already had a clear acceptance, if not expectation, and indeed at one with the thought that our 'hole' might not be big enough!

He continued (unnecessarily in my view), 'I had to walk through all t'mourners, back to grave wi' t' spade. 'Ad bin doubtful that 'un would go in when I sawrit. Looked a bit of a big 'un when it come into church, didn't fit not even near. Covered the whole grave both ends and sides.'

'Both ends and sides?' I said, not believing my ears. 'What did you do?'

‘Well the bearers shifted it off, while I jumped in th’ole and chopped sides out and down. Couldn’t chuck any stuff out so just ‘ad to bury it shallower.’

‘What did the mourners do?’

‘Funny really…’ ‘Funny’, I thought. What on earth could be funny about that? Terrifying, embarrassing, almost any word but ‘funny’.

‘Yes, they all sang hymns. Lots of ‘em, seemed like, took us a while,’ said Alf.

‘Lots of what, hymns or mourners?’ I queried.

Alf, face cracking into a laugh and with a definite glint in his eye, said, ‘both,’ and chortled. This man must have a skin of leather not to have been totally embarrassed.

I looked out of the car window and it was all too like Alf’s story. The service was over and the coffin was being carried out by the chap’s sons (I now know) plus one other. As they turned out of the Church porch the main wreath fell off the top; whether this was a son buckling with grief or the fact that the fourth bearer was comically taller than the others, wasn’t clear. All we saw was this massive floral anchor tumbling off the side as if to have been deployed like its real counterparts, or was it the old Pilot mucking about, dropping anchor for one last time? As it hit its seabed, or the path in this case, one of its great arms broke off. A number of non-prime mourners were on their knees in a flash to effect a repair, and by the time it reached the graveside it looked like an anchor once more, and when it was laid down you'd have been hard pressed to notice there was anything wrong with it.

From our position we could see the backs of the mourners while the interment took place.

'I hope it goes in,' whispered Alf. I had never had my fingers crossed that tightly before or since, and now had the unnecessary benefit of his experience. I shuddered at the thought - my skin was not as tough, thick or weathered as that of my partners. I would far rather he had saved his Cathedral story for later in the pub.

'Looks like it 'as,' Alf said.

'Did you think it wouldn't?'

'Wasn't so very sure,' he said, laughing like Mutley.

Formal proceedings over, the assembled throng stood about chatting. There was going to be quite a wait, but slowly and surely they manoeuvred the cars in the restricted lane and drifted away until we were finally left alone.

We approached the grave with trepidation. The coffin wasn't on top. Always a good sign, and I just hoped it had gone flat down and not cockled up at an angle. We looked in and were greeted by, well it has to be said, as good a view as you could hope for given the circumstances. There it lay absolutely level and at the bottom of a perfect grave, if such a thing exists. It was a beautiful coffin, like Teddy's had been at Preston Banks. I thought again it was a shame to bury such wood and workmanship. If this wood had been formed into a different shape it would be adorning a stately home as a table, or the like. I sighed for the wood but also a sigh of relief that it was, lovely or not, in.

'Job's a good 'un,' said Alf matter-of-factly.

'Yes, great fit,' I replied. It was however beginning to dawn on me that it was indeed a great fit, indeed a very good, not to say extremely good fit. A tailor-made fit, in fact you could say.

Alf was taking the greengrocer grass off when I said, 'Alf, that is a good fit?'

'Aye, thought it would be a bit tight, only glad Harry's lads did the lowering in. Sometimes when relations lower they make a right mess of it.'

'A bit tight.' he went on.

I could have screamed at him. The rings on the ends of the coffin were up and had deeply scored the soft earth of the grave ends as the coffin was being lowered. The same applied to the side handles - deep cuts in the sides, not unlike glacial striations. Trying to pull out the ropes and sheets was a task in itself, and the purple sheets were trapped between the walls of the grave and the coffin. This was tight beyond belief.

'Alf,' I said, 'can we hold on a minute while I pop to the car?'

'Yeah,' he said innocently. He would not have been so keen had he known I had bought that tape measure. My reason for going to the car was twofold. One I needed a sherry (often a misused marriage, 'need' and 'drink', but not this time), and secondly, I wanted that tape. When I returned, I quite unceremoniously got into the grave with Captain Trevor McBride, Pilot of the Bay, as engraved on his plaque along with his dates and an anchor.

'How big did they say this coffin was, Alf?' I said, quite convinced that we had been given the wrong measurements and if so it would have to be mentioned to the undertaker as a matter of priority, to give us a bit more tolerance in future.

'Six foot two,' Alf replied. I apologised to the good Captain for the intrusion, then knelt on his chest area reaching to the head end with my admittedly unsatisfactory floppy tape. The Captain and I must have been inches apart, as I nearly rested my head on his, reaching back with my tape. I held the tape in my fingers against the polished wood as a marker, and repeated the process to the foot end. It was four feet plus two feet two inches long making the advised six feet two inches: how could this be? This coffin must be nearer six feet six inches long, had to be?

'Alf!' I hollered up from the depths.

'Yes, PJ?'

'Where's your flipping stick?' Unavoidable language was deployed, I'm afraid, and 'flipping' had not been the result. I immediately apologised to the Captain. Mind you, after the floral weighing anchor incident I imagine the Captain might have used some choice and no doubt quaint naval expressions too. Alf appeared, towering above me at the graveside, and handed me his stick; some seed of a thought was beginning to grow in me. We laid it along the side of the grave so that it was at about mid-chest height for me as I was standing on our ever-patient Captain. I measured it with Alf, not once or twice but three times to confirm my worst fears.

'Alf, you said this stick was six foot six, positive you were, so is it me, or is this stick six foot two and a half inches?'

'Seems to be,' Alf said, now getting a little sheepish.

'So those undertakers just got a very stout box into an unforgiving hole, with a quarter of an inch at each end?' I asked with all the calm I could muster.

'Good fit,' he said.

'You're right,' I replied. It was indeed a good lowering job the professionals had done today. No it wasn't, I corrected myself, it was nothing short of divine intervention that they managed it, quite miraculous. I had successfully run cars whose pistons didn't fit as well as this client in his final resting place. I don't know if Alf realised how close to catastrophe he had taken us and how close the Captain had sailed. Surely he must have done, but if the rightly upset and watery eyed relations had tried to lower their dear Captain in, as they often wished, we would have needed a day and a JCB to put it right.

Doubtless Alf would have chortled through it like a naughty boy. He didn't seem to take life altogether all that seriously, I felt; he gave the impression of somehow being immune to it all. Soberingly, perhaps after his wartime experiences there was little that life could throw at him that would give him any cause for concern. However, admittedly all was and had ended well. Tyler would without question have gone ballistic, but it was over and the coffin was in, but wow that was close. We pulled the sheets out, and every one of them ripped. Captain McBride must have been determined to take something to the bottom with him, even if it was only four halves of purple sheets… He would surely have approved of it 'ship shape and Bristol fashion'.

We filled the grave in. I gave Captain McBride my usual send-off with an additional apology for having had to kneel on him.

When we'd finished Alf said, 'I remember now.'

'Remember what?'

'Be a couple of days ago, I was at the pheasant pens.' Along with the tape measure, no doubt, I imagined. 'Pen gate was swinging in the wind, and I needed to prop it open with something, so cut a bit off me stick. I forgot I'd done that.'

'Oh golly, Alf!' I exclaimed (I didn't exactly say that...). 'That memory loss could have ended in a real nightmare,' I said with admirable patience, which I thought well beyond the call of duty, it has to be said.

'Sorry… it could, couldn't it? I didn't think that would have happened,' he characteristically replied. Oh my dearest Alf neither, in a million years, did I, I said to myself reluctantly smiling within.

That was so close to embarrassment and every form of PR disaster, thought PJ for all concerned. Alf couldn't have picked a higher profile local to have courted such a disaster. The local television news cameras weren't there admittedly, but everybody else was!

We finished around six thirty and hospital visiting started at seven. I'd said to Sam that we might go straight to the hospital if there wasn't time to come home first. We joined the others at Tyler's bedside. He looked loads better, and was sitting up and chatting.

'What have you two been doing?' His sense of humour was back: we looked a right state - we'd brushed off what dirt we could, but we really were unacceptably grubby for a hospital. Alf was very self-conscious and clearly wanted out of there. He was old school, and thought you should have your Sunday best, or at minimum a tie on, to visit a hospital.

Tyler said, knowing full well what we'd been doing, 'You haven't come with your tape measure, 'ave you, Father, 'cause I'm not quite ready, not dead yet.'

This got laughter from all assembled and he had no idea of the nerve he had unintentionally touched, and indeed no, we absolutely hadn't got a tape measure and hadn't had for days. It was a blessing that Alf didn't at that moment produce one from the depths of a pocket, but he didn't. I wasn't sure I could have stood that.

In a quiet moment Tyler asked me how Alf and I had got on. Well, I thought, I couldn't tell him the truth there and then, his stitches might come out.

I whispered, 'I'll tell you a tape measure story when you're out of here.' As a taster I did say, 'Alf gave me a stick, and he hadn't disappointed…' I winked at Tyler and raised my eyebrows a little, and a knowing amused glint flashed across his eyes.

He knew…

Chapter 14

THE VICAR OF BRUNTON

The Vicar of Brunton had by all reports had something of a baptism of fire when it came to Alf's shall we say sometimes lax and unorthodox methods, and had (not altogether surprisingly) been traumatised by the experience. A grave had been dug some weeks before, largely by Alf whilst Tyler had been convalescing, and the Vicar all but needed counselling.

I couldn't help for the first day, but I had passed my 'working with Alf' test now and Tyler wanted me to go and help fill it in. The Vicar, who was new to Brunton, had come from an inner-city parish. This showed, and nowhere more obviously than with burials: he had never had a church with a graveyard. He had had a concrete block called a church, in a housing and shopping centre in some new town in the Midlands, where the graveyard for the now few burials was some anonymous field far removed geographically from the church itself. The consequence was hard to believe, but he had never seen a grave being dug - other than by an archaeologist. He had just attended the city cemetery, which no doubt housed the crematorium as well - more a sort of theme park 'one stop, get rid of your body shop'. I bet his former church had looked more like a multi-storey car park than a church; it probably was to ancient rural churches what the teepee at Liverpool and the modern effort at Coventry are to cathedrals.

Brunton Church had its own graveyard, as was more usual round here. Although an extension graveyard was planned and land earmarked nothing further had happened. The amount of bureaucracy involved in getting all the interested parties to reel off report after report - from groundwater to wildlife - for this extension proposal was eye-watering. You almost needed a faculty from the Church Diocese to even change a light bulb, meaning this extension was for the time being stuck solidly in the system under a weight of paperwork, and would probably remain there for years or until we were leaving bodies on the top of the grass. But for the moment at least there was room immediately surrounding the church.

The overriding reason for there being space left in this little churchyard was because the church had suffered a fire some two hundred years previously, and a substantial portion of the burial record was lost. This loss was not total but applied to a large area near to the church building itself. It was typical of many of the ancient graves here that they had no headstones and were not marked in any way. The record was the only pointer as to what might be there. Then, as now, headstones and indeed graves were an expensive commodity. Also it was not uncommon in the old days for paupers or people who simply couldn't afford to bury their dead, often children, just to bury them in secrecy in consecrated ground - 'dodge them over the wall' - so these wouldn't have shown on the record anyway. There were examples where these illegally positioned graves crossed each other, one cutting through another. I often thought it was a godsend that such illegal burials took place in the dark, as the sight must have been one of unimaginable 'Hollywood' horror.

Alf cackled away every time he talked of the Vicar of Brunton. The story was always the same, but always caught his audience by surprise. This involved the digging of a particularly sad and deep grave for a lady only in her fifties, deep enough to take relations above. It was then it struck me that graves were sort of the wrong way up in many ways. Obviously the first client by necessity had to be the deepest, but this meant subsequent clients, if present, would to all intents and purposes be looking down their own grave on the day of their forebear's funeral... Hey-ho, not entirely comfortable if indeed considered.

The grave Alf was digging was in the old part of the churchyard on this occasion, with no records. He was digging through all sorts - wood, handles, rotted fabric. Sometimes, he said, he'd even come across some soil. His punchline though was when he dug up a 'girt big thigh bone', just as the Vicar was walking across to greet him: 'Fella fair turned a rite ashen colour,' said Alf. 'He'd seen yon bits of wood and handles, and now this great bone on top of heap.'

The Vicar had said, 'What is that?'

'Oh that, Vicar, it's a ruet, a big tree ruet, often get 'em,' Alf replied, aware of the Vicar's discomfort.

The Vicar said in a concerned, 'Beam me up, Scotty' tone, whilst turning to go, 'Oh, gosh, well just make sure it all goes back in the hole afterwards, Alf.'

'Will do,' Alf replied. He reckoned the Vicar had swallowed his explanation. I was less sure of Alf's appraisal as to what the Vicar made of it and thought his acceptance of it as highly unlikely. Firstly, because a thigh bone looks, well exactly like, how can I put it, a thigh bone. Secondly because of the speed with which the Vicar had left, suggesting some recognition of the displayed biology. It has to be said that thirdly, there was a further difficulty with Alf's explanation. There was no evidence, contemporary or otherwise, of a tree sufficiently big enough to have bits of root of this size for miles.

Alf's tale reminded PJ of reading about Victorian burials in London at the height of their population boom. It was historically reported that far more burials were required than land available, and apparently the digging through of Alf's 'ruets' was commonplace (and by grisly reports not long after they had been 'planted'). Thankfully they invented the 'cemetery' as opposed to 'churchyard' as the solution and the rest, as they say, is history.

It was at Brunton not long afterwards, when Tyler could bear convalescing no longer, that we went to do a new quadruple. This was going to look more like a mine shaft than a grave. We gave ourselves two clear days to dig it. The 'silly after-Christmas season' had passed and we were now into the summer season. In the warmer months the Grim Reaper had to get more inventive and beckon folk with a new menu of assorted temptations and certainties, like motorbikes for the racers and over-fifties, climbing for anyone, helicopters for all, and other such absurdities. There was a question often asked in jest by many an undertaker's crew which went as follows: How many retired climbers do you know? The answer, inaccurate as it was, was always the same. One, Chris Bonington; all the others have fallen off!

This grave was because of one such tragedy, involving a lad in his twenties working on an old car. Cars had been his passion, by all reports, and one got the distinct impression of overalls and transmission fluid. Something dread had occurred to him, we didn't know exactly what. However, not unusually he'd been helping a mate out with his car at the time, doubling the tragedy all round, with one death and one life having to live with it.

Bearing in mind the intense pressure on grave space here, the Vicar, in conjunction with the family and undertaker, had decided to put him close to his grandfather, and not in the section near the church where Alf had frightened the Vicar with his 'ruet'. To this end they had allotted a space between two existing graves. It was the width we would struggle with; this was going to be tight.

We had said to the Vicar that we would have to put the soil box on the neighbour's grave as there was no alternative. Tyler generally didn't do this after a complaint years ago, when a lady had taken exception to himself and Alf doing this at another churchyard. He had put the soil box on her husband; he was fine about it but his wife sadly not so by all reports, but there had simply been no alternative then either. Unfortunately, as we all too often know in this life, you can't please all the people all of the time; indeed nowadays it appears increasingly difficult to please any of the people any of the time, it seemed to PJ.

Both the neighbour's graves here had lovely black granite headstones, to make things even more awkward. In fairness though, no one in the past would have imagined another grave going in between these two. This was never a grave plot on the original plan; this was definitely extra infill.

We got set up. It was a nice sunny day. Tyler had positioned his fags on the neighbouring stone and hidden the sherry under his jacket which he had taken off. The jacket didn't quite fit the tombstone like a mannequin or I'll swear he'd have hung it on it.

'Should you be drinking that?' I said to him.

‘No, shouldn’t be smokin’ these either, picked ‘um up on the way out of hospital’ he laughingly replied, gesturing to his glowing cigarette. There really was no hope. That was that, and all that was said on the matter.

We got the sod off and our shift pattern sorted out. The digging wasn’t that bad, no rocks or rubble, but it was a shade on the friable side, so sometimes you could shovel it rather than dig it.

‘We’ll get it down to double depth then call it a day,’ said Tyler. ‘We’ll have to pop up to Seascale Cemetery on the way back to get some more planks – we might have to shore the bottom bit up.’

‘Okay,’ I replied.

We duly boarded over the hole and left for the night. There were big black Victorian gates into this graveyard, very ‘Harry Potter’-esque, which we heaved shut behind us.

We didn’t need to go back early to Brunton; we were well ahead with a day in hand. On our arrival the next day Tyler said,

‘I’ll finish this last bit, in case we need to shore it up.’

‘Okay,’ I agreed, and shifted the planks off, but immediately I was faced with a problem, unknown territory for me, as one of the sides had tumbled in.

‘Tyler… Houston, we have a problem.’

‘What’s up?’

‘It’s fallen in a bit.’

Tyler came across from getting the barrow and looked in.

‘Oh, that’s not too bad, I’ve seen worse,’ he said. ‘If you get in and shovel that lot out straight into barrow, I’ll take it away.’

‘Wilco,’ I said.

When I got in the damage was worse than I thought: the grass had held the surface edge up and the collapse started below it, showing the edge to an overhang. Worse still, the coffins of the two top residents of the neighbouring grave were plain to see. There can only have been eight inches between this grave and its neighbour and a dividing wall that thin had been unlikely to stay up.

Tyler surveyed the damage from above and said it would be all right. ‘Mourners won’t see ‘em. We’ll make the sheets hang as low as we can,’ he advised.

I greeted my two new companions with an apology, but they didn’t seem to mind the intrusion. I dug for about forty minutes, and Tyler wheeled the stuff away. I was down to about treble depth and the grass was now about a foot above my head. We’d had no further collapses - yet.

I looked up and said, ‘Tyler,’ believing him to be sorting the grass out or leaning on a gravestone having a fag. There was no reply. ‘Tyler,’ I repeated, raising my voice a little. Still there was no reply. I tried again. ‘Oy, Tyler, I can’t get out.’ Again nothing. Then very loudly and with increased desperation I said, 'Tyler, I can't get out of here, stop mucking about, can you hear me?'

Suddenly I stopped in my tracks thinking: What am I doing? I was invisible under the surface of a graveyard shouting 'I can't get out'. I hoped no passer-by had heard my cries, especially the Vicar. It would be the end of him, the big wuss. Mind you one more collapse could be the end of me. Now that would be a funny, even convenient, place to die - in a grave?

Tyler had just been down to the end of the graveyard and was walking back leisurely. When he got to me he said, 'Were you shouting?'

'No,' I lied.

'Could have sworn I heard something.'

'No, all quiet in here, you must be hearing things. Perhaps it was a resident,' I said.

'Yeah right.' Needless to say Tyler was understandably long past ghost and ghoul stories.

'Can you help me out?' I asked.

'Yes, brought the little ladder from home.' He lowered the ladder and I finally emerged.

It was a two-man effort from then on in. Tyler climbed down the ladder and finished the digging. The sides held up but he needed to shutter the bottom two feet to give some support to the gravesides above. I lowered planks using the ladder rungs as a slide, once Tyler had shuttered up the bottom foot, taking care there was still sufficient width between the staves supporting the planks for the new resident. I then went down to help with the second level of planks. We could see all three of the neighbours now on one side and hoped for no further collapses. We had it finished in plenty of time: the funeral was at noon the following day. We covered the grave, prayed for no rain, bade our farewell to our exposed residents, and left.

When we returned the following day we removed the covering planks with trepidation. We really did not want to see another collapse, and especially one that could have brought the neighbours in to join the party. We breathed a sigh of relief: the hole had stayed intact. I went down and did a quick tidy-up of a few bits that had fallen in but nothing to worry about, while Tyler arranged the planks to be used as standing boards. This was quite a job as the top of this hole was in such poor repair, due to the friability of the ground and the closeness of the existing graves. The immediate surround was not much more than overhanging turf.

Tyler said, 'Now don't you be knocking into the sides while you're parping about down there.'

'Parping about?' I protested. Wash your mouth out, I thought. I was doing the very important task of 'bits and bobs' leaf removal, but this time there was a particular rounded stone in the mix that I thought might be interesting. If I am honest my leaf removal was, on this occasion at least, a smoke screen. The stone was a pink granite which only emanates from one location on earth, great for mapping the extremities of the ice sheets during the various ice ages Britain has withstood.

'I don't want a geology lesson now, PJ, just chuck it out and let's be 'avin' yer,' T said. 'Right, you position these sheets down the side to cover them coffins. I've got a hammer and nails if need be, or just trap 'em in planks.' I complied with this but not before putting my find firmly in my pocket. Sheets done I checked the base of the hole for any other bits, and then climbed out.

'Do you do all this checking to wind me up?' said Tyler.

'I think it's a touch of OCD.'

'What's that!?'

'Well if I knew that I'd be featuring in the *Lancet*, now, wouldn't I, Obsessive Comp—'

Tyler interrupted, 'Isn't that what you do to a boil?'

The penny didn't drop for a moment… lance-it, got it. Realising the conversation had gone decidedly off-piste, I simply answered, 'Ah-ha, so it is,' and left it at that.

All was ready and, as T intended, we were quite close to the wire in order to leave the grave unattended with minimum fuss, vibration and time, for fear of collapse. However today we were well equipped: a nice day, a full packet of cigarettes, a choice of sherry or cider, at which I asked T had his lottery numbers come up. No, he said, he was just feeling flush. We watched the funeral participants arrive and go into church, then we disappeared into our hide and waited, but here unusually you could not see the graveside proceedings from our hiding place.

'Sherry, sir?' offered Tyler, 'as an aperitif?'

'Delighted, sir,' I replied, continuing the stately politeness he had begun.

We settled down and started to put the world to rights, like a right old pair of fishwives. The mourners emerged some thirty minutes later. You could tell the Vicar had done a professional job. Some of the retired or locum vicars could get really carried away, dragging the service out to four pints that would equate to forty-eight non-alcohol minutes or even an hour, but not this one. This was a definite quick two-pinter, had we been near a suitable pub. I think the experience of Alf's 'ruet' of before had damaged him and put him off the whole business of burials. He didn't seem to like funerals at all and the sooner they were over the better, it appeared. He was far happier and more at home with his happy-clappy, guitar-playing morning service.

The mourners stood around the grave for a while; they often did when the deceased was young and this sadly was no exception. Many of this lot must have been his car-loving mates, evidenced by the suits that had clearly been dusted-off and didn't quite fit, along with the poorly tied and ill-fitting ties. Their fingernails would likely be an oily black sight to see.

They stayed long enough for us to enjoy a further round of drinks and by the time we finished they had gone. We picked up our spades and set off to the grave. We were in good spirits, in more ways than one, and all had gone well and to plan so we wouldn't be long filling in and finishing off.

If we had had smiles on our faces they were soon wiped off. As we unsuspectingly peered into the depths, our hearts sank and spirits plummeted. T said nothing initially then said quite quietly, breathing like a tradesman about to give an estimate, 'Oh…' I thought that was quite restrained, as I have to admit that I was thinking considerably more colourful language and in a far larger quantity. The coffin was in the hole, which was the only good thing to say about it. Despite our best efforts the entire side, opposite to where you could see the neighbours, if not for the sheet, had collapsed. They quite surprisingly had gone ahead with the burial. Well, lowering is all it could be described as, as buried the coffin was not. It was sitting almost toppled on its side; you could see as much of the side of it as you could the lid. I looked at Tyler, reluctant to say anything. He just looked back and said resignedly, 'It'll 'ave to come up.' I think he was beyond swearing.

'Up…'

'Yeah, will 'ave to come up and out. This hole is meant to take four, we'd be lucky to get two in if we leave it like this. Besides, bin paid for, digging for four, and there's no room in here,' he said. T resorted to some very expressive words on such occasions, I remember thinking. The non-swearing had obviously worn off.

‘Get the grass off the soil box and get the barrow, PJ, we’ll ‘ave to get ‘im out and then dig out everything what’s fell in and take it away. We’ll ‘ave to do it sharpish, don’t want ‘im on top for long. C’mon, fag break, ‘cause we can’t stop this till it’s done.’

With that we retired to our lair and while T had a cigarette, and we both had a drink, I asked, ‘T, has this happened before?’

‘Yeah,’ he said, ‘not as bad as this though. Generally just fill ‘em in anyhow, but can’t do that here; they more than need the other three spaces in here.’

We took away the grass and planks around the top as we wanted the minimum distance to lift. Dead weight is an entirely accurate term and there were only two of us; it had taken four persons to lower the lad in. T positioned himself at the head end – he wasn’t as heavy as me but much stronger – leaving me the lighter foot end. The ropes to the coffin were still attached.

T said, ‘Yer church bell-ringing skills will come in here, ‘cept this time the weight’s below yer.’

‘Yes,’ I sort of agreed, and we laughed…ish. We needed something to smile about.

‘Get yourself to that end and wrap the ropes round your hands. Shout if you need a rest and we’ll get it on to the edge of the hole,’ T said. When were in position he said, ‘On count of three, lift.’

Well heavy wasn't the word for it. Our friend here wasn't helping, although I'm sure he would have, if he could.

'Let the foot come my way a bit, then I can rest end on this end,' said T, 'then we'll do the same your end.'

'Okay,' I replied.

Things were going more smoothly than I'd thought when there was a significant jolt in the proceedings, followed by a shout. Now either our client had, heaven forbid, fallen out of the bottom, or something had gone wrong at Tyler's end, as the head end had lowered.

'Let your end go,' said Tyler, in obvious pain. This I did and went to his assistance. 'PJ, grab that plank, and stick it under box here, me leg's stuck.'

'On it,' I replied.

The grass edge of the hole had given way under Tyler's right leg. His weight along with that of the intended incumbent had been too much and his leg had slipped into the grave under the coffin, the coffin then sliding down his shin and resting on his foot.

'Jam it in there and tek weight off me leg.' This I duly did and levered the coffin up, until Tyler was free.

'Jam it in side, PJ.' Once the coffin was secure, I helped Tyler up. He had gone in far enough to be sitting on the grass.

'That hurt, took bark off me shin,' said Tyler. Now we all know that shin injuries hurt but for this tough old egg to say so it must have really hurt.

‘That looks angry,’ I said to T as he rolled up his trouser leg: the coffin’s edge had skinned his shin down the middle and it looked very sore indeed, not to mention bloody.

‘Angry, angry,’ said T. ‘It’s not angry, I’m angry.’

I helped him stand up properly and said, ‘C’mon, fag and sherry break – that’s going nowhere for a minute with that plank below it.’ I gestured at the coffin.

‘Good idea,’ replied T.

‘Did I mean fag break, or should I have said leg break?’ I said jokingly.

‘Sod off,’ was my humour’s reward. ‘God,’ he went on, ‘if I didn’t have bad luck I wouldn’t have any.’

‘What did you say?’

‘If I didn’t have bad luck I wouldn’t have any,’ Tyler repeated.

‘I love that. One to remember as I haven’t heard that before.’

We had another look at his leg; there wasn’t much we could do, our field first-aid box was limited. I was amazed there was a first-aid box in the car in the first place, but it soon became apparent that it was indeed more a box with ‘First Aid’ written on it, as it contained two elastic bands, a fading Mars Bar wrapper and a grubby but intact plaster. At least that was evidence that it had once held some useful content. Also present was an obviously rusty but unfired shotgun cartridge, well known for their use in first aid.

‘It’ll be reet,’ said T. ‘It’ll ‘ave to be, we can’t leave this now.’

He wasn’t wrong about that, this was no longer a scene of efficiency; it looked more like a bomb had gone off in a graveyard. We better secured the front plank and as I lifted the feet T pushed another plank below. We repeated this a couple more times and finally our client was back at ground level. We slid him off the hole and away, about four feet to give us room to work. We then both got in. We didn’t need the ladder for the descent, such was the extent of the collapse, but we had it within reach to get out. At least there was no digging to do, just lots of furious shovelling to expel this loose soil from the grave. You couldn’t see enough of the original grave floor to lay a pipe in, let alone get a coffin in. Embarrassing as it would have been for all concerned, it would have been better if the Vicar, or indeed the undertaker’s man, had said something before the lowering. We could at least have done an Alf and dug it out while they sang hymns around our heads.

We filled the barrow, then T said, ‘Just pile it in the soil box. We’ll take it away later if we have to. We’ll have to get ‘im in ‘ere as quick as. You remember all that stuff about Home Office permission and all that.’

‘Surely that doesn’t apply, he’s barely been in the grave ten minutes?’ I queried.

‘No, it does,’ said T. ‘Soon as coffin touches down, that’s it, can’t move ‘em.’

So there was no escape from the fact that with our coffin well and truly on the surface we were, to put it mildly, bending the rules. No sooner had T spoken than we heard the not so distant sound of the latch going on the large churchyard gates. Just when you think things can't get any worse, they have a horrible habit of doing so…

We stopped shovelling and switched to silent running. This wasn't going to look good, however you looked at it, regardless of whom our visitor might be. We looked at each other and waited for what seemed ages, not unlike waiting for a pot to boil. Finally, a figure appeared above us. It was the nervous, grave-hating Vicar, possibly the last person we wanted it to be. With his head some six feet above ours, his cloak gently waving in the wind, he looked a vision of authority and indeed fear. This was the view of him the dead must get, I thought (obviously if they had a view). It was like a scene from a horror film: planks scattered, sheets and greengrocer grass lying discarded in the breeze and, of course, the star of the show, the coffin, sitting proudly on someone else's grave. Boy, did we think we were in for it.

However, he simply said, in a quiet and measured fashion: 'I do not generally see the deceased on the surface after the funeral service, gentlemen.'

There was no opportunity to offer a defence, nothing to say, although I did think of saying, 'Neither do we.' But I thought better of it: it could have inflamed a tense situation and I'd have risked as sore a shin as Tyler's from his boot.

‘I will be in the vestry for fifteen minutes or so and do not expect to see the coffin on my return again. Ever. Is that clear?’

Again, he gave us no opportunity to speak or explain our intended action, but as he turned to go about his business, it had been made plain to us what his requirements and terms and conditions were.

‘I don’t think he’s very pleased,’ I said to Tyler.

‘Well, he can please ‘is self. Shouldn’t ‘ave let ‘em put the thing in in the first place, should ‘e. ‘C’mon, get stuck in, PJ.’

We went as fast as two can, well one and a half with Tyler’s injury, and cleared the hole out in double-quick time. We got the shutters out of the bottom, and one of the purple sheets which had been buried. We now had all neighbours on show and supervising, three on each side, and the head of the coffin in the next row down.

We climbed out, lifted and dragged our client back to his resting place and lowered him in for the second time. He was obviously still mightily heavy, and had got heavier as we had got weaker, but for the lowering at least we had gravity on our side. He could have had a chat going down to all his neighbours, as floors in a lift, who thankfully had not joined him. This grave was beginning to look more and more like a crater. We began filling in, in a more conventional manner, and one by one our now eight visible coffins were returned to their darkness.

Within minutes the Vicar returned. We thought, here we go, but he was surprisingly relaxed about things. God must have calmed him down a bit in his church.

He said, in a less authoritative way now, ‘Thank you gentlemen. Were those other coffins I could see in the sides?’

‘Yes, sir, indeed, really sorry about that, it is just this friable soil, we were hoping it wouldn’t fall in but these are so close together there was nothing left to hold the sides up,’ said Tyler in one explanatory breath.

‘Quite, quite,’ said the Vicar, ‘but you could see them?’

‘Yes, I’m afraid so,’ said Tyler. ‘Graves are just hiding places, sir, out of sight, out of mind, if you like. They’d be rum places if you took all the soil away.’

‘Oh, perish the thought,’ said the Vicar.

‘You “perish the thought”, sir, and we’ll bury it for you,’ said Tyler in an attempt at humour to lighten things up, or it may have been just nerves. However, we all - even the Vicar - chuckled at that: it had indeed been a traumatic and stressful few minutes for us all.

Before he went, he said to Tyler, ‘Is Alf your father?’

‘I’d like to say no, sir, and that it’s just a vicious rumour, but unfortunately yes, I am afraid he is.’

‘Quite a character, with his chortling laugh and his tree root,’ said the Vicar.

‘Yes, that’s ‘im, he does have his moments,’ said Tyler.

‘He’s been doing this a long time?’ the Vicar asked.

‘Since the Burma Railway,’ replied T.

‘Good Lord, that is a long time… and a shocking place to cut his teeth, so to speak. I don’t really care for all this gravedigging, you know. Never really got involved in disposal in the city parish I had. I’m not at all sure I’ll get used to this rural life.’

With that we all bade each other goodbye. PJ thought ‘disposal’, whether by fire or earth, such a clinical and almost distasteful word in many ways for the finale of an often loved, treasured and valued life, but when the chips were down, in essence, that is just exactly what funerals are. The funeral day just the ‘garnish’ around the plate to make the whole experience of bereavement as palatable as possible.

As we finished off, I said, ‘Very good that, T, that “perish the thought” joke.’

‘Ah well I’m full of surprises,’ he replied.

We laughed.

Weeks later we were waiting for a funeral and Tyler had bought a paper; not one of the rags, but one of the more sophisticated newspapers, and not a page 3 in sight. I didn’t say anything, but I surreptitiously watched him doing the crossword therein. He was right, he was full of surprises.

The Vicar wasn't joking about his rural life as within weeks we heard that he had indeed returned to the city. He had been just as prone to peering suspiciously down graves while pretending not to as the rest of us that was for sure. We all do it, believing we are unnoticed, as if therein lies a deep secret, or mystery, or even, PJ suspected, an answer.

I still wonder what we are all expecting to see…

Chapter 15

SETTLE DOWN

One day we went to dig in a small rocky churchyard, or more of a 'chapelyard' really, in a place called Leyrigg. The rocky description was obvious because there was rock outcropping through the rough grass. We were up in the hills here and I always wished I could meet the Abbot or Abbess who had positioned such chapels. There was no apparent immediate population to support, just a chapel on a hillside, and as usual enjoying a spectacular view including the lush valleys, no doubt full of soft deep soil, below. It was abundantly clear on these occasions that the senior ranks in the clergy who chose the position of these ancient chapels did not dig the necessary graves. They must have been chastised by gravediggers down the centuries, as even with our technology of jack hammers and the like, they were a nightmare to dig in. It was simple quarrying and we had none of Alf's 'gelly', thank the Lord.

Leyrigg was no exception. The grave was marked with a stick and was a single - they were all singles in these rocky spots as doubles were all but impossible. This plot was positioned under a big windblown tree, doubtless deeply envious of its counterparts in the valley. It had a visible root system clinging to the rocky hillside's surface, like the veins in an old person's hands and arms. We were prepared though; we had an electric jack hammer. We were not quite so prepared for the plug point to be inside the chapel which turned out, as you might expect, to be firmly locked. So much for the best-laid plans and all that. As a result, we abandoned our twentieth-century jack hammer as useless. We cracked on though - pickaxe, mattock, iron bar, the usual medieval suspects.

We tried to dig the sod off but there simply wasn't enough soil, so we pulled the grass off by hand in as big rafts as it would allow. It was very stony at the top, but it was a slate-type rock and had a cleavage, so it split better than it dug. As we went on it became clear that one side of this grave was going to be smooth following the cleavage of the rock down, with the other side roughly broken by the pick and bar. We toiled away, having the usual comfort breaks and occasional wander around the churchyard.

Some of the gravestones were technically at the wrong end of the graves, on the feet as it were. I think this was to encourage as many passers-by as possible to read them, as interested parties would be few and far between in this remote spot. At least if the stones faced the entrance there was a chance they would be read; if they'd been placed at the head end of the grave only the back of the stone would be exhibited to visitors on the way in. One chap had been an artist and his stone deserved viewing due to the patterns carved into the granite and around its edge. He had the grand name of Rupert de Montague; you could almost picture a fine, cravat-and-maroon-felt-waistcoat wearing gentleman poised at his easel, a masterpiece flowing from his brushwork, perhaps puffing contentedly on his pipe.

So not only was the land around this chapel awful for digging but also bad for access, and the whole place was built in such a way that it was all back to front. Whatever we might think of our planning departments nowadays, this location and positioning surely would never have got through.

I went to get the wheelbarrow and T said, 'PJ, sort through the soil box leaving the rock and little stuff.' This I duly did, and we continued although progress was slow.

'Fancy a pint?' said Tyler out of the blue. Was he hallucinating? Seeing people through exhaustion, or perhaps even talking to himself?

'Me?' I said, wondering who he could conceivably be talking to.

'Yes, course you, you melon, who else is there up 'ere?'

My question was indeed a stupid one, but in my defence I retorted, 'Well it's not the most obvious question to be asked by a man in a grave in the middle of nowhere.'

'Well, do yer?'

I thought I would humour him and replied, 'Great, love one, first-class idea.'

I thought he would say, 'We'll go on the way home,' or some such remark, but no, he said,

'Righto, c'mon, let's go.' He must have nicked a couple of pint pots from the pub and bought some tinnies for a change, I thought. But no, we boarded the car.

'Shouldn't we put the planks over the hole and hide the tools?' I asked.

'D'you really think someone's going to trail up here to fall in a hole or nick a spade or both, in the next half an hour?' was my almost rebuking immediate reply. I had to concede he had a point; it was unlikely. 'If they want to nick a spade from up here, they can 'ave it.'

With that we set off. After about three miles we came to a crossroads, with two routes crossing like ribbons laid across the landscape into which they disappeared. In one of the angles of the crossroads there was a farm with a concrete yard abutting the road. The yard had assorted old tractors and machinery apparently abandoned in it, on a highly polluted and muddy and uneven surface. As we got out of the car we could firstly smell, secondly hear, and thirdly see a big old barn full of pigs, who were crowded round the entrance to their quarters. You could see others running back through what was left of a field on the other side of the barn. I think they thought the sound of our engine signalled feeding time, but we were sadly to disappoint them on this occasion.

I said to Tyler, 'Well, this is all very interesting.' I was secretly thinking he needed sectioning if he thought we could get a pint here. Mind you, in fairness, he hadn't said a pint of what. T looked at me and gestured upwards to the corner of the yard above a heavy wooden door, where swung an old sign simply saying 'Mable's'.

We went in and were presented with a rudimentary pub, simple in its layout and, judging by the three pumps on show and a solitary bottle of whisky, adequately if sparsely stocked. At the back of the bar there were two barrels at an angle, with jugs nearby.

After some several minutes a lady out of a Dickens novel appeared and said, 'Now then, Tyler, I know why thy's 'ere.'

'I'd love to come more, Mable, but I only come for one thing,' he chortled, as Mable poured a Guinness.

She then addressed me. 'We's call 'im the Grim Reaper up 'ere,' she said. 'Only comes when someone's deed… Who might you be?'

Before I could answer Tyler said, 'This is PJ, Mable, 'e's my new posh helper.' 'Posh helper'? I thought. Almost a compliment, if a little loaded.

‘What d’you drink, Mr PJ?’ she said mischievously.

‘May I have a pint of bitter, please, dear lady.’ At this both Mable and Tyler laughed heartily.

As she pulled me a pint she said, still laughing, to Tyler, ‘See what you mean.’

The beer was nothing short of fabulous, and we were soon onto our second. Mable had got the fire going.

‘Who’s yer buryin’ now then?’ she said to Tyler.

‘Don’t know. Thought you might know or ‘ave heard, Mable?’

‘Nay, but it’s a big spot up ‘ere and there’s quite a few offcomers moved in t’ valley below… ‘appen one o’ them, or someone from away.’

If it had been someone from the extended farming community you could bet your bottom dollar she’d know.

We got up to reluctantly leave. This was an eye-opener of a pub and I loved it. On our way to the door Mable said, ‘What time’s funeral, Tyler?’

‘Half past two.’

‘Yous comin’ ‘ere first then?’

I for one was really hoping T would say yes, but I was quietly confident as it was like an invite. Tyler replied, ‘Love to, Mable.’

‘I’ll run you up a bit of a sandwich then.’

‘Great, that would be lovely, thank you,’ I replied, hardly able to contain my enthusiasm. We got back in the car.

‘Like it up here now, PJ?’

‘You’re not kidding.’

‘These sheep farmers like a pint or eight at end of the day.’ he smiled.

After my limited experience of sheep, I could see that sheep farming on this scale and up here was not for the faint-hearted, but Mable’s must certainly rank as a perk. She didn’t appear to close either: if she was awake then the bar was open.

‘I thought it was a pig farm,’ I said.

‘Nah, just a bit o’ a sideline, an ‘obby.’

Well I thought I was an ‘obby farmer’, but clearly I was nowhere near even that.

On our return to Leyrigg, enlivened by that ale and Guinness, we threw ourselves back at our task. The rock was splitting quicker now and the barrow wasn’t so heavy. I felt like an Irish navvy of the nineteenth century whose staple diet included fabulous amounts of ale to give him energy.

‘Finished,’ Tyler announced, ‘that’ll do. When it’s in we can pile the top up a bit, not like these others’ – he gestured around us – ‘but a bit to account for settling.’

Some of the surrounding graves were frankly ridiculous, as the spoil had all been left on top of them. The angular stone would lock together and these heaps would never settle; they were simply an eyesore and made any form of grass-cutting impossible. It almost looked as if they had simply put the coffin down and encased it in rubble, which had now sprouted hardy, wispy and tufty grass. It could only be down to the idleness or inexperience of long-gone gravediggers; probably just local farm lads, so inexperience was the kinder thought.

I woke the next morning full of excitement at the thought of lunch. I was looking forward to Mable's beer and sandwich. Tyler picked me up about eleven o'clock, so we had time to have our pre-arranged lunch and do the finishing touches to the grave, more commonly known as 'tarting it up a bit', ready for the two-thirty funeral. What could be better? We got to Mable's, to the same friendly greeting, and after pouring the beers she presented us with two sandwiches and a piece of pork pie. The sandwiches made the door stop cliché look mean, and the pie and pickle were to die for. I don't think either Tyler or I had ever had such a lunch and we did it justice. The old farm dog, Kimi (the 'i' having been affectionately added on retirement Mable said), that had been curled up by the fire with just one eye open didn't do too badly either; she seemed quite happy in retirement, especially today. She had greeted us with a cursory sniff of Purdey and Stromble no doubt and then lost interest and started making preparations for a hard afternoon's kip. I felt right at home and like I had known Mable and her place for years.

Tyler said, 'We better get up there about two o'clock, just to put grass out and sheets down, and we'll be reet.'

We paid Mable a pitiful amount - she wouldn't take a penny more than she asked for, so we made a generous donation to the Air Ambulance collecting box on her bar instead, about which she was really pleased.

''bout the only ambulance that can get up here in winter,' she said.

'Aye,' Tyler said, and that I could believe. There was a faded article from the paper pinned to the beam above the collection box, with a picture of Mable standing by a helicopter in recognition of how much she and her hill-farmer clients had raised one year. It certainly wasn't her only claim to fame in my book, nor an insignificant donation.

We got back up to Leyrigg about ten past two. We were fine for time as the grave itself was not on a direct route to the chapel door.

While we were sitting in the car I said to Tyler, 'There's not many here for a half two start.'

In fact, more accurately, there was no one there, not a car or person for miles. I went on, 'Must be one of those Manchester-type jobs like matey-boy at Tewthwaite.'

'Aye,' said Tyler.

Then just for good measure I said, 'You didn't get this one off that answering machine of yours, did you?'

'No,' was the firm, reassuring reply.

'And there isn't somewhere else that sounds like Leyrigg?'

'No. Mind, there is somewhere called Greyrigg.'

'I do hope you are joking?'

'No, no, there is, but up in t' Lake District somewhere,' he said, laughing to himself and at me.

'You!' I exclaimed, simply making him laugh all the more.

'Well,' I said belligerently, 'Where's your – this - funeral then?'

'I'm not sure,' said T, this time not very reassuringly. 'You go get the planks off and I'll bring the grass – oh and 'ere, take soil box and ropes, will yer PJ.'

I made my way to the grave weighed down by my delicious but huge lunch. As I approached I noticed the planks were off and stacked neatly by the side of the raw hole. They were on for sure last night, but I wasn't unduly concerned. I got to the graveside yards before Tyler who looked like a green Star Wars type wookie walking across, greengrocer grass trailing everywhere.

I looked down and called, 'Tyler, you won't be needing that stuff today.'

'What?'

'The grass and sheets.'

'What about them?' he said, nearing.

'You won't be needing them today.'

T looked down. 'Oh bother!' he exclaimed (as usual not the exact quote). 'What on earth is that doing there?'

'I don't know,' I said sheepishly. He dropped the greengrocer grass and purple sheets on the grass.

'Ah well, we better get on with it.' He sighed.

The problem was our undressed grave had, to our considerable surprise, got a coffin in it. Now it shouldn't be unusual, or a complete surprise, to anyone, let alone a gravedigger, to see a coffin in a grave. They sort of go together like bread and butter or bacon and egg, but on this occasion unusual it certainly was, as this coffin shouldn't have been there… yet.

I apologised profusely to an Edith Redfearn, who had made the ripe old age of ninety-four. Both Tyler and I were stumped as to how this had happened, and his professional pride had taken a serious blow. This should never have occurred. Tyler had his faults, as do we all, but shoddy presentation for the mourners was not one of them. We filled it in in almost complete silence, packing the rock back in, the slate-like faces of the stones against the side of the coffin almost bricking her in, one after the other. I could tell Tyler was frustrated and really wanted to complete this so that he could start finding out what had happened. We left a small bump on the top for settlement and we were done. Unusually there were no flowers.

We went back to Cliff Field but my description of lunch to Sam would have to wait. We had a quick sherry and shared with Sam the ideas we had had on the way home. There was only one plausible explanation, which was that we had got the time wrong. Tyler wanted to know how and why. The job hadn't been right, and he needed to get to the bottom of it and know why. Was it his fault, Alf's, the undertaker's, or had he himself forgotten something? Or was it another blow dealt by that blessed antique answering machine?

He borrowed Sam's phone and rang the undertaker. All Sam and I could hear was a series of yesses and noes, with intermittent laughter. Tyler had a deep voice, like Alf's, when he was being serious.

He looked relieved as he announced, 'It's his fault; he put his hand up. He told us half past two, but should have been half past twelve.'

'Was he all right about it?' I asked.

'Aye. Couldn't be much else, could he? I think he's been grovelling to the relatives, though. We were the least of his worries. Mind you, give 'im credit, he apologised to us as well when I told him I wasn't happy.'

The following week we were in Wragg - another unusual name for a village I always thought. Boulders are a gravedigger's worst enemy, always uncooperative, and boy, this deposit was a classic, chock full of them. This churchyard was built on boulder clay, in the same way as the glacial drumlin at Preston Banks churchyard, the difference being that this deposit was not in the form of a hill but was a level deposit, no doubt filling in a previous valley floor. The other difference was that, unlike Banks, the clay part was soft and diggable but the boulder part was random, frequent and unforgiving. This grave, when we had dug it the day before, was almost fifty-fifty boulders to clay. The biggest boulder in here had required the roll-up-a-plank-a-bit-at-a-time treatment; the smallest was about the size of a cricket ball. The boulders were well-rounded sandstone ones making the larger ones really difficult to manhandle – where were the World's Strongest Man competitors when you needed them?

'Wheel away as many boulders as you can, PJ,' Tyler had said. 'There's a boulder tip at the bottom corner over there. Shake off all the clay you can.'

'Why are we taking them all away, T?' I asked. My only theory was that they would make an awful clatter onto a coffin, or worse still could go through the lid, and Tyler would not risk that.

'Why do you think?'

I explained my theories, which he almost laughed off. There would only be us listening to the clatter, he pointed out. 'Who's going to hear it out here?' were his exact words, and if the lid split so be it, it would do anyway in time. He then began to tease me, like I was stupid, with a *Twenty Questions* type format:

Q. What are we digging? A. A grave.

Q. What sort of grave? A. A Double

Q. What does that mean? A. Someone's died

Q. What sort of someone? A. A married person

Q. What sort of married person? A. Likely an old one.

And so on… I still didn't get it.

'So,' said Tyler, 'we've established we likely have an older married person, just from deduction.' He raised an eyebrow. 'Agreed?'

Q. What might happen next? A. I don't know.

I conceded I was stupid…

'C'mon, PJ, use your loaf. The other partner might die?'

'So?' (I was being particularly thick now.)

'So! So listen, you daft egg, let's just say this is for hubby, and wifey is to go on top? And if he's old, unless you're Rod Stewart, she's likely to be old also? Are you following me so far?'

'Yes.'

'Well how much did you enjoy manhandling them boulders out yesterday?'

'Not much,' I conceded, and 'those', I thought (but T was too old to change his ways grammatically now).

'Well if we put 'em back and she pops her clogs, we've got to get 'em out again haven't we, to do the reopen?'

I got it then, slow even by my standards, I had to admit to myself. 'I really never thought of that, T.'

'No, I know you didn't, that's why it's took me twenty minutes to explain it to you. Gravedigging rule, never put big stuff back onto first one in a double 'cause you're likely the poor bugger who's going to have to get it out again. I did one at Lealeet once and did I curse the so-and-so that dug the first hole and filled it in with near solid rock knowing it would 'ave to come out again. There were no beer tins in it though, so can't 'ave bin old Dick who did digging before me. Do that and you're gambling that the second one of couple will live longer than you or your gravedigging career.'

Well, there was a first. I'd never heard of gravedigging being called a career before, but I think it is still some way off the National Curriculum or a degree course. Mind you, when you see some of the apparent nonsense that is 'degree course-able' nowadays, I don't know so much. If you can do a degree in some colossally overpaid individual called 'a footballer', gravedigging must surely have a chance.

Finally, though, we got the grave finished and it was quite a neat one. One or two large holes in the sides where boulders had been, all in all quite a smart job. On some occasions, not this one fortunately, we'd had to move graves because some boulders were just too big to dig out or jack-hammer through. This one was okay, although the finished product looked like we had been digging through plasticine. T said another way with big boulders if you couldn't lift them, especially if on your own, was to roll them back and to along the length of the grave, digging either side until below the finished coffin depth. He was full of tricks. (I had to admit to myself that I wouldn't have thought of that either…)

When we returned the next day, the weather was good, and it seemed all would go like clockwork. The village of Wragg was just a stone's throw away, and was home to a classic country pub. Not a 'Mable's', but I think she has her own special place in the hierarchy of pubs. Tyler however assured me this pub was a quaint place, horse brasses and that sort of thing, and I was looking forward to it.

We went into the graveyard past the boulder pile, our fresh ones showing up on top as they were still damp and had bits of clay stuck to them. I asked T why this pile was so visible. Usually these waste piles were hidden away behind bushes or a natural feature, but this one was near the gate, bold as brass.

T said, 'Why do you think?' I thought: What's up with him lately? He was answering every question with a question. 'Well, think about it,' he said.

'Er…' I mumbled, searching for a reply.

'Look, how many graves are there in here?' Another question. I was beginning to think I was indeed at gravedigging school. Perhaps I would be awarded a diploma? A 'Diploma in Gravedigging', the letters 'D.I.G' after your name. PJ was easily amused and distracted but thought it best not to share with Tyler for the time being.

'I don't know, hundreds.'

‘Yeah, hundreds, so if all them holes produced as many rocks as ours, and they hadn’t been put back in, we would be walking through a moonscape with boulders everywhere.’

‘I suppose we would…’

‘The pile there is so locals, builders and that, can take ‘em away.’ It appeared that anyone (strong) could just help themselves. What a good idea, I thought; they would make fine rockery and garden stones.

Tyler added with a grimacing smile: ‘Graveyard recycling it is, and there’s not much in here you want to recycle is there?’

‘No’ I replied.

What a thought: recycling bodies. Mind you, PJ always thought crems should have a power station the other side of their evergreen hedges. It still seems crazy to burn one infinite natural resource, namely us ‘the general public’, with another but finite resource, namely gas, which involves immense industry and danger to those who extract it, as experienced by PJ in his oil rig days. True “People Power” PJ smiled to himself but doubted such common sense would ever catch on though. ‘Aunty Freda’ keeping the living room lights on, would no doubt be viewed with outrage and not be seen as a vote winner. Be deemed as ridiculous by some anonymous chinless Whitehall wonder, happy with our current unsustainable and polluting method…, or increasingly would it? We have all burnt a pork chop under the grill though haven’t we? (I rest my case). We could indeed cremate one client with the next perhaps, a true ‘chain reaction’.

Our grave had held up beautifully, and it really was a nice morning. The grass was covered with dew and cobwebs; these spider characters were such a busy lot. I jumped in to do my usual summary clean-out; good job on this occasion as there was a small, almost spherical boulder plumb in the middle of the grave. The coffin would have rocked like a seesaw, not to mention the backache it would ultimately give the client. I showed it to Tyler, who said well done. I nearly went for a cup of sweet tea and a lie-down: he was usually unmerciful in his condemnation of my little tidy-ups.

'That needed to come out,' he said. 'It's just when you parp about with leaves it gets on my goat.'

'Well,' I said, 'leaves matter; they have rights too you know.'

'Don't start,' said Tyler, so I didn't.

This grave was really smart, I would say nice, but it is difficult to get the word 'nice' and 'grave' into the same sentence, unless other words in the sentence are Fred West or Hitler, or any number of other evildoers you can think of. However, this grave was a good one, very neat, and it was against a large hedge that bordered and enclosed the Vicar's garden.

We often saw the Vicar on his train, the ground vibrating gently before a booming voice called out, 'Morning, chaps.' His track circumnavigated the garden boundary; he had both a diesel and a steam motor unit. It is a lasting memory to see a Vicar, robe blowing in the wind and his dog collar on, all topped-off with a blue oil-stained Fred Dibner hat, thundering past astride his own train. It could fair lick along as well.

We left the grave at about eleven o'clock, and went to the pub. The funeral was at half past, so we had a good hour and a half. There was a pool table in the pub, so we had a few games. I didn't think I was bad at pool, having played a bit at university, but Tyler made me look like I was playing my first game. He was very good, advertising a misspent youth. I asked him where he had learned to play like that, growing up in a small village in the days before under-eighteens were allowed in pubs, and out of the two pubs only one having a table.

'There used to be a coffee shop opposite the station, where all us young 'uns met, bit like *Happy Days* and Fonzie. Learnt it there, as there was nowt else to do except play pool and Salty.'

'Salty?'

'Yeah,' said Tyler, grinning as if he was fifteen again.

'What's Salty?'

'Not what, who.'

'Okay, then who's Salty?'

'You learnt pool in the coffee shop, and about girls with Salty… She was very friendly and accommodating.' I reminded myself of how lucky and privileged I had been going to an eye-wateringly expensive boys' boarding school. Girls for us lived in zoos, and that was it, only the food was salty.

‘Why was she called Salty?’ I asked, almost dreading the answer.

‘Ha-ha,’ laughed Tyler, ‘because she made you thirsty for more.’

‘Oh,’ I said, not really knowing what to say and feeling green with envy of his youth.

All too soon it was time to go back to work. It was great to have a job where, when you went back, there wasn’t some clever clogs self-righteous manager telling his line boss that he could smell drink on you. Yes, that was great, and it was a beautiful summer’s day to boot. We went and sat in the car; we could see the grave about a hundred yards away. Tyler produced two pork pies from his sherry carrier bag.

‘Lunch,’ he said, ‘thought I’d treat yer.’

‘Thank you,’ I said. I meant it, too. It was kind of him and that pie really hit the spot. He was not well known for buying solid foods.

We saw the burial take place with no obvious problems, well not from our distance, and the officials and mourners slowly moved away. A lady lingered a little while on her own, before a younger lady and gentleman came back for her; they were only waiting out of sight in a bend of the Vicar’s hedge. We guessed it was Mum saying her final farewells to her husband, and she was being looked after by the children. We went over when they had gone and inspected our handiwork. All was fine, coffin neatly in, a good fit. The sheets and everything were intact.

‘Right,’ said Tyler. ‘Let’s fill it in. Oh PJ, while I think about it, was that five two, or five two? Just can’t remember.’

‘Five two, as you very well know.’

‘Thought so,’ laughed Tyler and started pulling the ropes out. He was, of course, referring to his victorious pool score.

It was all going very smoothly. T asked me to start taking stuff back to the car and trailer, which I did. As I was dismantling one side of the soil box, while Tyler was shovelling in from the other side, my side being empty, I did notice that there wasn’t much soil, well, clay left in the box.

I said, ‘Have we got enough stuff here to fill this to the top?’

‘Nope,’ said Tyler in a very matter-of-fact manner.

‘Well what are we going to do?’

‘Just take all the stuff away and we’ll see how we are doing.’

Ten minutes later we were finished. Everything was cleared away, the last grain of soil scraped in and we had not gained the surface by some way.

‘Eighteen inches,’ Tyler announced.

‘As much as that?’

‘Yep. Makes you realise the volume of rock we shifted out in them boulders.’

‘Yes, it does,’ I said, giving up on the ‘them’s. ‘So what’s next?’

‘We’ll have a walk round to see if there is any soil lying about or any graves with too much on. You go up that way to the left, I’ll do the other.’ T lit a cigarette and off we set.

We met back at the grave with bad news.

‘No good?’ T asked.

‘No.’

‘Me neither, but I think I’ve solved it though.’

‘Do tell.’

‘It’s simple and just round the corner. C’mon, I’ll show you.’

We walked along the hedge until it curved away from the car-park wall. ‘*Voilà,*’ said Tyler. I looked into the corner.

‘Grass cuttings!’ I exclaimed.

‘The very same. If we pack ‘em really tight down they’ll be fine.’

‘You sure?’

‘You got a better idea?’

‘Well,’ I burbled, ‘as it happens, no…’

‘Get the barrow,’ T said, and we were off.

Digging grass cuttings with a spade is not easy – in fact it’s close to impossible – but it was our only hope. We resorted to loading the barrow by the armfuls, it was miles quicker. After we had filled the grave up to overflowing, we began jumping up and down on the grass in an effort to compact it.

I said to T, ‘I hope no one sees us doing this, it must look a bit odd.’

‘Just keep at it before anyone does see us.’

We stopped for a sherry and fag break, then went for more grass.

‘One more trip should do it,’ said T.

I was surprised by just how hot the grass was inside the heap, steaming hot, and this was a warm day. We repeated the trampling procedure, put the sods of turf back and positioned the flowers. We swept away the few tell-tale grass cuttings round the edge and all looked well. Tyler always left a grave on the assumption that the relations would be coming back later in the day or soon after, so he wanted it as smart as was feasibly possible.

‘Good job,’ he said. ‘Fancy losing at pool on our way home?’

‘Don’t mind if I do.’

‘Masochist…' he said gleefully

‘I don’t think so. My time will come.’

Tyler looked at me; if he’d had glasses on he would have been looking over the top of them. ‘Really?’ he said confidently.

The next two or three weeks were routine on the gravedigging front. Tyler was doing a lot of groundworks; it was that time of year, with mowing and so on. He came to Cliff Field one day to do some fencing work in the jungle for Sam. Before he started we had a beer in my workshop/shed.

‘The Vicar at Wragg rang me this morning,’ he said.

‘Wragg?’

‘You know, Vicar with train and Fred Dibner hat.’

‘Oh Wragg… What did he want?’

‘He asked if we could pop back to that grave near his hedge that we did three weeks ago.’

‘The grass-cutting hole?’

‘That’s the one.’

‘What’s up?’

‘Well, Vicar said it’s settled a bit, and could we go and sort it out.’

‘Oh, settled a bit, has it? You didn’t tell him?'

‘No, but I did say we’d sort it out… We can load up some soil from Seascale.’

When we went the following day, we could see that the Vicar’s ‘settled a bit’ was, to say the least, generous. It had settled over a foot; the flower remains and grass had all gone down with the surface.

The Vicar spotted us while we were trying to put it right. ‘Morning, chaps.’

‘Morning, sir,’ I replied with equal cheer.

‘I’ve never seen one settle as much so quickly.’

‘No, I haven’t either,’ said T in his poshest voice.

‘You’d think it had been filled in with grass cuttings, wouldn’t you?’ the Vicar continued in jolly tone.

I looked at Tyler with a degree of panic, but he simply said laughingly, ‘Yes, you would, can’t understand it.’

‘Well, I’ll leave you to it. Thank you for coming back to rectify it so quickly. Cheerio.’

‘Cheerio, Vicar,’ we chorused.

‘You don’t think he knew about the grass cuttings, do you, Tyler?’

‘Course he knew,’ came the reply.

Chapter 16

SMASHING!

One day I was driving up the lane to Cliff Field on my way back from the local builders supply merchants. I had been to pick up some blocks for Stan in the skip on the back of my Fordson Super Major tractor. It was as old as I was but a great workhorse. As I passed Sooty's he flagged me down. I stopped and switched off the engine. It was fantasy to think you could have a conversation with the tractor running; it worked fine, but the silencer left a great deal to be desired.

'Hello,' I greeted Sooty.

He didn't answer but glanced around like Inspector Clouseau as if checking that we were alone. Still without saying anything, he gestured me down from the tractor and towards his den in his ex-garage. I followed his lead and went in.

Sooty said in a low voice, as if he feared the den was bugged, 'Got a new brew for you to try.'

The level of secrecy was for the benefit of Esme, Sooty's wife of a hundred and fifty years or so who, whilst Sooty lived in his garage, lived in her kitchen. Territory reigned supreme, with Sooty only allowed inside the house, PJ suspected, after the newspapers had been put down. She appeared to be almost surgically attached to a large, rarely silent, pressure cooker. Sooty was utterly convinced that Esme was blissfully unaware of his ale-brewing activities yards from her back door, which was as unlikely as it was ridiculous.

His house was a classically designed three-bedroom semi, with garden front and back. Sooty had given over his entire back garden to vegetable growing. He had dug the lawn up years ago. Whilst this veg garden was not enormous it was necessarily well organised and beautifully kept, including a greenhouse.

Sooty handed me a large plastic yoghurt carton. 'Just tap any soil out of that,' he advised.

I did my best but could not get it entirely clean: this beer was to have an additional earthy element, if not 'rooty'. The beer was in a plastic barrel up on his workbench; he took my yoghurt pot from me and filled it to the top, followed by one for himself. Although the sides of the yoghurt pots were not transparent, I could see that this brew looked very appetising indeed, with a creamy foam top on a clear brown base.

'Sorry I've got no glasses,' Sooty apologised. 'I'll have to pinch a couple from the kitchen, when she's not looking.'

It struck me that men never really grow up. I took a good swallow from my yoghurt pot, taking care not to lacerate my lips on the less-than-kind (for drinking purposes) rims on the vessel. The beer was surprisingly pleasant in comparison with some home brews I have had over the years.

'What do you think?' said Sooty, before I had finished this first draught.

As soon as I'd said 'Smashing,' which I'd genuinely meant, it was obvious I had spoken too soon. I was aware of a very distinct aftertaste, sort of familiar but hard to pinpoint. I finished my pot, and was again hit by this peculiar taste, but still couldn't put my finger on it. My pot was generously replenished, though I did notice that Sooty hadn't guzzled his beer with the same enthusiasm.

I was about halfway down when Sooty said, 'Do you think it's got a bit of an aftertaste?'

Trying not to appear impolite, I said, 'Well it's got a lovely colour and texture, but now you mention it, I can detect something after I've swallowed it.'

‘Aye,’ said Sooty, ‘hits you right in the back of your throat, doesn’t it?’

‘Yes,’ I reluctantly agreed. At least I knew it wasn’t just me.

‘I can’t understand it… Never happened before.’

I didn’t want to insult the man’s intelligence or upset him and wanted to employ tact, but I felt I had to ask the obvious. ‘Did you change anything that you did last time?’

‘No…’ was his clearly musing reply.

I felt like Jonathan Creek trying to explain the apparently impossible. I thought I would start at the beginning and it didn’t take long to have a fair guess at the problem. I asked if the kit was out of date and was assured that it wasn’t.

‘Did you sterilise all your equipment?’ I enquired.

‘Yes.’

‘Did you use Camden tablets?’

‘Ran out.’ I began to wonder if my investigation was making progress. ‘I used boiling water,’ Sooty added.

‘Well that should do, I would have thought,’ I said, still puzzling over the cause.

He more worryingly went on: ‘And just to be on the safe side, gave the barrel a rinse, yeah good rinse, with a drop o’ bleach.’

‘Drop o’ bleach!’ My brain screamed, before my stomach panicked. Bingo! Our mystery taste was revealed. I had never knowingly drunk bleach before. I did know of a lady who had drunk bleach, she was one our clients. I finished my drink, now looking forward to the whack in the throat. It didn’t disappoint: the aftertaste was unmistakably that of a branded domestic cleansing product, that claimed to kill 99% of germs. PJ just hoped that the one percent of him would survive!

I thanked Sooty, restarted the tractor and was away.

When I told Sam the bleach story, she laughed. ‘You won’t need worming or your colon irrigating any time soon then. No flies on you,’ she said. That wasn’t very reassuring, I thought. She had a cruelly mischievous streak sometimes.

A couple of days later Sooty came down the drive to Cliff Field pushing his wheelbarrow. This only ever meant one thing; he had cropped some veg and was bringing the outer leaves or stems for the sheep. They knew the score too as they bleated anxiously when they heard the squeak of the barrow wheel. Today it was sprout stalks. Often he would hide a bottle of his latest home-made wine under the veg - a pea-pod brew or similar - so that Esme wouldn’t know. He really did believe he could deceive her after donkey’s years of marriage. Pull the other one, Sooty, you must think she was born yesterday, which very visibly she was not.

He pulled up next to our coal bunker, cleared a way through the sprouts, and produced like a rabbit out of a hat the whole barrel of beer.

‘I thought you enjoyed this so much the other day I would give it to you,’ he announced proudly.

‘Oh, thanks,’ I said as enthusiastically as possible, which was no easy task.

‘Can you let me have the barrel back.’

‘Yes, no problem, thank you…’ (if it doesn’t dissolve PJ thought, but didn’t say).

I could have tipped it out there and then but that would have been unforgivable. I ran it off from the coal bunker at about two pints a day, concerned that the daily decrease should look credible on Sooty’s frequent visits and also concerned not to risk dissolving the limestone chippings beneath. After all, they had survived four hundred million years or so of what the planet could throw at them, but I felt that Sooty’s brew could be a step too far and spell their end.

Tyler tried some, as free booze was always of interest and could not be passed by lightly, but even he could not do this stuff, which sort of said it all.

Three weeks after the bleach incident, Sooty and I met again in his garage. This time I was walking past when he whistled to me. I could not help noticing his changed appearance. Gone was the bald Sooty. Well, bald except for a monk-like band of grey hair; not a full circumference, more of a horseshoe shape. Now suddenly and apparently overnight he had developed a full head of hair. A greater transformation there could not be, it was ridiculous. Firstly the hair was mousy-blonde in colour, presumably Sooty's original colour, and it was so obviously a poorly fitting toupée. We have all been in that situation where you bite your lip or clench your mouth muscles in order to suppress a laugh. Well that was the position in which I found myself and, as a consequence, in some difficulty. 'Should have gone to Specsavers' without doubt.

I went into the garage trying desperately not to laugh or simply stare at this thing on his head. It was a good job he didn't walk in the woods, as I dare say someone would have tried to get a shot off thinking it was a passing squirrel. From Sooty's manner I could tell he was in a serious mood, and the fear that he had bad news distracted me from the aberration on his head - if an eye had 'peeped' of this growth it would not have been a complete surprise.

'You'll have a drop of wine, will yer, PJ?' he said.

Despite my palate and throat screaming 'no, don't do it' (they only recently having recovered from the bleach) my mouth said: 'Great, thanks that would be lovely.'

This time he tapped the soil out of the yoghurt pots himself. I didn't bat an eyelid at that: it's funny how you get used to things. I sipped at the wine almost dreading swallowing it after my recent experience, but I went for it. My worries were unfounded, it was really quite pleasant, though from what it was made I couldn't even guess and it was probably better not to know.

Sooty was very Tom and Barbara, for anyone who remembers *The Good Life*. If it had been any part of a fruit or vegetable it would make wine was Sooty's view.

We stood facing each other. I was trying to look at anything but his head. I said, 'You look very smart today, Sooty.' I deserved an Equity card for that, acting beyond the call of duty, but laugh I did not.

'Terrible thing,' Sooty said, with no clues as to what he was referring to. However it was a perfect description of his toupée, but he surely couldn't have meant that. You wouldn't wear that thing then criticise it, or would you? Perhaps it was he who should have the Equity card. He was wearing his best, but 'not new' is a fair assessment, brown pinstripe suit and a black tie though, looking as smart as I'd ever seen him, which sadly wasn't saying a lot.

'Yes, terrible,' he went on, still in a darkly serious mood. 'I've been to Clampton, to my friend's wife's funeral, terrible thing, big funeral.'

'I'm sorry to hear that, Sooty,' I sympathised.

'Ah well… comes to us all, and she had done all right at eighty-four.'

'Indeed she had,' I said. 'What was her name?'

'Flo.'

I didn't know why I had asked really. Utterly irrelevant, but you just do, don't you?

'Terrible thing,' Sooty said yet again.

Surely Flo's death couldn't be described as a 'terrible thing'? We had established her age, and that she was popular. 'Big funeral' had been my clue there. Again I was beginning to feel like Jonathan Creek. I couldn't resist any longer, as I wanted to know why this particular death had been any more terrible than any other, so I thought I'd go fishing with his own term to see if that would flush out an explanation with an attempt at open questioning.

'Yes, Sooty, it is a terrible thing, but as you say it happens to the best of us, this dying, you just never know…?' said with as encouraging a quizzical look as I could muster.

'No, no, lad, it's not her dying that's terrible,' he said whilst topping up our glasses (to describe yoghurt pots through rose-tinted specs). Great, we were getting there, it worked I thought.

'It's what happened…' he tantalisingly started.

Oh do tell, Sooty, please. My curiosity was fit to burst. Another prompt was needed. Hopefully he didn't want me to chance the impossible guess. 'What was that then?' I said.

'What? What happened?' said Sooty.

Yes, yes! I screamed inside, 'what happened?' While Sooty had gained a full head of hair overnight I was about to start pulling mine out. Come on man, let's be having you. Get on with it. The suspense was becoming intolerable, so no further delay please…

‘Well,’ Sooty said, ‘do you know Clampton?’

Phew I thought a start: ‘Well I know the supermarket and the traffic lights.’

‘That’ll do. Just before the traffic lights there’s a car garage?’

‘There’s a Chinese between the lights and the garage.’

‘That’s it. Well there’s a road on same side as Chinese opposite the garage?’

‘I know the one.’

‘Flo and Ed live up there, where it rises quite steeply before dropping away.’ said Sooty

‘Got you.’ I chirped, strongly resisting the sore temptation to make fun that they were not known as ‘Ed and Flo’ or they would have sounded like all things tidal.

‘Well, they live in row of terraces near top. Railway houses, you know. Well, we were all in the house and milling about having a sherry, like you do, and there were some floral tributes laid out on the little tiled yard outside the front door.’ He picture-painted.

C’mon, Sooty, spit it out. That would have been good advice for that beer but it didn’t, fortunately, apply to this wine, which Sooty was topping us up with again.

‘Well, the hearse arrived and parked outside the house, and the driver and undertaker got out. The undertaker went to talk to Ed with the usual reassurances, while the driver began picking up the flowers and wreaths to load onto the coffin in the hearse. That’s when it happened. Terrible.’

Oh please put me out of my misery. I was so immersed in his story I had quite forgotten about the bird’s nest on his head. Pray, what happened? He was the master of doe-eyed hesitation.

‘Never made a sound. First I knew was somebody shouted. When I looked and saw it, it was terrible.’

Was I going to have to go down and beg on bended knee? I would if it would help.

‘The hearse ran off down the hill,’ he said in a half-whisper.

What! I thought. It did what? Did I hear that right!?

‘Sooty!’ I exclaimed in abject bewilderment. ‘What?’

‘It ran off down the hill. Driver dropped everything, the floral displays, the lot, but nothing he could do. He ran after it, but it was no good, it was well away.’

‘It ran off down the hill,’ I repeated, although how I talked with my mouth aghast and open I don’t know. The seed of a completely inappropriate but unavoidable laugh had been sown in the pit of my stomach.

‘What happened next?’ I said excitedly, as provided this hadn’t ended in utter carnage it had the potential to be explosively funny.

‘Well,’ Sooty explained, ‘we all ran to the pavement and looked.’

‘And?’ I said impatiently, supressing a picture of all aboard a ship running to one side for a spectacle. Surely it couldn’t have been that bad, I thought, or it would have been on the local news, even national.

‘Well, it ran across the main road about a hundred yards down from where we were and, errr...’

Errr what, Sooty? Keep going, PJ inappropriately thought.

‘It hit the car garage across the road; wallop, right into the showroom pillar. The front of the hearse was smashed to bits, horrible crunching sound. Another foot or so either way and it would have gone through the plate-glass windows and into the new cars,’ he said without a flicker.

I, for once, found myself in uncharted waters. It was a godsend Tyler wasn’t here, or he would have started, but for the moment I was fine. The toupée story had been confined to the comparatively ‘really sensible’ bin. Provided tragedy had been averted, this was developing into a scene from a *Carry On* film, although to Sooty it was deadly serious. Even those words ‘deadly serious’ made me chuckle. My mind was accelerating unstoppably, no doubt like the hearse. I could see the headline: ‘Corpse Killed in Car Crash’.

‘What happened next,’ I asked Sooty, with a very straight face.

‘Well…’ (I wished he would stop starting almost every utterance withthe word ‘Well’, as this funeral had not gone ‘well’ at all by the sound of things).

He continued: ‘The undertaker and the driver went off down the hill, with one or two of the mourners.’ In a ‘search and rescue’ mission I thought, quickly telling myself: Shut up, PJ.

‘Someone said one of the mourners was a policeman, so off they went. We were all ushered back into the house and front yard. They were over an hour coming with a new hearse. When the police had got there they had cordoned it all off, but had to get a truck to winch the hearse off the building so they could get the coffin out.’

This was just getting better. I wanted to cry, it was undoubtedly a classic. ‘Flo had Flown’ good and proper, right down the hill. Just wait till I told Tyler.

Tyler and I, and more particularly Alf, had been involved in some funereal disasters along the way, but this time we weren’t involved. Usually such disasters were nothing of the sort, just straightforward human errors, but a snapping hand-brake cable at a critical time like that must surely be the work of God, and God with a brilliant sense of humour at that. That would also explain why no one was hurt as, joking apart I thought maturely, this could have been a newsworthy tragedy.

Sooty poured me another glass of his wine, which was now acting like laughing gas. I looked sheepishly up at him, but I could hold it no longer.

I smiled uncontrollably, and sniggered. It was like holding back indigestion in polite company, then it happened. I laughed. I couldn't help it; it wouldn't have mattered if Sooty had laid me out, I would have been like a dying fly. To my huge relief, and I think his too, he laughed as well. He had likely been wanting to for hours but respectability had prevented him. Despite our difference in years Sooty and I had a lot in common. We were as instructed in *The Bucket List* – 'laugh until you cry'. He opened another bottle of wine and we made a start on that. Thank heaven we shared more than just the wine by way of a sense of humour.

'I don't suppose anybody at the funeral thought it was funny at the time, did they, Soot?' I said.

'No,' he replied, 'but they might in a year or two. And Flo would have loved it. I nearly did laugh when I saw it,' he confided. I had thought as much. Sooty was all right.

When we became human again, and I'd done my thank-yous and was turning to go, Sooty gave me the wine bottle, looked at me and said, 'PJ, tell me really - we are friends despite a few years - what do you think of my hair?'

Thank the Lord I hadn't got a mouthful of wine or I would surely have lost it or tasted it through my nose. 'Some people think it's mine but it's a toupée you know,' he reliably informed me.

'It's fine, Sooty,' I said, turning away quickly, absolutely bursting inside. Was he for real? He surely had a mirror and a wife? Spoke volumes about how often Esme looked at him. Finally I laughed a bit, the steam valve releasing from the pressure cooker inside me. He laughed with me and to this day I think he thought the hearse story had just tickled me again. If only he knew.

On my return to Cliff Field Tyler was in the kitchen having a brew with Sam.

'What the hell's happened to you?' they chorused as I sat down, bottle of wine in hand. I couldn't talk. The pressure cooker blew. I laughed and laughed so much it hurt, and yes, I ticked my Bucket List and laughed until I cried.

I shared the bottle and told them, and they laughed until they cried too, with Tyler spluttering through his wine for reassurance at one point if Sooty was absolutely sure that his dad, Alf, wasn't involved.

Chapter 17

ROPED IN

There were some rural churchyards that Tyler and I rarely visited. It wasn't that they lacked a proper church, it was just that they were located in areas with a dwindling population. Far fewer people lived in these places than in the past. Youngsters were increasingly finding getting to bed at five in the morning at university far more appealing than getting up at the same time on the farm. Along with this, many of the farms had been converted to houses or holiday lets. Whilst working communities in Victorian times, these places were now largely populated by offcomers in Range Rovers, with two kids, not twelve. However there were a few die-hard farmers up here, whose elderly families still supplied us with the odd client from time to time, and who had escaped the increasing popularity of the regional crematorium.

Foxfield was one such place; a lush leafy valley below and forbidding barren hills above, with a few farms dotted on the hill slopes way into the distance. I imagined that at night-time, with the lights twinkling, it would look like a view in a Tolkien landscape. You could see why many youngsters had opted for the softer option of life in the city, rather than the harsh realities of sheep farming up here which would be no walk in the park in the winter. Herriot's stories came streaming back.

Tyler said, 'Get the planks from the trailer, PJ,' waking me from my daydreaming.

'Oh, yes, right,' I said.

'Not waking you up, am I?' Has to be said T had certainly got the measure of me.

We set up where marked, about halfway down the graveyard; well more along than down really as it was parallel with the road on a break of slope. The road was just below us, with the graveyard and church on a very old man-made terrace supported by a huge limestone retaining wall. There was evidently a lot of rock around here, so we weren't surprised when we tried to push our spades into the ground to find that it was another of those more quarrying than digging jobs.

‘I’d forgotten this was so flipping rocky,’ Tyler didn’t say. ’It’s that long since I’ve bin up here. Go get the stuff, PJ.’ We were getting to the point in our relationship where a simple gesture or word like ‘stuff’ said it all. The time for necessary explanation over, my training was clearly nearing its end. So I duly went for the ‘stuff’.

The location of this plot said something about the decline of these remote farming communities. The plot was positioned in a line with the others like the tideline on the beach. We were about halfway along the graveyard, the part to our left being full and the part to the right never allocated and therefore empty. The planners in their day had never anticipated that the churchyard would become underused. It was unusual as most villages were having to expand for incomers, but Foxfield had slipped through the net of modern life. The indigenous people had all but petered out and the newcomers had not filled the void. It was too bleak and poorly serviced for the nouveau retired, and had been left to its fate. The graveyard overlooked a big, even by today’s standards, railway viaduct that Mr Beeching had famously (or infamously) closed in the 1970s. It had gone from state-of-the-art engineering to a grass-grown footpath simply overtaken by time. The level of engineering and the amount of work involved in the building was unimaginable, but you could almost see and hear the passing steam trains. I had to snap out of another daydream or I’d soon be appearing in *The Railway Children* - always fancied that…

‘Oy,’ shouted Tyler.

‘Jenny Agutter,’ I said.

'What?'

'Jenny Agutter.'

'Jenny who? What are you on about?'

'Jenny Agutter, she was in that film *The Railway Children*, about steam trains, years ago?'

'I know the film and I know who Jenny Agutter is. Every red-blooded male knows who Jenny Agutter is after *Walkabout.'*

'*Walkabout?'*

'Look it up. Now are we going to dig this hole or live in the heyday of steam all day?' said Tyler purposefully.

No answer was required.

We got stuck in to this rocky ground quicker than I thought. The rock was broken and weathered at the top, not like Leyrigg where it had indeed been more like quarrying slate. Doubtless this rocky terrace was old broken-rock infill from when they built the retaining wall and church. How these structures were built with horse and cart, and no electricity or petrol, only heaven knew.

'Is this a single?' I asked Tyler.

'Yeah, thank God, they're all singles up here.'

What had looked like it might be a nightmare didn't turn out too badly. It was solid rock all right, but a bit like Bonfire Night treacle toffee, and had been broken into manageable pieces which you could far from dig, but rather cajole and lever out. As the toffee would have a tooth filling out with ease and no remorse, these angular lumps of rock would make a mess of your finger, given half the chance.

About two feet down Tyler said, ‘Come on, sherry and fag time.’ We willingly downed tools and sat looking at the spectacular view.

At this point the undertaker unexpectedly showed up, seldom a good or welcome sign. Nine times out of ten it was bad news and they were coming to inform of some fiasco. But not today; think he must have been just keeping out of the office. Couldn’t blame him, they were not the cheeriest of working environments. Dead quiet…

‘Now then, lads, how’s it going?’ said our suited friend.

‘So, they’ve run out of people up here then, Frank, ‘ave they?’ Tyler said.

‘Yep, no bugger wants to be a hill farmer, ‘specially now the boss is in Brussels.’

Frank was a new undertaker to me, who clearly didn’t mind us supping sherry; he said he would have joined us if it wasn’t for his car. Frank always drove a big old black Bentley, Tyler had told me. Not so much to make funerals more special or necessarily ‘posher’, and neither of course was it his. He just liked driving it and took mischief in it being his company car and a perk of his job. Tyler also said it had been known to double-up as a ‘foreigner’ wedding car on occasions, in a ‘waste not want not’ role. Tyler introduced us; another cunning move by the old so-and-so as I got the next question.

'What's your opinion on our membership of the European Union then, young PJ?' Blimey obviously Frank was the only resident of these inclement Isles who didn't immediately start a conversation by talking about the weather. Such a broadside heavy and unanswerable question took PJ quite by surprise. Indeed, a question well before it's time as things have turned out. Tyler, you beggar, I thought as he sat there contentedly smiling through the cigarette smoke a la Dufresne on the Shawshank roof in anticipation of my answer. He'd given Frank a cig too, and their gazes burnt into me.

'Er…'

'Come on lad. Well?'

'Er…'

Tyler wasn't such a so-and-so as it turned out because he said, 'C'mon, Frank, who's going to hear 'is or any opinion up 'ere? If they don't listen to the lot in London what chance 'ave we got?'

'Ah well,' said Frank, 'important question though.' How little did he know. He flicked his cigarette end into the grave. 'Well I'll be off. See you both tomorrow.'

'See you, Frank, thanks for popping in,' said Tyler. As Frank left the churchyard for his car, Tyler said, 'Dipstick…'

I agreed and looked, although unnoticed, disapprovingly in his direction in relation to the cigarette end; even Tyler didn't do that and neither should he have. I hopped in and retrieved it.

'Thanks for getting me off the hook then, T,' I said.

'Thought I'd just let 'im start, just to show you. He kept me an th'owd fella two hours once with his politics. I don't know why he doesn't pack in this undertakin', and instead of mekin' coffins, mek 'imself an orange box, he's a pain in the backside when he gets goin'.' Tyler cackled. With that we cracked on, Tyler digging, getting rock out, and me wheeling it away.

'Just pass us the tape, PJ, will you,' said T. 'Hold yon end and read it off please, and thanks for getting that fag end out.'

'Please'? I thought. What did he want? I really shouldn't be so suspicious, and he wasn't meant to notice my fag end foray. I expected a normal telling off for rescuing bits, but fag ends were a No in Tyler's graves. Perhaps we were getting to be a team after all.

'What we at?' T asked.

'Six foot spot on,' I replied.

'Just measure width, will yer?'

'Twenty-eight.'

'That'll do then, we'll just keep going down. Don't tek any more rock away, PJ, just stack it in box.'

‘Okay.’

‘I’m a bit worried about why Frank came ‘ere. He’d be checking sommat.’ said Tyler.

‘Checking what?’

‘Well he’s not trailed up ‘ere to talk about the European Agricultural Policy has ‘e, or fer t’ good of ‘is ‘ealth.’

‘Might have done… Everyone back in the office might be so bored with him, and we are a bit of a captive audience.’

‘Fair enough.’ said T acknowledging the thought as credible.

I could tell something was niggling Tyler. After another hour of my turn in the hole he said, ‘That’ll do.’

‘I think it might have to.’ I said. I was on solid rock now. This had been put here by God as sea bed some four hundred million plus years since, was as hard as iron and as a result my rate of progress had slowed considerably, and I was about knackered.

‘This is bedrock now, T. The last ice age never moved this stuff, pure planet.’

‘Nah, that’ll do, not going near that. What is it?’

‘About four feet.’ We really could understand each other now with a combination of hand signals and part-sentences.

‘Let’s be off,’ said T. ‘We’ll come back a bit lively tomorrow with some more planks. We’ll have to build up a bit ‘o staging, but it’ll do.’

‘That was surprisingly tough, that one, T,’ I said, reaching for the sherry. ‘I’m about all in.’

‘You’ve done all right there, PJ. Glad to have you here. They’re hard work, these loose rocky ‘uns.’

With that we put the planks over, mothballed the grave for the night and were gone.

In the morning Tyler picked me up and we loaded the trailer with planks and blocks of wood and the like.

‘How much are we taking?’ I asked T.

‘Just enough,’ he said. Enough? I remember thinking, what does that mean? It looked to me as if Tyler had forgotten we were going to Foxfield, and was geared up for Glastonbury, but hey-ho what did I know.

We arrived at Foxfield about ten o’clock. The funeral was at midday so we had plenty of time. We moved the planks and I jumped in to do my usual tidying up. Tyler still had something on his mind, but I couldn’t put my finger on it, so I thought I’d grasp the nettle.

‘You all right? You’ve been a bit quiet since yesterday, what’s up?’

‘It’s that undertaker coming up here business. I reckon I know why, but we’ll see. Sorry, it’s nothing, but he’s been on my mind.’

‘No, it’s okay, as long as you’re all right.’

‘Yes. Oh and thanks for asking, I’m fine,’ Tyler reassured. (PJ was always concerned about Tyler’s stomach problem and knew him to not be one to make a fuss).

We pottered on in a leisurely fashion. I was the gofer getting all the planks and blocks of wood, while Tyler constructed the grave surround.

‘When are you expecting them?’ I said out of the blue.

‘What? Twelve o’clock. Should be here a bit before.’ T answered.

‘Oh,’ I said, raising my eyebrows.

‘What?’

‘I thought they might be here before that.’

‘Who?’

‘Well up here it would have to be your favourites, The Rolling Stones’

‘Flip off.’ wasn’t my retort. T got the message, though. He really did seem to be getting carried away with his ‘bit o’ staging’; no visible gantries yet though.

About eleven o’clock I said to him, ‘Hey-up, he’s back.’

Perhaps that was it: he’d got the time of the funeral wrong, because he had already checked we were in the right place.

‘What does he want?’ I stupidly asked.

I just looked at Tyler as if I knew. Even to me he looked agitated for an undertaker on his big day.

‘Morning Frank,’ said Tyler.

‘Morning, guys.’ We were in no hurry and sat on the enduring stage structure Tyler had built.

‘Just waiting for the lighting towers to arrive,’ I said, but my joke fell on stony ground. Something was afoot. Frank’s level of agitation was palpable. Tyler passed round the sherry and cigs; Frank declined the sherry, but accepted a cigarette.

‘What’s up, Frank?’ said Tyler. ‘Is it us?’

‘No, no. I’ve just been up to Burrows’s farm where we’ve put old Alice in t’parlour.’

‘And?’ Tyler was good at this. He was really confident with undertakers. Increasingly they were younger than him it has to be said, but more importantly they needed him far more than he needed them.

‘What’s gone wrong at the farm?’

‘Oh, nothing was when I came away – there’s no mobile coverage up there.’

‘What, happened?’ T persevered.

‘It was the office; they rang. Old Alice was a Church bellringer in her youth. There’s bells in here but no bell-ringing team any more. They have the team from Greywind across valley come when needed. Well, with it being a weekday only one of them could come, and he's just rung the office to say he can't make it, he's ill. Well I promised them that the big bell would be tolled for half an hour. They all made such a fuss about how haunting it sounds resounding across the valley, and how Alice would have been so proud and would have loved it. She never missed listening to the bells from her chair in later life.' Frank paused and drew long and hard on his cigarette.

I was about to say 'I c…' when I was on the receiving end of a firm 'shut up and stay down' hand signal from Tyler. He was going to get his own back for that two hours of politics he and Alf suffered, I could tell.

'Oh dear,' said Tyler, 'that's a bugger.'

'You're not kidding and that's an understatement, T, that's no lie,' retorted Frank. 'They are all old codgers, them bellringers. It's a right anorak thing to do, isn't it? Nobody wants to do it nowadays, and where am I going to find a bellringer, a bloomin' bellringer, in the next twenty minutes? A needle in a haystack would be easier. Just rang the office but no signal again and to top it all I told them at the farm to set off when they heard the bell,' Frank finished forlornly.

'Something's been worrying me too, Frank, since yesterday.'

'What's that, T?'

'Well you came up 'ere for something yesterday, didn't you, but you said nowt.'

‘Well er…’ Frank spluttered.

‘My guess is that you came ‘ere to tell us sommat, but you were too late, am I right?’ said an as usual perceptive Tyler.

For what it was worth I hadn’t a clue what Tyler was talking about. Perhaps this was why he had been a little preoccupied.

‘I reckon you delivered old Alice up home,’ Tyler went on, ‘and came here to tell us she was four foot something and six stone soaking wet, and that you had wrongly told us to dig a hole six foot by twenty-eight inches. You thought you’d save us some work, but when you got here the size was already done.’

‘I hadn’t the heart to tell you, I knew you’d be mad. I’ll pay more, T. You’ll be able to get two of her in that hole,’ Frank said.

‘I knew it,’ said T, looking at me, and if he were at a desk he would have thumped it. ‘We wasted about half a day, did a load of lifting and humping away we didn’t need to yesterday. PJ, what do you think of that?’

I wasn’t best pleased either, as I was knackered last night I chirped up.

‘I’m sorry, guys,’ Frank said, and promised to see us right.

He still had his bellringer to worry about, it just wasn’t his day.

As he was about to leave Tyler said, ‘Frank, why don’t you ring the bell yourself?’

‘I can’t do that,’ he said sheepishly.

'You could run up Tower and hit it with a stick or you could get a carrier pigeon to fly to the farm with a message to tell them to set off' Tyler went on, twisting the knife and he was loving it. 'Do you pay bellringers when they turn up?'

'Yes,' said Frank nervously.

'How much?' Tyler queried.

'At the moment anything … I'll never find one now, only got fifteen minutes. I'll go and ask the bloke who opened the church if he can, or if he can ring someone.'

'Likely his phone won't work either.' Now T was just being rotten.

'Oh, hadn't thought of that,' sighed Frank.

'Old codgers, anoraks, them bellringers, PJ, did you 'ear 'im? Now that's not very nice, is it?' Said T almost unable to contain himself.

It dawned on Frank, the penny dropped like a stone. Excitedly he said, his head at an angle and eyes bulging,

'Tyler, can you do it, ring bells? Tell me you can?'

'Well after all the name-calling I'm not sure I can remember how…'

'I'm sorry, Tyler, about those things I called you, er, bellringers,' he grovelled. 'I'll pay.'

'How much?' Tyler replied, quick as a flash.

'Forty?'

'Sixty.'

'Done, done,' almost squealed Frank. 'You'll do it?'

'No,' said Tyler, drawing on his cigarette in cruelly cool Hollywood fashion, at which poor Frank deflated almost physically like a popped balloon. I actually felt sorry for him. Tyler had extracted his revenge, squeezed it, and then some.

'But he can,' Tyler added, gesturing my way. 'Been doing it for years, but may be not an old codger if that's what you specifically need? Certainly an anorak, though, you've got my word on that.'

Who needs enemies?

Sam and I had joined our local bell-ringing group and graduated to team members. The requirements for team membership were fierce, one head, two arms and the ability to count to at least six preferred; indeed tough stuff. What really sorted the 'men out from the boys' (an out of date saying if ever there was one), the 'wheat from the chaff' (probably better), though, was an unwavering enthusiasm and absolutely nothing better to do, in our case, on a Monday night. Increasingly people wanted Church bells ringing at all celebrations - funerals amongst them - to celebrate life and lives, as opposed to the soulful lonely somber 'bring out your dead' tolling of old, although still popular by tradition.

Learning bell-ringing was an experience and what a motley crew we were, ranging from a globetrotting medical charity worker, a scratch golfer, a 'Duracell bear' powered non-stop teacher, a farmer, a welder, our very own actor no less and at least a brace of librarians. It was suspected that librarians liked bell-ringing, or campanology (kæm.pəˈnɒl.ə.dʒ naturally to a librarian), as it was the only waking activity where they were actually allowed to make a noise.

Until then, PJ had only ever associated bells with boarding school, hand held affairs, and it was indeed good to know they had long been adapted to be something pleasant, and weren't just sounds to be obeyed. Church Bells were of course the pre-electric summons or reminder that God wanted to see you and was open for business. School bells were programmed into pupils as stimulants of pre-ordained instructions to 'get up', 'go to bed', 'lights out' and so on, usually wielded by a power crazed Prefect dementedly ringing it for all it was worth. The distinction between 'Prefect' and 'God' was blurred at PJ's school, particularly so by the said Prefects themselves. They were a breed apart and commanded unquestioned obedience more akin to prison warders really. The 'storm troopers' of the school, 'Darth Prefect' was to be feared, and his bell the 'light saber' of its day.

Frank looked at me as if he was smitten. 'PJ, you are my saviour, I love you.'

'Well I don't know about that, Frank,' I said laughing a little uncomfortably.

'No, my saviour,' he repeated with emphasis.

I asked Tyler if he'd be okay finishing off. He was, after all, my boss to all intents and purposes and I knew my place.

'Off you go,' he said. 'I'll be fine. Besides there'll be no funeral if you don't summon them by tolling that bell.' He grinned from ear to ear. His revenge on Frank had indeed been sweet, and for him gleefully long.

Frank turned to Tyler as we were about to go to the tower and said, 'You knew, you knew all along.' Tyler just raised his eyebrows, widened his eyes and tapped the side of his nose, before returning to his fixed grin, as good as to say 'moi'?

'He's a rotter, he is, that Tyler.' Frank looked at me for support (and most definitely didn't say quite that, well not in those precise words).

I have to admit to cracking a smile myself.

'C'mon, Frank, let's go and ring that bell, we've got about five minutes until we start.' I felt sorry for him, if only a little, as the stress relief was tangible.

'What do you mean, "we",' protested Frank in a panicky voice. 'I don't know how, I can't,' clearly Frank thought it was now a two man job.

I couldn't do it; he was crying out for another wind-up but I couldn't do it.

'Let's do that again, Frank,' I said. 'C'mon, Frank, let's go and ring that bell, 'I've' only got five minutes before 'I' start.'

It was a surprisingly large church for a small village, and just confirmed how much the community must have shrunk since the heyday of the railways. And the six bells wouldn't have been bought with saving stamps that was for sure. I started tolling the bell bang on time. A bit like my grave-tidying routine I had my own little ways.

I'd tolled the bell at funerals before.

I asked Frank how old Alice was: she had died in her ninety-fourth year. So, grave dug and ready, all I could do for Alice now was to toll that bell ninety-four times.

When the funeral was in progress, I quietly slipped out of the back of the church and went back to my real job. I returned to find Tyler sitting by the wall near the grave with his trademark *Shawshank Redemption* smile on his face, a look of inner contentment.

'Have you been hitting that sherry a bit hard, T?' I asked.

'No,' he assured me, 'just been sitting here listening to your handiwork. Very even dongs, if I may say, not at all bad.'

'Well thank you, kind sir,' I replied, thinking he was taking the mickey.

'No, really sounded good, even one of undertaker's lads said he could shed a tear to order, listening to it, very sad.'

'You should learn to ring bells, T,' I said. 'Another string to your bow, arrow in your quiver?'

'Yeah right,' was my brief but clear answer. Years later he did have a go, though, but that is a whole other story.

I went over to the grave to admire Tyler's finished product. It was a lovely job. The graveyard sloped slightly towards the road, and T had cleverly used this natural contour in building his surround. He had filled in the slope, so that to the eye the ground looked level. As it was far from level, it gave the grave an exaggerated depth: clever stuff really. There were no leaves in the bottom or I would have had to go in. It looked a good six feet deep, when in fact I knew it wasn't an inch more than four, base to grass. It wasn't down (or up) to us whether a grave's depth was acceptable or not, that was up to the Vicar. He had five churches to service up here and was pleased to get a congregation at all, regardless of occasion, so provided the coffins weren't visible afterwards it was sort of taken as okay. Tyler's professionalism, though, meant they were always deep enough. Besides you would have needed explosives to get this grave any deeper.

Sometimes funerals went on a bit, and this was the Vicar making the most of having a congregation, willing or not, believers or not, and seizing the chance to proclaim the message. It was simply too good an opportunity to miss.

'Good job that, T,' I said. 'Have you had them this shallow before?'

'Once, but there t'vicar had run out of room. I mean really run out.'

The fella was only in his forties, a bigwig consultant at the local hospital. He mistakenly, as it turned out, used to go to work on his motorbike. The same old story had befallen him; some old dear pulled out and did for him. 'Didn't see him, Officer,' and that was it, police inquiry over. They could get more of a punishment for a parking misdemeanour. Funny thing was, as Tyler observed, the lady was going to the hospital for an appointment (so the local newspaper reliably reported therefore it must be true…), and there was a distinct possibility that her appointment was with the fella she ran over on the way.

Tyler went on: 'Well the Vicar said he'd have to go in with 'is parents. I told him it was full. He just said there was nowhere else until the new extension opened across the road, and we couldn't leave him lying around on top till then.'

'What, he actually said that?' I exclaimed.

'He did.'

Since doing this job PJ had heard people say some silly and obvious things, but that was up there coming from that source.

'Why didn't they just close the churchyard, and go crem-only until the new area was available?'

'You tell me PJ. Too obvious likely.'

'How deep was that then?'

'Thirteen inches wood to grass. You should have seen the staging I built for that one, you nearly needed ladders to get up to the "ground level" around that one. Looked stupid. That coffin was lowered through mainly fresh air, hey but none of my business, and nobody noticed.'

'Was that at Wilton-on-Sea?'

'Yeah, how did you know that?'

'Oh that'll be the one where you were leathered on sherry and a visit to The Blue Anchor. Oh and you got a flat tyre in the churchyard and naturally didn't have a spare wheel. Hence being there longer than expected and somebody had to come and pick you up.'

'Yeah, that's the one,' Tyler said slowly, but reasonably unashamedly, clearly hunting for an explanation as to where I had gained this knowledge. 'The old fella's been telling his tales again at dominoes in the pub hasn't he?'

'No,' I said in Alf's defence, with eyebrows raised.

'Well how do you know all that then?'

'I was the silly beggar that picked you up, that's how,' I reminded him.

'Oh,' said Tyler sheepishly. He was that leathered he had forgotten. I loved it. 'Sorry about that,' he muttered contritely but that would do. There but for the grace of God and so on, thought PJ.

Alice's funeral went off hitch-free. No one would ever know that she was nearly as far from the sides of her grave as she was from the surface, which was, once Glastonbury had been deconstructed, only two feet above the lid. She had looked like a pencil case in a dry dock, bless her. Tyler had a bit more fun at Frank's expense over the sizes, but all's well that ends well and we parted amicably. Tyler was fifty quid to the better on top of his fee for the grave-size fiasco, and I sixty up, thanks to Tyler's unyielding negotiations. It was definitely my round.

As we were packing away it struck me for no particular reason that Alice had had a life nearer to how life should be. An outdoor life, uncluttered by modern nonsense such as computers, mobiles, holidays and materialistic things. A life in which you worked hard, lived hard, had little time for recreation, got killed in wars or lived to a ripe old age as she had. I had noticed a war memorial close to the Church entrance; even the sheep farmers up here had made that sacrifice.

We had buried lots of people who had died young as a result of accident or illness, which sometimes made it easy to forget that the vast majority of our clients were old people, for whom life had gone entirely to plan and who had died in their own beds, often in their sleep. Remarkably unremarkable old folk all of them, which we all hope to be. Indeed most funerals also went off perfectly smoothly and without event or mess-up. Despite its mystery, the job of gravedigger was no different to any other: we did our best, but just sometimes that wasn't quite good enough.

'Hello, hello.' A voice woke me from my musings.

Tyler had his arms full of greengrocer grass, our last load. 'You go, will yer,' he said.

'Hello,' I called, in no particular direction, and saw a man approaching. He wasn't one of the undertaker's lot, they were long gone. He looked every bit the mourner - you know the type, shiny suit that didn't quite fit, somebody else's borrowed black tie, Hush Puppies, usually in the wrong colour.

'Hello,' I said, in his direction this time.

‘Glad I caught you.’ He was completely out of breath, and looked like he could do with a lie-down and a cup of sweet tea.

‘You are the gravediggers, aren’t you?’ Oh here we go, I thought, another obvious remark. ‘No’ sprang to mind, but I behaved.

He produced two five pound notes from a worn envelope. ‘Thank you, thank you,’ he said, ‘so glad I caught you.’

We looked quizzically at him and Tyler started to say, on sight of the money, ‘No, no…’ but the man carried on regardless.

‘These are for you.’

‘No…’ T attempted again.

The man simply raised his finger to his lips in silent gesture to politely discourage Tyler and said slowly, deliberately and with importance:

‘It has them here on the envelope, my instructions.’

Then shaking our hands firmly in turn, he presented us each our fiver.

‘It’s a tip, to say thank you, she was most insistent,’ he emphasised. ‘It’s from Alice.’

We humbly and quietly thanked the man, which he brushed aside with a further polite ‘no need’ gesture and a generous smile. He then tipped his head respectfully to Alice and walked slowly away in a dignified manner.

Tyler looked at me and I at him, and suddenly the enormity of what we did, and what Tyler had trained me to do, was clear. In that second, in that look, PJ knew by Tyler's eyes that his training was complete. PJ was now that most mysterious of things, a gravedigger.

No words were spoken and we gently finished our task for Alice Burrow and I performed, with real affection, my now time-served, Night Night God Bless routine and we were gone.

That was the first and last tip we were ever given. We never did know who the mysterious figure was, and had never indeed met dearest Alice, but it was, without doubt, the most important fiver we had ever held.

Printed in Great Britain
by Amazon

35205182R00244